A PROPHET WITHOUT HONOR

To Dolores Young

John 15:7

A PROPHET WITHOUT HONOR

Charles R. Bembry Jr.

iUniverse, Inc.
New York Lincoln Shanghai

A PROPHET WITHOUT HONOR

iUniverse books may be ordered through booksellers or by contacting:

iUniverse
2021 Pine Lake Road, Suite 100
Lincoln, NE 68512
www.iuniverse.com
1-800-Authors (1-800-288-4677)

ISBN-13: 978-0-595-37477-9 (pbk)
ISBN-13: 978-0-595-81870-9 (ebk)
ISBN-10: 0-595-37477-8 (pbk)
ISBN-10: 0-595-81870-6 (ebk)

Printed in the United States of America

Dedication to Charles (Specks) Bembry and Timothy Bembry. I love and miss you.

Mark 6:4

But Jesus said unto them, A Prophet is not without Honor, but in his own country, and among his own kin, and in his own house.

Acknowledgments

To Tonetta Rumph, Tracey Mills, for your patience, encouragement and help. Also to my mother Ernestine Bembry for believing in me.

Prologue

The communication devices allowed us to speak to each other in the murky water, and with night vision cameras we finally found the exhaust valve. Oppenheimer called me back to the surface. I slowly spread the light across the swamp, searching for alligators lurking in the water. When I reached the surface, Oppenheimer waved me on board. Just as I stepped onto the boat, a great gush of water poured out of the canal from the explosion. I turned back to Oppenheimer, and only remember seeing his arm with some blunt instrument hurling down towards my head.

I don't know how long I was unconscious. When I woke up, I heard the water crashing into the edge of the marshlands, and I was near my red pickup truck. I still had my diving suit on, and there was a bloody gash over my right eye. As I squinted to clear my vision, I could see some raccoons trying to get the candy bars from the glove compartment. I was groggy and my head was pounding. I strained to remember what had happened. I struggled to my feet and waved the raccoons off. There was a first aid kit in the truck; I doused iodine over the gash on my eye and screamed in pain. Able to see with only one eye, I managed to drive the truck back to Harpo's place. That's where this all started, as best I can remember.

"Harpo, where are you?" I yelled out, compounding the pain in my head. I walked back through his office and fell, causing even more injury to myself. It was dark in Harpo's office, and I realized that I fell because I had tripped over his body.

"Harpo, get up. Man. Get up."

I turned on the lamp and noticed the large blood stain on his back. "My God, Harpo, what have you gotten me into?" I asked, talking to the dead man.

In another room, further back in his office, I heard some noise, like a radio, but it was a small television. A news anchor was reporting a story about the FBI searching the home of a local civil rights leader in New Orleans named Clarence Reed.

I thought I was dreaming. I raised myself to my knees, then to my feet, and slowly walked to the television to hear more details.

The reporter continued, "Hold on folks—we have some breaking news. We have just confirmed that C-4 explosives have been found in the homes of Thomas Gere and Gerald Akins. The police and FBI are now looking for Gere, Akins, and Reed in connection with the Mississippi River Queen bombing."

I fell to the ground as if someone had punched me. How could the FBI have named me as a suspect so soon after the bombing? I needed to think…to retrace my steps. The last thing I remembered was Oppenheimer. I looked around Harpo's office searching for anything I might need, especially money. About ten minutes had passed when the newsman came on again to confirm that two bodies had been found and they were, in fact, my good friends Gere and Akins. The FBI was now at my house. My poor mother was standing on the porch in tears. It angered me that she was being humiliated like that. I had heard enough. I ran out of Harpo's office, started my truck, and drove as deep as I could into the woods, but I started feeling drowsy. The last thing I remembered was passing out while I was driving. The truck must have run off of the road and slammed into a group of trees.

The crash must have been loud enough for a local named John Cavier, a backwoods farmer some fifty yards away, to get up and investigate. I was groggy but I saw him coming towards me with a flashlight and two dogs that looked like hounds at his side.

"You all right, boy?" Cavier asked, pointing his shotgun nonchalantly in my direction.

"I don't know. I think I need a doctor," I said, slurring my words while leaning over the steering wheel.

"Sure, boy. Stay right there, and I'll fetch up some help."

I learned later that Cavier had gone back to his house and called the police. In a few minutes he returned and said, "Now you just sit right there. You that boy they looking for who killed all them people on the riverboat?" Cavier asked, his shotgun pointed at me.

"Who's that?" I asked. Cavier turned around to look. Wincing with pain, I rushed the old man and knocked him out, but not before he was able to let a shot go and barely miss my head. I ran for the woods. The police, with FBI agents, arrived about ten minutes later.

"That nigga' got the drop on me and headed for the woods," Cavier told the police.

They called for helicopters to survey the area. Later, I learned that the voice I'd heard from the helicopter was that of FBI chief Jon Tulle. "Give it up, Clarence Reed. This is the FBI," he shouted down as the helicopter put its spotlight on me.

Bleeding, hurt, and exhausted, I couldn't go any further and I stopped. As they came to get me, the only thing that I could think about was who had led the authorities to me. Gere, Akins, and Harpo were all dead. Suzanne was in New York and she wouldn't have mentioned to anyone that I was doing this job.

Oppenheimer ratted me out. I swore that even if it took 100 years, I'd make him pay. That was my last thought before I passed out and the FBI handcuffed me.

Chapter 1

Malcolm arrived at his father's home just before dusk. His younger brother, Joe Jr., ran out to help get his bags and the children out of the taxi. Malcolm heard a shout echo throughout the house that he had arrived. His father, the Reverend Josiah Stinson and a pillar of the community, always filled his home with family, friends, and nearly half of the neighborhood. As Malcolm walked into the living room, he found his father surrounded by his church elders.

Josiah stood up.

"Praise God! My boy's home," Josiah said, as he threw his arms open. The crowded room became silent as the two men hugged each other and cried.

"Where's mama?" Malcolm asked, wiping his tears.

"In the kitchen. She's taking this real hard, son. So be strong. Now, where them little ones at?" Josiah said, as Serena and Joshua popped into view from the crowd. The reverend's smile was big as a crescent moon when he picked up Serena.

Malcolm made his way into the kitchen. The smell of fried chicken, gumbo cakes, and pies filled the air. Lois Stinson sat at the kitchen table surrounded by the churchwomen, reminiscing about Elaine. Others fixed plates of food to send out, assembly-line style. The kitchen was a mixture of sorrow and laughter. Malcolm edged his way into his mother's view.

"Hi, Mama," Malcolm said, smiling at Lois. She began to cry uncontrollably and she opened her arms to Malcolm.

"She not suffering anymore, baby. She's right there in the arms of Jesus." The women in the kitchen said a concerted, "Amen."

"Where, them grandbabies of mine?" As he turned to call Joshua, he heard a chorus of, "Mommy, Mommy."

Malcolm turned again to look at his mother, who had a solemn look on her face. "She came in a couple of hours ago. Even though she's not your wife anymore, I told Papa Joe we had to tell her. She hopped on the next plane," Lois said, shrugging her shoulders.

"Look, Daddy. Mommy's here," Serena said, while Sara carried her and kissed her as she walked toward Malcolm.

Malcolm was seeing her for the first time in nearly four months, since the divorce was decreed final. It was the longest time they had ever been apart in their ten years of marriage. She had cut her hair to an almost boyish length, and her eyes sparkled in the kitchen light.

"Hello, Malcolm. How have you been?" she asked.

"Good. And, yourself?"

"Okay. Malcolm, I think we need to talk about some things…"

"Things? I believe we discussed everything. From this point on, it's basically 'have a good life, see you when I see you.'"

"I knew you wouldn't make this easy. Okay. We need to talk about the kids…"

"What about them? They're in my custody. I don't see anything to talk about. Let me guess. You'd like to see them sometimes," he said sarcastically.

"Yes, on a regular basis," Sara replied firmly.

"Right now, Sara, I'm going to bury my sister. In spite of your abandonment of the kids, I will discuss it with you later. So leave your phone number with my secretary, and I'll get back to you in a few weeks."

"A few weeks?" Sara's jaw hardened.

Standing close to her he could smell her perfume. Suddenly angry that he was aroused by her nearness, he barked at her right there in the kitchen. "You haven't seen or spoken to them in three months. So why are you in such a hurry now?"

"There you are, son. I've been looking all over for you. Excuse me, Sara, but Malcolm and I have some important business," said Reverend Josiah, as he grabbed Malcolm's arm, escorting him out to the backyard.

"What's wrong with you? Everyone is mourning for your sister and you're fighting with Sara."

"Sorry, Papa Joe. She wants to see the kids and it just pissed me off."

"Let things settle down for a while and in time you'll be able to talk to her in a civilized manner. After all, they need to see their mother."

Josiah walked Malcolm to the far end of the backyard where a big oak tree had a swing tied to it. "Remember this tree?" Josiah smiled, as he looked up at the rope tied to the tree.

Malcolm looked and said nothing.

"Boy, I remember when the three of ya'll would fight over who would get to swing first. You used to always let Elaine go first," Josiah said, as tears welled up in his eyes. "Have you made any plans yet about what you're going to do?" the reverend asked, sitting down on the swing.

"I don't know yet, Papa Joe. I had planned to stay in Hawaii for a couple more weeks to think about things," Malcolm said.

"Have you read anything about what's going on down here since the bombing?"

"Not really. I guess I've been a little self-indulgent lately," Malcolm said, gazing at the stars. He felt relaxed away from all the people.

"Malcolm, this young man that they've arrested for the bombing is a member of our church. He's a good man. I would never say that this man isn't capable of doing something, but he had no motive to do this. In the last four months I've talked to him…"

"What's his name again?"

"Clarence Reed. I had the NAACP representing him, but last week he released them from his representation."

"Why's that?" Malcolm asked curiously.

"He didn't feel comfortable with them. They represented his father at one point, but lost the case."

"His father?"

"That's another story. But getting back to Clarence…"

"Papa Joe, if you want me to recommend somebody…"

"I do, son, I want you to recommend yourself," the reverend said, as he stood and looked Malcolm straight in the eye.

"Oh no, Papa Joe, I'm not ready to tackle something like this. Not now. Do you know what a trial like this would entail? The cost would be considerable, not to mention…"

"No. I don't know. What I do know is that my baby—your sister—is dead. An innocent man is in jail. And the killers are out there laughing and roaming free, ready to kill again. I was hoping that, as a lawyer, and the man I raised, you would want to see justice done…like freeing the man they wrongfully accused, and maybe, luring the real criminals back so someone can catch them. But it seems to me, that you think it's all right for your sister's killers to roam free."

"Papa Joe, I'm not saying that. It's just that my life has fallen apart, and I want to get things back into their proper perspective," Malcolm said.

"And I'm saying to you, what could be more proper than to vindicate your sister's death?"

"How would I be doing that?"

"By, freeing Clarence Reed. By not letting the federal and local authorities sentence the wrong man to death," the reverend stated harshly.

A tall, robust, Black man smoking a big Havana cigar approached them. "Evening, Reverend. My deepest sympathies to you and the Mrs.," Campy said, hugging the reverend.

"Thank you, Campy. I don't think you've ever met my oldest son. Malcolm, this is Campy Frazier, hopefully the next governor of Louisiana."

"Pleased to meet you, Mr. Frazier." Malcolm waved the cigar smoke out of his face.

"Smoke bothers you, Malcolm?" Campy asked, putting the cigar behind him.

"A little. I gave up smoking cigarettes about six months ago," Malcolm said, coughing.

"Was it hard?" Campy asked, looking for a place to put out the cigar.

"Somewhat. I had cold-turkey withdrawal symptoms for a week, then just the will not to smoke anymore," Malcolm said, proud of his victory over tobacco.

"I was talking to Malcolm about Clarence Reed's trouble finding a good attorney." The reverend moved away to watch some kids playing by a tree he'd recently cut down.

"It's a real shame. Hell, everybody in Louisiana knows he didn't do it, but the feds need a scapegoat and unfortunately, Reed is it," Campy said, putting out his cigar on the tree. "Are you the lawyer or the soccer player from Europe?" Campy asked.

As Malcolm began walking back to the house, he stated, "The lawyer."

"What you think, Rev? Is he biting?" Campy asked.

"With Elaine's passing, it's harder to persuade him. I was going to wait another week, then call him while he was on vacation in Maui, Hawaii. It's hard for me, Campy, pushing him to do this. But my baby is in the hands of the Lord now. We'll wait until after the funeral and approach him again. Elaine always looked up to her big brother, and he's taking this real hard. But I know my boy won't let her killers just walk away. I have a feeling the good Lord will touch his heart and he will represent Clarence," the reverend said, throwing his arm across Campy's broad shoulders as they walked back to the house.

Malcolm made his way through the crowded house to find his mother. "Mama, can we talk for a minute?" he asked, helping her up from her chair. They walked through the house to Elaine's room upstairs.

The noise faded as they closed the door. Malcolm stared around at Elaine's things. Not much had changed from her school days. She had just moved to Los Angeles a year earlier. Lois sat down on the edge of the bed.

"I hope you're not upset that Sara is here. I feel like she's still family, even though you're divorced. And Elaine, well, she liked Sara a lot," Lois said, looking intently at Malcolm.

"It's not a problem about Sara. I guess I just overreacted. Mama, I've been through a lot this last year. Papa Joe has asked me to represent this Clarence Reed," Malcolm said.

"A, fine young man. Elaine admired him. In fact, she fancied him. They'd dated off and on, but nothing serious. Malcolm, all I can say is he's not capable of doing what they're saying. He is a young man of integrity, and in my heart I know he's not responsible for Elaine's death," Lois said, reaching her arms up for Malcolm. He sat down next to her on the bed and they hugged.

"No one can be more devastated than I am, sweetheart. I think defending Clarence would be just what Elaine would want you to do. After all, you told me a few weeks ago that you wanted to leave New York. It would be good to have you and the children living here. Who knows? You could even start your own practice in New Orleans. Lord knows you would have enough business," she said, rubbing his wavy hair and holding him as he softly sobbed.

"So you think I should take the case?"

"It's not what I think. It's whatever you want."

"If I do, the kids and I would have to live here for awhile. I haven't sold my condo in New York, yet."

"I wouldn't have it any other way," Lois said, keeping her arms wrapped around him and rocking him gently.

CHAPTER 2

At the cemetery, Malcolm and his father stood on each side of his mother to support her. Elaine had been well-liked, and there were over a thousand people at the cemetery. People who didn't even know her showed up. After Elaine was laid to rest, and Lois was in the limousine, the reverend pulled Malcolm aside. "Have you given it any more thought?" he asked Malcolm as they walked.

"Thought about what, Papa Joe?" Malcolm replied.

"About, the case, son, the case. Clarence Reed?"

"Why are you so obsessed with my taking this case?" Malcolm asked with a frown on his brow.

The reverend stopped walking and looked Malcolm directly in the eye. "I'm not obsessed. My daughter—your sister—is in the ground and the wrong man is in jail."

Suddenly Malcolm's mother fainted. He and the reverend ran to help her. "Someone get that ambulance over here. Hurry!" the reverend hollered as he held his wife.

After a few minutes Lois was in the ambulance. They treated her while they rushed to DePaul Hospital. A police escort led the way, while a parade of cars followed.

Lois Stinson was in the emergency room for over two hours. The doctor reported that she had had a minor stroke, and that he wanted to observe her in the hospital for a few days.

When the family was finally allowed to see her, Malcolm, the reverend, and his brother Joseph went into the room to see the drained but alert Lois. She wanted to talk to the reverend alone first, so Malcolm and his brother waited in the hall.

"Thank God she's going to be all right," Joe said.

"Excuse me, gentlemen. I have to go in there," a woman said, in a soft French Creole voice.

"By all means. That's our mother in there, so please take good care of her," Malcolm said, staring at the beautiful creature.

"Don't worry. I will," she replied, smiling sweetly at Malcolm, just inches from his face.

"She's gorgeous. Maybe I need a checkup," Joe said, staring at the nurse. "I wonder who she is. I've never seen her before."

"Yeah, like you know every woman in New Orleans—you've been in Europe for over a year," Malcolm said, still staring at the nurse.

Their curiosity overcame them, and they walked into the room. The nurse was viewing Lois' chart when she turned to Malcolm. "We'll be moving Mrs. Stinson to a private room."

The reverend was sitting on the side of the bed as they approached. "Roberta, you've never met my sons. This is Malcolm and that's Joseph," said the reverend, eyeing his boys.

"Pleased to meet you, gentlemen. Now if you folks don't mind, Mrs. Stinson needs some peace and quiet," Roberta said while she scribbled something on the chart. She said good-bye to the reverend and told Lois that everything would be all right. When she left the room, Malcolm followed.

"Excuse me, Roberta? Just what is her condition? The doctor told us she had a mini-stroke. So what exactly is a mini-stroke?"

"It's not as bad as it sounds. I guess the shock of Elaine's death was more than she could handle."

"By the way, if you don't mind my asking, how do you know my folks?"

"I attend your father's church. I've heard about you and your brother. You must be the lawyer from New York," she said, walking backwards down the hallway. Malcolm kept pace with her.

"That's me. I'll be in town for a while, so maybe I'll see you around," Malcolm said. He stopped walking. Roberta was just as alluring walking away as when she was coming.

"Probably." She swayed down the hallway, turned the corner, and glanced back at Malcolm. He was still staring at her as she disappeared.

"What a woman! That's the first interesting woman I've seen since Sara. Maybe there's still hope for me," Malcolm said, laughing.

"There are a lot of pretty women in New Orleans, brother," Campy said as he walked up behind Malcolm.

"How are you, Mr. Frazier?"

"Just fine. How's your mama?"

"The doctor said it was just a mini-stroke. She'll just need to rest for a few days and she'll be fine."

Malcolm went back into the room with Joe and Lois. Campy started to come in, but was waved back by the reverend, who came outside. "She's fine, Campy. A little rest and Lois will be back on her feet in no time. Praise God," the reverend said as he walked Campy out of Malcolm's earshot.

"I want you to contact that district attorney, Michael Ducruet, and tell him we'll be down to see him tomorrow."

"What happened? Did Malcolm change his mind?" Campy asked with grave concern.

"No, not yet, but Lord forgive us, his mother is putting the finishing touches on him now. For the life of me, Campy, I don't know why he has such a hard head."

"Yeah, I wonder," Campy said and they both laughed.

Lois had finished the job after twenty minutes. Malcolm was getting in the car to go home when Campy asked him, "Think you'll be able to see the district attorney tomorrow?"

"I guess this was a conspiracy for me to take this case," Malcolm said while everyone stood silently around the car. "So let's go meet this Ducruet and our client tomorrow," Malcolm said with a smile. Everyone else smiled, too.

"Ducruet is the devil incarnate, son. He's put more black men in jail than any other D.A. in the history of Louisiana," the reverend said as they rode home.

"Look, let's face it. A lot of black men are committing crimes, but the problem with Ducruet is that he always goes for the jugular. He pushes for blacks to be locked up for ten, twenty years when, in actuality, the crime only calls for a year or two. We need to tighten the reins of the judicial system here in Louisiana, and go after the big white-collared criminals. We've got to get rid of these politicians, and I'm not just talking about the white ones. It's the black ones as well," Campy said irritably. "I'm going to call David Segal."

"Who's he?" Malcolm asked.

"He's a civil rights lawyer—the partner of the lawyer found dead in the river with Akins. I think you should let him tag along with you when you go to meet Ducruet, and when you go to Angola prison to see Clarence," Campy said as they pulled up in front of his house. "We'll meet at Ducruet's office at ten a.m. Good-night, gentlemen."

When Campy got out of the car, two burly black bodyguards were waiting for him.

"Campy's a politician, but he has a good heart. Clarence Reed is a good political move for him, so his help will benefit us," the reverend said, wiping sweat from his forehead.

"What do you mean, benefit us, Papa Joe?" Malcolm asked.

"Nobody does something for nothing, whether he is black or white, and when you meet some of these politicians, you'll understand what I mean. And, son, whatever you, do when you meet Henri Joret—and you will—remember, he's the worst of the lot. He's the black man's enemy in Louisiana. To put it another way, he's like David Duke, except he wears a mask to hide his evil intentions and crooked ways," the reverend said. Before Malcolm could ask him any more questions, the old reverend had fallen fast asleep.

"He's tired. I know I am," Malcolm said to Joe.

"So, you are taking the case?" Joe asked.

"It looks that way. How long you staying in town?"

"Well, I was going to stay a week or two and catch up with the team in Barcelona, but now I'll stay till Mama gets back on her feet."

"Good. She'll be happy to have us both here for a while," Malcolm said, then fell asleep, as Joe sped down the highway home.

* * * *

On December 22, David Segal, the civil rights lawyer and Aaron Gere's former partner, arrived at the Stinson home early in the morning. The reverend opened the door to let Segal in. "It's been quite a while since I last saw you, David. How've you been?"

"Very well, Reverend Stinson. My condolences to you for your loss."

"Thank you. Come in. My son is eager to meet you."

"I've heard some good things about your son. When Campy called me last night and told me he was going to represent Clarence, I did a little research. And I must say I'm impressed," Segal said, following the reverend into the living room.

"Malcolm, you almost ready?" he shouted upstairs.

"I'll be right there," Malcolm shouted back.

"Are you coming down later, Reverend?" asked Segal.

"I'm ready now. There's no rest for the weary, David."

"Listen, Reverend, we've worked together on many cases, but do you think your son is the right one for this job? I mean, the Southern Poverty Law Center has some very capable people who can handle a case like this."

"I understand your concern, David, but Malcolm is one of the best in the country—and I'm not saying that just because he's my son. I think Clarence will be very comfortable with Malcolm representing him."

Malcolm ran down the stairs, rattling off instructions to his children who followed him.

"Malcolm, I want you to meet David Segal," the reverend said. They shook hands and walked outside where Campy was waiting. The four got into one car, and Campy's entourage followed.

"I guess I should start by briefing you about Michael Decried. He's the federal prosecutor of New Orleans who's aspiring to be the attorney general of Louisiana, if Henri Joret wins the governor's election," David said. He sat next to Malcolm in the back seat.

"Hell, David, call a spade a spade," Campy said.

"Well, for example, he's a big advocate of gambling in Louisiana. The incumbent governor made a real effort to prove that Joret had ties with noted criminals in Louisiana and Mississippi. Word has it, though, that the local Mafioso booted him from their inner circle about two years ago," David continued.

"Why's that?" Malcolm asked.

"He wanted more of the profits than they were willing to give him, so their business relationship became strained. I don't know what your experience is with the Mafia, but they can be very pesky, if you know what I mean," David said.

"Mr. Segal, you have no idea what experience I've had with them. Believe me, I understand fully. You seem a little upset talking about them," Malcolm replied, looking at David intently.

"I believe they are responsible for my partner's death. He had a few run-ins with them, but nothing like this. Let me be honest with you, Malcolm. A lot people were killed last Fourth of July and nobody knows who did it. The government's evidence points to Clarence. But, if the crime families are at war, Clarence may very well be the patsy they need," David said seriously.

"Even if that's the case, why frame Clarence?" Malcolm asked, as they pulled up to the federal building in downtown New Orleans.

David stared at the swarm of reporters outside the federal building. "Who knows? Maybe a smoke screen, or worst—that Clarence actually did it," David whispered to Malcolm.

"What's all this? Something going on here today?" Malcolm asked.

"I, uh, took the liberty of informing the press that Clarence was going to talk with his new lawyer today," Campy said cautiously, chewing on his unlit Tiparillo.

"Maybe you should have asked me first, Campy. One, we don't know if he wants my representation, and, two, I haven't cleared it with my law firm in New York. Thank you very much," Malcolm said bitterly.

Malcolm got out first. Campy's men formed a gauntlet around Malcolm as they entered the courthouse to meet District Attorney Michael Ducruet, who was watching the media show from his window. And he wasn't watching alone.

Malcolm and the crew made their way past the wave of questions being tossed at them.

"Malcolm Stinson, is it true you've come from New York to defend the accused terrorist bomber, Clarence Reed?" a reporter shouted. David Segal had arranged for Malcolm to make a motion P.O. Vice. The meeting with the judge took 30 minutes.

When they arrived at Michael Ducruet's office, they were surprised to be greeted by a comely black woman in her late twenties. She had luminous eyes that seared through Malcolm. Joret had told Ducruet to change his image by bringing in black personnel, ammunition when Ducruet was accused of being prejudiced. She smiled and asked with a slight French accent, "May I help you, gentlemen?"

"I'm David Segal, and this is Malcolm Stinson. We have an appointment with Mr. Ducruet."

"One moment, please. I'll check with him," she said, smiling at Malcolm. From Ducruet's office, hostile voices could be heard.

"He'll be with you momentarily. You can have a seat."

David started reviewing some papers. Malcolm stayed and talked with the secretary.

"I'm curious. How come a pretty woman like you is working for Ducruet? I mean, I hear so many bad things about him, like sentencing black people to jail," Malcolm said, leaning on her desk.

"Girl's gotta eat and pay the rent," she said flirting with Malcolm. The phone flashed and the secretary led them into Ducruet's office.

Malcolm and David approached Ducruet who was sitting in a big burgundy leather chair, facing the window.

"Have a seat, gentlemen," he said, turning around to face them. Ducruet was a man in his late forties, impeccably dressed in a light camel-colored suit. "Can I get you anything?" Ducruet seemed surprised to see Malcolm standing there. He stood up to shake David Segal's hand. "And this is your assistant?" he asked, shaking hands with Malcolm.

"No, Michael. This is Malcolm Stinson. He will be the attorney representing Clarence Reed," David said, watching the bewildered look on Ducruet's face become a small smile. Malcolm noticed a man sitting in a corner of the office, but didn't mention anything about it.

"So where are you from, Mr. Stinson?" Ducruet asked, glancing over at the stranger in the room.

"I've practiced law in New York City for the last ten years, but I'm originally from New Orleans. Excuse me, I couldn't help but notice that you were not alone here. May I ask why that person is sitting over there?"

The man's silver hair looked distinguished at his temples and his dark thick eyebrows highlighted his hollow black eyes. He was a robust man of about sixty-plus years. The man turned around and stared briefly at Malcolm. He pushed himself up from his chair, exhaling loudly. He walked over to the edge of Ducruet's desk and sat on its corner. "Good morning, gentlemen. I'm Henri Joret, the next governor of Louisiana. David, who did you say your friend here is?" Joret asked, flashing a smile.

"Mr. Joret, this is Malcolm Stinson," David said. Joret made no move to shake hands with Malcolm, but neither did Malcolm. "Henri, this won't take long if you don't mind, I just have to go over a few things with these gentlemen, and then we can continue our business," Ducruet said, leaning forward on his desk. Joret got up and started to walk out of the office, then stopped at the door, and turned back. "Malcolm, my friend, I want you to review all the discovered evidence. Take your time, and when you finish, I'll tell you what I'll do. Instead of having Mr. Ducruet here ask for the death penalty, I promise you that Reed will just get life imprisonment. Now that's a fair offer. I know what you're thinking. It's too early in the game to make a call. But once you review everything, I'm sure you'll see we've got your client every which way from Sunday. Deal?" Henri said, extending his hand to Malcolm.

"No deal. Besides I haven't heard anything from Mr. Ducruet yet, and even more importantly, from my client, Clarence Reed. Are you Mr. Ducruet's spokesman?" Malcolm asked, leaning back in the chair.

Henri Joret smiled. "This is Louisiana, not New York or California. I run things here, Mr. Stinson, and the more time you spend here, the sooner you'll find that out. I have an election coming up in a few months, and I will win. The incumbent has problems with the law and Campy Frazier can't do much harm.

So you see, I'm practically a shoo-in, and whatever I say goes," Joret said. His eyes pierced through Malcolm.

"I'm so happy for you, but no deal." Malcolm turned to Ducruet. "Can we get on with our business, or would you like to schedule this meeting for another time?" Malcolm asked, ignoring Joret.

"Maybe that would be advisable. I understand you want to visit Clarence Reed today. I'll arrange it. Say about two p.m.?" Ducruet asked as he walked around his desk to show Malcolm and David out.

"Hold on a minute here. You haven't been listening to what I've said, boy." Joret's voice had suddenly risen three decibels.

"Frankly, I don't care what you have to say, and I'm not your boy," Malcolm said, standing to leave.

"Well, then you better be prepared to see your client fry, and I'll make sure it's a national spectacle. Don't mess with me, Malcolm Stinson; you've never seen the likes of me before," Joret said. Then, in a suddenly calmed voice, he said, "I know you must be a very competent lawyer up there in New York, but you're going to go down on this one, my friend." Joret gave Malcolm a sinister smile.

Malcolm walked to within inches of Joret's face. "When the opposition comes on to me like this, I know something is wrong—there's something they don't want me to know. So, Mister-want-to-be-governor-of-Louisiana, you've got yourself one hell of a fight coming. Chew on that for a while, Mr. Henri Joret," Malcolm said vehemently.

"Mr. Ducruet, we'll be in touch. Let's go, David. It's beginning to smell in here," Malcolm said, and he walked out of the office with David hot on his heels.

* * * *

"Now, Henri, calm down. You brought that all on yourself."

"You listen to me, Michael. I want a speedy trial, finished before the election. I'll show Mr. Malcolm Stinson a thing or two before it's all over," Henri said, turning beet-red. "I believe this boy's going to be a lot of trouble," Joret said, watching the reporters outside the window crowd around Malcolm as he left the building.

"Michael, would you excuse me for a moment? I'd like to make a private call."

Ducruet left. Henri picked up the phone, leaned back in the chair, propped his feet on Ducruet's desk, and dialed a number in Montreal, Canada.

"We may have a potential problem down here," Henri said, when Monet answered the phone.

"Oh? Such as?"

"The NAACP has been knocked out of the box, and now Reed has some slick, black New York lawyer, Your Honor."

"What's the difference, Henri? The evidence speaks for itself. So what would you like me to do?"

"I was thinking, well, you still have your boys in the neighborhood?"

"They are within reach."

"Good. Then I want them to keep an eye on this lawyer. His name is Malcolm Stinson. And, Monet, you might want to bring in someone special for this."

"Do you really think this is necessary, Henri?"

"Listen to me, Monet. I can't afford for anything to go wrong. Nor can you. We both have a vested interest here. We can't afford to be careless. Do I make myself clear?" Joret growled.

"I get your point, Henri. They'll be on the job in a couple of days. Good enough?"

"I suppose so, except for one thing. I need reports of their work. Is that a problem?" Henri asked.

"That might be. I'll let you know."

"Good. I'll be in touch. Goodbye," Henri said. As he hung up, Ducruet walked back into the office.

"Michael, we need a speedy trial here..."

"Henri, do you realize how much evidence has to be reviewed by both parties first?" Ducruet said.

Henri got up from the desk, and grabbed his raincoat and porkpie hat. "Michael, do you ever watch Star Trek: The Next Generation?"

"I don't understand. Um, I might have caught an episode or two, why?"

"Well, again, I'll reiterate. I want a speedy trial, and, in the words of the infamous Captain Picard, make it so. Have a good day."

Chapter 3

Suzanne Joret drove her forest-green BMW through the winding roads of the flatlands of the Louisiana Delta. It was sixty-one degrees on this Christmas morning, so she opened the sunroof. She was happy to be visiting her mother, bringing an elegant silk scarf she'd bought for her on a recent trip to New York. But she was not thrilled to see her stepfather, Henri Joret.

Usually, at this time of day, there would be people walking along the roadside or other cars creeping through the country. But since it was Christmas morning, no one was on the road. Suzanne missed Clarence and had a sudden urge to change her route and go to the Angola Prison instead. But Clarence felt it wasn't in their best interest for the public to know about their romance.

She slowed down and drove through the rows of chinaberry trees that lined the entrance to the 1850 refurbished antebellum house. Suzanne dreaded spending time with her half-brothers and their families. She never got along with them when they were growing up. She was the oldest child, but the only one unmarried.

When she arrived at 9:45 a.m., there were no other cars. When no one responded to the doorbell, she started to walk towards the rear of the house, where she knew the maid and cook would already be preparing Christmas dinner. Suddenly, the huge front doors opened, and the housekeeper greeted her. Suzanne entered the house and called up the winding staircase to her mother. Suzanne saw the door to Henri's study slightly ajar. Alva, Suzanne's mother, hated the room and usually kept it closed and locked. Entry to it was forbidden.

The room was more like a museum than a study with antique artifacts on the walls. A large Confederate flag hung on the wall directly across from the door.

Taxidermy owls, hawks, and a four-foot alligator were spread around the room. Ten years ago, Henri had had the walls knocked out to display his showcase of rare coins he had collected since he was a boy. Suzanne remembered his telling her that the coins were valued at $300,000.

She had played hide-and-seek in this room years ago. Since it was forbidden to enter, it was the perfect place to hide. She walked in to see if any changes had been made in the last few years. Even though she had visited the house many times since she had moved out seven years ago, she hadn't been back in Henri's study. She glanced around at the different artifacts but quickly became bored with the room. As she turned to leave, she noticed the phone on the desk. She thought this would be a good time to call Sun Reed, Clarence's mother, to wish her a Merry Christmas. When she put the receiver to her ear and stared to dial, she heard two men talking. She covered the receiver gently with her hand and listened.

"I don't like the idea of this New York lawyer coming down here to represent Reed. Sandchester gave me a preliminary report last night," Henri said, speaking softly.

"What sort of report? And who is Sandchester?" Jean Claude Monet asked.

"Sandchester is my campaign manager, and his report says this Stinson boy is one damn good lawyer. Hell, I want to know who's footing the bill for Reed. From what I understand, this Stinson boy charges big bucks for his representation. Hell, I can't imagine a firm like his taking this case pro bono. Too much is at stake for his firm to foot the bill."

"So why are you worried? We know what happened as far as Reed is concerned, a job well done," Monet said, laughing.

"I suppose you're right. My sources from the feds say they're not paying any attention to Reed's allegation about another man being involved. And get this: they're charging him with the death of Harpo Stevens, as well," Henri said.

"You see, all's well, except for one little problem."

"What do you mean problem? I thought we didn't have any," Henri asked.

"I hear, through the grapevine, that my American cousins are not thoroughly convinced that Reed and his accomplices committed the bombing. So be careful if you get a visit from New York, from one Victor Zano," Monet said, cautiously.

"Um, when should I expect him?"

"Anytime, any day, it's nothing you can't..."

"I'm sorry, Ms. Suzy, but I had my pots cooking, and I smelled something burning when you came to the front door," Colette said when she popped her head into the study.

"What the hell was that, Henri?" Monet asked excitedly.

"I don't know. Hello? Hold on. Let me see."

Henri put down the phone and rushed out of the room, calling his wife, Alva. There was no response. He flew down the spiral staircase to the phone in the study and flung the door open.

"Suzanne! What are you doing here?" he asked accusingly.

"I was looking for Mother. I called out and no one answered. I saw the door open and came in to make a call. I heard voices on the phone, and hung up. Is something wrong?" she asked innocently.

"I heard another voice on the phone," he said, walking slowly toward her.

Suzanne took her eyes off of Henri, and reached for her bag of Christmas gifts and very nonchalantly replied, "Oh, that was Colette. She came into the study at practically the same moment I picked up the phone. Do you know where Mother is?"

"Probably in the greenhouse," he answered, as Suzanne scooted past him. He watched her suspiciously. Henri waited until Suzanne was out of earshot, then picked up the phone.

"Monet? You still there?"

"Oui, what happened?"

"It was just my stepdaughter. My children are coming over for Christmas dinner. She just picked up the phone to make a call. She didn't hear any of our conversation."

"I hope so, for your sake."

"What the hell does that mean?"

"It means there are no loose ends on my part. Let's hope there are none on yours, Monsieur Joret. But anyway, you're probably right. Forgive me for being so forward. So, don't forget about a visit from Zano."

"You were telling me about Zano. What if he comes looking for you?"

"No need to worry, my friend. He can't connect me with anything. So go have fun with your family and Merry Christmas to you. Au revoir," Monet said, cheerfully.

"Yeah, Merry Christmas to you, too," Henri replied. He stood there for a moment, wondering if Suzanne had heard any of their conversation. He would try to rest his suspicions by questioning Colette.

Suzanne flew into the kitchen where Colette and four other housekeepers were busy cooking the Joret gala Southern gourmet Christmas dinner. Suzanne grabbed Colette and walked with her towards the greenhouse.

"Now, Colette, you've known me for over twenty years and we've been friends, haven't we?"

"Why yes, Ms. Suzy, whatever is the matter?" Colette asked, as Suzanne held her arm firmly.

"If Mr. Joret asks you how long I was in the study—no, better yet, how long I was in the house before you came and spoke to me—you tell him that I had just walked in. Okay?"

"Don't you worry any, Ms. Suzy. I'll take care of it. We women have got to stick together. Right?"

"You're absolutely right, my sister," Suzanne said, as she gave Colette a kiss on the cheek, and then rushed away to greet her mother in the greenhouse.

"Colette," Henri yelled out, rushing into the kitchen.

"Yes, Mr. Joret," she replied, softly.

"When Ms. Suzanne came into the house, how long was it before she used the telephone?"

"Uh, I answered the door, and she said hello, and she wanted to know where Ms. Joret was. I told her I didn't know. She said she had to make a phone call, and went into the study. I took about five paces, then remembered that Ms. Joret was in the greenhouse, so I went back to tell Ms. Suzanne. As I walked in, she was just picking up the phone. Is there anything wrong, sir?" Colette asked, innocently.

"No, I was just wondering. Thank you," Henri said, walking away. The other cooks quietly gave Colette a standing ovation for her performance.

* * * *

Jean Claude Monet was the head of all the crime families in Montreal, Canada. But for him, it wasn't enough to run drugs, illegal numbers, prostitution, and private gambling parlors. He wanted more. The American crime families had drawn the line, forbidding him to cross the U.S. border.

He stood at his condo window overlooking a wintry Montreal. With him was Otto Salinger, his trusted colleague for the past twenty years. He was a former boxer and a good businessman. This was the one man Monet trusted more than any other.

"Otto, do you know what my key to success has been all these years?" Monet asked, looking out at the countryside.

"Good business savvy?" Otto replied.

"Yes, but the key is to know the people you deal with in business. Take, for example, our friend Henri Joret. He has aspirations to be Louisiana's next governor, and after that, maybe President of the United States. My, my, wouldn't he be someone to have for an ally? So, as I was saying, here's a man whose wife is a socialite, and whose three hard-working sons have families. But the black sheep is the girl, Suzanne. She's actually Henri's stepdaughter."

"So, because she's a stepdaughter, that makes her a black sheep? I was the stepson and I turned out alright," Otto replied.

"No, I didn't mean it like that. She's a television news reporter, and she really has no real, oh, what is the word I'm looking for…"

"Allegiance?" Otto blurted out.

"Precisely. No allegiance to Henri," Monet said, with fire in his eyes. And that is why we can't afford to take any chances on whether Ms. Suzanne Joret overheard my conversation. Otto, I want you to call Jasper. Tell him to have the Dalton brothers put a tail on Suzanne Joret, immediately. I want wiretaps in her house, in her car, and on her. I want to know who she talks to, who she spends time with. Tell Jasper I want this done yesterday. I'm going to my ex-wife's for Christmas. Call me later tonight to tell me of your progress. Au revoir and Merry Christmas, Otto," Monet said, grabbing his coat.

"And what if the girl knows something?" Otto asked.

"We'll kill her," Monet calmly said.

*   *   *   *

By 4:00 p.m., the Stinson house was full of family members. Elaine's death so close to Christmas made it hard for them to truly enjoy the holidays, but the reverend insisted on spending Christmas with family and friends. He thought celebrating the joy of Jesus' birth was far greater than his daughter's death. Even as a minister, he struggled with this thought. He had relatives from California, and all over the South, who'd come to spend the holidays with him and Lois.

Malcolm relished having a home-cooked meal—something he hadn't enjoyed in months. Sara was a better-than-average cook, and he considered himself an amateur gourmet cook. But the long hours at work made it hard for him to indulge in his passion for cooking.

The children were having the time of their lives, meeting and getting reacquainted with cousins and new friends. Conversations and laughter buzzed through the Stinson home.

The reverend found Malcolm on the back porch with some church deacons. He was slouched on the sofa, half asleep.

"You know what they say about you folks when you have a full stomach," the reverend said to Malcolm.

"Don't even go there, Papa Joe. There must be millions who are feeling the same way I do right now," Malcolm said, with a sleepy laugh.

"I want you to meet someone," said the reverend, helping Malcolm up from the couch.

"You sure those deacons haven't had a little Christmas cheer? They're awfully groggy for just eating a heavy meal," Malcolm asked, as he cleared his head.

"No, they haven't. I don't stand for that sort of thing. So many churches worship God on Sunday, and act like the devil on Monday. No, sir, I have some righteous men serving with me," the reverend said, as he stopped in the hallway.

They entered the living room that probably had at least twenty people scattered about in various conversations. The reverend stood by the doorway until he saw a bald-headed man, with a salt-and-pepper goatee. Once he got his attention, the three men left the house and walked down the quiet street without saying a word. Once they were out of earshot, the reverend introduced Cephus to Malcolm.

"Cephus is a homicide lieutenant here in New Orleans. He's a trusted friend and I believe he can help us," the reverend said, as the three men stood under a streetlight.

Up the street, two FBI agents were cursing each other for not bringing ultraviolet equipment to take pictures at night. They agreed to keep this out of their report, but would try to recognize who was walking with Malcolm. They did their best with binoculars under the dim light, but were already too close and didn't dare risk moving closer. All they could do was sit and wait.

"Thank you for your confidence. Let's walk down to the corner and over to the next street," Cephus said.

"I've got a house full of people. You two chat awhile. I'll see you later," the reverend said.

The FBI agents started to creep behind Malcolm and Cephus.

Malcolm started to talk but Cephus shushed him. They reached the end of the block, and Cephus motioned for Malcolm to follow him. They ran to the end house and peeped around the corner. The FBI agents were on the move.

"What's the matter?" Malcolm asked.

"I've been a cop for twenty-five years and have seen my share of stakeouts. I noticed two men in that car when I pulled up to your house. Since we started walking the car has been moving. Can you run?" Cephus asked a startled Malcolm.

"Follow me," Cephus said, and began trotting through the backyards to the Stinson home. Thirty-eight-year-old Malcolm was in fairly good shape, but he could hardly keep up with the lean fifty-year-old Cephus. They stopped for a barking pit bull making his backyard patrol. Malcolm could keep track of Cephus because of the moon gleaming off of his bald head.

"You see them?" Malcolm asked, watching Cephus look for the car coming slowly down the street. The old pit bull was tired and didn't bother to bark.

"Why would somebody be following you here, Cephus?"

"What makes you think they're following me, Counselor?"

"I can't imagine why anyone would follow me."

"Think again, new hotshot lawyer for Clarence Reed. And they—whoever they are—probably want to keep tabs on your whereabouts."

"Maybe they are the real bombers of the River Queen, or the prosecution, or even the police," Cephus said, waving Malcolm to keep low. They went to the far end of the big backyard and pretended to be having a friendly chat. Through the fence, Malcolm and Cephus could see the car, that had been following them, going back up the block.

"You're back in New Orleans, Malcolm. Watch your back while you're here. The reason I say that is because the feds keep the local police away as much as possible on this case with Reed."

"Why's that? I mean, this is your jurisdiction."

"But it was treated like a terrorist attack, and the feds took over. Anyway, I did some poking around and found out some very interesting things."

"Such as?" Malcolm asked, listening intently, while searching to see if anyone tried to come close.

"I was there on the night of the bombing. I've never seen such devastation, not even in war footage. Bodies were ripped apart and spread all over the river and the French Quarter. They still haven't found all of the bodies yet, probably because they don't know exactly how many people were on the riverboat. You know anything about the Mississippi River, Counselor?" Cephus said, watching a young man who was observing them.

"Not much. My father always kept us away from the river because of the currents."

"Exactly. Currents. There must be at least five different currents in that river that can trap bodies for months, even years. They still drag the river and find bodies. Listen, we're going to have to talk some other time."

"Don't look now, but you see that young dude over there talking with that old man?"

"Yeah," Malcolm said, glancing out of the side of his eyes.

"That boy claims he has changed his life by going to church, but I've seen him hanging around his old boss, Benny Dubois."

"Who's Benny Dubois?"

"The question should be who he's not. Dope pusher, pimp, arms dealer, muscle man. You name it, he does it. His main thing is drugs; he uses teenage kids as pushers. If the kids get busted they go to juvenile court. The punishment is not as stringent as for an adult, but when they get older, say 18, he uses them for other duties, mostly recruiting other teenage kids. I've seen him hanging around the Desire housing projects. Your father claims he's trying to work with him, but some kids are just incorrigible."

"Did you tell my father he was incorrigible?"

"Yeah, why?"

"When you tell the reverend a person in incorrigible, that makes him try even harder. Cephus, Pete Neil is my private detective from New York. I'd like to have him around, mean, give him the scoop on how things work down here."

"Sure, I suspect those guys following us were feds," Cephus said, looking at the young boy.

"Why feds?"

"You know Jon Tulle?"

"All too well."

"I heard he's poking around asking questions about your father and you. One more thing: pay close attention to Akins and Gere's autopsy reports. And I would make it my business to talk to Clarence Reed's mother. Also, his secret girlfriend, Suzanne Joret," Cephus said, and then broke out in laughter.

Once inside, Malcolm pulled Cephus to the side. "I forgot to tell you that Pete is an old-school, former Irish cop. You wouldn't have a problem with that, would you?"

"Do you trust him?" Cephus asked.

"With my life."

"Then I half-way trust him. But since your father tells me you're on the up and up, I'll work with your friend Pete Neil."

* * * *

The teenage boy, Joy Boy, pulled out his cell phone to call his old boss, Benny Dubois, as soon as Malcolm and Cephus were inside the house.

CHAPTER 4

Jasper Yates came to America when he was twelve years old, but he never forgot his German roots. He didn't have much of a legacy from his father, an American soldier who'd gone AWOL. In Germany, a man could take on his wife's last name—so when Jack Philips married Ilsa Yates and became Jack Yates, it wasn't out of love. It was to escape court-martial.

Jasper had been a Navy SEAL lieutenant for ten years. He enlisted in the Navy when he was eighteen years old, became a SEAL right after his twentieth birthday, and quickly moved through the ranks to lieutenant. Early in his Navy career, he was introduced to hate organizations by a sergeant who later became the Ku Klux Klan's grand dragon wizard in Alabama. That's where Jasper learned how to pull recruits from the SEALs.

Jasper had connections throughout the entire country, and he would direct men to the KKK, Neo-Nazis, or new groups in their home states. He had even made allegiances with certain splinter groups of the Irish Republican Army. He would take two-month furloughs every year and fly to West Germany to teach paramilitary operations to German Neo-Nazi groups. He solicited through his former troops to the KKK, to take paramilitary training. He led them in practice target-shooting, and laying of explosives and grenades. Jasper also taught hand-to-hand combat, specifically the art of silent killing. For bold Klan members who wanted to see real combat action, Jasper would arrange for them to participate in the Croatia war. Few Klan members had the heart for it; most of them just wanted to play war games and preach American racism. They were consumed with their hatred for blacks and Jews.

Jasper was well-liked and respected by the various heads of the Neo-Nazi cell groups. On weekends, he showed the classic Klan movie favorite, "Mississippi Burning," for his friends from the States.

Jasper had done mercenary work in Panama, Grenada, Honduras, Nicaragua and several African countries. He'd met Jean Claude Monet on a ski trip in Austria, where they'd become good friends and business partners.

On Christmas day, he was chopping wood on his twenty acres of land in Idaho. He lived alone in a wooden cabin that he'd built by himself. He was once married, but his wife and only child were killed in an auto accident in Baltimore, Maryland, and he had never married again or even had any relationships. He lived in Kootenai County, which was surrounded by Coeur d' Alene. It was a sportsman's paradise, with sixteen deep lakes, and fifty-four miles of navigable rivers. This was his home.

Returning to the cabin, he found his beeper screaming for his attention. When he stripped off his sweaty clothes, his physique was that of a man twenty years his junior. He was clean-shaven with a square face, and dark hollow eyes. He called the number on the beeper.

"Monsieur Monet. I see you've tried to get me several times. How can I help you?" Jasper asked, in his best French accent.

"My assistant Otto has been calling all day. I see on the weather report that you're up to your ass in snow," Monet said, jokingly.

"Yeah, but I don't mind."

"Well, pack your shorts. You're needed in New Orleans."

"Really? Something new?"

"Somewhat. My colleague is getting a little paranoid about some new lawyer handling the Reed case and he wants him tailed."

"Let him hire a private detective. I don't do that sort of work."

"It's worth another hundred thousand for a few days or weeks of work. Also, you might have to terminate someone, depending on what you find out."

"Since you put it that way, it does sound rather enticing."

"Jasper, two things: you'll need the Dalton brothers to help you, and my partner, Henri Joret, wants to be able to get a progress report from time to time."

"You know, Monet, I don't work like that."

"He's paying and, friend, he pays well."

"We'll see. Once I get into New Orleans, just tell him I call the shots. Now what is this lawyer's name?"

"Malcolm Stinson. Au revoir, my friend."

Jasper hung up, then replied, "And a parlez-vous to you, too. Damned Canadians."

* * * *

Malcolm waited in Cafe Du Monde in the French Quarter. It was one of the first businesses to reopen three days earlier. There had been extensive damage to this longtime establishment. Malcolm sat quietly watching the business people, and the fragment of tourists who were more interested in the remains of the explosion than the mystery of New Orleans and the French Quarter. He sipped on hot coffee, and ate beignets topped with powdered sugar.

Malcolm remembered the fun times he and Sara had had here on their fly-away weekends to New Orleans before they married. He thought about the Giamanco trial, and how it had strained their marriage that last year. How would this trial affect his children?

Over the steam of his coffee, he saw a sultry woman with short hair and wearing a revealing red, dress. From where he sat she resembled Sara, and for a moment, he thought it was Sara. Why did she have to come to the funeral? Everything had been fine until he saw her again.

The woman winked at him as she passed by. He stared at her until she was out of view. Then, a familiar voice interrupted his thoughts.

"There you are," greeted the reverend, as he and Campy approached Malcolm.

"About time you two got here," he barked.

"We had to take care of a few things. You okay? You seem a little upset. I saw that pretty woman walk by here. She sure looked like Sara to me," the reverend said, sitting down.

"Sorry, Papa Joe. She did remind me of Sara. Is she still here?" Malcolm asked, intently.

"No. She left for New York this morning, and left a number for you to call her."

"Look, guys, this seems like a family affair. I'll be over by the car when you're ready to go to the prison," Campy said, walking away.

The reverend sat down next to Malcolm and put his arm around him. "We've never talked about the divorce. It's not my business, but I am your father, and you can talk to me. Son, the good Lord does everything for a reason. Even though His word says He hates divorce..."

"Then you're telling me He had reason for Elaine to be killed?"

"I can't answer that. It's a question I'll ask Him the day I see Him. Listen, you got the kids. Why not start over right here in Louisiana? You turned out all right. Shucks, it'll be good for the kids, too. Leave that dirty New York City. For the life of me, I don't know why you were so fascinated by that cesspool."

"It's not bad if you know your way around. I'll be alright, Papa. Let's go meet Clarence Reed now. Did little Joe take care of my flight for tonight?" Malcolm asked, as they got up to leave.

"Sure did. I had a deacon run him out to the airport to pick up your ticket. Flight leaves at 8:05 p.m. on Delta and arrives at 11:15 p.m. at La Guardia. Anyone picking you up?"

"I'll take a cab."

"Come on, cheer up. You're about to embark on your greatest case ever."

"Sure. Or maybe the most dreaded case ever," Malcolm said, as they were on their way to the Angola prison.

* * * *

It took them most of an hour to reach the Angola Prison. Meanwhile, Clarence was entertaining another visitor. Her chestnut hair cascaded across her warm almond face. She crossed her long, sculptured legs. Suzanne Joret was there, using her status as a reporter to see Clarence Reed.

"How've you been, Clarence?" Suzanne was careful with her words, seeing the guards nearby. Clarence caught on instantly.

"Praise God. Pretty good, Ms. Joret," he replied.

Suzanne's eyes slowly filled with tears. "So, how are they treating you in here?"

"I've stayed in better places," Clarence said, with a slight grin.

"Rumor has it that you've released the NAACP for your defense. Is it true?" she asked, pulling out a pad, as if she were conducting an interview.

"That's correct, Ms. Joret. My prospective new lawyer is on his way, even as we speak."

"And who is this person?"

"He's Reverend Josiah Stinson's son from New York City. I believe his name is Malcolm. Supposed to be some sort of big-shot criminal lawyer."

"Is there any particular reason you released the NAACP?" she asked, already tired of playing this stupid game of questions and answers.

"I can only say, at this time, that it's personal."

Suzanne paused for a moment and stared at Clarence through the glass, wanting desperately to touch him. "I assure you, Mr. Reed, that we'll back you in finding out the truth about this tragedy," she said, as a tear rolled down her face.

Clarence couldn't take it anymore, either. "Thank you for coming, Ms. Joret." He put his hand on the glass, and quickly removed it, trying not to let his affection for Suzanne be seen by others. He mouthed the words, "I love you," then called for the guard.

In an attempt to compose herself before she left, Suzanne wiped her eyes, and then met her camera crew outside. In the parking lot, four cars were pulled in near the KETV van, and Malcolm and company exited the cars.

Suzanne walked up to Reverend Josiah. "Hello, Reverend." She hugged him, burying the tears in his chest.

"Now, now, honey. It's going to be all right. I want you to meet someone. This here is my son, Malcolm. He's going to free Clarence," the reverend said.

"Pleased to meet you, Mr. Stinson. I hope you're as good as Clarence says you are. Clarence's life is depending on it," she said, wiping tears away.

"I hope so, too, Ms...."

"Joret, Suzanne Joret."

"I'm quite sure we'll work it out," Malcolm said, solemnly.

"Remember, Mr. Stinson, this is Louisiana." She reached in her pocketbook and handed him her card. "Call me if I can help in any way," she said. After kissing the reverend on the cheek, she left to meet with her camera crew by the TV van.

"What was that all about?" Malcolm asked, curiously.

"She and Clarence were about to get married before all this happened," the reverend said. "Only his mother and I knew about their romance."

Malcolm turned and glanced at Suzanne. "I like Clarence already. He's got good taste in women. She's ravishing."

"Keep your mind on the business at hand, son," the reverend said, taking Malcolm by the arm.

From the public parking area, Malcolm, David Segal, Reverend Josiah, and Campy Frazier walked up the dirt road to Angola prison. The first out-cove was a wired fence with a glistening razor wire on top. A pudgy red-faced guard, whose clothes seemed a size too small, met the four men.

"Afternoon. What can I do for you all?" he asked, chewing on tobacco and spitting a glob next to Malcolm.

"We're here to see Clarence Reed. I believe Federal Prosecutor Ducruet called ahead," Malcolm said, disgusted that the guard spat so close to him.

"Umm, nothing on my board here. Wait right there. Let me make a phone call." He walked away to a little shack, and then was back in less than a minute. "You're the lawyer?"

"Yes."

"I was told that another lawyer named Segal, and a reverend, and some guy named Campy…"

"That's us," said the reverend.

"Alright. Then I need everybody to sign this here clipboard."

Once they all had signed it, he motioned them on to the main building. There was another row of barbed wire fences and more guards. The guards motioned for them to follow them inside. They walked past three trustees who were slowly mopping the floor. One guard instructed the group to line up against the wall so he could frisk them, while the other guard kept watch. He patted the four men down. They emptied their pockets of all keys and sharp instruments, pens, and knives. Two guards led them on a ten-minute walk through an area isolated from the rest of the prisoners. One of the guards, a black man named Calvin, led them up a flight of stairs and put them in a room.

"Only two at a time can see Reed," Calvin said, pulling out the keys and unlocking the door. Inside the room was a wire mesh fence, set up so that a maximum of six pairs of people could meet.

Once inside, Malcolm asked Calvin, "Just where exactly are we?"

"We're in the MSU, otherwise known as the Maximum Security Unit," Calvin said, pointing to a booth that Malcolm could use.

"You mean you're keeping him on death row, and he hasn't even had a trial yet?" Malcolm asked.

"My sentiments exactly, but they say it's for his own safety. I only work here. There have been a lot of death threats, though. Now, if you'll have a seat, Clarence will be out momentarily," Calvin said, as he locked them in. Only Malcolm and the reverend remained in the room.

"What sort of place is this, Malcolm?" the reverend asked, slowly sitting down.

"It's where they keep the convicted murderers. We need to do something about this," Malcolm said, and then banged on the door to call Calvin back.

"Yes, Counselor. They're bringing Clarence in now," he said, peeping through the slot in the door.

Malcolm came close to the door and whispered to Calvin. "I saw two men in blue wind-breaker jackets as we were coming in. They didn't look like prison guards."

"They're FBI agents. They're here to make sure nothing happens," Calvin replied, looking around to see if anyone was watching.

"Nothing happens? What do you mean?"

"Reed has had some serious death threats here in prison. Some of the inmates had relatives in the bombing and have vowed to get their revenge against Reed. That's one reason for keeping him here," Calvin said, slowly closing the door.

Behind Malcolm, another door opened and an expressionless Clarence Reed entered, dressed in orange prison fatigues, with chains on his wrists and ankles. He weakly smiled when he saw Reverend Josiah. As he sat down, the guards released Clarence's chains.

"How you doing, son?" the reverend asked.

"I'm at peace, Reverend. God has reason for this. I'm just hoping I can bear it out," Clarence said quietly.

"Clarence, I want you to meet my son, Malcolm. He's the lawyer from New York I told you about...you know, the criminal lawyer," the reverend said.

"Hello, Mr. Stinson," Clarence said.

"Just call me, Malcolm. Pleased to meet you, Clarence," Malcolm answered. "How have they been treating you here?" Malcolm asked, leaning on the counter of the booth.

"It's better now. When I first came, they treated me like I'd killed the President of the United States," Reed said. Then he changed course on Malcolm and the reverend. "Reverend, I appreciate everything you're trying to do for me, but these people want me dead, or in jail for the rest of my life. I want a good Jewish lawyer," Clarence said.

Malcolm sat back in his chair and just looked at Clarence for a second. Then he turned toward his father with a slight smile.

"What in the devil are you talking about, boy? Malcolm is one of the best criminal lawyers in the country. Sure, there are a lot of Jewish, and every other kind of lawyers, who would want to represent you for the publicity."

The reverend stood straight up and walked toward the door. "What else are they doing to you in here, Clarence?" the reverend asked in disbelief.

Malcolm spun around in the swivel chair. "Papa Joe, can you give Clarence and me a few minutes to talk?"

"Sure. Now you listen to Malcolm. Ever since the day I met you, I've never lied or deceived you. So please listen to Malcolm," the reverend said, as he walked out of the room.

Malcolm turned to Clarence, and stared directly into his eyes. "Look, I don't know where this Jewish lawyer thing came from, and frankly I don't care. I came here for two reasons: first, my father believes you're innocent, and secondly, to find the men that killed my sister. I understand you cared about Suzanne. Do you think she would want her brother to find the killers?" Malcolm said, intently.

"This is Louisiana, Mr. Stinson, and a lot of white folk want quick justice, and it seems as though I'm their man."

"So, why give them that satisfaction? Let's fight them."

"Your father tells me that you've practiced criminal law for about ten years. You had any cases like mine?"

"Not bombing cases, but there are many similarities to murder cases."

"Well, let's not let them get away with this, Mr. Stinson," Clarence said, with a smile. "Okay, where do you want to start, Mr. Stinson?"

"First, call me Malcolm from now on. Second, sign these papers that authorize me to be your lawyer; and third, tell me everything said and done from about three months before the bombing," Malcolm said, pulling out a small notebook from his jacket.

Clarence went over everything that he could remember. The most significant point was the phone call from Harpo Stevens, and his subsequent introduction to a German with grayish-red hair and matching goatee, named Oppenheimer. He needed some divers to unclog a pipe from a chemical plant. The job was to pay $3,000 for one day's work.

Malcolm wanted a full description of Oppenheimer: what he looked like, how he talked, how tall he was, and how much he weighed.

The guard came in and told them that that was all the time they would have that day. Malcolm told Clarence that he would return soon for more information, and assured him that everything would be fine. At least that's what Malcolm was hoping for.

"Well, what happened? Did he agree?" Campy asked Malcolm, as the reverend looked on.

"Let's get busy, gentlemen. They're holding an innocent man in jail," Malcolm said with a smile. The reverend embraced him.

When the four men were led out of Angola Prison, the media awaited them. Television, print, and radio were represented.

"What's all this?" Malcolm asked Campy.

"Good to have some publicity. Up until now, everything's seemed to be downhill for Brother Reed, so let's give the media some good news," Campy said, with a proud look.

Malcolm stopped before the barrage of reporters, as one of Campy's henchmen made way for him to the car.

"Mr. Stinson, are you here to represent Clarence Reed?" a reporter asked.

"I have only one statement to make. I'm now representing Clarence Reed, and I will prove that he didn't commit these heinous crimes he's being charged with here in Louisiana," Malcolm said calmly, and then thought of planting a tidbit for the real terrorists, if they were listening. "We also plan to bring the real terrorists to justice before this trial is over. Thank you. I have nothing further to add at this time," Malcolm said, as he was hurried into the car.

* * * *

While reviewing some evidence with a team of explosive-residue experts, an agent interrupted the heavily-built chief inspector of the FBI, Jon Tulle. "Inspector, excuse me, but I think you should watch this," the agent said, and turned on the television. Suzanne Joret was giving her report.

"In the bombing case of the gambling riverboat, the accused Clarence Reed, who just days ago fired the NAACP lawyers, hired a new lawyer today. Malcolm Stinson, a New York criminal lawyer, was seen today leaving Angola Prison, where Clarence Reed awaits his day in court. There is word going around that this highly acclaimed trial could begin as early as November of this year."

"I can't believe this. Stinson, here in New Orleans," Tulle said in a fury.

"Jon, did you know his father is a minister here in New Orleans, and this Reed fellow is a member of his father's church?" asked the inspector of the Explosives Residue Team.

"Listen, guys, I'll get back with you tomorrow on these things. There's something I must take care of now," Tulle said, as the agents began to leave his office. "Wait, Hansen, I want you and Crawford to follow Mr. Stinson. I want to know about everyone he talks to, and every place he goes. We're not going to let the same thing happen here that happened in the Giamanco case." He leaned back on his chair, and took a deep breath. "So, go, go, go!" Tulle barked and waved them out of his office.

He turned to the only agent that remained in his office. "I will know everything Stinson knows, come trial time. And if this Ducruet can't handle this case, we'll have to get rid of him. I want to know everything about him, too, so let's hop to it," Tulle said, reaching for a cigarette.

* * * *

Malcolm stopped at his parent's house to see the children and pack for the cold New York weather. By the time he reached the airport, the two FBI agents were already on his trail and boarded the plane with him.

CHAPTER 5

Weinstein, Abrams & Calucci was the third largest law firm in New York City with over 500 attorneys working in one building. The firm also had offices in Chicago, Los Angeles, Toronto, and New Orleans.

They hired only the top legal minds, and had a small, but excellent, litigation department. They had a reputation of hiring vicious law students. Ten years ago, they had seen promise in one such Harvard Law School student. His name was Malcolm Stinson.

Originally, Malcolm wanted to work in the insurance department, which charged $300 to $400 an hour. However, the senior partners thought otherwise. The firm hired few women and minorities, but Malcolm was not a token minority; he more than met their standards.

For two years, the FBI had investigated Franco Giamanco's businesses, and in 1992, he was arrested for racketeering, money laundering, and murder. Giamanco's father, Vito, the Brooklyn crime boss, approached the firm for legal help. The public was shocked that a prestigious law firm like Weinstein, Abrams & Calucci would consider Giamanco as a client.

Even though it was kept quiet among the senior partners, Malcolm Stinson was chosen to represent the crime boss's son. Giamanco paid $1,000 an hour, and it was well worth it. After a three-month trial, Franco Giamanco walked out of the federal court a free man. Malcolm had beaten the government, but had made a mortal enemy, as well.

Although it was a major victory, Malcolm suffered dearly for it. The months of long hours had severely damaged his marriage. Malcolm won the battle, but lost the war. He lost his wife and family for a criminal, someone whom Malcolm had always suspected was guilty.

He gazed out the frosty window of the cab approaching the law firm. He checked his watch, trying to decide what he would be able to accomplish today. He was determined to be back tonight and spend Christmas with his children. Malcolm arrived at six a.m. and went directly to his office. He passed a solitary maintenance man who was methodically polishing the marble floor.

There was mail sitting on his black leather couch, and photographs of Sara and the children were still positioned on his desk. He hadn't gotten around to removing them yet. He sat down at his desk in his cushioned, high-back chair, picked up the phone, and called Pete Neil, his private investigator and longtime trusted friend.

"Good morning, Pete. Happy holidays to you," Malcolm said in an early morning, chipper voice.

"Must really be nice there in Hawaii for you to want to call and wish me holiday cheer," he replied.

"Actually, old buddy, I'm right here in the city."

"Don't tell me you got snow sick. Why are you calling me so early in the morning? For your information, detectives usually work late nights. That's when all the crazies come out and you discover things."

"Well, that may very well be true, but I have some good news for you."

"If it's a job, forget about it. I'm thinking about moving to Florida for a few months. Really, this winter thing has started far too early and I'm sick of snow already," he said, and then paused.

"Pete, Pete, are you awake?"

"Yeah, stop shouting!"

"I do have a job for you, but it's not here."

"Is it warm?"

"It's warmer than it is here, and there's no snow."

"I'm listening."

"You heard about the New Orleans riverboat bombing in July?"

"Yeah..."

"I'm the defense lawyer for the guy they arrested for the bombing."

"Really? That sounds good, laddy," Pete said, as he sat up in bed. "Sounds like you'll need some detailed private eye work."

"Absolutely, my friend. When can you go down?"

"Oh, a couple days after Christmas. I promised my aunt I'd come for Christmas dinner."

"Good. By the way, have you been to New Orleans before?"

"The stories I could tell you. Check me in at The Orleans in the French Quarter. I like that place."

"Pete, this is going to be a serious case. Maybe even more involved than the Giamanco case."

"You sound worried, is everything alright?"

"I'm fine, just tired. I've been busy these last few days."

"I'm curious. How did you go from taking a trip to Hawaii into a major federal case in Louisiana?"

"My sister died in the River Queen bombing, while I was in Hawaii and…"

"I'm sorry. Say no more, my friend. I'll see you in N'Awlins in a few days. Call you as soon as I arrive."

"Thanks, Pete, and Merry Christmas."

"Merry Christmas to you."

* * * *

Malcolm looked through his law books searching for any cases about bombing trials. He checked his office for anything he might need in New Orleans. Then he took the elevator to Walter Baer's office on the fiftieth floor.

Walter Baer had worked at the firm for over thirty years. He married Leo Abrams' daughter twenty-seven years ago, and they had three children. Eighteen months ago, just when Walter was considering retirement, his wife died of breast cancer. To fill the emptiness her loss left, he kept working. As he waved him in, Malcolm opened the door and saw Walter looking over some papers. Malcolm thought he was looking like a college professor more than a lawyer.

Walter stood, expressionless at first, and then embraced Malcolm with open arms.

"Good to see you, Malcolm. Now have a seat. We don't have much time."

"Well, what's going to happen?" Malcolm asked, sitting back in the leather chair.

"There'll be a war with Rothman. When he makes a decision, the others usually fight him, but in the end, he wins. I had a brief conversation with him this morning, and he wants to hear more about your reasons for doing this. And if Calucci objects, we can sway him by throwing the Giamanco case in his face."

"I can't understand why Rothman hates me. Did I ever do anything to him?" Malcolm walked over to Walter's window overlooking Central Park.

"You don't understand it? He's a top criminal litigator, and so are you. He had that heart attack two months before Giamanco brought us the case, and he couldn't take the case—so you got it, and the glory. That's what pissed him off. I thought you knew that," Walter said, adjusting his bow tie. "Rothman will attack, Abrams will act as a peacemaker, and then we'll play it by ear. So tell me what you know about the case, and why you want to take it." Walter sat back to listen to Malcolm's story.

For the next two hours, Malcolm told Walter everything he knew about the case, allowing him to advocate the firm's accepting the case. At ten a.m., the two men took the elevator up to the executive conference room. The pro bono department, developed as a moral responsibility, had incurred a heavy cash overflow. Hours were donated to the homeless, ghetto kids, drug addicts, illegal aliens, and death row prisoners. A case like this was unheard of in the firm's history. Walter knew it would be hard.

The secretary whisked Walter and Malcolm into the conference room, which was dominated by a long mahogany table, with ten chairs on each side. Weinstein was on the left, and Calucci sat two seats from him. Rothman was placed in the dead center of the table, and Abrams sat in the last seat on the right. All were facing Malcolm and Walter.

"Come in, gentlemen. Have a seat," Abrams said softy. Malcolm and Walter sat in the middle, directly across from Rothman.

"Good morning, gentlemen," Walter said, sitting down.

"Good morning," Malcolm replied, gauging their expressions for any signs of hostility. Only Rothman seemed on the verge of exploding.

"We know why we're here this morning. Malcolm, as we all know, has been with the firm for over ten years," Walter said before Rothman interrupted him.

"Easy, Rothman. We haven't even started yet," said Abrams, a small man with flowing white hair. "Malcolm, we know that you had your reasons for announcing your representation of this Clarence Reed fellow. But it's customary at this firm for lawyers to consult with the partners first. You know the magnitude of this case; the cost alone will be phenomenal," Abrams said, stopping to sip his tea.

"Imagine, my foot. You put this firm's image in jeopardy. No telling what sort of backlash we'll get from negative publicity. I'm sorry. Defending some demented freedom fighter is out of the question," Rothman barked at Malcolm.

"Gentlemen, at one time or another, each of you have told me that I've done exemplary work here for the last ten years. Not once have I ever embarrassed this firm…"

"That's true, Malcolm...but why do you think this is an open-and-shut case? What facts do you have to go on that can prove this man's innocence?" asked Weinstein, chewing on his pipe.

"I don't have all the facts yet, but think for a moment. Why, and how, did the FBI capture Clarence Reed so fast? What kind of tip did they get to know where to find him and make an arrest? Put yourself in Reed's shoes for a moment. If you had planned to bomb a riverboat, wouldn't you have also planned an escape or covered your tracks? Two of the alleged bombers were found dead in the water. Clarence was found somewhere in the bayou by the feds. The man is no dummy, and I believe he didn't do it," Malcolm said, exasperated.

"Then who did?" asked Rothman.

"Let's wait just a minute, here. A few years back, we all sat at this table and discussed the strategy Malcolm would use to defend Giamanco. That wasn't a popular case, but it didn't hurt the firm's image, now did it, Carl?" Walter said, looking at Calucci.

Carl Calucci was the youngest partner. His eyes were deep and piercing, and he glanced up at the ceiling for a moment before he spoke.

"Malcolm, suppose we agree to your handling this case pro bono..."

"Carl, we don't need to take on a case like this now. People in this country are very paranoid about terrorists..."

"Barry!" Carl Calucci said, staring at Rothman.

"As I was saying, the reason I'd be in favor of this Clarence Reed, is because he is half-black and half-Vietnamese," Carl said, as Malcolm nodded. "So, Leo, think about this. I've researched this case, and what intrigued me is that Clarence Reed's mother is Vietnamese. My research shows that the New Orleans Asian community has grown dramatically since 1990, making solid business growth. We could market new businesses in the Vietnamese community in Louisiana, while handling this case. We can send some of our people down to that little office, where our lawyers are drowning in paperwork. Some new blood will find some new prospects," Calucci said.

"What sort of business are you talking about, Carl?" Leo asked, suspiciously.

"Insurance defense, commercial litigation, criminal defense." Calucci walked around the big conference table, until he got to Malcolm's chair, where he stopped and continued his pitch. "By taking on this case pro bono, we gain the community's confidence. We'll even take on smaller pro bono cases, concentrating on the Asian community. And by winning the case, Malcolm opens the door to the Louisiana market for us," Calucci said, grabbing Malcolm by the shoulders, showing his confidence.

Barry Rothman was stunned by Calucci's pitch. His tactics for knocking down the case evaporated. Rothman looked to Weinstein for help.

"It doesn't sound all that bad, Carl," Weinstein said.

"What do you mean it doesn't sound bad? This whole idea is preposterous," Rothman said in a fury.

"Need I remind you what your job is, Mr. Rothman? You manage who the cases are assigned to," Calucci replied harshly.

Carl Calucci kept up his campaign for the case, while this unexpectedly dumbfounded Malcolm and Walter.

"I can put together a good team to take to Louisiana in no time," Malcolm said, with confidence.

"When do they expect to go to trial?" Leo Abrams said, glancing at the steaming Rothman.

"I have to make a motion for a change of venue first, and then see what happens. There's a civil rights lawyer there named Segal—and this is just rumor—he heard from some sources that the government is looking for a speedy trial. If that's the case, we may be looking at late fall next year," Malcolm said, staring at Leo Abrams.

"Malcolm, there is one thing," Calucci said, making his way back to his seat. "I don't think taking a team down there is a good idea. We don't want to appear overwhelming. I suggest you bring in whomever you need, one at a time, handling the case with one assistant and one law clerk from down there."

"One assistant? A case like this with one assistant?" Malcolm said in shock.

"Yes, one co-counsel and—Barry correct me if I'm wrong—don't we have a second year lawyer in criminal litigation here, who happens to be Korean or Vietnamese? I'm not sure which," Calucci asked Rothman.

"Yes, her name is Lucy Yee and she's half Vietnamese and half Korean. The damn trial will be internationally represented."

"I understand she's very bright and capable in criminal litigation, and quite beautiful," Calucci said, with a grin.

Malcolm took a deep breath and leaned back in his chair. The room was silent.

"I suppose you'll need your usual staff—one by one, of course—a jury consultant, a government law expert, a legal aid, and your private eye?" Leo asked.

"I definitely need Pete Neil. The others I'll work out, one by one," Malcolm replied sarcastically, looking in Calucci's direction.

"Alright, let's see what happens after your motion for a change of venue. I agree with Calucci—just the one Asian lawyer as co-counsel. Carl, when can you have Ms. Yee in New Orleans?" Leo asked.

"Barry, how long? What is she doing now?" Carl asked.

"I'll have to check, but we could probably have her there right after New Year's," Barry said.

"Sol, you have any problem with this arrangement?" Leo asked, looking down the long table at Sol Weinstein.

"Sounds kosher to me," Sol replied.

"Then we're all agreed. Malcolm, you've got yourself a pro bono case," Leo said.

Malcolm and Walter felt a sense of victory. Barry Rothman was steamed in defeat. In parting, everyone exchanged holiday greetings, and then Leo asked Malcolm to stay for a moment. Malcolm sat next to Leo in the empty room.

"Malcolm, as you remember, I was the one who recommended that the firm hire you ten years ago. I've known Carl Calucci for over thirty years, but I didn't want to push the issue too much because I knew that you wanted to take it. I had some other questions about this case, but frankly I was surprised, and I suspected you were, too, when Calucci campaigned to take this case..."

"Thank you, Leo."

"But keep this in mind, Calucci helped me establish this firm, but ever since the Giamanco case, he's—I don't know how to explain it—but, he hasn't quite been the same. So," Leo pointed his finger at Malcolm, "watch your ass while you're down there, and be cautious of this woman, Lucy Yee. It's rare that Carl would come right out and recommend one specific lawyer as co-counsel in a big case, especially a second year lawyer," Leo said, sipping his tea.

"I was surprised myself. I mean, what's the catch here?" Malcolm said, looking over his shoulder to make sure no one else was in the conference room.

"As business goes, it makes marketing sense, but it's still unlike him to push a pro bono case. I'm going to ask you a straight question, and I want a straight answer. Is this case for publicity, or is it a good case you can win?" Leo Abrams whispered.

"It's probably both, but mostly the latter," Malcolm replied.

"If there are any problems, contact me or Walter immediately—none of the others. Do I make myself clear?" Leo instructed.

"Yes, sir," Malcolm saluted, with a smile. He shook hands with Leo Abrams and left him to finish his tea.

Malcolm didn't see Calucci, Weinstein, or Rothman again. He walked to Walter's office and found him deep in thought. "Hey, Walter, why so gloomy? That was easy. A few conditions, but what the hell, I can work around them..."

"I've worked with Calucci for over twenty-five years and have never seen him take on a project like that before, especially a pro bono case. My God, Malcolm, the man practically gave it away—no argument, no cross-exam, no discussion, of any kind. I tell you, son, there is something definitely wrong. I can't, for the hell of me, figure it out. Well, we'll see what happens. What are you doing for Christmas?" Walter put on his overcoat, never looking at Malcolm.

"What's bothering you so much? He gave us all the right reasons for doing the case pro bono."

Walter didn't answer.

"Walter, over here." Malcolm waved to get his attention.

"Yes. I'm sorry. Excuse me, Malcolm, but this is quite baffling. What did Leo say to you?"

"Nothing much, except to be careful in Louisiana...and to bring home a victory. He did have some concerns, and I have reservations, too. But let's see what happens and take it from there."

"Of course, you're absolutely right. I'm probably giving it more credence than I should, under the circumstances. Let's not sneer at our good fortune," Walter said, putting his arm around Malcolm as they left the office.

"Now, what did you say you were doing for Christmas?"

"I've got a 6:00 p.m. flight back to New Orleans. I'll be in touch," Malcolm said, hugging Walter. "Oh, Walter, when do you think I'll meet this Asian lawyer?"

"Call me after the New Year. By then, I'll have everything set up. Say hello to the kids for me. And, Malcolm, I wouldn't worry too much about the toys for the kids; I sent some things to New Orleans yesterday. Merry Christmas, my friend," Walter said, as he hopped into the limo.

* * * *

The two FBI agents were grateful to not have to spend Christmas in New York, thus sparing them hazardous-weather duty for the night.

* * * *

The almost-empty flight went directly to New Orleans. Malcolm's brother met him at the airport. The kids were asleep. Reverend Stinson was sipping hot cider with Lois and admiring the Christmas tree.

"Mama, how are you feeling?" Malcolm asked, dropping everything to attend to her.

"I'm fine, Malcolm. I was just stressed out—just needed some rest…"

"You're right about that. As soon as she got home, she went right out shopping," the reverend said, standing to pour himself more cider.

"Now, Josiah, you didn't think I was going to let those children have a sad Christmas. My Lord. Malcolm brings them back here with all that beach-wear clothing. I know it's warm down here, but Hawaii, it's not. At least not at this time of year. Besides, I went out with Roberta."

"Roberta?" Malcolm asked.

"Yes. You know the nurse you met in the hospital…" Lois' face lit up. "She spoke very favorably of you, Malcolm."

"Now, Mama…"

"Oh, hush, boy. The girl was just helping me buy the children some clothes. And I've invited her over for Christmas dinner."

"But you're supposed to be resting. Why are you going to cook all day?" Malcolm asked, with concern.

"You're right, son. That's just why I asked her to come over and help with the cooking," Lois said, grinning.

"This is the first Christmas that you and the kids have ever spent with us," the reverend said.

"I know, and the first Christmas they'll spend without their mother," Malcolm said.

"She called a little while ago. I just told her that you weren't here, so she said she'd call back tomorrow to speak to the children. And some boxes came from New York—Walter Baer sent something," Lois said, slowly standing to her feet. "Well, I'd better get some rest. It's going to be very busy around here tomorrow. Now I hope I can leave setting up the children's toys to you two. I bought them some clothes and a couple of special gifts that I'll give them personally. Goodnight, darling." She kissed the reverend and Malcolm, then went up to bed.

"Papa Joe, I know it's Christmas and all, but I have to ask you this."

"Sure. Anything."

"The firm has agreed to take the case pro bono with certain conditions; not to worry, its nothing I can't work out. And I'm bringing in a private detective friend of mine. He's been very helpful in past cases. By the way, what is Cephus's last name?"

"Pradier, why?"

"Just curious. I hope he'll be able to work with Pete Neil. He's a good detective. If anybody can find these terrorists, he can. Usually, he works alone, but my concern is that he's a hard-nose Irishman, and Cephus is a tough old black cop. Somehow I feel trouble brewing there," Malcolm said, throwing some tinsel on the tree.

"Don't worry, son. Those two hard-asses should produce some results in our favor," the reverend said.

Malcolm looked out the window into the dark, not paying any attention to the two cars up the street. One car was the FBI, and the other, Benny Dubois and two of his cohorts.

Chapter 6

The cable van arrived shortly after 2:00 p.m., the day after Christmas. The warehouse district, better known as the Soho of the South, was Suzanne Joret's residence. She never wanted to move into the loft condominium, but her mother Alva insisted on buying it for her twenty-fifth birthday. The area, renovated for the 1984 World's Fair, was known for its art galleries, the Contemporary Arts Center, and the Louisiana Children's Museum.

Suzanne left every day for her news anchor job at 2:30 p.m. Three men, wearing Southern Cable uniforms, broke into her apartment shortly after 3:00 p.m. The men quickly inserted bugs into the apartment's two telephones, into two lamp tops and, as an added bonus, installed a micro-television viewer in the ceiling. They could see and hear everything Suzanne did in her apartment. They were in and out in less than thirty minutes. Then they moved to the television station, where they found Suzanne's BMW and placed a tracking device in the well of the rear tire. Jerry was an expert at breaking into cars. The alarm went off, but within seconds, he cut the screeching sound. A bug was also placed in her mobile phone.

At the Asia Delight Chinese restaurant, Jerry bought a T-shirt, and an order of chicken in lobster sauce. He wore the Chinese T-shirt to make his way past security at the television station and deliver the food to Suzanne. At 6:15 p.m., Suzanne went to give her nightly newscast. Jerry placed bugs in Suzanne's telephone and then left the Chinese food on her desk with a note saying, "Enjoy, from a friend."

Just as easily as he entered, he left. Recorders and television monitors were up and running. Now, they waited.

When the newscast was over, Kathy Summers, Suzanne's research assistant, met Suzanne with information for the ten o'clock broadcast.

"All right, here it is. There were 100 people who applied and paid fees from $1,000 to $10,000 for video poker licenses. The gaming control board has no plans to refund the money in the thirty-three parishes that voted out video poker. The existing outlets can operate until 1999. Hello? Suzanne? Are you listening to me?" Kathy asked.

"Forget that for now. I need you to find out how many Monets there are in Canada," Suzanne said, looking to see if anyone was listening.

"Canada? Suzy, that could take days."

"You're right. Let's try Quebec first—better yet, Montreal. Yeah, Montreal. That's the last place they visited," said Suzanne.

"Montreal? Last visited? Who?"

"What's the name of the cute guy I told you about, the one who works for my father's campaign?"

"Oh, the blonde Adonis?"

"Yeah, him. He takes care of the bills, hotels, telephones, and campaign funds. He even pays my parents' household bills, including the telephone bill. So, what's his name?"

"Dale Old Bridge."

"Right. Get Dale on the phone and make arrangements—no, I'd better do this. It needs a personal touch. Just get me his number. And work on those Monets in Montreal."

"Are you doing a story on Canada or something?"

"No, but I'll fill you in later, when I know more. Let's go," Suzanne said, as they arrived at her small office. "What's this? I didn't order Chinese."

"Someone's treated you to dinner. Maybe you have a secret admirer," Kathy said, opening the food boxes. "Well, are you going to eat it?" Kathy asked.

"No. You go ahead; take it with you while you make those calls," Suzanne instructed.

By the end of the ten o'clock newscast, Kathy had Dale Old Bridge's telephone number, and a listing of 133 Monets in Montreal, Canada.

"This isn't going to work; it's too time consuming. I'll have Dale give me the specific number I'm looking for," Suzanne said, then dialed Dale at home.

"Hello?"

"Hi, Dale."

"Yes?"

"Suzanne Joret. How are you? We met about a month ago at my father's campaign fundraiser in Lake Charles," she said.

"Oh, yes. I remember. How are you?" he replied.

"Great. Dale, I was wondering...I'm trying to help Mr. Sandchester out. You know him, right?"

"Of course, the campaign manager."

"Well, he's so busy, and this is rather private, but I'm trying to find a number that, silly me, lost. I was wondering if you could help me out."

"What sort of number?"

"Actually, it's a telephone number in Canada, probably Montreal. You wouldn't know anybody there named Monet?"

"Can't say that I do, but I probably could retrieve the Canadian number for you. How about I just give it to Mr. Sandchester tomorrow?"

"Oh, no. I sort of don't want him to know I'm doing this—it is for my father, and he'd appreciate it if you would give me this information. We just want to make sure there's no problem with foreign campaign contributions," she whispered.

"Well, how soon do you need it?" he asked.

"How about tonight?"

"I just got out of the shower. It's really been a long day..."

"Dale, I'll tell you what...you get the number, and I'll buy you a late-night dinner. We'll get to know each other better, I mean, after all, we're on the same team. So, what do you say?" she asked.

He hesitated for a moment. "Give me about an hour. Where do you want to meet?" he asked.

"How about the Camellia Grill on Carrollton?"

"Okay. See you in an hour."

Dale hung up and got dressed. He'd admired Suzanne from a distance, and tonight was going to be his chance to get to know her.

He rushed over to campaign headquarters, and in a few minutes, he'd tracked down the information Suzanne needed.

Suzanne hated to use Dale like this, but it seemed necessary. She'd used Kathy's phone and Jasper and the Daltons didn't know about her meeting with Dale, but they followed her anyway.

At midnight, Suzanne arrived at Camellia's Grill and found it nearly full. Out of the twenty-nine stools, only four were free. The grill was filled with late-night diners: university types, ball-goers, and after-rounds physicians. She spotted Dale at the end of the counter.

"Good to see you, Dale," she said, as she continued her charade by kissing him on the cheek, making the young man blush.

"So, what looks good on the menu tonight?" she asked.

"I like the potato omelet, topped with onions, chili, and cheese," he said.

"That's too heavy for me. What else do you recommend?"

"Pecan waffles or the pecan pie."

"Pecan waffles sound good. So, how long have you worked for my father?"

"A year. I'd previously worked for Mr. Sandchester in Baton Rouge."

"So you two are rather close, I take it?"

"Not really. He just likes my work..."

"What exactly is your job?"

"I would say I'm the office facilitator. I make sure everything runs smoothly—travel arrangements, campaigning meetings, paying the bills, overseeing the campaign funds—that sort of thing," he said.

"Did you find that number for me?"

"Oh, yeah, I have it right here...uh, Ms. Joret, I only did this because you're the boss's daughter. I could lose my job if any..."

"Your secret is safe with me, Dale. Don't worry about a thing."

He handed her a piece of paper with four Canadian telephone numbers. She examined them closely. "That last number is the most recent call to Canada. Didn't your parents go to Canada two months ago?"

"Yeah, um, it was about two months ago. Dale, did you notice any date by the numbers?"

"I didn't write them down, but the last number was in October," he said, as the waitress brought their food.

"My, that was quick. Bon appétit." Suzanne watched this nice-looking man devour the potato omelet. They sat at the counter and talked for almost an hour before Suzanne was ready to leave.

"Well, Dale, I thank you for being such a dear. But I have an early appointment for a story on tomorrow's newscast."

"Could we get together sometime and go out on the town?" he asked.

"That sounds wonderful. But you know I work in the evening, and I'm going to be traveling a little for the next few weeks. So, I'll tell you what, the first chance I get, I'll call you and take you up on that offer," she said. Dale smiled. He would have accepted anything she said.

He walked her to her BMW. She gave him a hug and another kiss on the cheek, then quickly got in and sped off.

Jasper and the Daltons followed close behind.

*   *   *   *

Suzanne arrived at her warehouse loft shortly after two a.m. She didn't notice anything unusual. Exhausted from the day, Suzanne ignored the message light flashing on her answering machine, managed to get undressed and crawled into bed.

Jasper and the Daltons took turns throughout the night listening and viewing her as she slept.

As soon as she lay down, she jumped up to raise the heat—the temperature had dropped to the low thirties, which was low for New Orleans this time of year—then quickly got back into bed. She still ignored the blinking light on the answering machine.

The next morning, the phone woke Suzanne at 8:30 a.m., but was just a call from the station about a story for that night's newscast. She made her way to the kitchen area and fixed some cinnamon raisin oatmeal, whole-wheat toast, and coffee. She noticed her cupboards were bare, and made a mental note to go grocery shopping.

After breakfast she decided to sleep some more. All in one motion, she lay down on the bed and hit the flashing light on her answering machine. There were four messages.

"Hello, Ms. Joret. We met briefly a while back. My name is Malcolm Stinson. I would appreciate it if you could give me a call. I think we need to talk." He left a local number.

Beep.

"Now, Suzy, I won't take no for an answer. Your father and I are attending a gala affair in Lake Charles on New Year's Eve, and I want you to go. So call me. Mother."

Beep.

"Suzanne, it's Kathy. I just want to know if you're going ahead with the story about gaming licenses…oh, yeah, I didn't make any of those calls you wanted yet, so let me know what you want to do. Bye."

Beep.

"Hey, Suzy baby. It's Reuben. How are you doing? Now listen carefully, I'm only going to be here for a few days—actually, I'm leaving town on New Year's Day. But we need to get together. I'll give you an exclusive on what happened to Bob Cummings, my photographer. I know who killed him. I have pictures, honey. I'm in Baton Rouge, so here's a beeper number to contact me, preferably in the daytime on New Year's Eve." He left an 800 number.

Beep.

In the van across the street, Jasper and the Dalton brothers perked up like guard dogs when they heard a disturbing noise.

"Did you write that number down? The son-of-a-bitch is here in town. He won't get away this time," Jasper growled.

Suzanne was shaken by Reuben's call.

She replayed the messages and wrote down Malcolm and Reuben's numbers. Her thoughts shifted to Henri Joret's phone conversation on Christmas. She went to her dresser, where she put the telephone numbers that Dale Old Bridge had given her the night before. She looked in the mirror and thought she needed more sleep, but the name Monet echoed in her mind. She dialed the most recent number that came from her parent's home. Suzanne already spoke with a light French flavor, so beefing up the French accent was easy for her.

"Bonjour."

"Bonjour. Is this the Monet residence?"

"Oui, whom may I ask is calling?"

"I'm from the French Alliance. So sorry to disturb you so early in the morning, but we're doing a telephone survey on how people feel about the French seceding from Quebec in the second upcoming vote. The French advocates narrowly lost the first time, and we're hopeful we'll be successful this time."

"Well, I can't speak for Mr. Monet, but I have heard him on numerous occasions talk about the separation, and he is completely allied with the French position."

"That's wonderful. And to whom am I speaking?"

"Oh my, I'm Gertrude Brushard. I work for Mr. Monet."

"That is truly wonderful. By the way, for the record, Mr. Monet's first name is?"

"Jean Claude."

"Oh, is that the Jean Claude of..."

"Of Monet Pharmaceuticals of Canada," she said proudly.

"Why, of course. How silly of me. It's a pleasure to know that such an influential man is on the French side. Merci for talking with me. Au revoir."

Suzanne showered and got dressed. She called Malcolm, but he wasn't in. She left a message that she'd call him back later. She decided to call her mother later from the television station. She got in her car and tried to call Kathy, but her cell phone was dead, so she stopped by the Children's Museum and called from a pay phone. She later realized that this kept Kathy out of danger.

"Good morning, Kathy."

"What can I possibly do for you this early, boss?"

"I need you to find out everything you can on a Jean Claude Monet."

"Isn't he some sort of martial arts movie star?"

"Wake up, Kathy. This is important. Monet Pharmaceuticals, of Canada. Get me everything you can by tonight."

"Suzanne, what about the story on the gaming licenses?"

"Look, the wise guys probably controlled the vote to just the new applicants, so we'll just play with that and not mention their names. We'll call them 'the gamblers.' Now get on this Monet project, ASAP."

She was being watched from the other side of the street.

* * * *

"So what do we do now, Jasper?" Jerry asked, as Suzanne got back in her car. "Hello, Monet?"

"Jasper. Good to hear your voice. How goes it?"

"You tell me. She just called your house."

"What are you talking about? I just walked in."

"We're surveying her calls, and she just called your house and talked to Gertrude Brushard."

"My housekeeper? Hold on a minute. Mrs. Brushard," Monet called out.

"Yes, Mr. Monet?"

"Did I just have a call from a woman?" he asked.

"Why, yes, sir. She was taking a survey for the French Alliance about the French secession in Quebec. Why? Is there something wrong?"

"What else did you tell her?"

"Not much, other than that I heard you talk about agreeing with the secession. That's about it."

"Thank you, Mrs. Brushard. That will be all." Monet waited until she had left the room. "Jasper, where is she now?"

"We're following her."

"Good. Keep a good eye on her, and be ready to bring her in at any moment."

"Then what do I do with her?"

"Let's see what else she's up to, and then we'll push her to find out how much she knows. Call me back later tonight, around ten."

"Ten-four," Jasper replied. "Gentlemen, it looks like we're going to do a good old-fashioned interrogation."

* * * *

Suzanne was annoyed that she'd committed to speak to a women's association for battered women. It was a great humanitarian gesture during the holidays, but the timing wasn't good. I'll give my speech, have lunch, then head back to the television station, she thought. But, for the first time, an eerie feeling came over her—a sense that someone was watching her.

* * * *

On December 29, Pete Neil changed his plans and chose to spend New Year's in New Orleans rather than New York. Malcolm met Pete at the airport. They talked about past cases and arrived at the Orleans Hotel in the French Quarter just after 2:00 p.m. Malcolm had also reserved a room for Lucy Yee, his co-counsel, who would arrive, according to Walter Baer, on January 2.

As Pete dropped off his bags, Malcolm called Cephus Pradier, who suggested they not meet at the police station. The designated place was a thirty minute drive for Malcolm and Pete, and Cephus gave Malcolm specific instructions, so that they wouldn't be followed. They left the hotel, drove to the other end of the French Quarter, and parked the car in a lot. Then they walked four blocks to where a blue Ford van picked them up and took them to their final destination. The FBI agents lost Malcolm and Pete, and the best that they could do was trace the license plate of the blue van. A young black man in his early twenties drove the van, but he didn't talk to Malcolm and Pete during the trip to Cephus's car.

"Have they started giving you material for discovery yet?"

"Not yet, probably in another week or two. David Segal took care of the motion for me. Since I'm the new attorney, the judge will listen to my motion for a change of venue," Malcolm said.

"When is this supposed to happen?" Cephus asked.

"January 10, in front of a Judge Harlan Michaels. You know him?"

Cephus let out a long whistle. "Yeah, and he's a mean mother, too. Watch yourself with him. He won't give you much room to breathe."

"How do you know this judge?" Pete asked.

"I've had some experience with him in court. He's not partial to black lawyers, or those from out of town, so you'll be getting the double whammy," Cephus said.

"So, you're telling me that the black lawyers never contest his decisions?"

"Oh no, not at all. They've taken him to appeal court many times, but to no avail. Oh, and one other fact you should know: when Henri Joret was a state senator, he was instrumental, I hear, in getting Judge Michaels elected. Need I remind you that next year is an election year for Henri Joret?"

Cephus turned on Highway I-10 and headed toward downtown New Orleans. "I don't want to tell you how to do your job, but there are some key players here that you need to talk to…" he continued. "Clarence's mother, Sun Reed, can fill you in better than I can on some of the events leading up to the bombing. She wouldn't talk to me, but I know she knows something."

"Why wouldn't she talk to you?" Malcolm asked.

"Mainly because her husband was killed by a couple of red-neck cops, so she doesn't trust the police, period. No matter what race. As you spend some time here, you'll find out why that is."

"Who else do you suggest I see?" Pete asked from the back seat.

"Several people. Have you watched the news here yet?" Cephus inquired.

"I've caught some. Why?"

"Check out Suzanne Joret on Channel Eight News. She may be helpful."

"A newswoman? Do the media aid and abet the criminals down here?" Pete asked.

"No. I don't think so, Pete, but who else?" said Malcolm.

"Victor Zano. You might need a little help to see him, though. When you're ready, let me know, and I'll see if I can arrange a meeting."

"Let me take a wild guess here—the godfather of soul, he ain't—so he must be the godfather of New Orleans," Pete said.

"Your bloodhound is very perceptive. The Luppinos run things here, but the big boss is Victor Zano of New York," Cephus said, glancing at Malcolm. Cephus pulled off I-10, and on the side of the road was Malcolm's father's car that he'd left in the New Orleans lot.

Malcolm and Pete got out the car. "Thanks a lot, Cephus, for everything," Malcolm said. "I hope after talking with these people we'll find out some things. By the way, who do you think is tailing me?"

"Could be the feds, the Luppinos, the real terrorist, or a combination," Cephus replied.

"Well, I'm glad you don't believe Clarence did it," Malcolm said.

"No, I don't believe he did it. Don't ask me why, it's just a gut feeling. But I also feel that if Clarence didn't do it, the real folks won't stop at anything to keep you from finding out. Oh, I almost forgot, there is one more person who could prove to be very beneficial to you."

"Who's that?" Malcolm asked.

"Professor Thomas Hickman. He teaches political science at Tulane University," Cephus said.

"And how can he help me?"

"He has a very interesting hobby."

"What's that?"

"Oh, that's a surprise. You can't miss him. He's a very distinguished fellow with a close-shaved salt-and-pepper beard. He usually wears a bow tie and he talks like he's from Massachusetts. You'll like him. I'll let him tell you what his hobby is, but don't take this lightly. Make sure you touch base with him," Cephus said, as he put his car in drive, and headed down I-10 for New Orleans.

CHAPTER 7

Reuben Caulfield made arrangements to meet Suzanne at eleven a.m. at the Carly Hotel in Baton Rouge on New Year's Eve. He waited two hours, but she never showed up or called. He went to New Orleans to find out what had happened.

He hadn't talked with the police or the prosecutor's office about Bob Cummings's murder since July. He wasn't a suspect, but they wanted him to come in and talk. Any dispensation would be considered via telephone. Reuben had expressed a concern for his life. Two of Deputy Chief Waller's eyewitnesses wrote statements saying that they had seen two young white men chasing Cummings and Reuben. Reuben told the police that he didn't know Bob Cummings was dead until the next day, when he'd heard it on the news. He filled them in on what had happened that day, but had left out the part about the photos he had of the men, in particular Deputy Chief Waller, and the unknown others. He wanted to give the story and photos to Suzanne, who could tie Waller to Bob Cummings's death.

He borrowed a friend's car and drove to New Orleans. He looked around carefully when he arrived at Suzanne's warehouse loft. He and Suzanne had once had a fling that lasted six months.

He entered her building and rang the doorbell. No answer. After several minutes, he remembered that she used to leave a magnetic key box under the mailbox. It was still there. He walked through her apartment remembering the old times. The scent of her perfume lingered in the air. As best he could tell, nothing was out of order. Looking for paper to leave her a note, he noticed her answering machine blinking four messages. He hit the play button.

"Change in plans, dear. Your father and I are leaving town for the evening. Talk to you when we get back...Oh, Happy New Year."

Beep.

"Suzy, it's Reuben. I'm waiting here at the hotel. Are you coming or not? Give me a call at the number I gave you."

Beep.

"Are we riding up to Baton Rouge in my car or yours? Preferably yours, I hope. Call me. Kathy."

Beep.

"Ms. Joret, you don't know me, but if you want some information that could free your friend Clarence Reed, meet me tonight at seven o'clock p.m., off Hollow Road in the bayou. Please be prompt. I'll explain later, but your parents' safety depends upon your showing up tonight."

Beep.

That voice sounds familiar. Where have I heard it before? It's 6:55. Won't make it in time. Ah, hell, I'd better go anyway, he thought. He popped the cassette out and placed it in his pocket.

*   *   *   *

At seven o'clock p.m., Suzanne, the brazen reporter that she was, showed up alone at Hollow Road. She drove her BMW slowly down the dirt road that ran along the bayou canal. She stopped and slowly opened her window. "Hello? Is anyone here? This is Suzanne. We had an appointment for seven o'clock p.m.," she said, turning off the ignition.

She heard sounds of the bayou—the water swishing upon the shore, and splashing sounds that she didn't realize at the time were alligators sliding into the water.

She decided it was safe to get out of the car. As soon as she did, a man dressed entirely in black and wearing a knit hat that revealed only his eyes and mouth, came from behind the car. He grabbed her and put his hand over her mouth. She struggled, but he was stronger and pinned her to the car. Then two other men, also in black, walked out of the darkness.

"Ms. Joret, I'm so happy you heeded my warning," said one of the newcomers. "Now I'll keep my promise and give you an exclusive scoop. For now, your parents are safe, simply because we have you. My, you've been a very busy lady, poking your nose in places where it doesn't belong. But I'll explain all this later.

You're going to be my guest for a while, and we'll get to know each other better," Jasper said, as he softly stroked her face.

She pulled her leg back toward the car, then hauled off and kneed Jerry Dalton in the groin as hard as she could.

"Put her out," Jasper ordered. Jim Dalton held a chloroformed cloth up to her face until she passed out. They put her in the back seat of her BMW and drove deep into the steamy bayou.

Having witnessed the abduction, Reuben left, going directly to Baton Rouge. The next morning, he was on a plane back to New York City and the safety of Greenwich Village.

* * * *

The Reverend Josiah led a New Year's Eve candlelight vigil at the church. His heart was heavy as he preached about life evolving from death, using Elaine as the example for his sermon. Malcolm sat in the front row with his mother and the children. Roberta had managed to get a seat for her and her five-year-old daughter next to Malcolm. There were tears when the reverend began preaching, but there was joy in the Lord's house when the New Year rolled in at midnight. The church's recreation center served a free meal for all who attended the service, and anyone else who dropped by.

"We didn't get a chance to talk much at your parents' house on Christmas," Roberta said. She poured some punch into Malcolm's cup.

"No, we didn't. I was kind of busy that night. Sorry about that."

"Mind if I ask you a question?" she said, sitting down next to him.

"No."

"At Elaine's wake, was your wife the woman with the short haircut?"

"My ex-wife. She came to pay her respects. But, ah, let's not talk about her."

"Bad memories?"

"You could say that."

"I know all about that. My divorce was horrible. My ex was a self-indulgent bastard. Forgive me. When I think of how good I was to him, it makes my blood boil."

"Where is he now?"

"He remarried, moved to Lafayette, and had another baby with his new wife, in addition to the two she already had. He works off the books doing God knows what, so he doesn't give me any child support. But that's okay. As long as he doesn't come around, I'm fine. Although Larissa, my daughter, is starting to ask about him..."

"Larissa, is that a female version of Larry?"

"Very perceptive, Mr. Stinson. His name is Larry. He wanted a son, so Larissa was the alternative. I guess he knew we wouldn't have any more children together. What about your lovely children? It's rare for the man to have custody."

"That's a long story, and to make it short, she didn't exactly want them," he whispered, with his back turned to the children.

"So how long will you be in New Orleans?" she asked.

"I don't know, but it looks like this trial will start in the fall."

"Good. I mean, that's good, because I can show you some of the changes in Louisiana."

"That'll be nice. I'll be looking forward to it."

"Daddy, can I go over to Larissa's house tomorrow?" Serena asked, pulling on Malcolm's pants.

"I don't see why not," he replied, as she ran off to play with the other children.

"You'll have to excuse me for a little while. I have to go back and help serve the food. I'll catch up with you later, okay?" Roberta said.

"Happy New Year, Malcolm," Cephus said, extending his hand.

"Happy New Year to you. This is the first time since I left home that I've spent New Year's Eve in church."

"I've been coming ever since I got shot."

"Got shot?"

"Yeah," Cephus took a deep breath. "About six years ago, I got caught in the crossfire with some thugs in Metairie. For all intents and purposes, the doctors said I should have died. I took four bullets. Your father and his elders prayed for me at the hospital," Cephus said, as the Reverend Josiah walked up to them.

"I was just telling Malcolm how your prayers helped me after I was shot."

"It was the movement of God, son. The bible says that the fervent prayer of a righteous man availeth much. Thank you, Jesus." He continued to eat his salad.

"That's all you're eating, Papa Joe?" Malcolm asked.

"Didn't you read that article in USA Today about blacks in the south having a higher rate of blood pressure? I'm changing my eating habits because my doctor suggested I change," the reverend said.

"Who are those characters over there?" Malcolm asked.

"That, my friend, is Benny Dubois—dope pusher, pimp, con-man—you name it, he does it," Cephus said, sipping on his punch.

"God will convict criminals even if the law can't," said the reverend, while looking at Cephus.

"Well-dressed guy," Malcolm said.

"That he is, son, and he gave a big offering to the church tonight."

"You condone that, Reverend?"

"Cephus, you need to start coming to my Bible study classes. The Word of God says the wealth of the wicked is laid up for the righteous. Better to give that money to the church to do God's work, than let some kid suffer from an overdose or something terrible. Oh, by the way, Malcolm, Roberta volunteered to get Joshua in school for January, and half-day care for Serena, but you'll probably have to go with her. I hope you don't mind, but I don't want your mother under too much pressure," the reverend said, as Lois waved him over.

"So, Cephus, what happened?" Malcolm asked.

"What happened with what?"

"The tail? The car following me?"

"Oh, I almost forgot. Well, a friend of mine on the force knows a guy in the FBI, and it seems Jon Tulle has a thing for you. So watch your step."

"I don't understand why he's following me."

"From what I gathered, it has something do with what happened between you two a few years ago. He doesn't want it to happen again."

"I beat the government in a murder case for a Mafia kingpin's kid in Brooklyn. It was the saddest day in my life as a lawyer," Malcolm said.

"You know, I was just thinking. The Luppinos don't deal much with black cops. So when the time comes, Benny Dubois just might be our in," Cephus said, looking at Benny, who was returning the stare.

"Why do you say that?"

"Well, Benny's like a sergeant in the field. He gets flashy with his money and women, but he works for the Luppinos, who, like I told you earlier, take orders from Victor Zano."

"So how does he tie into the Reed case?"

"I don't know yet, but I have a feeling he does, or knows someone who does." Cephus and Malcolm mingled with the other church members, but Benny kept a watchful eye on Malcolm until he left. Outside, the FBI was filming everyone, including Benny Dubois.

CHAPTER 8

Suzanne awakened and took a deep breath of the murky swamp-water air. Her head felt heavy, and her hair still covered most of her face. Her first reaction was to push her hair back, but she discovered that her arms were tied with cord to the chair she was sitting on. She looked around the room and saw the three men gaping at her.

As she continued looking around the room, she saw two single beds on the far side, a small black stove, and a mini-refrigerator. The sidewall held a world map, an old Confederate flag, and pictures of Hitler watching his troops march in Berlin during World War II. There were pictures of an Aryan group dressed in full battle garb. She rolled her head around and saw posters of naked women. Next to the pictures of the women was one of a black man hanging from a tree and a group of Klansmen standing proudly by.

The shack sat on a small island in the canal. The island was just big enough for the shack and it was necessary to use a boat to get from the island to the mainland. While it was possible to wade through the five-foot deep water from the island to shore, there were hundreds of alligators surrounding it. The front of the shack had a lower level that sat three feet off the water, and it had the modern conveniences of electricity and hot and cold running water.

Suzanne sat at a table while the Daltons watched her from the other side of the room. Jasper walked across the room and stood next to her. She peeked through her hair at her admirers.

"Now let's see what we have under this beautiful head of hair," Jasper said, pushing Suzanne's hair away from her face.

"What the hell do you want from me?" Suzanne spewed.

"My, my, is that any way to greet someone? I believe the polite phrase is something like, Bonjour, comment allez-vous," Jasper said.

Suzanne snarled and instantly shot back a French expletive.

"What did she say, Jasper?" Jerry asked.

"I don't know, but we can assume it wasn't very nice. Isn't that right, Ms. Joret?" Jasper said.

Suzanne smiled at his comment. "So what's the deal? Ransom? Sex? Information? What do you want from me?" she bellowed.

"Let's start with that last one—information." Jasper sat on the edge of the table.

"What sort of information?"

"Why are you interested in finding one Jean Claude Monet in Montreal?" Jasper asked.

"She doesn't know what you're talking about."

Jasper signaled for Jerry Dalton to play the tape of Suzanne's conversation with Monet's housekeeper. Then he showed her photos of her having dinner with Dale Old Bridge. "Maybe some sort of news story? Or better yet, what did you overhear in the phone conversation between your distinguished father and Mr. Monet on Christmas Day?" Jasper studied her reaction as she listened to the recording.

She managed to keep a blank look, as if the call meant nothing. Jasper walked over to the picture of the black man hanging from the tree. While looking at it, he said, "You know, in a few months, that's what they're going to do to your black lover—no, excuse me, your mongrel lover."

"I don't know what you're talking about."

"Oh, but I think you do. We've studied the Joret family extensively. We have photos and videos of your many secret rendezvous with Reed. I must admit you two did an excellent job of keeping your little tryst quiet. But we caught on to you. I think it's disgusting. A beautiful woman, like you, disgracing your race with a mongrel. So, Ms. Joret, just tell me what you heard on Christmas Day and this will be all over."

"You're going to let me go?"

"Of course, why would I need you? The fellows here might think differently though." Jasper grasped her face in his hands. "You do have such luscious lips. Well, too bad, you're not my type." The Daltons looked on in confusion.

"You like boys? Okay. Let's go on to something else. What…"

The cellular phone in Jasper's coat pocket rang.

"Hello, Jasper?"

"Monet?"

"Have you got her yet?"

"She's sitting in the living room, as we speak." Jasper walked outside on the small porch to talk privately with Monet.

"And what does she know?"

"So far, she's not admitting anything. We've really just started questioning her."

"Give it until morning, then kill her. And get back to trailing Malcolm Stinson. Has she talked to him?"

"I don't know. Like I said, we've just started questioning her."

"Find out. If she has, we might have to deal with the lawyer."

"By the way, while we're in the request mode, we have a little unfinished business. Our agreement was that I would pay off all the soldiers that participated, and then that money would be reimbursed to me. It's been months now, and I only have $500,000 in my Cayman account. I believe you owe me another half-million."

"Now, Jasper, are we going to let a little money come between us? After all, since you've been in business with me, you have made over what...two million? Surely we're not going to let a measly five hundred thousand interrupt our business," Monet said.

"You're absolutely right. I'll expect it in my Cayman account by the end of business next week...or we will talk about other business arrangements." Jasper hung up before Monet could say anything else.

"Jerry, Jim," Jasper called out.

As they came out, Jasper reached inside a bucket and pulled out a handful of dead fish and threw them into the murky canal waters. Within seconds, the waters moved furiously as alligators raced for the free meal.

"This is what we are going to do. Jerry, you and I will go back to New Orleans to keep an eye on Mr. Stinson. Jim, you stay here and watch our guest. Give her water and one decent meal a day. Apply the ankle chains on her feet and cut the ropes so she can use the bathroom. Don't let her out of your sight, even for a moment. When you sleep, chain her to the stove. She can't move that. I'll call you every six hours. During the day, feed the alligators and let her watch. She'll tell us, in due time, what we need to know."

"And when she does, can we get rid of her?" Jim asked.

"We'll see. We might need to use her as a bargaining tool." Jasper walked back in and spoke to Suzanne.

"I have to leave now, but I'll see you soon. Hope you'll enjoy your stay." He started to walk out, but stopped at the doorway.

"Oh, Ms. Joret, one more thing. The next time I see you, I hope you'll be a little more cooperative, because I assure you, I can be most persuasive. Enjoy your stay. If I see Clarence Reed, I'll give him your regards," Jasper said. He laughed as he walked to the boat, and then turned to Jim standing on the porch.

"Oh, Jim, another thing. Don't lay a hand on her. No funny business, because if there is, you'll be the alligators' next meal. There is a reason for all this, and sexually abusing her doesn't fit into the scheme of things. Do I make myself perfectly clear?"

Jasper climbed into in one of the two aluminum boats and sat down with Jerry right behind him. Both boats had small outboard motors, but were also equipped with oars. The alligators watched as Jerry rowed to shore and then they scurried across the water. Once on shore, Jerry shot a couple of bullets in the air to scare off the alligators.

The two men drove the blue van to the river and used a flat raft, stable enough to hold the van, to pull them across the river, with a cable attached to a tree. On the other side, they hid the raft in the bushes. There was only one other road to get out, and the Dalton brothers cut down a big tree that would take three or four men to move, and laid it across the road to block it. Jim walked back inside when the van taillights disappeared.

"Now this can be easy, or it can be tough. It all depends on you, Ms. Joret." He sat on the chair across from her.

"Who are you, and why are you doing this?" she asked.

"All in due time, honey."

Suzanne's bravado was waning fast and her expression was tense and forlorn.

"How long will I be here?"

"Can't quite say—depends on what Jasper wants to do with you."

"Jasper is the older man?"

"And Jerry is my big brother. You look awfully uncomfortable there, so I'll tell you what we're going to do. I'll put handcuffs and leg irons on you, then move you over to the bed so you can get a good night's sleep. You'll be able to toss and turn a little in your sleep, but that's all the movement you'll have."

After he applied the leg irons and handcuffs, Jim cut the rope. "I don't want you to get the wrong impression of me, Suzanne—you don't mind if I call you Suzanne, do you?" he said.

No reply.

"My brother and I are highly-trained professional soldiers," he continued, "so don't get any funny ideas about escaping." He assisted her to the bed and locked her chains to the stove. "There, you're all set for beddy-bye. Oh, like I was saying, if you try anything stupid, I'll kill you. I want you to know that." He moved to the other side of the room to the other bed. "By the way, Suzanne, Happy New Year." He smiled, and then dimmed the light for the night.

"Are we safe in here from the alligators?" she asked across the dark room.

"Safer than gold at Fort Knox. Goodnight." He closed his eyes and was asleep in a few minutes. Suzanne spotted the luminous dial on the clock over the stove. Twelve fifteen. She didn't fall asleep for hours. With Jim Dalton across the room, and the sound of alligators swimming around the shack, she was nervous. Tears rolled down her face, and she thought this might be her last New Year.

CHAPTER 9

On January 5, outside of the Louisiana Federal Court House in New Orleans, reporters clustered in groups, awaiting the arrival of the opponents in the U.S. vs. Clarence Reed case. All of the major media were represented.

Malcolm arrived with what the press described as two of Campy Frazier's muscle men. Michael Ducruet arrived with his legal team dressed in dark suits and carrying leather briefcases. Jon Tulle and six agents sat behind Ducruet's team. Malcolm sat with Clarence Reed and David Segal. Cephus Pradier and Deputy Commissioner Waller sat in the rear, with two policemen. A beautiful Asian woman also sat in the rear.

At precisely 10:00 a.m., all arose. "The honorable Judge Harold T. Michaels, presiding," said the bailiff. The courtroom was silent as everyone stood and checked the expression on His Honor's face. Segal's knowledge of Michaels was summed up in one word: bastard.

"Good morning, gentlemen. I have reviewed the motion for a change of venue and I see no reason to grant your motion, Mr. Stinson," the judge said. His thick eyebrows peeked through over his bifocals to watch Malcolm's reaction.

"As Your Honor is well aware, I have just started representing the defendant. In the short time I've had to prepare for this hearing, I have witnessed at least a half-dozen television network specials about this case that could have prejudiced the public against my client. CNN continues to run story after story like a sit-com. These reports show my client in a bad light to the public. And, particularly here in New Orleans, a portion of each television news broadcast contains a story about Mr. Reed." Malcolm moved from behind his table.

"This is a little out of the ordinary—and I beg you to bear with me, Mr. Ducruet—but, Mr. Stinson, where would you suggest we change the venue to?" The judge asked.

"Anywhere except the state of Louisiana. Preferably Iowa," Malcolm said.

He heard the snickering in the background and looked at the judge.

"Mr. Stinson, I'm not going to belabor this issue. Considering what you've just said, can you prove that pre-trial publicity has tainted the jury pool for this trial? Can you prove that any newspaper, magazine, or television report can ascertain unequivocally your client's guilt?" He stared at Malcolm.

Ducruet sat relaxed with his legs crossed. He was enjoying every moment of the judge's argument with Malcolm. Malcolm turned his back to the judge and returned to his seat.

"No, Your Honor," Malcolm quietly answered.

"And do you have any evidence specifically indicating that there is any citizen on the jury rolls who is biased?" the judge asked.

"Not at this time, but I will explore any potential prejudices during voir dire," Malcolm said.

"Within reason," said the judge.

Michael Ducruet got up graciously, as if he had the judge on his team.

"Your Honor, if I may interject something about these delaying tactics by the defense."

"No, you may not. Sit down, Mr. Ducruet." Then the judge instructed the court clerk to read the defendant's plea.

"By order of the State of Louisiana, for the charges of terrorism and murder in the count of 1,267 people who were murdered on July fourth, nineteen hundred and ninety-eight, how do you plead, Clarence Reed? Guilty, or not guilty?"

An eerie silence fell over the courtroom, as if the spectators expected Clarence Reed would make some outlandish confession and save everyone time and money.

Clarence stood and solemnly said, "Not guilty."

"Therefore," the judge continued, "the grand jury, Mr. Reed, has found substantial evidence to the above mentioned charges of terrorism and murder in the first degree. Therefore, by the power vested in me, the court date is set for August 17, 1998. Voir dire will begin August third. Are there any questions, gentlemen?" The judge looked at both counsels.

"No, Your Honor. The state will be prepared," Ducruet said.

"Your Honor, that is just eight months away, and we haven't started discovery yet," Malcolm said.

"Then I suggest you get busy, Counselor."

"Your Honor, can the state tell us here, today, what information they have and when they will have it available for the defense?" Malcolm stared across at Ducruet.

'Well, Mr. Ducruet, can you answer Mr. Stinson's question?" asked the judge.

Ducruet looked down the table at his six assistant DAs as they shuffled through papers for an answer.

After about three minutes of shuffling papers, and begging the court's indulgence, Ducruet addressed the question.

"Sorry, Your Honor. We have four thousand statements from potential government witnesses, more than three thousand photographs, one hundred videotapes, information on over ten thousand items of physical evidence, and one hundred and fifty laboratory reports. Included in this information are seven hundred statements from people who have information about the other suspects in the case," Ducruet said, finishing his list.

Even for Judge Michaels, the list was extensive. His eyes shot up and seemed to get lost in the thick fold of his eyebrows. He folded his hands into a steeple and cleared his throat. "Do your best, Mr. Stinson. I'm quite confident that a lawyer of your caliber will be ready by August."

"Your Honor, in order for my client to get a fair trial by law...the government has had six months to review all of the evidence. I don't have a problem with the amount of information, Your Honor, but August is pushing it. I don't understand why the court is pushing for a speedy trial..." Malcolm questioned. He stood with his arms spread open, as if he were hoping to receive a blessing from Judge Michaels.

"No one is pushing for a speedy trial, Mr. Stinson, but the calendar is open for August, and eight months should be sufficient time for you to prepare."

"Well, Your Honor, it may mean that I will have to reject thousands of pieces of evidence," Malcolm said.

Judge Michaels didn't like this at all. "I suggest you start meeting with Mr. Ducruet." The judge grabbed his gavel.

"Anything else, gentlemen?"

Ducruet and Malcolm both shook their heads in unison.

"Good. Then court's adjourned." He slammed down his gavel and walked off the bench.

Malcolm walked over to Ducruet. "I'll be at your office first thing tomorrow morning. I'll bring a U-Haul truck. Should I pull it around to the back of the federal building?" Malcolm asked sarcastically.

"Just give me a call. We'll make arrangements at that time. Have a good day, Mr. Stinson." Ducruet turned his back to Malcolm.

Malcolm leaned over the table to Clarence. "I'll be in to see you the day after tomorrow."

"What's going on, Mr. Stinson? Five hundred of this...seven hundred of that—what's the point? I don't understand," Clarence said, as the bailiff came to take him back to prison.

"I'll explain when I see you. Take care of yourself," Malcolm said.

Angry at what had occurred, Malcolm gathered his things and rushed out of the courtroom, with David Segal trailing behind him. A herd of reporters were waiting outside the courtroom for a statement. Malcolm noticed a beautiful young Asian woman with her arm raised wanting his attention. He kept walking, but could smell her Chanel perfume. She called out, "Mr. Stinson, I'm..."

"Right now, I'm not giving any statements to the press..."

"I'm not from the press. I'm from the firm. Walter Baer told you I was coming."

At the mention of Walter's name, Malcolm turned and walked back to her. She had long dark hair in a braid that reached halfway down her back. Her eyes were olive and warm, with a mysterious twinkle. This woman was exquisite.

"So you're Lucy?"

"Yes, Lucy Yee. Sorry I'm a few days late, but I had an emergency in my family and..."

"Hey, it's alright. Come with me." Malcolm tried not to stare.

"When I found out that you'd be here, I rushed over." She kept up with Malcolm's rapid pace. Court police, behind a ribbon-like barricade, restrained the first waves of reporters. They shouted out to Malcolm for a statement. Malcolm stopped suddenly.

"All I'm going to say for now is that Clarence Reed is the victim of a major conspiracy, just because he believes in the civil rights of people. We will prove, beyond a shadow of a doubt, that he is the victim, and not the assailant, as the government wants you to believe." Malcolm walked out of the federal building, where another group of reporters wanted a statement. He repeated the same statement, and then grabbed Lucy Yee by the arm, escorting her to a waiting car provided by Campy Frazier.

* * * *

Michael Ducruet was on the steps of the federal courthouse, giving his short dissertation on how the government would prove that Clarence Reed bombed the gambling riverboat. Ducruet stopped during his statement, watching Malcolm's car drive off, and then turned to his assistant.

"Find out who the Asian girl is," he whispered.

Jon Tulle stood with four agents atop the federal building stairs. "This case is so big, it'll make up for that blunder in New York, so let's get busy and give Mr. Ducruet our undivided attention." He laughed, and then walked down the stairs to his waiting car.

* * * *

Across the street, Jasper and Jerry Dalton were dressed in sanitation clothes and moving quickly to their van. Everyone had come to court.

* * * *

In the car, Malcolm explained to David Segal and Lucy Yee what had to be done. "The firm is letting us use space at our satellite office, but I still don't know where it is. Lucy, find out and set things up for us. We'll need a conference room and what…five or six computers? Walter told me they'd accommodate us with that. David, we're going to need help getting through all this paperwork. It is all a ploy by Ducruet for us to lose our focus. Tonight, I'll make arrangements for some experts to come in: forensics, autopsies, fabrics, fibers, blood types, and explosive specialists—the kind of people who induce yawns during a trial." Malcolm pulled out a small notepad from his jacket.

"Do they have fingerprints that link Clarence Reed to this bombing?" Lucy asked.

"We'll know once we start discovery," Malcolm replied, while he wrote something in his notebook.

"Drop me off on Bourbon and Canal. I'm meeting someone for lunch. What are you going to do today?" asked David Segal.

"I was thinking the same thing—lunch. What say you, Ms. Yee?" Malcolm asked.

"Sounds good to me," she replied, with a smile.

"I'll call you tonight, David. And, thanks." The car pulled up to the curb to drop off David. "So, what's your pleasure, Ms. Yee?"

"Really doesn't matter."

"Chinese?" Malcolm stuttered.

"I am Asian, but I've been Americanized."

"Good. Let's have some Italian. I know a good restaurant here in the French Quarter."

"Where to, Mr. Stinson?" the driver asked.

"Antoine's," Malcolm replied.

The driver dropped them off.

"My, this place is quite lovely," Lucy Yee said, following the maitre d'. They were seated and given a wine list.

"Do you eat here often?" she asked.

"Not really," Malcolm replied, putting down the wine list. The waiter came. Lucy ordered a glass of Chablis, and Malcolm ordered cranberry juice with lime.

"Too early in the day for you?" she asked.

"No, not at all. I don't drink."

"Oh."

"I quit smoking a few months ago, so I try not to have alcohol or caffeine, or any of the things I associate with smoking. Tell me about yourself," Malcolm said.

Lucy raised her head and took a deep breath. "Let's see. I'm originally from California…West Covina. When I was sixteen, I moved with my parents and two brothers to Fort Lee, New Jersey. I attended NYU Law School, specializing in criminal litigation. I have been with the firm for two years and I've read a lot of your cases."

"I don't know how I missed you," Malcolm stated.

"I studied your case file in the Giamanco case—a brilliant piece of work."

"Thank you, but I'm interested in why you entered criminal litigation."

"Why not? Asians need lawyers, like anyone else. That's what I eventually hope to do. I want my own practice one day."

"Mr. Calucci recommended you. How do you know him?"

"I don't know him personally, but I guess he'd heard about some pro bono work in the Bronx."

"I was told you were Korean. Is that correct?"

"Yes and no. I'm Korean and Vietnamese. It's a long story."

"Sort of like Clarence. He's Vietnamese and black."

"We should get along just fine." She smiled, and Malcolm did, too.

"Malcolm, I know this isn't my business, but in this morning's New York Times, there was an article that mentioned your name." She reached into her over-sized pocketbook.

"Oh, it's not unusual for them to report about the case," Malcolm said.

"It's not about the case; it's about your ex-wife." She handed him the paper.

Malcolm read the front-page headline aloud, softly. "'EX-WIFE OF NEW YORK CRIMINAL LAWYER ARRESTED FOR STOCK FRAUD.' That's quite a caption. Poor Sara." Malcolm read the article, but as he put the paper down, another article caught his eye:

DAUGHTER OF GUBERNATORIAL CANDIDATE MISSING

"What's this?" Malcolm asked himself.

"What's what?" Lucy asked.

"This woman. An anchorwoman for a local television station, here in New Orleans, is missing. She also happens to be the daughter of a bastard named Joret, who's running for governor. I've left a few messages on her machine asking her to contact me, but she's never returned my calls."

"Does she play some part in Reed's case?"

"Oh, no. She interviewed him, and as part of investigating Clarence's case, I want to talk to her. That's all. Have you ever been to New Orleans, Lucy? This city has a murder rate higher than New York, so watch your step. Do you mind if I keep this paper?"

"No, go right ahead. So boss, what's my first assignment?"

"Nothing for today. Get some rest, and I'll pick you up, say about nine. David and I will visit Ducruet."

"Who exactly is David, and isn't Ducruet the prosecutor?"

"David Segal is a civil lawyer whose partner was killed in the riverboat bombing. He's offered his services during this trial, and knows his way around the legal jungle down here better than I do. So far, he's been a great help. Ducruet is the prosecutor. You'll meet all the players soon enough. Hell, I'm still meeting them."

They left Antoine's, and Campy's driver dropped Lucy at the Hotel Orleans.

"There's a friend of mine working on the case with us—a private detective named Pete Neil. I'll have him give you a call tonight or maybe you two can meet for dinner. He's in Room 503, if you have any problems, and here's the phone number where I'm staying. There's someone there most of the time, so any messages will get to me. Well, that's it for now. Welcome to New Orleans. I'll see you at nine sharp. Goodnight, Lucy." Malcolm left her in the lobby.

* * * *

Pete Neil had another assignment, and spent the day riding Cephus' beat. At first, they didn't talk much. Cephus wasn't the trusting type.

"So, Pete, what did you do before you became detective?" Cephus drove toward the Desire housing projects.

"I was a homicide detective, like you—12 years on the force."

"What made you quit?"

"I didn't exactly quit—well, in a way, I did. Internal Affairs investigated some cops who were taking bribes from local Harlem dope pushers. I never took a bribe, but, unfortunately for me, my partner was on the take. At first I didn't suspect him, but he came right out and told me. When he offered to let me in, I said no. We were friends, but not brothers, if you know what I mean."

"What? Was he black…Spanish?"

"He was Irish, like me."

"Hmm." Cephus watched the young drug pushers in the street who were watching him.

"Well, anyway, there was a big inquiry, but the commission didn't have anything on me. I knew that, but stranger things have happened in the NYPD. So I elected to resign and face some trumped-up charges that would have black-balled me, no matter how I looked at it. I took my retirement money and started my own private detective business, and the rest is history."

"How did you hook up with Malcolm?"

"Strange, the way we did. I was looking for a missing person, and he was working with another detective, who couldn't produce anything for him. Well, it turned out that my missing person was involved in the murder case Malcolm was working on. We clicked, and have been working together for about seven years now."

"Well, you've got to make a living somehow, I guess," Cephus said, as he parked his unmarked police car on the street in front of the Desire housing projects. The young black boys slowly scattered when they saw his car.

"So, is this where we're going today?" Pete kept a watchful eye on the boys.

"No. I just stopped here for a minute to check things out. We're going to a funeral."

"A funeral?"

"A sort of re-opening of a case I had back in June of this year."

"What do you mean, re-opening?"

"Ten days before the riverboat bombing, three black boys, two fourteen, and one sixteen, were murdered with a hunting knife, from what we gathered."

"So, today's funeral is for someone who died the same way?"

"Yes, but there's something distinctive about these deaths; they were stabbed in the back, sodomized, then the killer cut off the boys' right ears."

"A real freak, huh?"

"You could say that. Well, after the bombing, those killings stopped. But the dead boy today has the same M.O. as the ones in June. Our killer seems to be back in business." Cephus put the car in drive, and sped off.

"These kids who push crack, here in the French Quarter, all work for Benny Dubois. The three kids who died also worked for Benny. But just like anything else in our society, once this killer kills some white tourist looking for a high while visiting our fair city, we'll hear about it fast from the mayor's office. They don't care about the poor black kids, but the visiting tourists are a grave concern. It reflects poorly on the city, according to the politicians."

"It's like that all over, my friend," Pete said.

Cephus and Pete soon arrived at the home of Leroy Jenkins, the most recent murder victim. Outside the house were a host of Benny's juvenile soldiers. Cephus pulled up about two houses away, but in plain view of all who were standing around the Jenkins' home.

"You'd better stay here. I'll be right back..."

"I can handle myself. Trust me," Pete said.

"Listen, my friend, I remember once upon a time when the only suspects in a case were either some career black criminals, or career white criminals. But New Orleans has become a melting pot, for the Colombian Cali, Chinese Triad, Jamaican Posse, and the Japanese Yakuza, and the Luppinos still run things in New Orleans. Benny Dubois is the peacemaker and coordinator of them all; so let's walk lightly here. Let me handle this, okay?" Cephus got out of the car.

"Since you put it that way, okay."

Cephus approached the ten young black boys standing outside the Jenkins home. He walked past them into the house to pay his respects to the boy's parents: respectable, hard-working people. In a few minutes, Cephus was outside again. This time he walked right into the boys' huddle.

"Who's going to be the first to tell me what he saw?" Cephus asked. Hard looks were thrown at him. Then, an older kid nicknamed Trumpy Short—

because he always had money and was Benny's number one kid on the street—spoke up.

"Ain't nobody goin' to say nothin', Mr. PO-lice man, because we goin' to take care of it in the street, ourselves," he said, then started laughing. "We wait on the PO-lice to get this guy, social security will be paying him." All the kids laughed.

"What are you saying? He's a white guy?" Cephus asked, and the kids laughed again.

"You the law and you don't even have a clue. Let me tell ya', he's a white guy, about six-foot-three, stocky build with a ponytail. And I'm only telling you this, because if we find him first, he's going to beg us to put a cap in him. Now take a hike with your white boyfriend over there. If some white kid from the suburbs got killed, the killer would be serving time already..."

Cephus walked over to Trumpy, grabbed him by the throat, and slammed him on the hood of his shiny 500-S1 Mercedes-Benz.

"Let me tell you something. I'm nobody's joke in this town, and if I ever catch you putting a cap in anybody, you'll be begging me to put one in you. Now you get in your beautiful car here, and go home to your girlfriend, Benny," Cephus said. Four kids reached for concealed guns, but none pulled them out. Cephus let go, and waited for them to pull off in their expensive drug-bought cars. He walked back to his car straightening his tie. Pete sat in the car holding a 38-caliber cocked in his hands.

"What you doing with that?" Cephus asked.

"Your friends there were surrounding you, and reaching for things while you had that kid on the car. I found this in the glove compartment." Pete put the gun back where he had found it.

"Let me do the policing around here. Got it?"

"Sure, no problem. I really think I'm going to enjoy my stay here in New Orleans. Yeah, things are looking up."

As Cephus drove by, Pete waved at the kids still standing outside. They drove back downtown so Cephus could check whether any white criminals with ponytails had been released in the last year.

CHAPTER 10

On January 7, the Joret mansion was swarming with the FBI, state police, and the New Orleans Police Department. Alva Joret was a nervous wreck and chain-smoked Virginia Slims. Henri made some calls to Washington, D.C., and the FBI director put Jon Tulle on the case. Daryl Hayes, the black New Orleans police commissioner, was there with Deputy Commissioner Waller. New Orleans's black mayor called Cephus personally. This displeased Waller, but he had no choice in the matter. They could only report that they were still looking for a lead. The FBI had checked Suzanne's apartment and found nothing unusual.

The FBI agents questioned Henri and Alva until they could take no more. They examined the room Suzanne had stayed in on Christmas, but nothing resulted.

Had she been upset in any way? That was their last question before Alva, in a torrid rage, jumped up and ordered all the police out of her house.

They visited the television station and interviewed everyone from the janitor to the CEO. Kathy was given the drill because she was the last person who had spoken with Suzanne. Tulle led the questioning.

"The last time you spoke with Suzanne, you two were supposed to go to Baton Rouge. Why?"

"That's it, I don't know. All she told me was that she had a lead on a story and we had to go to Baton Rouge. Why?"

"But don't you set up her news items?" Tulle asked.

"Yes, but on occasion—and this unfortunately was one—she didn't tell me." Kathy was nervous and her mind was racing. She was afraid that if she told the

FBI about the inquiries in Montreal, whoever had came after Suzanne would come after her next. If that was the case…or had she been kidnapped? She kept the Canadian information to herself. Tulle continued to ask detailed questions about Suzanne's personal life for about an hour and a half. The FBI had no clues about what could have happened to Suzanne Joret.

* * * *

On the same day that the FBI and local authorities questioned everyone who might know something about Suzanne Joret, Malcolm and Lucy visited Clarence Reed at Angola Prison. Clarence had been removed from the maximum-security unit. They brought him to the visiting area, where there were cameras in each corner of the ceiling, and a partition down the middle that separated the prisoners from their guests. No glass, just a screen partition. Clarence was brought in by a burly, white guard, and then left alone with Malcolm and Lucy.

"How are you making out in here, Clarence?" Malcolm asked, with a smile. Clarence looked at Lucy pulling out a notebook.

"Praise God, brother, I'm well."

"Clarence, this is Lucy Yee. She's from my law firm in New York, and will be working with us on the case."

"Good. A pretty face will help in this time of adversity."

"She's a very capable lawyer. Now, today we're going to go over all the details again. When we last spoke, you told me about Harpo Stevens contacting you about this job. And that's when you first told me about the man named Oppenheimer. Did anything unusual happen? Or better yet, just tell me the turn of events, say, starting a month prior to Harpo's contacting you."

Malcolm let Clarence tell him everything that he could remember from the time that he had been arrested. He didn't leave out any details. The recalling of events took a little over an hour.

"Tell me what's happening with Suzanne, and about her possibly being kidnapped. Why would anyone do that?"

"I don't know. Cephus went to the Joret's house, so he should know something. As soon as he lets me know, I'll contact you and…"

"Listen to me, if anybody has a clue to Suzanne's whereabouts, it's her assistant Kathy. She would never make a move without Kathy's knowing about it."

"Well, I think they went to talk with her, and we'll follow up, as well."

"Forget the feds. Tell her I said to let you know what's happening. The only people that knew about Suzanne and me were my mother, your parents, and

Kathy. We became pretty good friends. If she doesn't want to tell you anything, bring her here. I'll get it out of her."

"Get what out of her?"

"If she hasn't told the feds yet, then there's something she knows, and for some reason she's keeping it to herself," Clarence whispered.

"I don't know if the cameras have microphones."

"So?"

"Do you trust Ms. Yee?" Clarence asked.

"Yes."

Clarence wrote down instructions for Malcolm. He and Lucy walked to one side of the room. The plan was for Clarence to talk to Lucy in Vietnamese.

"Ms. Yee, do you speak Vietnamese?"

"Enough to hold a decent conversation, I think. Why?"

"Just do me a favor. Follow Clarence's lead when we go back to him."

"Okay," she said. They walked back to Clarence as the guards watched closely. There were no microphones in the cameras. As they sat down, Clarence spoke in Vietnamese and Lucy understood. She looked at Malcolm for a moment, hesitated, then stood up. Clarence stood up, too. Malcolm followed suit, and remembered what Clarence had asked him to do. Lucy moved toward the screen with her back to the camera. She kissed Clarence, and Malcolm was taken by surprise. Clarence spoke again in Vietnamese, and Lucy replied pleasantly. Clarence said good-bye and walked toward the door, which was opened for him by the waiting guard.

Malcolm still wondered what had occurred when they reached the car. They were about a quarter mile away from the prison when Malcolm finally broke the silence.

"All right, is this some sort of Asian thing?" Malcolm asked.

"Not at all. Clarence wanted me to give you this note," she said, opening the note.

"Wait a minute. Let me open that please." Malcolm pulled off the road. A car following them whisked by. Its passengers were Jasper and Jerry Dalton.

The note read:

CHECK THE GLITTER DOME BALL IN HARPO STEVEN'S OFFICE.

CHAPTER 11

Malcolm dropped Lucy off and picked Pete Neil up at the hotel. They were going to go to Harpo Stevens's office. En route, he called Cephus, who agreed to meet them at Harpo's office. When they got there, they realized that the police had locked the door, so Pete picked the lock.

"So, Counselor, are you going to tell me what we're looking for?" Cephus asked, slapping at the cobwebs. It was nearly 6:30 p.m., and the visibility was poor, so Cephus used his flashlight. The place was in disarray. Harpo was not much of a housekeeper, and the police hadn't helped when they conducted their investigation.

"Point the flashlight up there, Cephus," Malcolm said, looking for a chair. There, undisturbed, was a glitter ball, the same type used at the New Year's Eve celebration. It was the size of a beach ball. Malcolm climbed onto the chair to get a better look. He asked for the hammer he had seen lying on Harpo's desk. He chipped a small hole, and used Cephus's flashlight to peek inside.

"Eureka! Gentlemen, I believe we have found gold in the glitter dome," Malcolm said, chipping a bigger hole in the dome.

"What's in there?" Pete asked.

"Maybe our first concrete clue." Malcolm unscrewed a camera from the pole that it was attached to inside the ball, and brought it down.

"Now, I hope that what we're looking for is in here. Let's see, we push this, and pull that. Pop goes the weasel, gentlemen, we have film," Malcolm said, gazing at the cassette.

"Okay, you've proven the inefficiency of the New Orleans Police, so what do you suppose is on the film?" Cephus said.

"I'm hoping we can get a glimpse of who was here that day of the bombing. And if I'm right, we might see this Oppenheimer fellow that Clarence was talking about," Malcolm said, putting the film in his shirt pocket.

* * * *

Jasper and Jerry were sitting in a van just up the road from Harpo's place, when they saw Malcolm and company coming in their cars. They ducked down, so that they would not be detected. They sat there for a moment as Jasper tried to figure out why the others were there snooping around.

"Well, are we going to follow them?" Jerry asked.

"No, we need to go inside and see what they were looking for, or worse, what they might have found," Jasper said, pulling in front of Harpo's office.

They looked around for nearly thirty minutes, but the sloppy office was just as confusing to them as it had been for Cephus and Pete. Only Malcolm had known what to look for in the office. Jasper noticed the fresh broken pieces of the glitter dome on the floor. He examined the dome.

"What do think, Jasper?"

"I think I might have underestimated the late Harpo Stevens. Let's go," Jasper said, gazing at the dome while he left. "If I'm correct, Harpo may have gotten Oppenheimer on film. I don't want you to mention this to anyone, especially your brother. This is something I have to fix," Jasper said, as they got back into the truck and headed out, cursing Harpo's name the whole time.

* * * *

Malcolm entered his parents' house and was greeted by his children, who had been running wildly and shooting water guns at each other.

"Where's your granddad, and why are you shooting the water guns in here?" Malcolm asked, sternly.

"Grandpa is taking a nap, and Grandma went out," Joshua said, timidly.

"Both of you, go upstairs to your room, I'll be there in moment."

"Oh, you're back. I just dozed off for a few minutes," Papa Joe said, stretching.

"Papa Joe, the kids were running wild with water guns. I'll deal with them later. But right now I need to use the VCR."

"Okay, I'll tend to the kids, while you gentlemen watch your movies," Papa Joe said, chuckling up the stairs.

"I hate to burst your bubble, Malcolm, but we did find five other tapes with nothing special on them. Just some locals going in and out of the office," Cephus said.

"Maybe so, but Clarence told me that Harpo normally changed the film every day. If there was something shaky on the film, Harpo would erase that day's film," Malcolm said, putting the film in the VCR.

"So how do you know that this mystery man, Oppenheimer, didn't come on another day and Harpo didn't erase the meeting?" Pete said.

"We'll see in a minute, but suppose Oppenheimer was there the day of the bombing and came into Harpo's office. According to the autopsy report, Harpo died the day of the bombing, so he wouldn't have had a chance to change the film," Malcolm said, fast-forwarding the film. "Well, what do we have here," Malcolm said, freezing the frame.

"Looks like the character Clarence described," Cephus said, in amazement.

"No, it doesn't look like. He is exactly what Clarence described. Now we have a picture of what Oppenheimer looks like. Maybe your people can clear up this picture, Cephus. Do you think this can be done discreetly?" Malcolm asked.

"I know someone outside the department who can help," Cephus said.

"Then maybe you can run his picture through your archives, and come up with something," Malcolm said.

Cephus left with the film. "Malcolm, do you trust him? I mean that video could be a big piece of evidence later," Pete asked.

"At some point, we have to trust other people, Pete, if we're going to make any headway with this case. At least it shows what Clarence says has credibility."

* * * *

Jasper and Jerry were driving back to the French Quarter. Jasper was angry that he had underestimated Harpo. He also knew now that couldn't underestimate Malcolm. He needed to find out just how much Malcolm knew. He knew it would mean he would have to go against his orders, but he wanted to follow Malcolm. Things seemed to be changing, and thoughts of terminating Malcolm began weighing on Jasper's mind.

CHAPTER 12

The four days of parading had reached its crescendo. It was Fat Tuesday—Mardi Gras. Malcolm was weary after the last six weeks of work. Eighteen-hour days, sorting through tons of paper work, and he felt that he still hadn't scratched the surface. Malcolm, Lucy, David Segal, when he could, and two of Segal's law clerks, pored over the four thousand statements from potential government witnesses. They studied the twelve hundred photographs, and one hundred videotapes. They hadn't even touched the eight thousand items of physical evidence, the one-hundred-ten laboratory reports, the two hundred individual telephone records, or the five hundred statements from people who said they had information about other suspects in the case. Malcolm tried six different deaf people, two of which who were touted as experts, but none could lip-read what Oppenheimer was saying in the video. Malcolm had arranged for two highly-profiled forensic experts to fly in from Connecticut. He even thought about setting up a shadow jury, but that would include an expensive jury consultant. Malcolm had experience in picking juries, but in this case, there were too many things to do; a shadow jury at this point seemed plausible.

Every day, Malcolm left the office and spent time with the kids, even if it was only an hour. Rothman called about Malcolm's expenses in New Orleans, but, Malcolm ignored him. Sara, his ex-wife, called asking for money, even though everything was properly disposed of at the divorce hearings. With her current legal problems, she tried to convince Malcolm to help her so that the mother of his children wouldn't go to jail. He would almost rather explain to the children why Mommy was doing ten to twenty in the state pen. Roberta made sure the kids got to and from school every day. The reverend and Lois helped, too.

Malcolm rose early the morning of Mardi Gras. He'd given everyone the day off, and he had decided to take the kids to see the parade. Cephus had called the night before about meeting him with some information. Malcolm was dressing Serena when Reverend Josiah walked in.

"Why in God's name are you taking those children to see that parade?" the reverend asked.

"It's just a parade, Papa Joe. I usually take them to the Macy's Thanksgiving Day Parade, but we were in Hawaii," Malcolm answered.

"Those parades are satanic, not to mention the lewdness of the crowd and all the drunks marching around. I tell you, there is nothing holy about the entire event—Mardi Gras is just what it portrays: a masquerade of deception," the reverend stated.

"Go upstairs and get your brother, Serena." Malcolm looked crossly at his father. "Papa Joe, you don't need to talk like that around her. Now, I know you may not see it, but those two are going through some emotional adjustments, and I don't need matters complicated by your telling them that Daddy is taking them to a bad parade," Malcolm said, following the scent of grits and eggs.

"That parade is nothing but debauchery..."

"Besides, Roberta is coming and bringing her daughter. And like I said, I have to meet Cephus there." Malcolm ate a biscuit.

"How come you don't eat my grits and eggs?" Lois questioned, mixing the scrambled eggs with cheddar cheese. "I remember a time when you couldn't get enough grits, sausages, eggs, and biscuits. What did they do to you up north?"

"Eating habits change as you get older. Oatmeal and a banana will do me just fine. And it would do you some good, as well, seeing that your doctor wants both of you to change your eating habits." Malcolm took a bowl and poured hot water in his instant oatmeal.

The reverend stood in silence for a moment. "Sweet Jesus in the morning. Is anyone listening to me on Sunday mornings, or am I just talking to myself? You mean to tell me Roberta and Cephus would come hear me preach the Word of God every Sunday, particularly this last Sunday when I preached about not attending Mardi Gras festivities? Lois?" the reverend said, exasperated.

"Now Josiah Albert Stinson, you hold on one dang minute. Didn't you tell me that every year, when you were a boy, everyone in Plaisance, Louisiana, got on a flatbed wagon drawn by two horses, and went to Mardi Gras?" Lois had her hand on her right hip, as the eggs sizzled in the frying pan.

"I wasn't a man of God then, but now I know better. Now I want to pass that wisdom onto my grandchildren, since my people missed the point." The reverend left the kitchen.

"You know, Malcolm, he's right. One mistake doesn't mean you have to repeat it," Lois said gently.

"We're going to the parade in Metairie, anyway. I am going to stay long enough to meet with Cephus, and talk for moment. Okay?" Malcolm kissed his mother on the cheek.

When Roberta and her daughter came to the house, the reverend answered the door. He gave her a strange look and said nothing, but lowered his head and shook it in disgust.

"Good morning," she said, watching the distraught reverend walk into his study.

"Did I come at a bad time?" she asked, looking at the reverend.

"No, he's just upset. He'll spend some time in prayer and be fine later on. Okay, we are all ready. Joshua, Serena, let's go." He smiled and patted Roberta's daughter on the head.

"You mean those children are going without breakfast? Good morning, Roberta. Ya'll had breakfast?" Lois asked, rushing to the front door.

"We had some toast and juice, Mrs. Stinson," Roberta said politely.

"Good, then you come and join the children. Mr. Health Nut here has already eaten." The children ran down the stairs. "Put down those jackets and march into that kitchen." Lois glared at Malcolm, who gave her no argument.

"I hope they haven't forgotten to bless their food," the reverend shouted out from his study.

Breakfast was eaten in a hurry, even though Lois wanted to stretch it out to talk with Roberta. It was nine o'clock and Malcolm was growing impatient. Lois glanced at him, and decided to release the children, fussing at them about putting on their jackets, even though the temperature was supposed to reach the low seventies on this Mardi Gras day.

Malcolm didn't want to take them to see the parade in the French Quarter, but preferred the parade in Metairie along St. Charles Ave. The French Quarter parade hosted the most elaborate gay beauty-and-costume contest in the world and it was very lewd. By the time Malcolm and his entourage had reached St. Charles Avenue at 9:45, the streets were packed with people. The parade made its way through, and the children were excited. The children marveled at the flamboyant costumes and bizarre make-up. They saw a variety of spectacles parading down the street, including tap dancing bottles of Chanel, The Rolling Stones,

Oscar Wilde, Nubian royalty, and French revolutionaries leading Marie Antoinette to the guillotine. There were even troupes of topless clowns. By noon, Cephus had come with his three children, but his wife who had listened to Reverend Stinson, boycotted Mardi Gras.

"Well, I'm glad you could join us," Malcolm said.

"Sorry, I got lost in the crowd down the street," Cephus replied, gathering up his kids.

"So, what's so urgent?" Malcolm asked.

"Benny Dubois wants to meet with you tonight, at Dooky Chase's. It's a restaurant outside the French Quarter," Cephus said. The crowd went into an uproar as the Thai royal barge came down the street. King Rex was the premiere float of Mardi Gras. Malcolm put Joshua on his shoulders and held Serena in his arms so they had a better view.

"So, what does that thug want to talk to me about?" Malcolm asked Cephus.

"I imagine it's about Clarence Reed, but he wouldn't tell me anything."

"Roberta, would you like to go to dinner tonight at Dooky Chase's?" Malcolm asked.

"Sorry, I'd love to, but I'll have to take a rain check. It's Mardi Gras, and we need a full hospital staff," she answered.

"Eight o'clock. I'll see you then," Cephus replied.

Malcolm took Roberta and the children to get some lunch, and then dropped her at home. As he drove home with the children, he sensed someone was watching him.

* * * *

Malcolm and Pete arrived exactly at 8:00 p.m., but there was no sign of Cephus or Benny Dubois. They waited for ten minutes, and then decided to take a table and order cocktails. The maitre'd approached Malcolm with a phone call.

"Hello?"

"Listen Malcolm, I'm sorry, but my kids got sick from some street vendor food. My wife is in Lake Charles visiting her mother. So I won't be able to make it," Cephus explained.

"Hey, it's okay. Pete and I will have dinner with this Benny character another time," Malcolm said, watching a beautiful woman walk by.

"I wish it were that easy. Benny will probably still seek you out. Just talk to him, appease him, and listen, I've sent someone else to see you tonight, as well. His name is Thomas Hickman, the professor at Tulane University," Cephus said.

"How will Hickman find me?"

"Don't worry; he knows what you look like. Give me a call later when you get home, and fill me in," Cephus said, and then hung up.

"So what was that all about?" Pete asked, also admiring the woman.

"Cephus isn't coming, but we're still meeting Benny Dubois, and a Tulane University professor, who's joining us for dinner to tell us about his personal hobby," Malcolm said, and rolled his eyes.

No sooner had Malcolm mentioned the professor, than a lean man with a meticulously cut graying beard, stood at the restaurant door. He looked around the room until he spotted his party, and then walked over, waving to Malcolm and Pete as if they were long-lost friends.

"Good evening, gentlemen. My name is Thomas Hickman. I hope Cephus told you I'd be joining you for dinner." The professor shook hands with them.

"Yes. Have a seat," Malcolm said.

"Thank you. This is the culinary divine of New Orleans. Talking about things over a good meal, you accomplish so much. It's an exhilarating feeling." The professor picked up the menu.

"What do you suggest, professor?" Pete asked.

"Let's see. Ah, yes. Let me suggest the crabmeat farci, or the shrimp clemenceau. Or if you prefer, the succulent catfish is prepared like no other in Louisiana. The sweet potatoes, your mother will want the recipe, and the bread pudding is exquisite." The professor buttered some cornbread and then the waiter took their orders. They took the professor's suggestions.

"Professor, what do you teach at Tulane?" Malcolm asked.

"Political science," he replied.

"Cephus mentioned something about a hobby that I might be interested in."

"Waiter, may I have a granger please?" the professor asked.

"Excuse me, but I'm not a drinker. What's a granger?" Malcolm asked.

"A martini with an onion, instead of an olive," he replied.

"So you were saying about your hobby..." Malcolm asked.

"Well, for the last ten years, I've been studying the movement and growth of..."

Before the professor could say another word, a burly black man with thick forearms and amicably dressed, asked the three men to come to a private room in the back of Dooky's. Malcolm boldly asked why.

"Because Benny would like to see you now. I suggest you start moving out of your seats, or would you like some assistance standing up?" he questioned. Knowing they were there to meet Benny Dubois, they followed the big bruiser into a small room, where Benny was dressed in an all black Armani suit with a flaming-red shirt, gold chains, and earrings in the shapes of German crosses. His ponytail kept his slick black hair in place. On one side was a black woman, with an hourglass figure in a skintight minidress, and on the other was a white woman, with the same sort of dress, only in a pastel blue. Their makeup was heavy, but they were beautiful, nonetheless.

"Sit down, gentlemen. I've arranged for your dinner to be served in here with us." Benny unfolded his arms from around the two women.

"Thank you," Malcolm said. "I understand you want to talk to me about something."

"Hold on a minute there, Counselor. This is my party, and I'll ask the questions," Benny said. "Now, I know you're Malcolm, and you must be the private dick, and you're not Cephus, so who the hell are you?" Benny asked the professor.

"Thomas Hickman, professor of political science at Tulane University. I don't believe we've met before," he said. Malcolm and Pete looked on in amazement.

"So why is this character with you tonight?" Benny asked.

"He's helping me with some research in the Clarence Reed case." Malcolm saw that the professor was getting ready to open his mouth, but Malcolm kicked him in the shins to quiet him.

Benny studied the professor while the waiters brought everyone's food. Benny ate a couple of mouthfuls of food before talking again. "I understand your bloodhound here, is interested in the murders of my former associates." Benny wolfed down his food as he talked.

"Well, we're looking at a theory that whoever committed the murders could be involved in the riverboat bombing," Pete replied.

"Why's that?" Benny asked.

"These kids were killed just before the bombing and Reed's arrest. With so much media attention on the Reed case, the killings have started again. It may be the same person," Pete said, then sipped his mint julep.

Benny paused for a moment, and then nodded for the two women to go powder their noses. "Last week, when Leroy got killed, another kid working with him saw the bastard attack one of my other runners." Benny became emotional for a moment, but then calmed himself. "This white guy in a long raincoat and French tam had Mole by the throat, holding a big hunting knife on him, and making him pull his pants down. But before this guy could rape the kid, his partner Binko ran down the street. And do you know what the bastard did? He cut off his right ear, then slit Leroy's throat. He got in a van. He had a long ponytail, longer than mine."

"How do you know if he had a hat on?" Malcolm asked.

"He dropped his hat while Binko chased him. Binko was packing and put a few caps into the van, but he still got away." Benny became agitated by just talking about it. "So, you tell me how I can catch this scum, and there's fifty grand in it for you," Benny said.

"That's a nice offer, but we're no closer than you are. You've told us more than we knew already. But would this kid Binko give a description to an artist?" Pete said.

"Where?" Benny asked.

"Down at the police station," Pete replied.

"No way, man. The cops will arrest him on some bogus charge. Then I have to go through all that rigmarole to get him out of jail. Forget it," Benny said.

"Cephus will take care of everything," Malcolm pleaded.

"Hello, Counselor, Cephus is still a cop and a good one at that, so it doesn't pay for me to take that chance. Cephus and I talk, but he hates everything I stand for. What makes you think he wouldn't take advantage of an opportunity like this to bust me? You got to do better than that for me to cooperate with you."

"How about we get a private artist, one who doesn't work for the police?" Pete said.

"That might work. You set it up," Benny said. One of his monstrous bodyguards whispered something into his ear. "Well, gentlemen, I have some urgent business to take care of. Enjoy your meal. It's on me. Au revoir." Benny wiped his mouth and motioned for the two women returning from the ladies' room, to turn around to leave. In a few seconds, they were all gone. Malcolm, Pete, and the professor were left alone in the private room to talk.

"Okay, that was interesting. So now we're working with a drug-dealing pimp, trying to find a lead. Before we were so rudely interrupted, professor, you were saying about your hobby," Malcolm said.

"I was saying, for the last ten years I've been studying the growth of hate groups in America and abroad," replied the professor.

"Hate groups?" Malcolm asked

"Yes. Aryan nations, Ku Klux Klan, Neo-Nazi's, remnants of John Birch Society, new groups like The Order, and let's not forget the militias…and there are many of them. For example, there's the Unorganized Militia of the United States who called for an armed march on Washington D.C. a few years ago to arrest congressmen for treason," the professor stated.

"How do you study these groups?" Malcolm asked.

"I have an elaborate system for checking their movements and growth. We communicate on the Internet as well. They don't know it's me, and I'm even a dues-paying member in some organizations."

"Why?" Pete asked.

"Because these hate groups that are just out in the open, or the ones that hide in militia groups, are a cancer that must be controlled," the professor said, looking for the waiter.

"This is very interesting, professor, and I see why Cephus wanted us to meet," Malcolm said.

Pete leaned over and whispered to him. "And why's that?"

"Because Cephus and I believe that maybe one of these militia groups could be responsible for the riverboat bombing," Malcolm replied.

"Professor, can you tell me of any militia groups that might be responsible for the bombing of the riverboat?" Malcolm asked.

"That's quite a mystery. Most of the area groups aren't taking credit for it. Their conversation on the Internet is that Clarence Reed should be made an honorary member. They claim he is the first black man to know that his race is wrong for wanting any equal rights."

"I don't follow," Pete said, confused.

"So far, Clarence is the only person charged with the bombing. He's black, but on the Internet, they call him the mongrel, because he is mixed. The militias are big on him because he is an ex-Navy SEAL. They think his being a former serviceman makes the militia's reasoning of blowing up the riverboat larger than the civil rights cause," the professor answered.

"Can we see some of your information?" Malcolm asked.

"Well, I suppose so. Cephus says you're all right. What about him?" the professor questioned, tilting his head towards Pete.

"He's all right. Unless, Pete, you belong to the IRA?" Malcolm asked, laughing.

"Very funny." Pete smiled back.

"Cephus is one of the bright spots in the New Orleans Police Department," the professor said. He tapped his finger at a spot on the menu showing the waiter what he wanted for dessert. "You guys want anything?" Malcolm and Pete both ordered coffee.

"Why do you say that, professor, or should we call you Thomas?" Malcolm asked.

"Professor will do. Hate group members are on the police force. In big cities like Los Angeles, police are known for being brutal' in New York they're known for corruption. Other big city police forces have reputations for being incompetent. Here in New Orleans, the police rank high in all three categories."

The waiter brought in the professor's bread pudding.

"Is anything being done about it?" Malcolm asked.

"Actually, there is. A new police chief has been brought in from Washington, D.C. But he's even having a hard time revamping the police force," the professor replied.

"Who are they, and why is that?" Pete asked.

"Why is because the police department is run by four assistant deputies and they run it like the mafia. God help us if Henri Joret is elected governor," the professor said.

"Why?" Malcolm asked.

"A few years ago, the Times Picayune broke a story that Joret had ties with the Zano crime family of New York. It was only speculation, but it was enough to put suspicion on Joret. Remember, he's a wealthy Cajun. It's really his wife Alva who carries the juice. Politically, her family goes back three, maybe four, generations in Louisiana politics. She's the backbone of Henri's political career. Fortunately for Joret, little attention was given to the story because Governor Edwards was having his own problems with gambling and organized crime. But I'd bet my last dollar Henri Joret *was* involved with those mafia boys then, too." The professor took another bite of his dessert and wagged his fork.

"Cephus told me that the new black police chief was having problems with some predominantly white police association of New Orleans," Pete said.

"That's true, and Clarence Reed comes in because he protested the organization! They felt that because the mayor of New Orleans is black, he pushed the issue of affirmative action to hire more black police officers. But the white police association is blaming much of the corruption on the black officers. Today in New Orleans, forty-five percent of the police force is black. And that bothers them something awful. The sad part is that many of the black officers are also corrupt. Think about it for a moment: all these years the whites controlled New Orleans, and now you have a black mayor, a black police chief, and forty-five percent of the force is black, in one of America's biggest tourist cities. That just doesn't set right with the upper echelon of white Louisiana." The professor finished his pudding. "Now, where is that waiter?" he questioned, searching for the waiter.

"You mentioned something about hate groups abroad?" Malcolm asked.

"Yes, they are all internationally connected. Places like Canada, Germany, England, and Australia. Believe me; Clarence Reed didn't commit this crime. Given some time, I'm confident I can pinpoint who did it. From the info I've gathered in the last six months, this was a special mission. The hate groups themselves don't know who committed the crime, but they all want Clarence Reed in on it. One night, you'll come over, and I'll show you what I have so far." The professor stood and shook hands with Malcolm and Pete. They complimented the waiter on an exquisite meal and left.

"This has been an informative night," Malcolm said.

"Do you think this professor is on the level? I mean is he all there? What kind of life does he have? This hobby seems more like an obsession with hate groups." Pete said.

"We don't know that. Let's just see what he has, first," Malcolm said.

* * * *

Once they were outside, two undercover FBI agents disguised as a black couple followed Malcolm and Pete to their car. Cephus was sitting in an unmarked car down the street. He had intentionally skipped dinner in order to find out who was following Malcolm. Pete and Malcolm drove off and the FBI followed. Cephus noticed something else as he started his car. A van with two men inside, Jasper and Jerry, had joined the caravan. They followed Malcolm to the hotel where Pete was staying, then on to Malcolm's parents' home. Cephus couldn't get close enough to write down the van's plate number. Cephus was even more concerned. He didn't know what to do to ensure Malcolm's safety.

* * * *

Jon Tulle was happy with the photographs and videotapes the agents had brought him from New York. As he thought things over in his office in Washington, D.C., he had doubts about the concerns the White House had about the bad publicity the case was receiving. Recently, all of the networks had presented various specials that raised doubts about whether the government was covering up again. Like Waco, Texas, or the Freemen of Montana, or Randy Weaver at Ruby Ridge. Except, this was a case of a black civil rights leader who had brought problems out into the open, like Martin Luther King, Jr. had.

Tulle was in the middle again, and if things went wrong, he could find himself in the tower in Juno, Alaska. Tulle had questions, for the first time, about Clarence Reed's guilt, but he still had to fight the war he'd waged against Malcolm.

CHAPTER 13

Henri Joret arrived early on this first Sunday in March. His appointment with Jasper Yates was at 10:00 a.m., and a torrential rain was falling. They were to meet in a deserted gas station, just off Route 10 in Slidell, Mississippi.

Jasper was on time, and the heavy rain was a good cover, if anyone saw them together. Monet had faxed Jasper's picture to Henri, so he knew what Jasper looked like, but he wouldn't tell Jasper that Monet had done this.

As a precaution, the prearranged password was "Louisiana's next governor will be black." Jasper left Jerry in the new van they had stolen and got into the black Lincoln limousine.

"Terrible day for a flood," Joret said.

"Can't be any worse than a black man becoming governor of Louisiana," Jasper replied, as they shook hands.

"William, you can move now," Joret instructed the black chauffeur. Joret put up the partition. "Well, we finally meet. I have to tell you that your work is impeccable. But when Monet and I set this venture up, it was to be done with minimal bodily harm…"

"Mr. Joret, the Fourth of July has come and gone. What's done is done, and neither you nor I can change it. Now, you wanted to see me about something?" Jasper asked firmly.

"Okay, let's get down to business. It seems that this lawyer Stinson is poking around in a lot of areas, so I was thinking that we could create some kind of a diversion. Something that would take his mind off the case for awhile," Joret said.

"What did you have in mind?"

"Another bombing."

"Of a gambling hall?"

"No, a church."

"When?"

"Let's say in about two months. The timing has to be perfect. The campaign will be going full swing by then, and he'll be coming into the home stretch of the trial. Let's say the first Sunday in May." Joret waited for Jasper's reaction.

"I assume you're talking about his father's church?" Jasper liked the idea; he had a slight grin on his face.

"You've done this before?" Joret asked.

"Just be confident that the job will get done," Jasper replied.

"All right. So you can do it?" Joret asked.

"First Sunday in May. Okay. You know my fee for this?" Jasper probed Joret.

"It's not the same as the riverboat, is it?" Joret asked.

"No. Two hundred thousand," Jasper responded.

"Two hundred thousand? Hell, I could blow it up myself, for that amount of money."

"Have fun. Drop me back where you picked me up, please," Jasper said.

"All right, you can't blame a man for trying."

"This is not a game, Mr. Joret, and I'm not your plaything," Jasper responded.

"Okay. It's a deal. Two hundred thousand."

"All right, I'll supply everything. Have I made myself clear?" Jasper asked. "If that's all, you can drop me off right here."

"But we're in the middle of nowhere," Joret stated.

"That's fine. No problem," Jasper said. "We'll be in touch." He got out of the car in the pummeling rainfall.

The limo drove off, and within seconds, Jerry pulled up in the van. Jasper and Jerry drove back to their hotel. They wouldn't follow Malcolm today; they'd rest and call Jim to see how he was doing. Heavy rainfall in the bayou always brought the alligators onto the island where the shack was built. Jerry knew Jim would be nervous. One year, the rain came up to the shack doorway, and flooded the place. The alligators were within feet of swimming into the shack.

"Jim, how's our guest doing?" Jim spoke into his cellular phone.

"She's fine. She sleeps and cries a lot. Outside of that, she's not a problem. What's the latest on the weather? The water here is rising fast, brother. I'm getting a little concerned," Jim asked.

"No need to worry. They say it's going to stop around one this afternoon. I'll call you back around then, or you call me and give me a status report on the water level. Ten–four," Jerry said, and hung up the phone.

"Can you believe that?" Jasper asked.

"Believe what?" Jerry responded.

"Joret asked me if I could find his daughter for him. If that isn't a laugh. Hell, if we had kept her blindfolded, we could have made a bundle for her return. Damn," Jasper said, disgustingly. "Well, anyway, we have another job to do, so tomorrow—no tonight, call Linus Smith in South Carolina. We'll need him for this job."

"What job?" Jerry asked, making a U-turn on Route 10 to head back to New Orleans.

"Another bombing. By the time we are finished with Joret and Monet, we'll all be millionaires," he said, laughing.

They went back to their hotel.

The rain stopped at noon.

* * * *

On Thursday, Leo Abrams died of a massive heart attack. Malcolm was wading through paperwork when he got Walter Baer's call.

"Malcolm," Walter said softly.

"Walter, how are you? Long time no hear. I've been meaning to call you."

"Malcolm, I'm calling to tell you that Leo Abrams passed away this morning," Walter said.

"What happened?" Malcolm asked.

"He had a massive heart attack early this morning at his home. He died before they got him to the hospital. And that's just the first of the bad news," Walter said.

"Did someone else die, too?" Malcolm asked.

"No, but you're not going to like what I have to tell you."

"Go on."

"I sent a clerk to Rothman, who overheard a conversation about your being taken off the Reed case…"

"No way, Walter. Why?"

"It seems as though Giamanco—the father this time—is going to be arrested by the feds for racketeering, and he's insisting that you represent him. The law clerk overheard Weinstein, Calucci, and Rothman fighting over the matter. I'm afraid they've decided to release you from the Reed case," Walter said.

"I'm telling you now, Walter, I'll quit first, before I represent Giamanco, so maybe you should let them know," Malcolm said.

"Well, don't jump the gun yet. Let's see what we can do. There's always a way to work things out," Walter said.

"Not this, Walter. Anyway, when is the funeral?"

"Tomorrow."

"I'll catch a flight out tonight. Bye."

Malcolm hung up the phone and saw his two law clerks and Lucy looking at him.

"Lucy, would you like to go to Leo Abrams funeral tomorrow?"

Lucy said nothing for a moment, and then nodded yes. "We'll be leaving tonight. Look, everybody, let's call it a day. We'll be back day after tomorrow."

There was a Delta flight, non-stop to Newark. At 3:30 p.m., Lucy and Malcolm boarded the plane together.

Malcolm gazed out the window all the way to Newark.

It was March and it was still cold in New York. Lucy Yee wasn't moved by Leo Abrams' death. She took a cab to Fort Lee, New Jersey, while Malcolm took one into the city. He arrived at his empty apartment just before 8:30. He'd forgotten to turn the phone off, and his answering machine was filled with messages. Walter Baer called within minutes of Malcolm's arrival.

"Malcolm, welcome back. We have to talk tomorrow. Well, actually," he stuttered, "Rothman wants to meet day after tomorrow about the future status of the Reed case," Walter said.

"And what exactly does that mean, Walter? If he thinks Giamanco can twist his arm for me to handle his case, well, he'd better be prepared for him to rip it off, because, Walter, I'm not going for it," Malcolm said.

"Now take it easy. Let's not make any irrational decisions," Walter replied. "Look, get some rest and be there at eight tomorrow morning. The funeral is at ten o'clock in Long Island, so we'll have time to talk. Okay? Goodnight." Walter hung up quickly.

Malcolm dialed the number Sara had left on the machine. He recognized the number, but wasn't sure where he had seen it before. The voice on the other end was Sara's mother in Connecticut. "Hello?" she said.

"Hello. May I speak to Sara?" Malcolm asked.

"Why, Malcolm, how are you?"

"I'm fine, Mrs. Dereford," he replied.

"You've been on the news a lot lately. How are my grandchildren? I haven't seen them in nearly a year, you know," she said.

"They're doing well. Right now they're living in Louisiana. Is Sara in?"

"Hold on. Sara! Telephone," she shouted into the phone. "So when will I get to see them? Easter, maybe?"

"I'll have to let you know," he said, as Sara picked up the extension.

"Please do, Malcolm. I would really like to spend some time with them. Malcolm, when you get a chance, call me; I'd like to talk to you," she said, as she hung up.

"Hello, Malcolm. Thanks for getting back to me," Sara said, sarcastically.

"Listen; don't start this conversation off on the wrong foot. What do you want?" he asked.

"Can I see you tomorrow?" she asked graciously, suddenly changing her tone.

"I have to go to Leo's funeral in Long Island at ten. Then I need to do some things at the office, so I'll meet you there around three," he said.

"We couldn't meet at the house?" she asked, sweetly.

"No, I have some other business to take care of while I'm here, and the office will be fine for our meeting," he replied, lying to her about other appointments. He didn't want to be alone with her at the house. At the office, he could be strong against anything she tried.

"All right, the office at three. I'll see you then. Oh, by the way, Malcolm, did the children tell you they want to visit me next week?" she asked.

"They told me you called about it. I don't know right now. I don't have the time to fly with them on the plane and come back, so I'll see about that," he said.

"I could come and get them. Let them stay with me for a month or two while you're working on the case…"

"And who's going to pay for all this air travel?" he asked.

"Well, right now you know I can't, but would you keep your children from seeing their mother?" she asked.

"Not less than six months ago in our divorce settlement, you received $100,000—that was the agreement because you wanted out of the marriage so badly. I took custody of the children, and you let some jackass invest your money into stocks, then you lose it all and get arrested for stock fraud, smearing my name across the New York Times. And you have the nerve to say that if I don't pay your way to see the kids, I'm denying them from seeing their mother? Let's just end our little talk right now because I'm getting pissed off. See you tomorrow at three. Good-bye." Malcolm angrily hung up the phone.

Walter picked up Malcolm up at 8:00 a.m. sharp. They discussed what could happen now that Abrams was dead, and nothing had really changed other than they might pull out of the Reed case. When they arrived at the synagogue in Long Island, nearly every lawyer from the firm was there. Others in attendance included politicians like the mayor of New York City, the governor of New York State, and both U.S. senators. There was a black coalition, as well as an Hispanic one, for the work that Leo Abrams had done in pro bono representation over the years. The New York media also attended the funeral. Leo had been a noble man and was loved by many.

The funeral took just forty-five minutes. Malcolm and Walter rode together to the cemetery. Once the burial service was over, the pinch began. Rothman made his way around to see Malcolm.

"Malcolm, how goes it?" Rothman asked.

"Good, Barry," he replied.

"Seeing that you're in the city, we want to have a little meeting tomorrow, say around ten-ish," Rothman said. He left as quickly as he had come, not waiting for an answer.

When Malcolm turned around, two of Giamanco's thugs were in his face. "Mr. Stinson, Mr. Giamanco would like to have a few words with you," a slick-haired thug in a blue pinstriped suit said, blocking Malcolm's path. They had walked about twenty yards along the row of limos, when Vito Giamanco stepped out.

"Ah, Malcolm. It's good to see you, my boy," Giamanco said, with open arms and an unlit cigar hanging out of his mouth. Malcolm didn't reply.

"Everything alright in New Orleans? I read about you almost every day in that big case. It seems to me the government's got nothing on that colored boy—the civil rights worker. Right?" Giamanco asked. Again Malcolm refused to say anything, he just looked at Giamanco.

"I've got a proposition for you." Giamanaco put his arm around Malcolm and led him towards the grass. "I've got a little problem with the feds coming up soon. So I'm going to need a little legal advice..."

"I understand that you already have an attorney. So why would you need me?" Malcolm asked.

"He's only good for certain legal matters. This is heavy-duty stuff, more up your alley, if you know what I mean. So, I'll tell you what, I'll pay you those exorbitant fees you charged me for my son, and I'll throw in a bonus of five hundred thou," Giamanco said, expecting Malcolm to take the deal. Instead, Malcolm removed Giamanco's arm from around him and stepped back.

"The answer is no. I already have a case that will take me the rest of this year to finish," Malcolm said.

Giamanco started to laugh. "Maybe you didn't understand me, because the way I hear it, you no longer have a case in Louisiana, so your calendar is free," Giamanco said.

"Excuse me, sir. I have another appointment," Malcolm said to Giamanco, then walked around him. Giamanco grabbed him by the arm.

"Nobody brushes me off. Understand that, boy?" Giamanco said, firmly.

"Why would you want a boy to do a man's job?" Malcolm pulled his arm from Giamanco. His sudden movement forced the two thugs to come closer to him. Other people at the cemetery were watching Malcolm and Giamanco stand face to face. When the police moved toward them, Giamanco backed down from the confrontation.

"This isn't over yet, Stinson. I'll be in touch," Giamanco said, as he climbed back into his limo.

Malcolm walked over to Walter, who was taken aback by the entire incident. "You okay, Malcolm?" Walter asked.

"Walter, have Calucci and Rothman already talked with this asshole and made a decision?" Malcolm asked, helping Walter back to the limo.

"I dare say I wouldn't be surprised. The meeting may be just a show for you." "Come spend the night with Martha and me. She was a little under the weather today, and couldn't make the funeral." Walter reached into the limo bar for some scotch.

"I'm meeting Sara this afternoon, and I want to look into a few things while I'm here. But thanks anyway, maybe next time," Malcolm said, as the limo drove them back to Manhattan.

* * * *

The FBI and the New York City Police videotaped the entire scene with Malcolm and Giamanco. This was the sort of information Jon Tulle fed on. He had always suspected Malcolm of being connected to organized crime. Armed with this new information, he would convince District Attorney Michael Ducruet to somehow show that Clarence Reed was also involved with organized crime…that maybe there was a war going on, and they hired Clarence to blow up the riverboat. Tulle couldn't wait to see the tapes.

*   *   *   *

"Malcolm, did you notice that the young lady working with you talked to Rothman for quite awhile? You don't think she was giving him a report about your progress?"

"There's nothing to hide, but I found it curious that she spent the entire time talking with him. And who was the other man standing with them?" Malcolm asked.

"That's Hugo Hurst, Rothman's boy. Good enough to be a lawyer, but not good enough to be a litigator," Walter replied, as the limo pulled up to the firm. "Well, call me tonight, and we'll talk some more about what to expect. If what Giamanco said is true, we have to decide what our next step will be. Malcolm, with Leo gone, I'm the only one there to intervene on your behalf."

"I understand, Walter," Malcolm said, as the limo drove off. He walked to his office and saw an unfamiliar face. "Where's Cindy?" he asked.

"She's out with the flu, and you are…?" she asked.

"Malcolm Stinson. This is my office," he replied.

"Oh, I have a message for you about a meeting tomorrow at…"

"Ten o'clock. I know. I'm expecting a woman named Sara—well, actually, she's my ex-wife—at three o'clock. Buzz me before you let her in," Malcolm said, and went into his office. He then stepped back out of the office. "Who sent you here to work?" he inquired.

"I'm from a temp agency," she coyly replied.

"Okay, but don't forget to buzz me first, before she comes in."

"Okey dokey," she said.

As Malcolm walked back into his office, he thought of an old college friend who handled cases of stock fraud. Arnold Levison had graduated from Harvard Law School when Malcolm did. They worked for different firms, but managed to remain fairly good friends. He dialed his number.

"Arnold Levison and Associates," the soft voice said on the phone.

"My name is Malcolm Stinson. May I speak with Mr. Levison?" he asked, cordially.

"One moment, please. I'll see if he's free," she answered.

"Malcolm! How the hell are you, my good man? It's been a few months of Sundays since I've heard from you," the joyful Levison said.

"I've been real busy."

"So I've seen on television. You're national news, handling that terrorist case. So how are the kids? Sorry to hear about your divorce," Levison said.

"Everyone is fine, and the divorce is just a fact of life. Actually, Arnold, that is partly why I'm calling you. Have you heard Sara was indicted in this stock fraud case?"

"And they mentioned your name in the Times."

"Arnold, can you help her out? I'd hate to tell my children one day that I did nothing to keep their mother out of jail."

"I guess we can do something. Send her over to see me."

"When would be a good time?"

"Oh, I don't know, tomorrow?"

"What about today, say around four?"

"That'll be fine. Who, may I ask, is taking care of the tab?"

"Send all the bills to me. How's the wife and kids?"

"All is well, my friend. You have to come over. I moved to Connecticut about a year ago. Best move I ever made."

"I will for sure, once I find out where I'm going to settle down."

"You're in New Orleans now, right? Love that city, man. Listen, I've got another call I've been waiting for, so just tell her to come over this afternoon. Hey, good talking to you, buddy." Levison hung up.

"Mr. Stinson, you have a call from a Walter Baer on line one," the temp said over the intercom.

"Yes, Walter."

"I want you to get me an account number in New Orleans, and quickly."

"Why?"

"What I suspect he will do tomorrow is pull out of the case. As the pro bono officer, I'm authorized up to $300,000 at one time, on my own signature. So let's get some of that money down to New Orleans. I have a feeling you're going to need some dough," Walter said, from his car phone.

"Call me back in fifteen minutes," Malcolm said.

Within fifteen minutes, Malcolm had Reverend Josiah's account number, and Walter electronically sent $300,000. Malcolm was grateful, and Walter reminded him to keep receipts for what he spent…even if he was taken off the case.

The temp buzzed to tell Malcolm that Sara had arrived. She was twenty minutes early, and barged in with the temp following her. Malcolm said it was all right. Sara looked exquisite today. She must have dolled up just for Malcolm. He watched her like some new love in his life, as she swayed over to the edge of his desk. She was wearing a ruby silk-dupioni caftan with fuchsia pants, and her high-heeled sandals exposed her fuchsia toenails. For the first time in over a year, they were alone together. "May I sit down?" she asked.

"Be my guest," Malcolm replied, gesturing to a chair.

Malcolm leaned back in the chair behind his desk, holding a pencil between his hands with his elbows on the armrests.

"So, what's so important that you need to see me in person?" he asked.

"For starters, I'd like for us to…be able to talk, without a lot of hostility in the air…" she said.

"My dear, I haven't the slightest idea what you're talking about," he said.

"…And I miss the kids. I know I agreed to your having complete custody, but can't we work something out, where I keep them for a couple of months, and you keep them for a couple?

"Pre-school…"

"Are you moving to Louisiana, Malcolm?" she asked.

"I don't know yet, but it's possible."

"I'll never get to see them, then. What's wrong with staying here in the city?"

"The country air was good for me, and it's good for them."

"You're doing this just to spite me," she accused him.

"Not at all." He stood to look out his window. She followed him there.

"This case I'm on may not be over until the end of the year, or maybe even early next year."

"Malcolm, that's months away." She stood behind him, and raised her arms to hold him, but hesitated, fearful of his rebuke if she touched him.

"I'll tell you what, maybe you can have them for the summer, but come September, whether it's Louisiana or New York, those children are going to be in school, and it won't be in Connecticut." He turned around and saw Sara's tears falling down her silky cheeks, her luscious lips inches away from his.

"I think I made a big mistake," she said, pressing her body against his. He looked into her eyes, and then suddenly plunged his tongue deep into her mouth. She moaned with passion as he leaned her against his desk, knocking everything off as their bodies moved. She wanted to undress, but he had her pinned to the desk. Malcolm moved her legs up and moved into a comfortable position. It was the same passion they had felt for each other ten years ago, or was it just lust from lack of intimacy? Then Malcolm fought his emotion.

"I can't do this, Sara," he said, as she tried to pull him back on her.

Exasperated and out of breath already, she yearned for him to fill her.

"What's the matter, baby?" she asked in a seductive voice.

"You defiled our bed for no other reason than your selfish pleasure and ambition. You betrayed your children and me, and now you think you want me again. I have some moral character, so enough is enough. Let's talk about your present problem." He stood up and moved away from her, straightening his clothes.

She lay there in disbelief that he'd taken her that far. Malcolm knew how to touch all of her sensual buttons. He knew that he was teasing her, and she was surprised at how much he enjoyed doing it. Later he'd be sorry, but for now, he relished the moment.

Sara took a deep breath, and then stood to straighten her clothes.

"You know that isn't right, Malcolm. You owe me," she said.

"Right. So, what's happening with this stock fraud case?" He moved to the couch across the room while talking to her.

"I've got a lawyer, but I have no confidence in him. That little bastard, Armon, is telling the D.A. that I ran the whole scam. Malcolm, all I did was give him money to invest. I didn't know what was going on, until the FBI banged on my door and arrested me. Malcolm, that's the God honest truth," she said.

"All right, listen, you still have time today. I want you to go see a friend of mine. His name is Arnold Levison. He handles stock fraud cases and he's very good. I spoke to him and he'll represent you—don't worry about the bill, I'll take care of that," he said sadly, as she hugged him. He'd stood his ground and he hadn't given in to her desires.

"You've always been my hero." She picked up her pocketbook and headed for the door. Malcolm gave her Levison's address. "Malcolm, I'm praying you can forgive me, and maybe we can give it another go. Ten years married and three years of dating; it's a long time to throw away. I don't think we've had our fill of each other. Just maybe we took—I took—a detour that harmed us, and the children." Tears rolled down her face. "I'm sorry for what I did to our family."

"It's not the forgiving that's hard. It's the forgetting, Sara. Take care of yourself," he said, as she walked out.

* * * *

Early the next morning, all of the players were assembled in the conference room. On one side were Calucci, Rothman, and Weinstein. On the other side sat Malcolm, Walter, and Lucy, who was now assigned to the case. Rothman started the meeting off with a bang.

"I'm glad everyone could make it. Since there are rumors about the status of this case, I put a stop on any monies being transferred from the firm to the Reed case yesterday. So, Walter, that three hundred thousand that you attempted to transfer to New Orleans was voided," Rothman said, with his head cocked to one side, looking at Walter.

Malcolm and Walter felt like reaching across the table and strangling Rothman. "We reviewed the progress of this pro bono case in Louisiana, and came to the conclusion that it had an adverse reflection on the firm's image. So now that Mr. Abrams, God rest his soul, is gone, we feel that representing Clarence Reed isn't in the firm's best interest. So Malcolm, take a couple of weeks to wrap things up, because we have a paying client…I might add…for you to represent," Rothman said.

"And just who might that be?" Malcolm stared at Rothman.

"Vito Giamanco, and we will bill him at top dollar," Rothman replied.

"What happens to Clarence Reed?" Malcolm asked.

"That's not our problem. Do you know how many lawyers are anxious to represent him? Hell, they don't care about negative publicity, but here, we do." Rothman tried to convince Malcolm that Reed would be all right.

"And this is your solution, to have me represent Giamanco?" Malcolm asked.

"It's not a solution. You work for this firm, and we appoint the cases to you."

"Well, I've been here for ten years, and I know when it's time to move on. You can take away the finances for the case, but I can leave here, still be a lawyer and represent Clarence Reed in August," Malcolm said.

"What are you saying, Stinson?" Calucci asked, astonished.

"That as of today, I resign from Weinstein, Calucci, and Abrams—or is it Rothman already?"

"Now wait a minute, you're taking this Reed case a little too far, Malcolm," Calucci said.

"Hell, let him quit. Who needs him?" Rothman said, leaning back in his chair.

"Hold it," Weinstein said. "No one's quitting anything. Malcolm, Leo Abrams was the senior partner, and he gave his blessing on this case. So we'll review this in three months to see where Malcolm is with the case, then we'll make a decision. Lucy will stay on, as will the private detective. Their salaries and expenses will remain intact, but we will limit other expenses to twenty thousand a month. So, Malcolm, do the best you can. If some difficulty arises, we'll talk about it. Fair enough, Malcolm?" Calucci and Rothman sat dumbfounded.

"Yes, sir, I guess that's fair," Malcolm said quietly.

"Now, I have another appointment, gentlemen. This meeting is over." When Weinstein got up to leave, so did everyone else.

"Well," Walter said, "we get to fight another day. I don't understand what happened in there, but you're still on the case. What's the matter? You don't seem happy about this." He and Malcolm left the stunned Calucci and Rothman at the conference table.

"Something's not right. He did this for a reason, and in July when the three months are up, I think he'll reveal it to us." Malcolm was shocked that Weinstein had taken such a position against Calucci.

He stopped and told Lucy that she didn't have to be back in New Orleans until Monday. It was Friday, and she'd love being home for the weekend. Malcolm said good-bye to Walter and caught the next flight to New Orleans.

* * * *

Outside, the FBI agents were playing with the videotape they would show to Jon Tulle. There would be peace, and a sense of progress, at FBI headquarters. They thought they had finally made some headway with their case against Malcolm.

CHAPTER 14

Suzanne Joret was dead tired. She felt the swamp on her body. The handcuffs were loose, but not loose enough for her to escape. She kept her sanity by talking with Jim, trying to find out what made him tick and hoping for an opportunity to escape from this alligator-swamp prison. She'd been there for two months, and wondered if anyone was still looking for her. Jim wouldn't let her read any newspapers or listen to the radio. Completely isolated from the entire civilized world, she was determined to escape. She would not die here.

On the second Monday in March, the early morning temperature was already in the mid-seventies. Suzanne no longer feared the swimming alligators that she could see from her seat—she'd even named them, to amuse herself. Suzanne considered herself lucky that Jim had followed Jasper's orders not to lay a hand on her, but from time to time, she caught him giving her looks that scared her.

This morning, Dusty Powell visited the Daltons' hideaway. The Daltons had been orphaned at age ten. Their mother had died from breast cancer, and their father, a former Klansman, died in a trucking accident a year later. Dusty was made their guardian; he hired Delia-May, a black woman, to watch the boys while he worked as a longshoreman. Ironically, for eight years, a black woman raised the racist Dalton brothers. Dusty was hurt on the job when the boys were in their teens. It was Dusty who introduced them to the world of hatred and bigotry. He took the boys to Klan rallies, and taught them about racism. After high school, the Daltons enlisted in the Navy, and two years later, they became Navy SEALs. In the Navy, they found another foster parent, Jasper Yates. He taught them racism for a profit.

Dusty lived a mile down the canal from the Dalton brothers and had been sick since November. While Suzanne was there, Jim visited him once a week. But on this Monday, Dusty—unshaven and smelling like a swamp rat—knocked on the door. Jim was in the bathroom when Dusty came in and saw Suzanne sitting hand-cuffed on the bed.

"Well, my, my. What do we have here? A love slave?" Dusty questioned, as Jim burst out of the bathroom with a knife in his hand.

"You ought to announce when you enter a place, Dusty," he said.

"Okay, I'm here. And who is this lovely swamp flower?" Dusty didn't take his eyes off Suzanne for a moment.

"She's a guest. She's tied up so she don't get lost in the swamp."

"Um, so you want me to believe that's why you got her hand-cuffed and all?"

"What do you want, Dusty? Don't mind her."

"I was wondering why you are always coming up to see me but never give me a chance to come up yonder."

"I'll tell you what, I've got to go to the store up the road, and when I get back, I'll tell you the whole story. Just watch her. Hear? No touching," Jim said, putting on a tee shirt. "I'll be back before you know it," Jim said, leaving the shack. Dusty waited until Jim got out of sight.

"So why don't you tell me, pretty lady...wait a minute, I've seen you before. Why, ain't you that gal from the television station that they're all looking for?" Dusty sat at the table close to Suzanne.

"What are they saying about my disappearance?"

"They don't know if you've been kidnapped, murdered, or been in an accident. It's just a plain old mystery to the cops. So, Jim and Jerry done kidnapped you. For what?" Dusty asked, curiously.

"Because they bombed the riverboat. They thought I knew all this information about them, which I didn't, until Jim boy here began spilling his guts for the last two months," she said.

Taking a chance, she turned on the charm.

"So, what's a sweet old guy like you, hanging around these parts for? I take you for a city-type fellow." She mustered her best radiant smile.

"You just trying to josh an old man," he said, but moved closer to the bed. "I ain't never seen anything as purdy as you out here." He rubbed her arms.

"That's too bad, you know, because I haven't had a man in months, and I think Jim boy is a little funny. You know what I mean?"

"I tell them boys that it ain't right for them to spend their young adult lives out here in the swamp, but ever since they hooked up with the Navy captain—what's his name?"

"Jasper."

"Yeah, him, them boys ain't been right. But what you say about you ain't had a man in while?" He kissed her neck. She didn't resist. She even faked a moan for him.

"How about we take care of a little business before Jimbo gets back?" He wrapped his arms around her and nibbled her ear.

"Well, that ain't fair," she said.

"What ain't fair, honey?" he asked, still kissing her neck.

"That you can hold me and have pleasure. I want to be able to hold you, and give you some pleasure," she said, with a sweet moan.

He paused and glanced outside. "Now, you got to promise to put these back on after we've finished."

Suzanne told Dusty where Jim kept the key to the handcuffs. She scanned the room quickly for a weapon. When he unlocked the handcuffs, she felt pain as she stretched her arms for the first time in months. Dusty dropped his pants, wanting her to take him in her mouth. She stood up and told him to lie down on the bed. He shuffled across to the bed and she grabbed the iron skillet from on the stove, and when he turned around to sit on the bed, she whacked him as hard as she could. He fell to the bed with blood gushing out of his ear.

She hesitated for moment to see if he'd get up. She had the iron skillet cocked and ready for another blow. Dusty moaned in agony, and slowly sat up on the bed. Then suddenly, to Suzanne's surprise, old Dusty moved like lightning, tackling her to the floor. He was on top of her, and raised his fist to punch her. She moved the pan in front of her as the punch was about to land, and Dusty's fist crashed into the iron skillet. He yelled out in pain. She scooted from underneath him and tried to escape through the door, but it was locked. She pulled frantically on the handle, not seeing Dusty stand and pull up his pants.

"You no good piece of trash. I'll kill you!" he shouted. As he lunged toward her, she threw the window open, holding on to the railing. Dusty, in the same motion, lunged after her. He rolled off the top of the little shack into the water. Still not aware of what had happened, he stood up and cursed her as the waters around him splashed. Before Dusty could take two steps, a small female alligator grabbed hold of his leg, and then another grabbed his arm. Within seconds, others joined in. Suzanne heard the fury of the water. She turned around, while still hanging on to the rail. There was no sign of Dusty—just some brown murky blood. She pulled herself up and made it down the stairs to the boat and then paddled to shore among the other alligators, who were waiting for her to fall into their feeding ground. She was exhilarated; she'd escaped.

Once she reached land, she didn't know which way to go. Anywhere away from the shack was good for now. She didn't take the road with the tree covering it. Then she remembered her car. Maybe they didn't find the spare key. Against her better judgment, she returned to the tool shed that hid her BMW. The door was locked so she looked for something to break it with, or maybe the side window. She banged on the lock. It wouldn't break. She took a tree branch she had found and broke the shed's window. Using an old cinder block lying nearby as a step-stool, she took one step up. A huge arm coiled around her waist and slammed her to the ground.

"You make one move, and I'll kill you," Jim said. He had a big ten-inch hunting knife ready to plunge into her. "Where's Dusty?" His hand was on her throat and his knee was in her chest.

"I don't know. He let me go and left." She gagged from the grip he had on her.

"Turn over," he said, and put the knife away. He pulled out a snub-nosed .38 Magnum pistol, grabbed her by the hair, and placed the gun to her temple. "Now, we're going to get in the boat, and if you make one sudden move, I'll put a bullet in your skull and feed your carcass to the gators. Do you understand me?"

She was exhausted and didn't fight back. He maneuvered the boat back to the shack and took a quick glance around, but saw no sign of Dusty. Upstairs in the shack, Jim saw that there had been a struggle.

"Where the hell is Dusty, dammit?" He smacked her around the room a few times. He was about to punch her, when the cellular phone rang. "Hello," he shouted.

"Hello, Jim. What's the matter? Why are you shouting?" Jasper asked. Jim didn't tell Jasper about Suzanne's escape attempt, because it was his fault.

"Nothing—just had the music up a little bit," he said, calmly.

"Music? I didn't know you were a music buff. You and our guest having a party? You do recall what I said about touching her?" Jasper said. "Let me speak to her."

Jim covered the phone and told her to say everything was fine, or he would throw her to the alligators.

"Hello," she said, in a quiet voice.

"Is everything alright, Ms. Joret?" he asked, politely.

"Why, that is so kind of you to ask, you Nazi bastard," she blurted out. Jim took the phone from her and pushed her back onto the floor.

"She's alright, Jasper," Jim said, keeping a watchful eye on her.

"She'd better be. She's very important to us, Jim. We'll need her down the road, so take good care of her. I mean it. No harm is to come to her…at least not yet. Is that clear, soldier?" Jasper asked.

"Understood, sir," Jim said, and hung up.

"I should just throw you in for the hell of it. Dusty better not have fallen in the swamp because of you. If he did, all bets are off and you're going in next. Now, come over here, and let's put those chains back on," Jim said.

"You know, you're not a bad lady. You seem prettier than you act. So, I'll tell you what, if you're nice, I'll tell you the story of what happened on the Fourth of July. I'll let you know all the gory details of your nigger lover, Clarence, and what part he had in all them people being killed," Jim said, securing Suzanne once again.

Without a fight, Suzanne let Jim put her back in the handcuffs and leg irons. She leaned over and cried. She wondered if anybody would ever find her. What was Clarence thinking, since she hadn't visited him? Did he know she was missing? Then a thought occurred to her. Is Henri Joret involved in this? The bombing? My kidnapping? What part did he play in this? Suzanne slowly gained strength from these thoughts. She was determined to survive this, somehow. But tonight, she would rest.

CHAPTER 15

Tipitina's was a jazz club named after a song by the famous New Orleans jazz musician, Professor "Fess" Longhair. Malcolm, Cephus, Pete, and Lucy arrived together at nine p.m. When they entered the club, a tornado of mambo, rumba, calypso, jazz, Mardi Gras Indian music, and the blues swirled around them.

The club was packed with people. To the left of the stage they noticed Professor Hickman sitting alone. Lucy swayed through the club, her radiant beauty turning heads away from the pounding music, as she made her way to the professor.

The professor was smitten with Lucy on sight. "That is a lovely dress you have on, Ms. Yee," the professor complimented.

"Why, thank you, professor. By the way, what do you teach?" Lucy asked, returning the professor's warm glance.

"Political science at Tulane," he said. This exquisite Asian woman captivated him. She found him attractive and amusing. For the next thirty minutes, the professor talked about the Korean and Vietnamese cultures.

"I thought we came here because he had some information for us," Malcolm said, sitting next to Pete and Cephus.

"You're the one who invited her. She's as enchanted by him as he is by her," Pete said. The next set of music was about to begin, and Lucy excused herself to go freshen up. Malcolm seized the opportunity.

"Look, professor, I hate to interrupt your little tryst, but you did tell Cephus that you had some information," Malcolm said. The professor was off in some other galaxy.

"You work with her, huh?" the professor asked.

"She works for me," Malcolm corrected him.

"All right. The other night I was on the Internet, and some Klan people are saying that a black group, in retaliation for Clarence Reed, is responsible for Suzanne Joret's disappearance."

"Why would a black group do something like that?"

"Well, everyone in Louisiana knows that Clarence and Henri Joret are mortal enemies. I mean, after all, there's affirmative action, abortion, civil rights, and the judicial system. If Henri said something was white, Clarence would say it was black. It's the rivalry they had. Then a guy named Zorro, from Michigan, spoke about giving the SEALs his approval for sinking Satan's river raft of chance during our beloved country's birthday. Now, what would that mean to you?" The professor beamed as Lucy returned to the table. He stood to help her into her seat.

"Okay, is there any way of tracking down this Zorro? Or even communicating with him?" Malcolm was intrigued by the professor's information.

"I'll give it a try. Come by one night, and we'll browse the Net. And bring Ms. Yee with you." The professor turned back to Lucy and enjoyed the music.

"It's no big deal. Clarence was a SEAL, so they could just be giving him credit," Malcolm said.

"Those guys talk that sort of trash to each other all the time. A statement like that is not going to help us," Cephus said, loudly.

The professor overheard their comments, as Lucy was engrossed in the music. He moved away from Lucy and moved his chair closer to the others.

"They did say something else, now that I think of it," the professor said. The three men urged him to continue. "They said the mongrel couldn't come to terms with the other monkeys, better known to them as Niggers, Apes, Alligators, Coons, and Possums: the NAACP. So they said, 'The mongrel was hanging on in prison, while the black deputy dog, from the cesspool capitol of America, would try his hand in white Louisiana's judicial system. Only to be swept away in the fall, by the white justice system of white America,'" the professor said.

"They say that sort of stuff on the Internet?" Malcolm asked, stupefied.

"I've seen worse. When you come by, I'll explain it to you."

Malcolm sat back in his chair, and noticed Benny Dubois waving to him from the bar. He waved back, and then told Cephus.

"I know. I saw him about twenty minutes ago. Strange, running into him so soon," Cephus said, then leaned over and whispered to Pete and Malcolm. "I can't keep an eye on you all the time, but Pete here, should be a little more careful about watching your back," Cephus said.

"Why?" Malcolm asked.

"Somebody else is tailing you. The night you met Benny at Dooky's, I followed you back to the hotel when you dropped Pete off. The feds were following you, but a van, with two white men inside, was also on your tail. I talked with Benny; he may be a criminal, but I believed him when he said it wasn't any of his boys. Someone else has a vested interest in your whereabouts, Counselor. Be careful around N'Awlins. There are a lot of two-legged things that go bump in the night. As a precaution, I'm assigning an unmarked patrol car to watch your daddy's house."

* * * *

Oak Alley, in Vacherie, was sixty miles upriver from New Orleans, where the oak trees pre-dated the 1839 homes. Plans were being made at Henri Joret's Greek revival home to adjust to the latest poll. The meeting's participants weren't going to like the news.

Todd Sandchester, a short thin man wearing a perfect hairpiece, had been involved in electing Presidents Reagan and Bush. For twelve years, he'd been an integral part of the Republican Party, resigning the year that President Bush ran against Bill Clinton. He made millions through the Reagan and Bush years, and had been taking a hiatus until Henri Joret pulled him out of retirement. Sandchester was fifty-one years old, and Henri wanted him for this gubernatorial election, and the next presidential election. Sandchester thought Henri was his best bet to enter into the higher echelon of American politics.

The meeting included Henri's top supporters—millionaires from Louisiana, Mississippi, Texas, and Alabama. Sandchester pulled Henri off to the side to review the plan, but Henri wasn't convinced it was the right political move.

"Todd, this just isn't right. First, we have to consider whether the other candidate would join our team, and, more importantly, whether these assholes will approve that action," Henri said.

"Just let me handle it," Sandchester said.

"I'm telling you, if it gets too hot and nasty in there, I'm pulling out and letting you take the heat. Understand?" Henri said, as Alva walked in.

"What are you two plotting now?" she asked.

"What we talked about the other day, Mrs. Joret—the other candidate," Sandchester said, quietly.

"You both act like a couple of mice sneaking around for crumbs. Let's go. I'll handle this," she said boldly, after having two double shots of Remy Martin. As they moved into the large living room where the six men were having cocktails, Sandchester grabbed her arm, ever so gently. "Mrs. Joret, this has to be handled quite delicately."

"Alright. You start, and if I see you're losing your audience, I'll save the game. Understood?" she said.

They composed themselves and entered the room, smiling and laughing. Alva Joret had four of them, and Sandchester and Henri each had one apiece. This rally of the troops went on for twenty minutes before Sandchester asked everyone to have a seat.

"I know you all have an idea why we're here tonight. The plain truth of the matter is that Henri is in a dead heat with his opponent. Our analysis shows that there are problems in the black community," Sandchester said smoothly, to Alva's satisfaction.

"What sort of problems?" asked George Meeke, a textile millionaire from Alabama. "Why don't we do what that senate woman did, and get the gambling vote out there? That will take us over the hump."

"'Well, that's the problem we're trying to fix by keeping away from those gambling folks. We don't want to go into office owing them anything. The reason our opponent is a few points ahead is because of that black candidate, Campy Frazier," Sandchester said.

"Hell, by election time, he'll know he can't win. So we'll throw him a bone," said a Louisiana magnate, Harvey Stillman. He motioned for the maid to freshen his drink.

"That may be the case," Sandchester said, "but what if he doesn't accept our bone? What if he wants to run? That could upset the entire race. Our facts show that Campy has ninety-five percent of the black vote, ninety percent of the Spanish vote, eighty-nine percent of the Asian vote, and this, gentlemen, is the most disturbing statistic, ten percent of the White vote. Our polls show we need at least ninety-five percent of the black votes to win."

"Those polls ain't worth a rat's ass," said Bill Hargrove, a behind-the-scenes political mover in Louisiana politics.

"Gentlemen, I cannot overemphasize the importance of these statistics," Sandchester said, ardently.

Then Cal Thomason, a wealthy rancher from Texas and longtime friend of Henri's, joined in. "So what can we do to change these statistics?"

Sandchester stood in a corner of the room with his hands clasped, as if he were getting ready to pray. He probably was. He moved slowly toward the room's center and swirled slowly around, glancing at each person before he spoke. He shaped his hands into a steeple and put them in front of his mouth, like a Buddhist priest, and stammered, "We have come up with a solution to this political dilemma."

Henri almost couldn't bear to hear the reaction.

"After examining every avenue and all possible alternatives, we have but one solution," Sandchester said to the silent room. He tried to swallow without anyone seeing him. Then in a flash of courage he announced, "We are considering bringing Campy Frazier onto the Joret ticket."

Sandchester's eyes moved rapidly around the room for their collective disagreement. As the harrumph rig raised the decibel level, Thomason was first.

"Let me get this straight. You want us to put some nigger on Henri's ticket. Henri, what the hell is this screwball talking about?" he questioned, with each word getting louder by the syllable.

"Now, now, boys, Todd here is a professional, and he's never been involved in a losing campaign. Hell, he was the one who suggested bringing Quayle on as Bush's vice-president. I was as startled as you all are. Why, my first reaction was an emphatic no until I realized that it would help win the election," Henri said.

"This is damn outrageous! A black as…as what? Lieutenant governor?" Ben Wellington, the Southern insurance magnate, said. "Never in Louisiana's history has such a thing been considered. Do you know how many white votes you'll lose? We'd be the laughing stock of the South—hell, the country."

One after another, they poured out their venom at Sandchester's idea. Alva had heard enough. She set down her drink and spoke quietly, yet forcefully.

"Now listen to me. This idea is not only good—it's phenomenal. Only the people in this room know this campaign's long-term goal—four years as governor of Louisiana, then on to the White House. What better picture to present to America in four years, than Louisiana's having had the courage to have a black man for lieutenant governor.

"Think of the other plans we have for our state to be a model for the rest of the country. We have one of the country's highest unemployment rates. With your help, we can dramatically change that in the next four years. Imagine, we will appeal to minorities all over the country. The white voters will also be impressed with what we do for the middle class," Alva said, empathetically.

"Alva, with all due respect to you and your family, this truly is ludicrous. Haven't you weighed the loss of white votes, compared to the black ones we would gain?" said Ashby Stanford, who owned three casinos on the Gulf of Mississippi.

"That's possible, but we have to sell the idea. After all, Campy is not like, uh...who's that black guy in New York always running off his mouth?" Alva asked, looking at Sandchester.

"Al...something?"

"Gentlemen," Alva continued. "Campy has been a Louisiana congressman for eight years and has done things not just for his black constituents. How do you think he came up with ten percent of the white vote? That is very big for an underdog to have that much power. He's a pillar in the community, and throughout the other parishes of this state.

"Imagine, if you will, making history, and then taking our ideas from Louisiana to Washington, D.C. You have to stop thinking in the old Southern ways. I'm sure you all have a particular interest you want satisfied, if you know what I mean. It's a win-win situation. My family has been involved in Louisiana politics for four generations. My grandfather took a lot of heat when he backed one loony man for senator, and then a governor, a man named Huey Long. It's the nineties, guys, so let's get with the program," she said, in a commanding voice.

"I don't know about this. It seems like a big risk," Thomason said.

"Has Campy Frazier accepted this offer?" Ashby Stanford asked, with grave concern.

"Why, no, we wouldn't have asked him before first asking your opinion about doing business with them. Also, the cost would be substantially less than if we did business with Ireland," Joret replied.

"So, when will the news break about Campy Frazier?" Ashby asked.

"Probably in a few weeks. We still have to work out the details on approaching Campy, and we have some other backers to consider," Sandchester said.

"This had better work, or you won't work in this country again," Thomason threatened, rushing to the door in a fury. The others mumbled their resistance to the idea, but still gave a nod of approval. Alva could barely hold herself together.

"I thought those assholes would never leave," she sighed, "Mr. Sandchester, I have a new project for you."

"Yes, Mrs. Joret. What can I do for you? Oh, by the way, thank you for your help," Sandchester replied, lighting a cigarette.

"I need you to find a good private detective. The damn police and FBI ain't worth a rat's ass...my baby is still missing..." she sniffled. "I want to find her—dead or alive—I want to find her."

"Alva, I've been assured by the top echelons of the FBI that they're making every effort to find Suzanne," Henri said.

"Todd, excuse us for a moment," she said, bitterly. Sandchester left the room and closed the door behind him.

"You listen to me, Henri. It was my father, and his money, that brought you to this point in your political career. The Jorets could have helped you financially, but your family never has supported your political career. It still pisses me off that you haven't given up this campaign to make an all-out effort to find Suzanne." She struggled to her feet, and made her way to the door. She grabbed the door handle, and just before she opened it, she said, "And, Henri, God help you if I find out that French bastard had anything to do with Suzanne's disappearance. If he did, your political career is over...and his criminal life, as well. I know she's not your blood, but she's mine."

Henri returned to Sandchester in the living room. They looked at each other for a moment. "What if she's right? What if Monet had something to do with Suzanne?" Henri asked, in a whisper.

"Why would she think that?" Sandchester asked, fixing himself a drink.

"Something that happened shortly before Suzanne disappeared."

"So, you think Monet is involved?"

"I would hate to think that, but if he is, I'll deal with him, in due time. But above all, my friend, Alva should never find out the truth."

"The week after Easter I'll set everything up. You needn't worry," Sandchester said, as he walked out of the house. He paused for a moment at the door and turned to Henri. "We should consider some alternatives to bringing Monet on as partner after the election. If this pans out to be true—his involvement with Suzanne, I mean—what would stop him from harming any other members of your family, if it suited him?"

"I think you're right. Let's explore a fail-safe plan where we can put the blame on Monet and put him into the hands of Victor Zano. The authorities would be too easy on the bastard. So get that devious little mind of yours working on a plan."

"I never did like Monet's involvement, but I understand he was a necessary evil for this ordeal. Goodnight, Henri," Sandchester said.

Henri wasn't satisfied with Sandchester's attitude in resolving this matter of Suzanne. He listened for Alva, who had made her way upstairs to the bedroom, crying and cussing about everything. He went to his study and walked directly to the safe behind the head of a taxidermy black bear. He had a phone inside, with a secure line that even the FBI couldn't tap without his knowing about it. He called the number.

"This must be important. We agreed that you would you only call this line in an emergency," Jasper said.

"Consider this an emergency. I have my doubts that Monet knows nothing of the disappearance of my stepdaughter. So let me ask you. What do you know?" Henri asked.

There was a momentary pause.

"I don't deal with abductions."

"Well, here's another deal for you. Get me information on whether she is alive or dead. It's imperative that I know," Henri said.

"How important is it to you?"

"It's worth another hundred grand."

"So, is she worth more if she is dead or alive?"

"Preferably, alive. More if she is alive."

"From what I know about these sorts of people, if she has seen them, they will kill her."

"So let's hope she hasn't seen them. I want her alive for now. And make it quick. It won't be long, if it's not too late already, before this Stinson character starts looking for her as well."

"Ok, I'll be in touch," Jasper said, and hung up.

Henri stood there, took a deep breath, and thought, Damn, he's got her, and if she has seen him, he'll kill her. Now, I have to get rid of Monet and Jasper. But maybe, just maybe, Victor Zano will take care of everything. He poured himself a shot of whiskey and felt relieved that he had two patsies for Suzanne, whether she showed up dead or alive. His next concern was to move quickly and carefully. And to get it done before the election, and before Malcolm Stinson finished the trial.

CHAPTER 16

On April 1, Sol Weinstein was listed in critical condition at Sloan Kettering Hospital after he'd suffered a stroke from an aneurysm. Barry Rothman felt bad for Weinstein, but was relieved he now only had to deal with Calucci to pull Malcolm off the Reed case. But he needed some concrete evidence to convince Calucci. Rothman called Hugo Hurst, his trusted aide—actually, he was a lawyer—a weak litigator, but like Rothman, a very capable office manager. Rothman and Hugo Hurst discussed the Reed case, and planned their next move about pulling the plug on Malcolm.

Three days later, Victor Zano met with Calucci at a restaurant in Little Italy.

"I'm glad you could make it, Mr. Calucci. Have something to drink?" Zano asked.

"Scotch, and a little water," Calucci answered.

"The reason I asked you here is…you know, of course, that Giamanco was arrested three days ago. I have a feeling he's going to be in for a while. A little birdie told me that no bail would be granted for him at tomorrow's arraignment, so he stays in the joint. Will Malcolm Stinson be back to represent him?" Zano asked, as the waiter brought Calucci his scotch.

"I don't know. I was ready to take him off the case when my senior partner overruled me and let him stay on it for another three months."

"Overruled, huh? Same partner who had the stroke the other day?"

"Yes."

"So that means until your partner returns—if he returns—you call the shots."

"Yes," Calucci said, sipping his drink and looking around, noting Zano's hoods in the restaurant.

"But what was his reason for overruling you?"

"I really can't answer that, but there might be something with the girl."

"Girl? What girl?"

"She's a young Asian lawyer that I originally thought Abrams had picked, since he's the one who mentioned her to me. But I found out later that Weinstein mentioned her to Abrams, and he's the reason she's on the case."

"Well, seeing that he had a stroke and all, I guess he's not talking. Um, what's her name?" Zano asked.

"Lucy Yee. Why?"

"Nothing, just curious. So, what's going to happen with the Louisiana case?"

"I'll review things with my managing partner, Rothman, and we'll make a determination then."

Victor Zano was thinking. There was silence as the waiter took their dinner orders.

"Calucci, I want you to do me a favor. If you pull the rug out from this Malcolm Stinson, do you think he'll give up the case?"

"No. I don't. Actually, I think he'll quit the firm before giving up the case."

"Good. Then you can do Victor a favor that I won't forget."

"What's that?"

"Let Malcolm and this Lucy Yee stay on the case."

"That sounds feasible, but if he gets mad and quits the firm, I can't let Lucy Yee stay on the case."

"When, and if, it to comes that, I'll take care of things from there. Believe me, I'm sure I can convince Mr. Stinson to be reasonable."

Calucci apologized that he had a previous engagement and had to leave. Zano and Calucci shook hands. Victor told his right-hand soldier, Carlo Tizzi, to contact Luppino in New Orleans. He wanted to meet with Benny Dubois when he got into town. There was an important job waiting.

* * * *

Easter Sunday found Malcolm and his children in a church packed full of people to hear the reverend's message: The True Significance of Christ's Resurrection.

Hundreds of people showed up impeccably dressed—the regular Christian church attendees, and the folks the reverend called the C & E people—Christmas and Easter service attendees. Unlike many black churches in the South, the reverend felt a church should symbolize what heaven is like. So he prayed and talked with people around the community, and in part, his prayers came true. The reverend felt that a church shouldn't be all one color, so his congregation was twenty-five percent white, ten percent Hispanic, and five percent Asian. The rest was black. The reverend felt resentment from some of the black group towards the other races coming in, though the tithes and offerings had hit an all-time low during this time. But the reverend stood his ground, and those who were angry left the church.

Malcolm was a proud father. His children were dressed up and acting respectable. Pete Neil came in late and sat in the back.

Sun Reed, Clarence's mother, sat in the front, as always. Lucy met her, and they sat together. Lucy was astonished by the happiness and joy exuding from the congregation.

Cephus, along with his wife and three kids, sat two rows behind Malcolm, who was sitting in the middle section's second pew. Roberta just happened to find seats next to Malcolm. There was no children's service today, so children were scattered throughout the church with their parents.

The church had a full band, and the musicians were mostly former rock and roll, jazz, and rhythm and blues artists. They had trumpets, clarinets, drums, guitars, a piano and an organ, along with a trombone and French horns. The high praises to God gave out a sweet, yet funky, hallelujah beat this morning. The choir was fifty strong.

The congregants were in the aisle dancing a Holy-Ghost jig in no time. The sanctuary resounded with laughter and joy as they sang "Joy in my Heart," an up-tempo song.

The music was loud and the sanctuary was getting warmer by the minute. The ushers opened the front doors to let the cool spring air in.

* * * *

Two FBI agents, who had parked down the street, were in their cars, bobbing their heads to the thunderous gospel music. Jerry Dalton sat in the driver's seat, tapping his fingertips on the steering wheel and slightly rocking his head, while Jasper cringed with disdain.

* * * *

When the music finally subsided, the people praised God with lifted hands and loud voices, thanking Him for His grace and mercy on their lives. The reverend got up from his chair and approached the pulpit.

"Don't stop now. Just keep on praising Him, for He is worthy! Jesus is our Lord and Savior. Psalm 150 says, "Praise ye the Lord. Praise God in his sanctuary, praise him in the firmament of his power. Praise him for mighty acts, praise him according to his excellent greatness. Praise him with the sound of the trumpet, praise him with the timbrel and dance, praise him with stringed instruments and organs. Praise him upon the loud cymbals, praise him upon the high-sounding cymbals. Let everything that hath breath praise the Lord. Praise ye the lord."

The reverend began sweating profusely, and he pulled out a small towel and dabbed at his face, and then reached under the pulpit for a glass of cold water. There was a sense of peace throughout the church. Even those C & E people felt overcome by the Spirit of God this Easter morning. The reverend then invited everyone to have a seat.

"Before I deliver God's message today, let us constantly keep Brother Reed in our prayers, while he is in Angola Prison. Elders and deacons, come assist me in laying hands on my son, Malcolm."

Malcolm looked quizzically at his approaching father.

"Lord, Father God, in the name of Jesus, we pray, Lord, that you impart your wisdom to your child here in the future months to come, as he goes out to defend your other child, Clarence Reed. Lord, he'll be facing an unfair judicial system that is filled with hatred and bigotry. Lord, give him favor in court and put a guard about him as he travels everyday. Lord, you say that you would make your enemies as your footstool and crush them. And I pray, Lord, that the real killers will be caught and brought to justice for this heinous crime they have committed before thy sight."

The reverend, elders, and deacons, all laid hands on Malcolm and asked the entire church to stretch forth their hands in agreement.

After the service, people milled around outside. Malcolm enjoyed seeing folks he hadn't seen in years. Others encouraged him about the upcoming trial.

Lois Stinson gave Pete her camera to take a picture of her with the children. At the same time, a reporter from the Times Picayune asked Malcolm for a picture for Monday's edition. The photographer asked Malcolm to kneel between his children, and to move in another direction, away from the sun.

* * * *

In the background across the street, dressed in telephone company uniforms, were Jasper and Jerry Dalton. They had inadvertently gotten in the picture, much to the photo editor's dismay. However, the picture still made the front page of Monday's paper, in spite of the telephone men in the background.

* * * *

After the photo session was over, Malcolm spoke to Sun Reed.

"It's a pleasure to see you again, Mrs. Reed. Forgive me for not seeing you sooner, but there's been a lot of preparation going on for this case. I was going to make it my business to see you soon. I see you've met my colleague, Ms. Yee." Malcolm had Serena hanging onto his pants leg.

"I understand quite well, Mr. Stinson. Your father is a good man and speaks highly of you. I have complete confidence in your representation of my son. And yes, Ms. Yee is very charming." Sun Reed smiled at Malcolm.

"What is a good day to visit you?" Malcolm asked.

"Wednesday would be nice, say around seven," Sun Reed offered.

"That'll be fine, madam," Malcolm replied, as he noticed David Segal waving for his attention.

"Excuse me, Mrs. Reed. Until Wednesday, then," Malcolm said.

He walked over to David Segal as the FBI took pictures from their car. "Well, this is a surprise. You were in the service?" Malcolm asked a distressed David Segal.

"I enjoy a good Christian service every once in a while—particularly now," David answered.

"You seem upset. What's wrong?" Malcolm asked.

"Listen, Gere was my business partner and friend. And I want to help you win this case. But I have to feed my family, too. I've got a big case coming up and possibly another one right behind that."

"What sort of case?"

"I have a group of clients who are suing a Louisiana company that makes breast implants. It's an ongoing case, and lots of Louisiana women may be entitled to big money if the settlement comes out soon. I'm negotiating for the complainants with some other lawyers. It's the Spitzfaden class action and deals with the Bristol-Meyers Company," David replied.

"I'm not going to be that much help to you anymore, and I'll also need my law clerks back. Sorry, Malcolm," David said.

Now Malcolm had a perplexed look on his face.

"I guess you have to do what you have to do. I appreciate all your help, David. Really, thank you."

Malcolm was holding the sleeping Serena in his arms, but shook hands with Segal. David walked away as the FBI took more pictures.

Malcolm looked for Joshua and found him with Roberta and her daughter. Cephus cleared his throat loudly from behind Malcolm.

"How's it going, partner?" Cephus asked.

"Not very well today, but the day is still young," Malcolm replied, adjusting his grip on the sleeping Serena.

"I hate to bring bad news, but we may also have a serial killer in our midst..."

"That sounds wonderful for an Easter Sunday," Malcolm said, sarcastically.

"Not only that. A report came out of Washington, D.C. that New Orleans has a murder rate eight times higher than the national average. Seventy-six murders per 100,000 people. The mayor is in a frenzy."

"Is this story going to have a happy ending?" Malcolm interrupted Cephus.

"I don't know. Anyway, the mayor wants fourteen million dollars to hike police pay and improve recruiting. So far, they've only found four million. They got together with the New York police, and are implementing the Comstat System to cut down the crime and murder rates. It's a state-of-the-art computer analysis of the latest crime patterns, with an emphasis on police accountability. They claim this system worked in New York," Cephus said.

"I remember when they did that in New York a few years ago. But I only know what I heard on the evening news," Malcolm said, trying ever so gently to wake Serena up.

"Well, they seem gung-ho on trying it in the Big Easy."

"Isn't it a theory that police could reduce crime, not just react to it?" Malcolm asked.

Serena whined as she woke up.

"Yeah, that's just what they're talking about. So I've been appointed to work with these guys from New York. The mayor wants four hundred more cops. But finding the money for them is another thing. So, my friend, until this is over, you'll be seeing less of me," Cephus said.

"What is this? Abandon Ship Day? First David, and now you," Malcolm blurted out.

"I didn't say I was abandoning you. I just won't have much time to help in the investigation. You've got your Irish private eye," Cephus said, as his children approached. "Look, got to go. I'll be talking to you." Cephus swung his little girl up into the air and left Malcolm standing alone with Serena.

"What's that matter, laddie? You got that 'I've lost my best friend' look," Pete asked, taking pictures as they walked.

"It seems that way. All of a sudden, David Segal has a heavy caseload and needs his law clerks. Cephus is involved in a police program to fight crime in the Big Easy. And I'm left with Lucy, and I'm not sure what she's capable of doing. So, what's your story?" Malcolm asked in disgust.

"Not a thing, my friend. I'm with you till the end," Pete said, encouragingly.

"Good. I'm sorry if I sound cross, but everyone's abandoning ship. I should have known better than to think that of you, though, my friend," Malcolm said, reassuringly.

"Well, now that you have that out of your system, let's go have an Easter feast and get out of the FBI's visual range. They've been snapping your photo ever since church let out. I'll get the car," Pete said.

Malcolm met Roberta at the bottom of the church steps. He had a tired look on his face that she sensed instantly. "Did the service drain you that much? You didn't move around much," Roberta said.

"No, it wasn't the service. I just got a one-two punch thrown at me. Well, let me take these two somewhere to eat. My parents are going to Reverend Taylor's house for dinner. They invited me, but there'll probably be thirty or forty people there for dinner, and I just don't feel like answering questions about the case all afternoon. So, what are you doing?" Malcolm asked, holding Serena up by her arms as she struggled to wake up.

"I cooked this morning, and you're welcome to come over for dinner. It will be just you, me, and the kids," she said, her hazel eyes glistening at Malcolm. He couldn't resist her offer.

"I'd be delighted," Malcolm replied.

Malcolm, Roberta, and the children left the church. Jasper and Jerry and the feds all quickly wrapped up their equipment.

Instead of taking the fifteen-minute drive to Roberta's house, he drove out toward the country.

"May I ask where we are going?" she asked cheerfully.

"Oh, I thought we'd just take a little drive before we ate. Sort of work up an appetite." Malcolm looked in the rearview mirror and noticed the same telephone van he'd seen at the church. While rounding a curve in the road, he noticed the FBI agents, two cars behind the van and its mystery men. He turned off onto a dirt road. He wanted to know who was following him. The van and the FBI followed suit. He sped up to almost seventy-five miles per hour, and Roberta started to get jittery.

"Is everything all right, Malcolm? You're driving awfully fast for a country drive," she said, nervously.

"It's not a problem. I just wanted to take a short cut. I'm going to slow down now," Malcolm said, as he made his way back to the main highway. Jasper was puzzled by Malcolm's actions, while the FBI agents were trying to copy the van's plates.

* * * *

"You suppose he's on to us?" Jerry asked, trying to keep a safe distance behind.

"I don't know, but let's not take any chances. Pull off on that road. Let's go visit your brother and Ms. Joret." Jasper looked in the side view mirror and noticed the feds. The van turned off and went down another dirt road. The FBI agents stopped at the crossroad and watched the van leave a trail of dust. They got the license plate number.

Malcolm had given his spies the slip for now. The FBI agents sped up but couldn't catch Malcolm. They lingered at the entrance to the main highway from the dirt road, but Malcolm was long gone. They sat there seething, realizing that Malcolm had given them the slip. Now they wondered, as did Jasper and Jerry, if he was on to them. The feds took solace that not much would happen since Malcolm was with a woman and three children. They drove back to New Orleans for something to eat, and then waited at the reverend's house.

* * * *

Malcolm drove on I-10 toward Baton Rouge. "How about you save that meal for tomorrow and we eat at a place called Silver Moon Restaurant?"

"In Baton Rouge?" Roberta asked.

"Yes. You know the place?" Malcolm asked.

"Alex, my ex-husband, took me there a couple of times," she said.

"Okay, not a problem. How about Corey's Corner?" he suggested, waiting for her reaction.

"Yeah, that'll be okay. I've never been there, but if you want to go to the Silver Moon, it's fine with me, too," she said.

"Corey's Corner. Something new for both of us," Malcolm said with a smile, as the kids complained about being hungry.

*   *   *   *

Jasper and Jerry arrived at the shack thirty minutes after they had lost Malcolm. Jim was sitting outside on the porch when they arrived. The air was already thick on this Easter Sunday, and the mosquitoes were biting.

Suzanne was sleeping on her side until she heard voices outside.

Jim thought about telling them what he suspected had happened to Dusty. Being the military man he was Jasper would blame him for leaving his post, which had resulted in Dusty's disappearance. For now, he wouldn't mention it. He had already briefed Suzanne, threatening that if she mentioned anything about Dusty even coming over, he'd kill her on the spot.

"How goes it little, brother?" Jerry asked, embracing Jim.

"Good, good. No problems. And you?" Jim asked, with the same eagerness in his voice.

"How has our guest been acting?" Jasper asked, walking into the cabin.

Suzanne sat up. Strained, her eyes were bloodshot and had formed little bags underneath them due to the lack of sleep.

"We just came by to see how things are going," Jasper said, looking for something in his trunk. He pulled out a magnum .38 revolver and a small telephone book, and then locked the trunk again.

"Jim, we'll be back on Friday to pick you up at 1800 hours. Make sure she's fed and secured. We have a little job to do next Sunday. On Thursday, Linus Smith will be coming here, so put him up for the night," Jasper said, checking the gun's chamber while loading it.

"Since when do you carry a gun? I thought you were strictly a blade man," Jerry inquired.

"Ever since those federal agents got our license plate number. We'll give Dusty back his van and use the Ford Fairlane until we can come up with something else. Jim, call Dusty and tell him that we need the Fairlane."

"Sure. The car is right outside. He left it here the other day. I helped him back to the road, uh, he was a little drunk, so I told him to walk home, seeing how he might drive right into the river," Jim said, hesitantly. Jasper shot him a mildly suspicious look.

"All right, my dear. It won't be much longer," Jasper said to Suzanne with a smile, as he started to walk out the door. Then he stopped. "By the way, I met with your daddy the other day. He seems slightly concerned about your safety. I believe his emotions were more for your dear mother than himself. Of course, I couldn't tell him that you're being wonderfully taken care of, but I tried out of innocent complacency to reassure him, in a moral way, that you were all right. When you think of it, actually, I was telling the truth, wasn't I?" Jasper said, smiling at Suzanne.

"What do you plan to do with me?" she asked, breaking her silence.

"Why, you're our ace in the hole. If anything goes wrong, I'll strike a deal with your daddy for your safe return."

"What makes you think he'll make a deal with you?" she asked.

"Oh, that's not a problem. I'm counting on a mother's compassion for her lost daughter. You know, momma's baby, daddy's maybe." Jasper roared with laughter.

"Why are you doing all of this?" she asked.

"For White America," Jerry quickly responded.

"Well, I'm white," she retorted.

"You've lain with a black man. Your integrity has been blemished, so you now fall in the same category as any one of them niggers. Hell, if this hadn't happened, you'd probably have some little jungle bunny baby by now. You should thank us for saving you from that fate," Jerry lashed out at her.

Suzanne thought it futile to continue the conversation any further. Jasper and Jerry watched her as she lowered her eyes and curled up on the bed.

Jasper and Jerry headed for the boat. Once on the boat, Jasper said to Jim, as they were scurrying across the water, "Take good care of Linus. He's bringing a special package for me. See you Friday and watch our guest carefully. She's very valuable to us."

Jasper and Jerry hopped in the Ford Fairlane and after three tries, the relic started up. Jim went back inside to Suzanne.

"You did real good, little lady. I don't see how a piece of trash like you is valuable to us; maybe because you're so attractive. Jasper will sell you off to a white slave market or something," Jim said, sitting down next to her on the bed.

Suzanne suddenly moved closer to the wall, startled by Jim's being so close to her. "Tell me, how do you people live with yourselves? I mean, you're so full of hatred that you can't even think straight," she lashed out at him.

"Hatred? Yes, in a sense. What is justice in America for the white man, the true American? Niggers ain't nothin' but entertainment. You don't know how hard it was for me in the military to serve with them. And look at your boyfriend. He was a hero in Desert Storm. We don't need these things to be happening in

America. Affirmative action, what a waste of time and money that is—or shall I say was."

"Look," Suzanne said, "I'm not going to discuss history with you, but think about it—three hundred years of slavery, then years of oppression, socially, economically, and educationally. My God, a window opens for thirty years and you say, well, you didn't make it, so let's go back to the fifties and sixties again."

"We're going to take America back from the blacks and the Jews. The riverboat was only the beginning," Jim said.

"How many of you were involved there in the riverboat bombing?" she asked.

"I forgot that you're a newswoman. I'll tell you, but not today. So you best be getting some rest," he said.

"What's up for the weekend?" Her curiosity piqued.

"I don't know, but whatever it is, it's going to be a blast if Linus Smith is involved," Jim answered, proudly.

"Linus Smith is a militia man, too?"

"His expertise is abortion clinics and churches." Jim laughed and went out to sit on the porch.

CHAPTER 17

Clarence Reed now resided with Angola Prison's main population, but he was in a restricted area that only had ten cells and only five other prisoners.

While Clarence was asleep one night, the other five prisoners were quietly moved into another area. Two men were led into the restricted area. One man named Rocco, stood six-foot-five and weighed 245 pounds. He had big forearms and a matching gut, and was a professional hit man. The other man, Louie, was six feet and weighed 230 pounds. He sported a tattoo of a naked woman wrapped with snakes on his chest. A prison guard on the Luppino payroll arranged for entry into the prison for Rocco and Louie.

Unlocking Clarence's cell, they pointed a flashlight in his face. Clarence, startled by the unusual visit, slowly got out of bed.

"Get up, boy. We need to talk," ordered Louie.

"What do you want?" Clarence asked, shading his eyes from the light with his hand. In an instant, Rocco rushed Clarence and smacked him with the back of his hand, knocking him to the floor next to the toilet.

"Move, nigger, when we tell you," Rocco shouted, standing over Clarence.

"Now we can make this easy or hard. The choice is yours," Louie said.

Clarence looked up at Rocco. "Don't put your hands on me again. Got that, fat boy?"

Rocco's anger flared at Clarence's statement. When he reached down to pick him up, Clarence's right foot slammed into Rocco's face, breaking his nose. Blood gushed out. Clarence was up on his feet in a fighting mode for mortal combat. Louie flung a billy club through the dark cell, smashing Clarence in the face. He fell back from the blow and Louie charged, pounced on Clarence, and threw two hard punches to his face. Then he sat on Clarence, pinning him to the floor.

Rocco could be heard in the background, shouting in agony. "He broke my nose."

"Never mind that, get over here," Louie instructed.

"What the hell do you want from me?" a bloodied Clarence cried out.

"We want to know who hired you to hit the riverboat, and who helped you," Louie said, sitting atop Clarence.

"Who are you guys? I can't help you because I don't know who did it. I was set up," Clarence managed to mumble in agony.

Louie motioned for Rocco to move his big foot, and then punched Clarence again in the face. Blood filled Clarence's mouth. Then in one swift move, Clarence drew his legs up, propelling Louie off of him. He rolled over Louie, landing on his feet. Rocco came charging. Clarence sidestepped him, forcing him to bang his head into the cell bars. Louie grabbed Clarence from behind, but Clarence managed to throw him over his shoulder. Clarence kicked Louie in the face several times, until a massive hand struck him in the head, sending him back toward the wall. All three were breathing heavy and waiting for the next one to make a move. A guard came from the outside.

"Time's up, fellows. The feds usually send someone about now to make a night check. My God! Look at you. Let's go. Get the hell out of there. You can't even take one nigger. Come on. Let's go."

Louie and Rocco got up to leave.

"You ain't heard the last of this, boy. You will tell us what happened," Louie said.

"Come back anytime, fellows. I don't have much company," Clarence sneered.

The guard rushed to get Louie and Rocco out of the prison quickly without being noticed. "Hell, don't you boys know what you're dealing with?" the guard asked.

"What are you talking about?" Louie asked, reaching for a handkerchief.

"I mean the guy is a trained killer. Did you think he was going to let you come in there and beat the hell out of him and say thank you?" The guard laughed while looking around the corner.

Louie grabbed the guard from behind. "Are you a trained killer, too?" Louie asked, holding the guard up against the wall.

"Take it easy, guy. I was just making a little joke," the frightened guard said.

"Well, I don't think you're too funny. Move it. Let's get the hell out of here." Louie pushed the guard ahead of him.

* * * *

Wednesday morning, Malcolm, Lucy, and Pete were wading through the tons of tedious discovery paperwork. At 11:40, the telephone rang.

"Malcolm Stinson?" the male voice asked.

"Yes?"

"I'm not important. What's important is that you go to Angola Prison to see your client."

"Why?"

"Let's just say he had a rough night," the caller said, and hung up.

"What's the matter?" Pete asked, when he noticed the curious look on Malcolm's face.

"There was a problem at the jail last night. Lucy, you keep at it. Pete, come with me."

"Maybe I should go too. You might need an interpreter again," she said, anxiously.

"I don't think so. I'll fill you in on what happened when we get back." Malcolm rushed out.

In less than an hour, Malcolm and Pete were at Angola Prison. They were immediately escorted to the warden's office. The warden was upset that Malcolm knew that something had happened before he had finished his investigation.

The FBI was standing by watching, while Clarence simply reported the night's events. The warden interrogated each prison guard that had been on duty the previous night. So far, he had made no headway. Malcolm waited for nearly an hour before the warden finished his interview and allowed Malcolm into his office.

"You made me wait for nearly an hour to see my client. Now, please, tell me what happened here last night." Malcolm stood in front of Warden Harold Ashburn, who was completely bald and had thick bushy eyebrows. He had been the warden for nearly twenty-three years.

"Have a seat, Counselor." His Cajun accent filled the room.

"I don't plan on staying that long. Why can't I see Clarence?" Malcolm said as he leaned over Ashburn's desk.

Ashburn twirled a pencil in his hand, and then he slowly looked up at Malcolm. "Nobody comes in here and dictates anything to me. You see, Counselor, any problems at Angola Prison I personally take care of. It's my responsibility if something goes wrong."

"What are you trying to say?" Malcolm lashed out.

"Last night someone roughed up your client. We don't know who yet, but we will. Supposedly, it was two guards, but I don't believe that."

"You can rest assured that there will be a civil suit..."

"Now don't go off onto some tangent about lawsuits and all. Hell, I don't even know if they were my men." Ashburn threw his hands in the air.

"Well, if they weren't your men, do you want me to believe that somebody just walked in here, attacked Clarence, walked out, and no one was the wiser?" Malcolm said, cynically.

"I am trying to be patient with you, Stinson, but don't push your luck. I'll throw you in a cell and wait for the charges and trial to come later," Ashburn said, slowly.

"You're as stupid as you look. I'll see my client." Malcolm sneered at Ashburn. The warden quietly glanced over his wire-framed glasses and waved Malcolm out of his office.

In a matter of minutes, two prison guards escorted Malcolm to the visiting area. Clarence entered the room with bandages wrapped around half of his head.

"My God! What happened?" Malcolm asked. Clarence told him the same story that he had told the warden, except for one detail.

"I left out one important fact. Those two guys weren't guards," Clarence said through his swollen lips.

"But you told the warden they were guards."

"I said they were dressed like guards, and it was dark."

"So how do you know they weren't guards?" Pete asked. "For one thing, they had a flashlight. I saw their faces. I've never seen them here before."

"Clarence, is there anything I can do for you?" Malcolm asked.

"No. I just hope I don't have more visitors anytime soon."

"I doubt you will. We'll file a civil suit against the prison. That should guarantee this doesn't happen again. One more thing, do you know which guard came and got the two guys out?" Malcolm asked.

"They call him Snake." Clarence gave Snake's physical description.

"I'm visiting your mother this evening. Do you have any messages for her?" Malcolm asked.

"Why are you going to see her?" Clarence inquired.

"I want to ask her if she noticed anything or anyone unusual before the bombing," Malcolm replied.

"Tell her I love her and miss her. I don't want her to come to the prison. She had enough of that when my father was alive. I have to go. I have a headache."

"One of us will stop by every day to make sure you're all right," Malcolm said as he and Pete left.

* * * *

Sun Reed was sitting in her parlor when Malcolm rang the doorbell. She was small woman with wrinkles around her eyes from many sleepless nights. She wore a traditional kimono, with her hair rolled up into a bun. She showed Malcolm her radiant smile.

"Come in, Mr. Stinson. I've been waiting for you."

"Thank you. I'm not late, am I?" Malcolm asked. He glanced at Pete, who had stayed in the car. Malcolm wanted to talk to Sun Reed alone.

"Would you like some tea?" she graciously offered.

"That will be nice. Thank you," he said, as she waved her hand for him to have a seat. Malcolm looked around the house. It was decorated in Oriental fashion with a hint of New Orleans flavor. On the fireplace were pictures of Clarence as a young boy and as a Navy SEAL. In the middle was a picture of a tall black man hovering over Sun and her little boy Clarence.

"Is that your late husband?" Malcolm asked, as Sun handed him the teacup.

"Yes, that's him. God rest his soul," she replied, politely.

"I can see the resemblance in Clarence."

"Um, yes, they do look alike. Was there something you wanted to talk to me about?" she asked, sipping her tea.

"Yes. I guess I'll start with the question. Did you notice anything peculiar about Clarence in the week before the bombing? Any kind of strange behavior?"

"No. Nothing strange...except for the fact that he was a little excited about some diving job for Harpo Stevens—I believe that's his name. Yes, that's him. He offered Clarence good money for a one-time job."

"Had you noticed anyone unusual around the house or the neighborhood?"

Pete was outside checking with neighbors about anything strange they might have noticed during the week of the bombing.

"Not really. Why do you ask?" She was confused by Malcolm's question.

"You see, Mrs. Reed, they found volatile explosives in Clarence's room and in his garage. So, I'm curious how these people planted the C-4 explosives. Can you remember anything abnormal?"

"The only thing I remember about the day before the bombing was that two white men from the gas company came to the door around eight that evening. They said there was a reported gas leak coming from my house."

"How would they know that?"

"They said a computer checks gas leaks in every home in New Orleans. I didn't think too much about it, modern technology and all."

"Where did they go?"

"They claimed it was coming from Clarence's apartment upstairs."

"Can you remember what they looked like?"

"One was older than the other. The older one did all the talking, and…they had gas company hats on," she said, as the scene became clearer.

"Did you tell the police or the FBI about this?"

"No. They never asked. They were only interested in Clarence's whereabouts prior to the bombing."

"All right. I'm going to get a sketch artist to come out tomorrow, and you describe every detail about the two men to him. Take your time and do your best. This may be our first lead as to what the men look like. Don't say anything to anyone else about this. I'll be right back. I'm going to get my colleague. I want you to meet him tonight. He'll return with the sketch artist tomorrow." Malcolm went outside to find Pete and was back in the Reed house in five minutes.

Mrs. Reed gave Pete a description of the two men. Pete wasn't a professional sketch artist, but as a former cop he could put together a fairly good description of eye color, hair, weight, build, age, and race.

"Well, that's a start," Pete said, closing his notebook. "Tomorrow we'll bring a professional sketch artist."

"Thank you, Mrs. Reed. I think you may have been a big help to Clarence's case," Malcolm said.

"Will you be bringing that lovely young Korean lawyer? I so enjoyed talking with her," she asked.

"Sure. She'll be with Pete tomorrow," Malcolm said.

"Good. I promised her a good Vietnamese meal. Did you know she's half Vietnamese?" Sun Reed asked, in a delightfully soft voice.

"Yes," Malcolm replied.

"Why don't you come, too, Mr. Stinson?" she asked, holding the front door as they were leaving.

"I'll be busy tomorrow, but maybe another time."

"Just let me know," she stated, as she closed the front door.

"Does that mean I get to eat, or just Lucy?" Pete asked, as they drove off. Malcolm laughed.

They stopped by Cephus Pradier's house. After talking with Cephus, they decided not to use a police sketch artist, but the college student Cephus used when the regular artist wasn't available.

* * * *

Zano proffered his hand to Benny.

"Benny, I hear you do excellent work for us here in New Orleans.

"We have a little problem here in New Orleans."

"What are you looking for?" Benny asked.

"It's not exactly what we're looking for, but more what we need. You see, we're not convinced that this Reed fellow committed this crime against the organization. But, if we're wrong and he did do it, we want to know who else was in on the deal. I don't believe the righteous civil rights leader woke up one day and God told him to blow up a riverboat…you read the Bible, Benny?" Victor stood and walked around the patio.

"I've picked it up on occasion," Benny responded.

"Well, I'm a good Catholic, and it would go against my Christian moral fiber to kill hundreds of innocent people, just to destroy a riverboat."

"So, do you want me to take Bible study classes?" Benny questioned, jokingly. No one laughed.

"No. I have something else in mind. I need you to watch this lawyer. I want to know everything he does.

"I'm not 007, Mr. Zano. Who's going to run my operation?" Benny asked.

"Don't worry about that. Arty will take care of everything. This is very important to me, Benny," Zano said.

"With all due respect, Mr. Zano, do you mind if I talk with Mr. Luppino alone for a moment?" Benny asked.

Zano walked back into the house. Benny walked around the edge of the patio. He looked back over his shoulder at Zano. "What the hell is going on here, Mr. Luppino? I thought I did a good job for you," Benny said, exasperated.

"Benny, just do what the man asks. He's my boss, too. Let one of your boys handle the operation. I'll even give you a couple of my guys so that everything stays on the up and up. All he wants you to do is follow the lawyer for a little while. You told me yourself that these hate group guys have bought products from you. Check with them, maybe they know something." Arty sat in a chair and watched Benny walk around.

"Hate groups? What do they have to do with this?" Benny stopped to ask.

"Mr. Zano believes that a hate group might be involved with the bombing."

"Let me ask you a dumb question that may not be any of my business. Have you guys considered another family doing this?"

"We would have known that by now; the family would have come forward. We don't operate like that, if we do something, we let you know why."

"So, you kill somebody and then you tell the other family why you did it?" Benny said, astounded.

"Something like that. This could be your ticket out. You've told me yourself you would like to move to New York. Here's your opportunity."

"Okay, if this is what you want, Mr. Luppino."

"Good, Benny. It will be over before you know it. Victor!" shouted Arty. Zano strolled outside puffing on his cigar.

"We're all set," Luppino said.

"That's real good. Just one other thing: while you're keeping a tail on Malcolm Stinson, I don't want anything to happen to him. Because if this Reed guy is innocent, we'll need Stinson to help flush out the real bombers," Zano said. "He's looking for the bombers and if he finds them, we'll be there," he said, shaking Benny's hand.

* * * *

Malcolm was at his parents' home. The kids were in school, and his parents had gone to a Bible study meeting in Baton Rouge. He made a call to a smalltime gangster in Manhattan who had worked for the Zano family. Pepe was the only name Malcolm knew him by, and it would take several calls to reach him. Pepe was a crook who kept himself out of jail, but he had one distinctive thing about him—he was Giuseppe Marazzi's grandson—and a member of the Mafia Crime Family Commission in New York. He had authority over Zano and Giamanco. Malcolm would be putting his life in danger to meet him.

Chapter 18

The breakfast meeting was scheduled for Friday morning, April 17, at the Lloyd Hall Plantation Restaurant in Cheneyville in central Louisiana. William Lloyd Hall's sixty slaves had built the plantation. The ten room, two-and-a-half story mansion had brick walls sixteen-inches thick, and was believed to be haunted. Hall had been hung for being a double spy during the Civil War and was buried on the plantation. His niece Inez had committed suicide there, and Harry Henry, a soldier who hid in the attic, was discovered murdered, and was buried under the house. Their apparitions were said to appear frequently. And the spirit of Sally Boston, the black nanny, was seen whenever young children were around.

Following Joret's instructions, Sandchester made arrangements to have a breakfast for Campy Frazier and his campaign manager, Ziggy Gaines. Gaines was a stocky man who'd been a football star at Louisiana State University twelve years before. Gaines was experienced, having done campaign work for former Governor Edwards, and was very skeptical about this meeting with Joret. He thought that Campy could beat Joret and the incumbent outright. Although some Louisiana politicians thought Gaines had delusions of grandeur, he stood firm on his position.

Campy and Gaines arrived at ten minutes after ten, with an entourage of twelve men; six stayed outside, and six followed them inside. Only Gaines joined Campy in the dining area.

Suspicion hung over the dining room's quiet, polite aura, where the only diners were Joret, Sandchester, Campy, and Gaines. To break the ice, Joret talked about sports.

"Campy, what do think about bringing another NBA team to Louisiana?" Joret asked, spreading his muffin with apple jelly.

"Couldn't do anything but help the economy—jobs, businesses. They just didn't do it right when we had one before. You scouting around for some investors?" Campy asked.

"I do have some folks who are interested. We have to take it to the NBA for consideration but, with a few calls here and there, I think we could have another team here in a couple of years."

"I don't see why not. They play college bowl games here; the Super Bowl, and I hear there are some investors in Shreveport looking to bring a professional baseball team to Louisiana. The only problem is, who will get the good paying jobs?" Gaines asked, with skepticism.

"I'm sure that people will be hired equally throughout the system for baseball and basketball. This is the new South, Mr. Gaines," Sandchester commented with a smile. Gaines returned an unbelieving glance.

"I thank you for this marvelous breakfast," Campy complimented, reaching for one of his cigars. "Seeing how we both ate out of the same pot and I haven't keeled over yet, I'm assuming we haven't been poisoned. So, what's this meeting all about?" The other three chuckled at Campy's remark.

Joret stood up from the table and walked to a corner of the room. "Campy, you and I have disagreed on a few issues over the years, but I've learned that sometimes you have to look at the big picture. Everyone in this state knows of your work in Congress, and of mine in the Senate," he stated. He paused in front of the first of twelve paintings that chronicled the life and ministry of Jesus Christ, called In the Bosom of the Lord, by Richard C. Thomas, a black Louisiana artist.

Joret walked as he talked. "I know affirmative action is a big issue, and I'm to blame for listening to people on my staff who thought otherwise—that it was politically correct to confront that issue. But after studying it more intently, I realized that it was not a good idea to attack and abolish affirmative action," Joret said, looking down at Sandchester.

Raising his arms in the air, Sandchester spoke up.

"All right, it was my fault. I looked at what California did, and I thought it was the most politically correct thing to do at the time."

"Henri, seeing that you're the host, and the breakfast was so wonderful, I hope that you're not going where I think you are with this little story," Campy said, lighting his cigar.

"What do you mean?" Henri asked.

"That you want me to drop out of the race for a political favor that you'll repay, once you've been elected," Campy said, with disdain.

"Au contraire, my friend, I don't want you to leave the race. But I'm getting to what I'm looking for in a moment," Joret said, continuing his walk. "I know that there are other issues that gravely concern you and..."

"Henri, I know your views of the police department—thinking that they do a wonderful job. We have the most corrupt police department in the country. I have a problem with Ducruet putting black men in jail for long periods of time, just for picking their noses in public." Campy puffed on his cigar, filling the room with the Havana smoke.

"You're right to a degree. Now we can look at the Ducruet problem and reach a compromise. The police department is involved in Comstat, that program from New York. The mayor is doing all that he can to raise the money, but you see, Campy, it's issues like these that our opponent Steeler is turning his back on. That's why we need to join forces and run that son-of-a-bitch right out of Baton Rouge," Joret explained.

"Before I address your statement on joining forces, there is the sensitive issue of Clarence Reed before us."

"All right. I was a little hasty in my position on the case, but at the time, all the evidence pointed toward him. And it seemed he had a motive as well, but I don't want to dig all that up right now. My position is to let the government boys do what they have to do, let Malcolm Stinson defend Reed, and let God be the judge," Henri stated.

"So, what's this all about? Joining forces?" Campy inquired.

"Campy, we can make history in Louisiana," Joret said. "I want you and Mr. Gaines to join my team."

"Your team? Doing what?" Gaines interjected.

"Well, you would be Mr. Sandchester's assistant, and Campy would run as the lieutenant governor." Joret stood up straight, looking at Campy as if he'd just given him a million dollars.

"I don't think so," Gaines spurted out.

"Hold on a minute. You mean I would run on the same ticket, as your lieutenant governor?"

"That's right," Joret said, with a smile.

"Campy, you can't be seriously considering this," Gaines said, sitting on the edge of his seat.

"Now, just wait a minute, Ziggy..." Campy puffed on his cigar and walked around the table. Sandchester said nothing, but he was waiting for his chance to convince Campy.

"Just think about it, Campy. White and black candidates running the Louisiana government," Joret said, with conviction.

"Now, if I were to accept your offer, I'd want it clearly stated in writing that I wouldn't be a lame duck lieutenant governor."

"Actually," Sandchester said, "we'll be addressing the very issues that you're talking about now in your campaign. Police problems create crime and unemployment for minorities, judicial system problems create teenage pregnancies, just to name a few. Campy, we're looking to make some big changes in Louisiana. So big, that the entire country will be watching us as an example." He gave his rah-rah speech, much to Ziggy Gaines' dismay.

A silence came over the room, as Campy thought, and Joret and Sandchester waited for his answer. Ziggy Gaines finally stood to voice his vehement objection.

"This grandiose vision for Louisiana's future sounds sweeter than rock candy, but what guarantee do we have that you'll keep your word? Your track record over the years, Mr. Joret, has not been friendly to the black community. For example, what sort of guarantees do we have for jobs and small businesses? Particularly in the state government. How are you going to fight off allies, if you implement better working conditions for the black community throughout the state? These are some of the concerns we would have to address, if Campy were to seriously consider your offer," Gaines said, looking straight through Joret.

"Mr. Gaines, do folks hold mistakes that you made years ago against you today?" Joret politely asked.

"Some, yes, but that's not the issue here. You profess to be a Christian man, Mr. Joret. So, you want us to believe that you are now a Saul, turned into a Paul?" Gaines asked.

"Yes. Yes, you could say that. I no longer look to persecute, but to liberate," Joret answered, reverently.

Campy was still mulling over the offer. He turned his head toward Joret and Sandchester. "Before I accept this, there must be some conditions met first."

"Such as?" Joret inquired.

"First, you must publicly denounce your position against affirmative action. Second, you must state that you are looking into revamping the police department in New Orleans. And third, whatever happens in Clarence Reed's trial happens, and you have no opinion on the outcome, other than that justice will be served. The other issues we'll deal with later," Campy said.

Joret stood still, trying hard to use his peripheral vision to see Sandchester, who spoke up for Henri.

"It's a deal," Sandchester said, hoping Joret wouldn't say anything to the contrary.

"Okay, Campy. It's a deal," Joret confirmed.

Campy, without hesitation or conference with Gaines, walked over to offer a handshake and seal the new political union. While his hand was still in Joret's, he said, "Just one other thing. I need a couple of weeks before we make this public, to talk this over with some people, and prepare them for the news. I don't want the folks that are backing me to hear it on the evening news."

Sandchester reached inside his coat pocket for a calendar. "All right. Let's see, two weeks will make it May first. We'll have a press conference in New Orleans, and you both will be there." Sandchester had a brusque look on his face.

Everyone was pleased, except for Ziggy Gaines. Campy gave him a look that said, Better do as I say, and shake hands. Gaines needed his job, so he reluctantly shook hands with Joret and Sandchester. Campy and Gaines gathered up the entourage and they went to their cars. Joret watched closely.

"I hope you're right about this, because if you're not, the gators will feast on your little carcass by the Fourth of July," Joret said.

"Believe me, the press will eat this up. We'll draw national attention. And folks in the state will see a real attempt to solve issues and create unity. Sure, we'll lose the bigot vote. But we'll gain a hell of a lot more votes—black and white," Sandchester boasted proudly. He walked out to make some calls, wanting to get the press conference going and start a buzz about what the Joret campaign would be announcing in two weeks, to change the governor's race.

Henri had let Sandchester in on most of his activities, except for his business with Jasper Yates. And the timing would be perfect, that first weekend in May. On Friday, they would join forces with Campy, and on Sunday, after the church bombing, their forces would be cemented. Henri knew the bombing would solidify his standing in the black community, when he'd publicly announce that every effort would be made to find the racist terrorists. He stood by the window, basking in the morning sun, as Campy and his entourage pulled off.

"I can't believe you accepted his offer, Campy, without considering the ramifications of such a drastic political move," Gaines said, sorely.

"Ziggy, my friend, you know the saying—politics sometimes makes strange bedfellows? I apologize for not taking the time to allow you some input in this, but my friend, this is a rare opportunity. For example, what if something were to happen to him in the next four years? Who would be governor? And this puts us in a great position to run after the four year term," Campy said.

"Or, what if something happens to you?" Gaines asked.

"That won't happen. Think, Ziggy. Even if he didn't endorse my candidacy for governor, he couldn't say anything negative about me, for fear that it would reflect badly on him. Besides, we'll make our own plans for running for governor. We'll have the experience of running Louisiana, and we won't sit back like a lame duck, no matter what Joret and that little weasel Sandchester try to do," Campy said, blowing the smoke out of the window.

"Make arrangements next week to meet with all of the ministers who support us," Campy continued. "I've got to let them down gently. I need to talk with Reverend Stinson first. As Stinson does, so does the rest of the clergy."

*　*　*　*

On Saturday morning at the Dalton shack, militia man Linus Smith, a former Navy SEAL who had served under Jasper Yates in Desert Storm, waited patiently for Jasper and the Dalton brothers to arrive. He had thirty pounds of C-4 explosives in his truck—enough to blow up an entire city block.

Smith was a thin, wiry man, with tattoos on both of his strong arms. He was dressed in battle fatigues, and hadn't seen Jasper, or the Daltons, since July Fourth of the preceding year.

Jasper, Jerry, and Jim pulled up in a van shortly after ten o'clock.

"Ah, Smitty, my boy. Been waiting long?" Jasper asked, with open arms.

"Not too long. I hope this isn't an example of being on time for this mission," Smith replied, while shaking hands with the Dalton brothers.

"I've cased the layout for our mission," Jasper stated, showing the First Baptist Church blueprints that Joret had provided from the city planning office.

"At 2300 hours, we'll make our way to the rear of the church. The door is a simple lock with a bolt and not connected to the alarm system. All of the other entrance doors and windows are. We'll weld it back together when we leave. Once we're inside, we can disarm the alarm system and walk out any exit. The explosives will be set in the basement by the boiler and affixed to a timer set for 1200 hours. That'll give plenty time for the congregation to arrive for the 11:00 a.m. service," Jasper said, laughing. Jim Dalton was troubled about killing all these people.

"Why can't we just blow the church up in the middle of the night? That should be sufficient," Jim suggested. Jasper's mood changed drastically, and he turned from the blueprints.

"If you don't have the stomach for this, Jim boy, maybe you should go back and watch over our guest," Jasper sneered.

"Just asking a question, that's all." Jerry patted his brother on the back.

"This is war, brother, and in war, there are casualties. Once you get your feet wet again, you'll be alright," Jerry said to Jim, assuring Jasper that his brother would be alright for the mission.

"All right, then. As I was saying, we'll place the bomb here in the boiler room, and by noon tomorrow our mission will be national news."

"That's right," Smith said, breaking into laughter and excitement. "These niggers ain't nothing but communists trying to hide behind God. Besides, we blow them up and they'll be meeting at Saint Peter's pearly gates, for their judgment of hell."

They sat down on a dead tree and talked about old times. All were laughing, except for Jim Dalton, who forced himself to blend in with the group. Jasper watched him closely, wondering if Jim could carry out the mission.

* * * *

Malcolm was in the office by noon on Saturday, eager to review the sketches that Sun Reed had described for the artist. Pete Neil was already there, trying to match a resemblance from a criminal mug-shot book that Cephus had lifted from the police department.

Lucy was on her way back from the post office, where she had just express-mailed copies of the sketches to Hugo Hurst in the Sheepshead Bay section of New York.

Jasper had worn a beard on July 4, and Jerry Dalton had worn a fake red moustache and a red wig with long hair pulled into a ponytail.

Malcolm had seen the photos the night before, and wanted Lucy to arrange for the college sketch artist to meet with him to redo the sketch without the moustache, and with some other modifications. But neither Lucy nor the artist, were there at noon. At 12:45, Lucy raced into the office.

"Did we have a late night, Ms. Yee?" Malcolm growled.

"No, sir. I just had to mail something at the post office before it closed," she answered in defense.

"So where is the sketch artist?" Malcolm asked.

"I tried reaching him last night and again this morning, but had no luck."

"All right. Look at these photos, and see if they match the sketch," Malcolm said.

Lucy said nothing, but sat right down and looked at the mug shots.

"Malcolm, we're wasting our time trying to make a match. Let's take the books over to Sun Reed, and see if she can identify the men," Pete said, flipping through a mug book.

"I suppose you're right. Find out where Mrs. Reed is. Cephus needs these books back by four o'clock. This won't disturb your schedule, will it, Ms. Yee?" Malcolm questioned, impatiently.

"No, sir. And again, I'm sorry."

"And what, might I ask, will you be doing for the better part of the afternoon?" Pete asked Malcolm, packing up things while searching for the telephone.

Lucy packed up her things and took one of the mug-shot books with her.

"The car is out back. I'll be there momentarily, Ms. Yee," Pete shouted.

Lucy left, disturbed by Malcolm's verbal attack.

"Take it easy on her, Malcolm. What's bothering you?"

"There's something peculiar about her. I can't figure out what it is yet...but keep an eye on her." Malcolm put a copy of the sketches in his briefcase.

"Alas, laddy, you haven't answered my question. What's wrong?" Pete asked, with concern.

"It's the whole case, Pete. There's so much work to be done. Before you know it, August will be here, and I'm afraid we won't be ready...but there is a sign of hope."

"What's that?"

"I deal with facts in a legal case, but thus far we don't have many. But, we do have three theories. First, if the riverboat was blown up as part of a mob war, this sketch will identify them."

"How's that?"

"Remember Reny James, the cop who helped us a few years ago with the Wilkerson murder?" Malcolm sat down across from Pete at the conference table.

"Oh, yeah. He helped in fingering those Jamaican Posse gang members."

"I'm going to send him the sketches and see what he can come up with in New York. He has photos of every crime family in New York, Chicago, Detroit, Los Angeles, and Las Vegas. He also has access to FBI data," Malcolm said, quietly.

"And what if he comes up with nothing?"

"Then that brings us to the second theory, which is a variety of people—militia groups, hate groups—that sort of thing."

"Who will give us that information?"

"Well, I've been thinking about it, and I think this professor guy can help us out."

"Sure you want to rely on that guy? He seemed a little flaky."

"I was thinking that, too. But Cephus says the professor has a vast knowledge of these groups, and a computer loaded with information. Who knows? He might even have some photos for us."

"And, your third theory?"

"The one I hate to think about…that Clarence Reed was involved in the bombing."

CHAPTER 19

April 19, 1998 was a significant day in Louisiana. The city of New Orleans was designated as the location for radical hate and militia groups to have their unofficial holiday parade. The Aryan Nation, The Order, The Ku Klux Klan, and military militia groups came from all over the country for the celebration.

They dressed in 17th century regalia to kick off the historical parade. April 19, 1775 was the date of the battle of Lexington. April 19, 1943 was the day Warsaw burned. April 19, 1992 was white supremacist Randy Weaver's stand-off at Ruby Ridge, Idaho. On April 19, 1995, Richard Wayne Snell, also a white supremacist and, like Weaver, a movement martyr—was executed for killing an Arkansas pawnshop operator. April 19, 1995 was the date of the Oklahoma City bombing. There were signs displayed for the Waco, Texas fiasco, and the Freedom Fighters of Montana.

The march began precisely at 11:00 a.m. Jasper, Linus, and the Dalton brothers marched with their hate brothers. It felt like a family reunion. In the midst of the hoopla, Jim slipped away to a phone booth.

* * * *

Malcolm woke up just as his mother and children were about to leave for church. He had stayed out late the night before with Roberta. They'd had dinner at a small restaurant on the Mississippi River, and then listened to jazz at the Alexandria Amphitheater. They walked and talked late into the night. Malcolm got home around five in the morning. When the reverend inquired about his going to church, his grunt indicated, "Not today." Somewhat perturbed, the reverend left the house at 10:00 a.m. to prepare for his sermon. His children came in after Lois had dressed them.

"Daddy, it's time to get up and go to church," Serena said, tugging at Malcolm's pillow. Joshua jumped on the bed and started bouncing.

"Serena, Joshua, it's too early for this," Malcolm cried.

"No, Daddy. It's almost eleven o'clock. Right, Joshua?"

"One arrow is on ten, and the other is on eleven," Joshua said, looking at the wind-up clock next to the bed.

Malcolm pulled himself from under the covers and took a deep breath, his eyes still half-shut with sleep. He pulled both children gently to him.

"Daddy had a late night and needs to get some sleep, so you go with Grandma Lois to church, and I'll see you when you get back. Maybe we'll go to the flower park," Malcolm said, trying to slip back under the covers.

"It's the Botanical Gardens, Daddy," Joshua said.

"No, it's not. It's the flower park," Serena burst out.

"Come on, Dad. You said you'd go to church with us. Then if you don't go, can I stay home, too?" Joshua asked, lying on his back next to Malcolm.

"No. Now get moving. Say a prayer for Daddy."

"We don't have to go to church to say a prayer, Daddy," Serena said. "Where were you that you stayed out so late?"

"I went out for dinner. Is that all right with you?" Malcolm asked.

"You didn't take me," she replied, shaking her head back and forth.

"Next time, all right, honey?" Malcolm said with a smile.

A gentle voice came from downstairs. "Let's go, children. Let your father sleep," Lois said.

"Okay, get going. Grandma is waiting." Malcolm got out of bed and led the children downstairs.

"You look terrible. I'm quite sure Roberta will be at church today." Lois stared at Malcolm again. "Yes, go back to bed. No one should see you today."

She whispered to Malcolm, "You're setting a bad example for these children—making the same mistake so many parents do, by just sending their children to church without them." She grabbed the children's hands and stormed out the door.

Malcolm made his way to the kitchen for some orange juice. He skimmed through some notes that Lois had left on the table in the hall. There were messages from well-wishers about his representing Clarence Reed. He found a message from Walter Baer, from two days ago, and one from a Reuben Caulfield. The name wasn't familiar, but it was a New York City area code. The message said, "Must talk with you. Urgent." Malcolm figured it was a new client from the firm in New York. But why would they refer Caulfield to him here in New Orleans? He made a mental note to call the number tomorrow. Some sausages were still on the stove, draining on a paper towel. Malcolm hadn't eaten pork in over a year, but who would know? He ate the sweet sausage, and added a biscuit, then settled down at the table with the Sunday Times Picayune.

The telephone rang. He let it ring five times before he picked it up.

"Hello, Stinson residence," Malcolm said.

"Is this Malcolm Stinson?" the muffled voice asked.

"Who wants to know?" From the tone of the voice, Malcolm thought it was another prank racist phone call.

In the background, he heard voices from the racist hate rally. Jim Dalton was in a phone booth. Although he was a Klansman himself, he couldn't kill the old black nanny that had raised him and his brother. He knew that she regularly attended the Zion First Baptist Church.

"Look here, boy, you know what time it is?" Jim questioned, muffling his voice.

"Who is this? What do you want?" Malcolm shouted through the phone, and then hung up. Jim called right back.

"That wasn't very nice, boy. You listen to me," Jim said. "Do you know the Bible?" Jim asked.

"Say your little racist remark, and don't call back here again," Malcolm said.

"There's a scripture that says, To be absent from the body is to be present with the Lord. Ever heard that before?" Jim said.

"You say that meaning what?" Malcolm asked with interest now.

"It's 11:38. You've got twenty-two minutes to save a few hundred people from meeting the Lord at one time. Get my drift? May the good Lord put wings on your feet," Jim said, and then hung up. If the black nanny didn't get out, he wouldn't feel guilty; he had warned Malcolm.

"To be absent from the body is to be present with the Lord…twenty-two minutes…the church…a bomb, my God," Malcolm said, as he rushed out the front door in his shorts and tee shirt. The church was a five-minute walk from the Stinson home. Malcolm ran like an Olympic sprinter in his bare feet. He made it to the church in less than two minutes. His mind was racing as he climbed the steps two and three at a time. There had to be nineteen or twenty minutes left, if the caller had been telling the truth. The ushers saw him coming through the front door in his shorts but didn't know what to do.

"Listen, I want you to go downstairs and evacuate everyone in the children's Sunday school. Fast. A bomb is set to go off in about fifteen minutes. Move it!"

The two ushers did as Malcolm asked, but two others fled the building. The choir was singing the last chorus of the morning's worship song. As the Reverend Josiah stood at the podium, singing along with the choir, he couldn't believe his eyes when Malcolm ran up to him. The choir stopped singing. Malcolm covered the microphone and whispered in his father's ear.

"We have ten minutes to evacuate the church. A bomb is set to go off at noon," Malcolm said. The reverend, shocked, paused for a moment.

"Brothers and sisters, please, do not panic. Everyone must leave the church quickly. Once outside, get as far away from it as possible," Malcolm said over the microphone. The church folk kept their seats and looked from side to side. When they didn't move after ten seconds, Malcolm shouted, "There's a bomb set to go off in ten minutes. Move out, now!"

The congregants, young and old, moved at lighting speed. In five minutes, nearly everyone was out.

Malcolm went down to the back exit door to make sure all of the children were out. Most had gotten out by climbing through the ground-level windows.

He looked anxiously for his children. "Serena, Joshua, where are you?" Malcolm shouted out the window. There was no response. He went outside and across the street. He saw that a Sunday school teacher had collected the children together. Malcolm instructed the teacher to move even further back. He saw Joshua and grabbed him.

"Where's your sister, son?" Malcolm asked, frantically.

"The last time I saw her was before they told us to leave. She and another girl went to the bathroom," Joshua said.

"Who is the other girl, son?"

"She's right there in the blue and red dress."

Malcolm raced over to the girl. "Where is the other little girl that went with you to the bathroom?" he asked, grabbing her arms in panic.

"I left her there. She was playing with the water and I told her to come on, but she stayed playing with the water." Malcolm ran back into the school. He saw that his parents and Roberta were safe.

"Son, where you going?" the Reverend Josiah shouted.

It was 11:56. Malcolm ran down the hallway, and could hear Serena banging on the door for someone to let her out. She was too small to grab the handle to get out. Malcolm swung open the door and grabbed her. He looked to see if anyone else was there. He opened the boys' bathroom and checked. The clock on the classroom wall said 11:59. With Serena in his arms, he ran back into the classroom and pushed her through the window.

"What's the matter, Daddy?" she cried out.

"I'll tell you later." He crawled out the window.

Everyone had escaped from the church and stood well back in a park. Malcolm ran with all his might, holding Serena, and made it across the street. Someone outside had called the police and a two-patrolman police car in the area moved slowly down the street in front of the church, watching people running deeper into the park. Malcolm and Serena ran further into the park, and the congregants followed. Someone yelled, "Duck! Its twelve noon."

Like a rippling wave, 350 people hit the ground. They lay on the ground for a minute. It was ten seconds before 12:01, when someone said, "Yeah, a bomb. Right. Twelve noon."

At 12:01, the bomb went off. The explosion was so powerful that the police car flipped over three times, nearly hitting some of the congregants. Though most of the people were at least 200 yards away, the blast knocked them down like wooden matchsticks. Bricks and wood flew aimlessly through the air, hitting people. Two houses next to the church property were completely destroyed. Malcolm covered Serena with his body, as dirt and rubble beat down on his back. After five minutes, an ash cloud filled the air, along with an acrid smell of burnt wood, paint, and brick. Malcolm lifted himself, picked up the crying Serena, and called for Joshua.

People were strewn everywhere, moaning from being bombarded with debris. Malcolm walked in the direction where he had last seen Joshua. He saw the reverend lying down and being helped by his mother. He had a small gash on his head and blood streamed down his face, but he was conscious.

"What happened, Malcolm?" the reverend asked.

"I don't know yet, Poppa Joe. Just thank God that whoever did this called in time to warn me."

"Called? What do you mean?" Mother Lois asked. She had small cuts on her legs and arms.

"Someone called the house and warned me. You all right here?" Malcolm's parents nodded that they were okay.

"I'm going to find Joshua. I'll be right back."

Malcolm walked through the park, when suddenly another explosion made everyone gasp and flinch. Malcolm found a crying Roberta leaning over her unconscious daughter.

"What was that? Another bomb?" she asked in fright.

"Probably not. Maybe just a gas line. How is she?"

"She's breathing. She must have a concussion. She needs to be hospitalized quickly. What happened here, Malcolm?" she asked, frantically.

"Ambulances will be here any moment. All of New Orleans must have heard that blast. I'll be right back. I have to find Joshua." Malcolm picked up Serena and continued his search.

A few feet away, children lay still on the ground, afraid to move a muscle. Malcolm saw Joshua.

"Joshua, are you all right?" Malcolm put Serena down, and examined Joshua like a doctor would.

"What happened, Daddy?" Joshua asked, tears streaming down his face.

"Take it easy, son. Did anything hit you in the head?"

"No, it was a big wind that made me fall down."

"Just lie there for right now, and young lady, you sit right here with your brother." Malcolm turned to attend to the elderly Delia May, the Dalton brothers' black nanny, lying on the ground moaning.

"How you feeling, madam?"

"I'm fine. Guess the good Lord decided it wasn't my time yet. How are you doing?" she asked.

"I…well, why don't you just sit on this merry-go-round. Or would you rather stay on the ground?" Malcolm had his arms around her.

"Well, I done messed up my Sunday-going-to-meeting dress already, so I'll rest on Mother Earth."

"Okay. I'll be back."

"Ain't you the reverend's boy, Malcolm, right?"

"Yes, ma'am."

"Go attend to 'dem children," she said, as Malcolm leaned her against a small tree.

Malcolm stood up and looked at the destruction. The fear was gone, but anger filled up the void. The spot where the First Zion Baptist Church had stood, with its beautiful architecture and grounds, sure looked like a bomb had exploded.

Bodies were all over, and people were crying, but none had died yet. Malcolm ran back to Roberta and her daughter. In the distance, he heard the sound of fire engines and ambulances approaching. The dust cloud over the park slowly dissipated.

Malcolm noticed that the two white officers from the turned-over police car had been thrown from it. They were the only casualties, thus far.

*　　*　　*　　*

Henri Joret was playing on a golf course just outside Dallas, when the news came over on a small television that was strapped to one of the caddy mobiles. Zack Hillerman, a wealthy banker from Texas and Henri's host for the weekend, called out. "Henri, I think you'd better come over and see this," Hillerman motioned to Henri, who was setting up to tee off on the sixth hole.

"Not now, Zack. I'm all set here." Henri tried not to lose concentration on his swing.

"No, Henri. You'd better come. There's been a bombing in Louisiana," Hillerman said. Henri dropped his club and ran to the small television, which was crowded with other golfers.

The news reporter showed scenes of the aftermath of the Zion First Baptist Church bombing. The reporter was interviewing the Reverend Josiah Stinson. Henri's mouth dropped and blood rushed through his face. He'd told Jasper the first Sunday in May. He excused himself and drove a cart back to the clubhouse where Sandchester waited, enjoying a Long Island Iced Tea. Henri shouted to Sandchester that they had to leave immediately.

"What's wrong?" Sandchester asked.

"What's wrong? You weren't watching the news?"

"No. What's happened?"

"The Reverend Josiah's church was blown up a couple hours ago."

Oh, Henri, this could be big trouble." Sandchester took another swig of his cocktail.

"Call the airport and have the plane ready when we get there. Every candidate in Louisiana will be there. Arrange for me to meet with the press and Campy…and hurry the hell up," Joret commanded, walking off the course.

"Sandchester, this Jasper Yates is getting out of control. There are two kinds of people like him, those who kill and pillage for a cause, and those who do it for money. Lucky for us, Jasper is one who does it for money. And that, in and of itself, should bring about obedience when given a job to do. But if Jasper continues to disobey my orders, I will personally put a gun to his commie head. And you will follow shortly thereafter, if you don't come up with a plan to control or terminate Jasper Yates," Henri said in a rage, storming toward his car.

* * * *

Investigation of the church bombing had begun. Lights were set up, and teams of the ATF and the FBI were working diligently. Church bombings had tapered off in 1997, and nothing this big had happened since the Alabama church bombing that had killed four young girls. Prior to this, the fires and bombings had all occurred when no one was around. FBI inspector Jon Tulle was on the scene with an officer from the NOPD and an ATF officer, who'd cornered Malcolm.

"So, Counselor, you're sticking with this story about discovering the bomb?" Tulle asked Malcolm.

"That's right." Malcolm was now dressed, but was tired.

"Mr. Stinson, we have several statements that you charged into the church in your underwear, shouting about a bomb in the building."

"You're sticking with this story, Malcolm?" asked Tulle.

"Mr. Stinson to you, and yes, I am. If there's nothing else, I need to be with my family." Malcolm made his way through the law officers.

"This is not over, Mr. Stinson," Tulle sneered, as Malcolm walked away.

Malcolm turned around to answer Tulle. "You better believe it's not over, Inspector."

CHAPTER 20

Three days after the church bombing, Malcolm, Pete, and Lucy visited Professor Hickman at his small Victorian home on Lake Pontchartrain's southern shore. Professor Hickman had lived there alone since his divorce five years ago. His two children were with their mother in New York City. When he became obsessed with militia and hate groups in America, he had converted his dining room into an observation headquarters. The professor sealed off the dining room containing his data and made it accessible by a false wall to the room.

Malcolm and company arrived at seven o'clock p.m. The professor opened the door, dressed in basketball shorts, a Jacksonville Jaguar football jersey, and Nike sneakers. His small living room was decorated with Picasso prints.

"Come in. I've been expecting you," the professor said, cheerfully. "I want to express my heartfelt feelings for what happened on Sunday. When you called me on Monday, I started doing some investigating," the professor stated, closing the door behind them. Malcolm looked around the living room of his small, but attractive home.

"Did you come up with anything?" Malcolm asked, waiting for the professor to offer him a seat.

"Yes and no. But before I show you anything, can I get you a drink? I have cranberry juice or sherry. Please have a seat," the professor said, pointing to his couch and chair. Everyone agreed on cranberry juice.

"So, what do you mean by 'yes and no?'" Malcolm asked when the professor returned with the beverages.

"Before I go into any details, do you know anything about hate groups? There's a reason for their madness." Professor Hickman sat on the arm of the couch.

"I don't follow you, Professor. May I exchange my drink for a little of that sherry?" Pete made a face after drinking the cranberry juice.

"For example, let's take the Aryan Nation. They're very popular, indicated by their rising numbers nationwide," the professor said. "The Aryan Nation's philosophy is that white people are the true descendants of the ancient Israelites, in direct line from Adam and Eve. Jews, they believe, descended from Cain, who was born not of Adam and Eve, but of Eve and the serpent. Cain's children fled into the woods, mated with the beasts, and produced the nonwhite—what they call—"mud races." To them, any one of us, with the exception of the private eye here, would be considered an interbreed," the professor said.

"You're kidding m! They really believe that sort of thing? I mean, I'm not a church-going person, but, hell, I know that's not how it went down in the beginning." Pete was flabbergasted.

"Yes…and there's more. You see, they also believe that there are twelve Aryan Nations: Finland, Sweden, Denmark, Norway, Germany, France, Spain, Holland, Iceland, Great Britain, and the United States. That's twelve, isn't it? Facts I know—math was never my forte."

"Who started all of this?" Lucy asked.

"Well, for years they've been camped up in Northern Idaho. There's a Reverend Wright up there who teaches this stuff. You have to understand that tax-resisters, militia members, right-to-lifers, home-schoolers, freemen, libertarians, Christian patriots, Evangelicals, and white supremacists all symbolize white people in America." The professor got up to feed the goldfish in his ten-gallon tank.

"What does all this mean?" Malcolm asked.

"They believe that America is going to hell in a hand-basket, full of colored people and government regulations. They think crime, drugs, decay, disease, unchecked immigration, and increasing social and economic stratification is destroying America. They want a safer, more wholesome life, governed and protected by traditional American values, meaning to them, values of the founding fathers—white Christians." The professor ushered them into his secret little hate crime control center.

"In this room, over the last five years, I have compiled information about practically every hate group in America, and most of the world." The false wall moved mechanically, revealing flashing computers and a map of the United

States lit with small, colored lights, designated by states and hate groups. There was one computer that was used for the Internet, and the other stored information on hate groups: locations, memberships, numbers, training cites, and cities and towns in all the states. Photos could be brought up of the Aryan Nation, Neo Nazis, The Order, Klansmen and military militiamen.

"So, what have you discovered that relates to the riverboat bombing?" Malcolm asked, as the professor browsed through the information.

"Well, in the last two days, no one has come forward to take credit for bombing your father's church. But, they are giving out heartfelt congratulations to whoever the brave souls were that...blew up the church of that lawyer's daddy, who is representing Clarence Reed." The professor looked up at Malcolm.

"And the riverboat?" Pete asked.

"The riverboat was put together like a special convoy...but no specifics have been given. I know you couldn't use this in court, but in months of studying the conversations, it is evident to me that Clarence Reed didn't commit the crime. But they are happy he's in jail, and not out in public promoting human rights. It's funny that they relate Reed to a 90's-type Martin Luther King, Jr., and—this isn't funny—that it was only a matter of time before someone would have killed him." The professor stopped the computer on Louisiana hate groups. The screen showed a chart of hate groups, their membership numbers, and locations.

"Where do you get all this information?" Pete looked around the secluded room full of charts and graphs on the walls.

"Sorry. That's privileged information. Can't reveal my sources."

"Can you tell us about any group that is prone to use explosives?" Malcolm asked.

"They're all prone to use explosives," the professor replied.

"This is very interesting, Professor Wilkes. Now, let's see if you can help me. I have rough sketches of two men. Can you identify them?" Malcolm pulled the sketches out of a manila envelope.

The professor examined the sketches closely.

"Okay. I'll scan them and run them through my system. It may take a little while. Have you tried running it through the FBI? Their system is more elaborate than mine, but mine is state-of-the-art."

"See if you come up with anything. I don't trust the feds. And right now may not be a good time to approach them with this. But let me know the moment you come up with something...day or night," Malcolm said, as he moved to leave.

Lucy made mental notes of the place as she left.

"Thank you, professor. If you identify those men, it may be our first big break in the case," Malcolm said, as he and Pete walked out the door.

"Do you have to go, Ms. Yee?" The professor leaned with one hand on the front door.

"I'm afraid so. Maybe another time," she said, smiling at the professor as she left the house.

Malcolm drove Lucy and Pete back to their hotel in the French Quarter.

* * * *

On Friday morning, Henri Joret was in his study reading a fax that he had received early that morning. Alva was still in bed recovering from a hangover. Her depression seemed to increase day by day; she worried constantly about Suzanne. No body, no news, no leads. Without the slimmest ray of hope, she believed Suzanne was still alive, but couldn't understand why there hadn't been a ransom. Was she in an accident and now suffering from amnesia?

Even Henri wondered what had happened. He was more concerned that either Jasper or Monet had betrayed him, by not letting him know that Suzanne was either killed or kidnapped. The very thought of either of them using one of his family members, without his knowledge or approval, infuriated him. Still, he had no concrete proof that this was true, but his gut feeling made him believe it. He wondered about Christmas Day when he and Monet had been on the phone. Did Monet make the decision at that time, or later, to have Suzanne disappear? He would attend to this matter soon but, for now, he had more pressing matters to consider. Tonight, Campy would break the news to his supporters about joining Joret's campaign.

Sandchester had informed him that Victor Zano wanted to meet with him. But with all that on his mind, he forced his attention back to the fax. Malcolm Stinson had a picture of Jasper Yates. What else did he know? How long before he finds out who Jasper is? Would the FBI be involved in finding Jasper? Something had to be done. Jasper had been found out, and now he must be eliminated. Henri had a little time to remove Jasper and Monet, but it would take careful planning.

* * * *

At 6:30 p.m., 110 men of the cloth gathered at an all-white Presbyterian Church, twenty miles outside of New Orleans. The church's pastor had offered the use of his church for Reverend Josiah Stinson to address a plan to prevent any more church bombings.

The preachers were seventy percent black, and for the first time in Louisiana, the races were mixing. The mixture wasn't fifty-fifty, but at least it was a start.

Campy was also present and asked the reverend for a little time to address the group. Up to this point, Campy hadn't approached anyone about his joining the Joret ticket. He thought he'd just announce his decision, and defend his position afterwards. Ziggy Gaines told him that was heading for disaster, but Campy preferred this approach.

Malcolm and Pete were also present. At the reverend's insistence, Malcolm sat in the front row, because Josiah wanted to show the crowd he was proud that Malcolm was representing Clarence Reed. Pete found a seat in the rear. Malcolm was a little disturbed by this, but appeased his father.

"I'm glad that you all could make it to the meeting tonight. God bless you for traveling from your homes. I'm not going to preach to you tonight, just enlighten you. I also want to give a special thanks to Reverend Gulklinson for the use of his beautiful church tonight." The audience gave a round of applause. The reverend led the group in a short prayer before he started the meeting.

"Also here tonight, is my son the lawyer, who, as most of you know, is representing our innocent brother Clarence Reed."

There was another round of applause.

"And last, but not least, our man for governor, Campy Frazier."

More applause.

"Over the last few years, I've seen attacks on our houses of worship. In 1995, church bombings and fires ran rampant. And in 1998, the devil is again showing his ugly head. Oh, I'm not going to preach to you tonight..."

Campy got up and tapped Malcolm on the knee, motioning him outside to talk while the reverend spoke. Once outside, Campy wiped the perspiration from his head with a handkerchief and walked around aimlessly.

"What's the matter, Campy?" Malcolm asked.

"I'm a man who stands by his convictions. I recently made a political decision. In my heart, I felt I made the right move, but tonight I'm getting cold feet about speaking to all those people. I mean, they've been the backbone of my campaign for governor, and I don't think they will understand."

"What sort of move have you made?"

Campy stopped walking and stared straight at Malcolm. "I agreed to run on Henri Joret's political ticket as lieutenant governor."

"You've got a big selling job to do. Why would you want to do something like that?"

"If those men continue to back me, Joret has the power to win the election, and we'll accomplish two major goals. First, we'll get rid of the incumbent asshole Steel—oh, excuse me—and for the first time, a black man will be one step away from becoming governor of Louisiana."

"You're going to wait for eight years for that?"

"No, no...Joret has other plans after four years. I believe he's going to run for the presidency, leaving me to run for governor. It's the perfect situation."

"But you know what kind of man he is, and what he stands for."

"You'll see his viewpoints change in the coming weeks. Malcolm, I know you've heard the saying, politics makes for strange bedfellows," Campy said, as he put his arm around Malcolm's shoulder. "You're an educated man. You should understand this."

"Yes. I've seen this sort of thing before, but Louisiana's different."

"That's why I need your help in selling this package."

Malcolm moved away from Campy's embrace. "No, Campy. I'm just a lawyer and the son of a preacher here. This is my birthplace, but I'm not a resident...I can't even vote for you. No way can I get involved. First thing Papa Joe will think is that I put you up to running with Joret. No, Campy. I have enough problems just representing Clarence Reed."

"Maybe a little support wouldn't be a bad idea. Those men in there respect your opinion."

"Campy, they don't even know me."

"Man, you are the talk of Louisiana. Come on, Malcolm. I need your help."

"Campy, you should be out here talking with my father, not me."

"All I'm asking for is a little support. Please, Malcolm."

"I can't promise anything, but let's see how it goes."

They walked back into the church. The reverend had covered most of his plan which called for around-the-clock protection for each church. He had even made up booklets for everyone attending the meeting. The Reverend Josiah glanced over with a little disdain as Malcolm and Campy came back into the sanctuary.

"I want you all to know that this June, when we go to the National Baptist Convention in Memphis, I will propose this program for national use. This was in the works before the bombing of my church on Sunday. It's not something I threw together at the last moment. It's time for action, my brothers. It's time to do the Lord's work outside of our own little communities. Oh, I'm not preaching to you tonight. Well, I've said I wouldn't keep you long. Read it. Pray about it.

And see if the Lord tells you to put it into action. God bless. Now, just a word from Campy Frazier before we leave tonight. Campy?" the reverend said. Campy walked to the podium, glancing at Malcolm.

Campy took a moment to gather his thoughts as the church waited for his familiar political revelry. But something was wrong with Campy this evening.

"Good evening, brothers, and just for the record, we as Christian men in the future, will not leave out the women. Reverend Josiah will get a little flack for not inviting any female preachers here tonight," Campy said, looking over at Reverend Stinson.

The reverend shot his eyebrows up to claim his innocence.

"I want to speak to you all tonight on a serious note. I'll be brief and to the point. I don't know how many of you know the history of the black man in Louisiana. His story is very much the same in any state in the South, or, for that matter, in this entire Union. But in Louisiana, when they freed the slaves, our white forefathers were so upset about black men being free that they did everything in their power to continue the trend of slavery. For example, after the freedom decree was declared, if a black man spit on the street, he was tried in court and sentenced to seven years of hard labor on a plantation chosen by the court. Also, if a black man was seen looking at a white woman, he received the same. Although other Southern states..."

"What's this speech all about?" Cephus, who was sitting next to Malcolm, asked.

"I think he's trying to soften the blow through a historical remembrance," Malcolm said, mockingly.

"So, through all the problems that we have faced as a people, we need to look at the future from a different perspective." Campy looked out at the mystified faces in the audience. "I have some news for you tonight. News about a different perspective for Louisiana's future. I want to be in the capitol come November, to play a big part in shaping the future of our state. So, I have decided to withdraw my bid for governor of Louisiana..."

There was a silent hush in the church, waiting for Campy to explain his dropping out of the race.

"Let's face it, gentlemen, Louisiana is not ready to vote a black man into office for governor..."

A preacher named Edward Hills stood up in the back of the church. "Even if you lost, Campy, it would show our people that we are still fighting, and that we can compete. It would be an example to our youth and their dreams of one day becoming governor. Campy, you still have to fight."

There was rush of mumbled approval for Reverend Hill's comment.

"Well, Reverend Hill, I had those same thoughts, and felt I couldn't give up either. So, I have decided on an alternative," Campy said to the audience of preachers. Campy placed both hands on the podium and leaned forward.

"After long deliberation with the Lord, a decision was made..." he lied. "I will close out my campaign, effective immediately, and join the Joret campaign, running as lieutenant governor," Campy revealed, looking straight toward the back of the church.

Reverend Hill was in the aisle, shouting now. "Let me get this straight. You want us to believe that you'll be the running mate of the man who's been our enemy for years? Campy, please!"

"Now, hold on one darn minute. I've met with Henri Joret and his viewpoints have changed," Campy said, trying to convince the ministers.

"Look, Campy, everyone in Louisiana knows that Michael Ducruet is in Henri Joret's pocket, and he's putting our young men in jail. And you're telling us that you want to be his running mate?" another minister from the left side shouted out.

Reverend Josiah wanted Campy to take the heat, because he hadn't discussed this with him first. Malcolm sat there shaking his head, and feeling sorry for Campy. It became an open forum to rip Campy for making such a choice.

After an hour of spitting their venom at Campy, the next phase started. The preachers withdrew their support for Campy.

After many pleading glances from Campy for help, Reverend Josiah finally stood up and approached the podium. He motioned for Malcolm to come up. Before speaking to the crowd, the reverend whispered into Malcolm's ear, "You think this is a good idea?"

"Well, if Joret wins, you got somebody in the big house you can call on. Support him now, and figure out the rest later," Malcolm replied.

The reverend put his hand over the microphone and whispered to Campy, "I'll deal with you later." Then, he raised his hands to the crowd to settle them down.

"Brothers, brothers, may I have your attention." As he spoke, the church full of ministers stopped their conversations and turned to the Reverend Stinson.

"Now, I know that the news we have just heard is shocking, but let's look at the reality of the whole scenario. Campy is a qualified politician who can run on his own for governor, but maybe the state isn't quite ready for a black governor. So, with that in mind, and understandably so, I recognize your concerns about Henri Joret. But having Campy as the lieutenant governor can only be a plus for us. We'll finally have someone on the inside that can be our internal voice. And who knows what can happen in four years? Joret may move on to something else, and Campy will have the experience of running state government. We'll be able to count on the minority vote, and make new friends in the white community that will give us votes for the next election. I think it's a good idea, and we should support him in this endeavor," the reverend said, waiting for a reaction from the group.

"What about his policies on unemployment for minorities, affirmative action, and police injustice? And, he's practically convicted Clarence Reed in the press," a minister shouted out from the back.

Campy made his way back to the podium.

"We have discussed these concerns, and within a week, you'll see his opinion change on those very issues," Campy politely replied. The crowd settled down.

Another minister got up and spoke.

"Reverend, you have been a spiritual father to us, and if you feel this is the right thing to do…I guess I have no choice other than to respect your position. So, I'm in support of Campy running with Henri Joret."

Then, like a domino effect, preacher after preacher got up and gave his support to Campy. Only a half dozen reserved their vote of confidence. But in the end, Campy and his supporters owed a great debt to the Reverend Josiah. Just when everything was back in order, a disgruntled minister got up to speak.

"I want to know how Malcolm feels about Campy's running with a man who wants to take Clarence Reed to the gas chamber."

Malcolm was hoping to not have to say anything, but the reverend motioned for him to take the microphone. He took a deep breath and addressed the crowd.

"Henri Joret's opinion of the case doesn't matter. It depends on the twelve jurors. Like Campy said, let's wait and see how Joret changes his opinion about the case. It's better to be on the inside looking out rather than the other way around. Don't you agree?" Malcolm said, as the ministers applauded him.

The reverend ended the meeting with a prayer and then turned to Campy. "They'll want to ask you a lot of questions, so when you're finished here, I'll be waiting for you at my house…"

The reverend, Malcolm, and Cephus left with Pete, who had enjoyed all the excitement from the back of the church. As they drove back to New Orleans, the reverend was furious. "When did he tell you about this, Malcolm?"

"Tonight, while you were giving your speech, we went outside to talk."

"When you think about it, it's not a bad idea. But, dang it, he should have told me first. Even if I disagreed with him, he should have told me. Heck, I kept all these people behind him. I'm going to light right into him when he comes by tonight."

"You still going to support him?" Malcolm inquired.

"I'll keep my word, but I'll voice my opinion on his approach, and clear things up, so that we don't have this problem in the future. Lord, help me, this has made me so angry I could cuss!"

"Reverend!" the three men said in unison. They all laughed, breaking the tension.

Chapter 21

It was 6:40 p.m. when the phone rang at the Stinson home.

"Hello? Who is this?" Serena questioned.

"Hello. Is your father in?" Reuben said, recognizing it to be a child's voice, and assuming it was Malcolm's daughter from the photo he'd seen.

"Yes, but who is this?" she insisted.

"Tell him it's Reuben Caulfield."

"Daddy, telephone. It's Reuben's Coffee," she said to Malcolm, who had just come home.

"Yes, how can I help you?"

"Mr. Stinson, I'm taking a big chance by calling you," Reuben said, cautiously.

"Why's that?"

"You never know who is listening."

"Listen, I don't know who you are, but I don't have any time for 'I Spy' games..."

"This is not a game, Mr. Stinson. It concerns your client. I have information that may be pertinent to your case," Reuben said.

"Okay. Talk. This line is clear. Take my word for it."

"How's that?"

"Trust me. It is."

"All right. My name is Reuben Caulfield, and I used to be a reporter for the Times Picayune. About a year ago, my partner, a photographer, and I were doing a story on the homeless in New Orleans while Deputy Chief Commissioner Waller met with two other men in a restaurant. I heard the commissioner convince the FBI that Clarence Reed committed the bombing. Afterwards, my colleague took pictures of the four men. They chased us and I escaped. Unfortunately, they killed my friend. Today, I was looking through some old copies of the Times Picayune, and saw these same men in the background of a photo of you and your children on Easter Sunday…Mr. Stinson, you still there?"

"I'm here, Mr. Caulfield. Do you have these photos?" Malcolm asked.

"Yes, I do."

"When and where can we meet?"

"I'm in New York."

"How about Friday, say one o'clock?"

"Sounds good. There's a park in Greenwich Village just before 11th Street and Hudson. I'll be wearing a Cincinnati Reds baseball cap, and carrying a Times Picayune. See you then," Reuben said, and hung up.

Malcolm called the firm, and Lucy was still working.

"Hello, Lucy."

"Yes, Mr. Stinson?"

"I want you to stop whatever you're doing and find out what you can about a man named Reuben Caulfield—he was a reporter for the Times Picayune about a year ago. See if you can get me his picture. I need it by tonight."

"But I was…"

"No buts. This is an urgent priority. Call me when you have everything. Bye."

Then Malcolm called Cephus.

"Hello. Cephus Pradier. Homicide."

"How you doing, buddy?"

"Good, and yourself, Counselor?"

"I've seen better days. Look, I'm calling to pick your brain a little. What do you know about a former reporter for the Times Picayune named Reuben Caulfield?"

"He was involved in a murder case about a year ago. His photographer was killed, a real nasty death. We didn't have any evidence on him. There were some witnesses that described a killer other than Caulfield. He mysteriously left town, and we never saw him again. Why?"

"I don't know yet. He called me to say that he had some information that could help the Reed case."

"Where is he?"

"He didn't say, just that he'd get back to me." Malcolm didn't like lying to Cephus. "Is the block for tapping my phone still on?" Malcolm asked.

"Yes. I had it checked yesterday. The feds can't say anything without explaining why they want your phone tapped. Let me know when he calls again. I'd like to talk with him, too. Maybe I could get some information on who killed that photographer."

"Will do. Thanks a lot, Cephus," Malcolm said, as he hung up. Next, he next called Pete at his cellular phone number.

"Pete, where are you?"

"In my hotel room."

"I'm going to New York to see Walter. I think they're going to try to pull out of the case again."

"That's too bad."

"I received a call from a guy named Reuben Caulfield, a former reporter from the Times Picayune. He has some photos that could help us in the case."

"I think I'd better go with you to New York. You shouldn't be alone in the big city."

"Maybe you're right. I plan to see someone else while I'm in the city."

"Like who?"

"Someone from the Italian Commission."

"Why are you going to see them? You know the feds will be watching."

"Exactly. That's why you need to come...so you can give them the slip while I go meet with the Commission."

"They've agreed to meet with you?" Pete asked.

"Just one integral part of the board. I'll try and get us a flight out tomorrow afternoon. Keep the line open. I'll call you later." Malcolm saw Serena waiting for him to pick her up. "And just what can I do for you, young lady?"

"Daddy, I want to see Mommy," she said in a gloomy voice. "I miss Mommy, Daddy. Joshua does, too."

Her teary eyes pierced Malcolm's heart. "I'll see what I can do, baby. Now take daddy's jacket upstairs." Malcolm watched his sad daughter drag his jacket up the stairs. He felt her pain, and his anger kindled against Sara. But this time he needed to do something. He knew the number of Sara's girlfriend in New York, where she was staying, and dialed, controlling himself from lashing out at her when she answered.

"Hello?"

"Hello. May I speak to Sara?" Malcolm asked.

"Who's calling?" the woman asked.

"Malcolm."

The woman covered the phone and asked Sara if she wanted to talk with him. She took the phone. "Hello, Malcolm. How are you?"

"I'm well. Thank you. The reason I'm calling...recently, Serena and Joshua have been asking see you, a lot. I think it would be nice if you spent some time with them."

"I wish I could, but so many things are going on now. And I don't have the time to really..."

"Sara, these are your children, too. And it's killing me to see them cry about not seeing their mother, and, frankly, I'm tired of making excuses for you."

"Malcolm, I don't have a place to keep them. There's barely room for me here. You know, you're living in Louisiana, and I'm here crammed up with my friends..."

"That was part of the divorce agreement, when you were running around with your stockbroker thief. You received money, no home."

"Let's not hash all that out again. Let's not argue. We're talking about the kids now, not us. Okay, I'm not working. Would it be too much to ask for some spending money, for clothes and trips? I'm speaking specifically for them."

"Sure, within reason. I'm coming to New York tomorrow, and will probably be there through the weekend. When I'm getting ready to leave, you can come over—say Saturday or Sunday...All right?"

"So, this is for now through September?"

"Right. How's that lawyer I recommended to you?"

"Good. He thinks everything will work out. I just want to thank you," Sara's voice cracked, and she began to cry.

"Sara, Sara, will you stop crying? Years from now I don't want the kids to think that I wouldn't help their mother stay out of jail."

"Thank you, Malcolm," she said, continuing to cry.

"You're welcome. I'm not heartless, you know."

"I never thought of you as heartless, just not very understanding at times." She wiped away her tears, and blew her nose. "So, I'll see you and the kids this weekend. Malcolm, it wouldn't hurt if we all spent at least one day together."

"No, it wouldn't, but I'll see how things go. Maybe we can. Expect a call from me, say, Friday night or Saturday morning. See you then," Malcolm said.

"Bye, Malcolm," she said softly.

* * * *

Three hours after Malcolm called Lucy for information on Reuben Caulfield, Henri Joret waited in his limo on a deserted back road in the bayou. After waiting for nearly fifteen minutes, Jasper Yates showed up. Jerry Dalton stayed in the van. With the church bombing fiasco behind them, Jasper had a new project.

"I have a new assignment for you—one I that hope you won't fumble," Joret said.

"Such as?"

"Malcolm Stinson is heading for New York tomorrow. He's meeting with Reuben Caulfield, a former news reporter from New Orleans. Do you know him?" Joret inquired.

"Can't say that I do. Why, is he important?"

"That's it. All I know is that he witnessed his colleague's murder about a year ago, and then escaped from New Orleans for fear of reprisal from the killers. Monet said you have some sophisticated surveillance equipment."

"Yes, I do."

"Good. I want to know what Malcolm Stinson talks with this reporter about. Can you handle that?" Joret asked.

"Not a problem, anything else?"

"Yes, as a matter of fact, there is. Any progress on the whereabouts of Suzanne?"

"Not yet, but I have some people in New Orleans checking some possible leads. We have better information avenues than the FBI and the local police, combined."

"I imagine you would; let me know the moment you do," Joret said, looking suspiciously at Jasper.

"That's it?"

"Just be careful, you know we're in this together," Joret said, as Jasper left the car.

"What's up?" Jerry asked.

"We're going to find something we lost months ago, and this time, make sure we kill it," Jasper said, laughing.

"What's wrong? You seem to have a worried look on your face."

"Nothing. I didn't like the way Joret was asking me again about his little Suzy. We'll need to make a decision about her soon," Jasper said with a concerned look, as they pulled away to prepare for their trip to New York.

CHAPTER 22

Willy Johnson and Dexter Holland ran a crap game scam in a Texas juke joint about five miles from the Louisiana border. A fight broke out when their scam was unveiled. Two men reached for knives to cut Willy and Dexter, but Willy and Dexter shot and killed both men instead. They fled the scene of the crime with no money for their efforts, in a stolen 1991 Chevrolet Impala with Texas license plates.

They drove all night and had passed several police cars in the night, without incident. Their gas was running out, but they only had four dollars between them. A few miles outside New Orleans, the gas gauge hit empty, so they got off the main highway. They needed to steal another car to get home to the Desire housing project, but robbing a gas station this close to home was too risky, so they drove into the bayou. Willy suddenly slammed on the brakes, while driving down a deserted road that ran parallel to a canal.

"What's wrong with you, fool? Ain't no damn air bags in this car," Dexter barked.

"There's a tree blocking the road, man," Willy said, putting the car in park and getting out.

"Who, in their right mind, would drop a tree on the road like this?" Dexter listened to the strange night noises in the bayou. "This place gives me the creeps. What was that?" Dexter said, reaching for his gun.

"Probably alligators. Look, Dex, see that light down yonder?" Willy said, standing on the tree. Dexter stood atop the tree to see, too.

"Maybe they can give us some gas. If not, we'll steal their car," Willy said, trying to move the tree. "Damn. This thing is heavy, man, and I don't feel like struggling to move it. Let's go. We'll take their car. There's got to be another way out of here."

"Willy, I don't know what you are thinking about. We are in the bayou. Nothing out here but alligators, rednecks, and wild animals. So, what makes you think we're going to walk up to that doorstep, and politely say, 'Pardon me, folks, but we seem to have run out of gas. Can you spare some petrol?'"

"Dexter, you may have a very good point, my brother. So let's just take their car, and get the hell out of this wild kingdom."

Willy led the way. He wore a black straw porkpie hat with a white band around it, and matching black and white shoes. His beady eyes pierced the night, and his two gold teeth reflected off of the half moon.

Dexter had a big nose and nearly half of his mouth was gold. He was small, but strong and agile. Willy was several inches taller, and lean. Willy and Dexter were two dangerous men who'd been in and out of jail for the past ten years. Nothing would stop them from getting what they wanted, and they were as black-bigoted as the Dalton brothers were white.

They moved closer to the house, squatting down as if someone might spot them in the darkness. Suddenly, a noise came from the canal right behind them. They both reached for their guns—Willy in one direction, and Dexter in another, a position of protection they'd practiced many times.

"What the hell was that?" Dexter strained to see through the darkness.

"Came from the river. Must've been a gator," Willy replied, with his finger on the trigger, ready to shoot anything that moved.

"What was that other noise?" Dexter asked.

Willy looked behind him.

"Nothing, man. Just a rabbit," Willy said, with a sigh of relief. "Look. There's a shed over there. Let's see if they got a car in there," Willy said, as he ran over to the shed. He used his forearm to wipe the layers of dirt off of the small four-pane window.

"Well, what's in there?" Dexter asked, in a loud whisper. "Willy, what's in there, man? Why aren't you answering me?" Willy lit a match and put his arm through the shed's broken window to get a better look at the car.

"Dex, you ain't going to believe this…"

Willy ran back to where Dexter was hiding behind some bushes. "Man, these backwoods folks doing all right for themselves. They got a Beemer sitting in there. Hell, man, it looks brand new."

"You telling me that there's a BMW sitting in that shed?"

"You damn right, Skippy. Can't be no more than a year or two old."

"What you think? We break in, hot-wire it, bust out of the shed, and drive off?" Dexter said, doubtfully.

"Nay, we need to secure the area."

"I was afraid you'd say that. I don't see any movement in the house. Plus we're going to have to ride that boat just to get there. You know these rednecks shoot first, and ask questions later."

They crept to the river and heard the rustling noise of alligators as they approached the boat.

"This ain't going to work. Damn, look at all them gators in the water," Dexter said, moving back, and getting ready to shoot at anything coming his way. They moved back behind the bush when they saw someone come out on the porch to look. Jim Dalton had a shotgun in his hands, and was looking over the area to see why the alligators were restless.

"Look, I say there's only him in there. Wait a minute. I got an idea," Dexter said, as Jim went back in the shack. Dexter moved back a few steps. That rabbit was still sitting there. Dexter reached down into his socks and pulled out a ten-inch hunting knife he had strapped to his leg, and then threw the knife at the rabbit, nearly slicing it in half. He rushed over and continued the incision, cutting the rabbit in half, then brought the bloody carcass back to Willy. The alligators smelled blood in the air and swam in their direction.

"Here, throw that part down river," Dexter said, as they tossed the rabbit halves down the river. As the rabbit hit the water, a mad frenzy ensued by the alligators fighting for the night's snack. They jumped into the boat and quickly paddled over to the island. Willy had his gun aimed at anyone who might come out of the house. Dexter was picking up speed as two alligators, that lacked the taste for rabbit, swam nearby. They landed and quietly climbed up the stairs.

Jim Dalton came out to catch a breeze in the swamp air. As he opened the door, the butt of Willy's gun hit him right over in the bridge of his nose, knocking him backwards into the shack. Jim dropped his shotgun and Dexter retrieved it, following Willy inside.

"Sorry for the intrusion, but we saw you had a gun…"

"Look, Willy, this guy's a big freak. Got the woman all tied up. We disturb something here?" Dexter asked, looking at the pale Suzanne, who was weak, but happy to see anyone other than Jasper or Jerry come through the door.

"We disturbing you, lady?" Dexter asked, waving his gun.

"No, not at all. I'm being held hostage here. Could you please help me?" she asked in a frail voice.

Dexter made his way around to see how Suzanne was tied up in the iron chains.

Jim was semi-conscious and lying on the floor. Willy stood over him with his gun pointed at Jim's chest, while he looked around the room and noticed the posters of Nazis and Klansmen. His eyes caught a photograph of a black man being lynched by a bunch of smiling white men under a big oak tree—it was even autographed by someone.

"Yo! Brother man, take a gander at our friend here's art gallery," Willy said, looking down at Jim with an angry face.

"You niggers better get out of here while you can. Leave the girl alone, and maybe I won't have them hang you like that picture up there." Jim was in pain, holding his nose as blood gushed everywhere.

"If that don't beat all…boy laying here, bleeding like a pig, making threats. Forget it, Dex. I'm just gonna put a cap in him and end his miserable existence." Willy aimed the gun at Jim's head.

"No," Suzanne pleaded.

"First of all, who's going to tell them? And second of all, why would you care? Seeing how he's been holding you hostage?" Willy said, cocking the hammer of the gun.

"Because killing him would be too easy. He needs to go to jail for the rest of his life," Suzanne said.

Dexter reached for some water to give Suzanne a drink. "Thank you," she replied.

"Okay. We'll put the leg irons on him. Get up, asshole," Willy shouted at Jim.

"Be careful. He's a professional killer," Suzanne warned them.

In unison, both men said, "So are we."

Dexter grabbed the keys off the wall and freed Suzanne from her months of bondage. Then he locked up Jim Dalton and gagged him. "Maybe we should just throw him over the side and let the gators choke on his racist ass. Or how about setting the place on fire and letting him burn?" Willy asked.

"Okay. Now what do we do with you, lady? What's your name, and why did he have you tied up?" Willy asked.

"My name is Suzanne Joret. I'm a news reporter for Channel Eight News, and I have information about last year's riverboat bombing. That's why they had me kidnapped." She was standing, trying to get the blood to run throughout her body again.

"Ah, sugar…Dex, she's a news reporter. We done told you that we're killers. We can't let you go now," Willy said.

"Wait a minute! You're the daughter of that guy running for governor. Yeah, there's a reward of one hundred thousand dollars for information leading to your safe return. You're not going to be ungrateful, and turn us in for helping you?" Willy asked, joyfully.

"Willy, is it? No, sir. I'll make sure you get every penny," she said, cheerfully.

"All right. That your car out there in the shed?" Dexter asked.

"Green Beemer?" Suzanne asked.

"Yup, that's it. You wouldn't know where the keys would be? Save us from hot-wiring it," Dexter said.

"No, but I keep a spare key in the well of the rear tire," Suzanne replied.

When Willy looked outside, it was as if the alligators knew the Daltons had company tonight—their little red eyes were speckled over the river looking up at the shack.

"Give me that pail. This redneck got any food in here?" Dexter snatched the pail from Willy. There was a mini-refrigerator containing ham, hot dogs, and a couple of steaks, along with some Spam, and a little gator tail. They opened the cans of meat and poured them into the pail. When Willy threw some of the meat off into the distance, the gators followed the trail. They dumped the rest of the meat on the far side of the island where there were more alligators. The three moved quickly down the stairs, only to be met by the biggest gator they'd ever seen.

"Damn, he's a big mother—must be an old guy. Probably feeds on the smaller gators for food." Willy leaned back on the stairs as the giant gator approached the bottom step with his mouth open.

"So, what do we do now?" Suzanne asked.

"In the words of Clint Eastwood, 'Dis here is a .45 magnum—the most powerful handgun in the world.' Now if I remember correctly, gators have very small brains, yet are very violent. So, once he opens his mouth..." Willy said, pointing the gun nervously at the alligator. When Willy took another step down, the alligator moved closer to the step and opened his mouth with a growling hissing noise. Willy shot him four times in the mouth, and the alligator went limp. They stepped cautiously over the lifeless reptile and into the boat, safely making the twenty yard journey, before the other gators pursued them.

Willy easily knocked the lock off the shed, and they backed up the green BMW while Suzanne directed them to the road leading to the river. Once on the other side, freedom shined for Suzanne. She was with two criminals, but she thought it was a far better cry than being with Jasper and the Daltons.

"Suzanne, right? I'm Dexter, and dis here is Willy."

"The pleasure is mine, gentlemen."

"Well, at least she's a lady. So, where we going?" Dexter made himself comfortable in the leather seats.

"Maybe my phone is still in the glove compartment," Suzanne said. Dexter pulled out the cellular phone, and plugged it into the cigarette lighter.

"They must have left it, hoping I would contact someone. Thank God for Kathy—she'd think of something like that. May I?" She reached for the phone. She had to take a moment to remember. She dialed Kathy's number, got her answering machine, but left no message. "My friend isn't home. Guys, there's something I forgot to tell you."

"What's that?" Willy asked.

"There were some very dangerous people working with that guy we left back there."

"Yeah, yeah, right, so why were you tied up like that, and how long have you been there?" Dexter asked, dialing a telephone number.

"This is almost June, so it's just about six months. And I know that they're the ones who bombed the riverboat and pinned it on Clarence Reed."

"Clarence Reed, the civil rights brother? Oh, man, we can't let this fly, Willy."

"So, you're the good Samaritan now?" Willy glanced sideways at Dexter.

"We need a place to chill out for awhile to figure out what we're going to do next. Since your friend ain't home, we got some friends in the Desire housing project. We'll need to get you some clothes and a bath—no offense, lady, but you smell like a swamp rat," Dexter said, reaching his party on the phone. "What's up, baby? Dexter, your lover man, here."

"Dexter Holland, where the hell you been for the last three weeks? If you think you're going to just walk in here and everything is fine, you got another think coming, my brother," said the voice on the phone.

"Now take it easy, baby. I got some good news for you. We headed for a big payday and it's totally legit. How my kids doing?"

"What do you care how they're doing? You not paying any rent or buying any food for them. Dexter, look, wherever you are, just keep going...what do you mean got a big payday that's legit?"

"I'll tell you all about it when I get there...uh, Willy and a guest of ours are coming, too. So cook up some vittles. You're going to like this. See you in a little while. Bye."

"Now listen up, folks, particularly you, Suzanne. I'm going to lay this story on my honey, but when I tell her about the money for the reward, it's going to be only fifty thousand; twenty-five thousand for each of us. The other fifty, we don't need to mention it at this point. Agreed?" Dexter looked over his shoulder at Suzanne.

"Not a problem, Dexter," Suzanne agreed.

"When we get to the projects, I'll drop you and Dex off. I can't leave a car like this out in front of the building. I got to hide it from our local undesirables," Willy said, and Dexter joined him in laughter.

It was 10:30 that night when they finally arrived at the Desire housing project. The night was warm, and many locals were just hanging out, with the police stationed at each end of the projects. Willy drove to the back of a project building to drop off Dexter and Suzanne.

After a lengthy talk, Dexter convinced his girlfriend that their money was to be made in harboring Suzanne. They let her bathe, fed her, and clothed her.

Suzanne would sleep peacefully for the first time in months. She didn't feel threatened by Dexter or Willy because they had a reason—even if they were criminals—to take good care of her until they got their money. Before she went to sleep, she called Kathy and left a number for her to call back.

Old man Sawyer let Willy keep the car in a garage behind his building, for the promise of a bottle of Wild Irish Rose wine the next day. Someone saw Willy stash the BMW and wrote down the license plate. They knew that money could be made by knowing the whereabouts of a brand new green BMW.

CHAPTER 23

Malcolm got up early to catch his eight o'clock flight to New York. The children were running about, making noise and a mess. Lois Stinson made breakfast for her son, while the reverend was on the telephone trying to rent a tent for church services.

Pete arrived to take Malcolm to the airport, and Roberta and her daughter arrived right behind him. When little Serena saw Malcolm with his suitcase, she asked, "Daddy, where are you going?"

"I have to go home to New York to take care of some business. But guess what? I have a surprise for you and Joshua," he said, as his son walked over, curious about the surprise. "Today is Thursday, and in two days, Uncle Pete here, is going to fly with you on an airplane. And you're going to see Mommy." Malcolm watched as Serena's sad face transformed into a happy grin.

"Really, Daddy? Mommy will be there?"

"Yep, and you two will spend the summer with her. How's that sound?" Malcolm asked, hugging both children.

"Goody! We'll all be living together again. Right, Daddy?" Serena asked.

"Ah, not quite, baby. Daddy has to take care of business here in New Orleans. But I'll come and see you during the summer. Promise." Malcolm saw the dejected expression on Joshua's face. "What's the matter, son? I thought you wanted to see your mother."

"Nothing. I thought you and Mommy had stopped fighting, and we were going to be a family again. May I be excused now?" Joshua pulled away from Malcolm's arms.

"Your mother and I are not fighting. We're just separated."

"You're not separated, you're divorced," Joshua said.

"What's divorce, Daddy?" Serena inquired.

"I'll tell you later. Joshua, you may not be able to understand right now, but trust me, everything is going to be all right. You'll feel better when you spend some time with your mother."

"It's not the same. You don't love her anymore."

"I do love her, but not in the same way. I'll always have a love for her because she's the mother of my children." Malcolm grabbed him gently and held him close to his chest. "Just give it some time, son. Everything will be fine. You'll see. I love you, and so does your mother, even if we are apart. You can understand that, can't you? Now, now. No tears. I'll tell you what, in a couple of weeks we'll go to a Yankees game, and we'll go up to Harlem to see the Rutgers Basketball Tournament, like we did last year. Okay?" Malcolm reassured Joshua, wiping his tears away.

Joshua just nodded in agreement with Malcolm.

Roberta was there to pick up the children for school; she'd witnessed what had just happened. "You must have been a very close-knit family." She walked Malcolm down the stairs to the car.

"Pretty much, with the exception of the last year or so of our marriage. He's a tough kid. He'll get through this...I hope. So, how've you been?"

"I'm good. Could be better if I saw you a little more often," Roberta said smiling, trying to cheer Malcolm up.

"In that case, we'll do something about that as soon as I get back."

"Which will be when?"

"Probably Monday."

"Malcolm, I may be out of line, but are you going to see her while you're there?" Roberta asked cautiously.

Malcolm looked deep into her eyes.

"No, you're not out of line. Yes, I will see her, but it's over between Sara and me. There's too much hurt between us to ever get back together again. My only concern is that my kids know her and love her, regardless of what she's done to me. If it weren't for the kids, I'd never want to see her again, at least on this side of heaven, but she is their mother. I haven't figured out what happened to her, and frankly, I don't even care any more. My only concern is that she love her children. I'll call you," Malcolm said, as he kissed Roberta sweetly on the lips.

* * * *

It was 9:50 in the morning when Kathy dialed the number Suzanne had left. The voice sounded like Suzanne's, but could someone be making a prank call? She dialed the number.

"Hello?" Dexter's girlfriend said, holding their seven-month-old baby in her arms.

"Can I speak to Suzanne?"

"Hold on a minute. Who's calling?"

"Kathy."

"Some girl named Kathy is on the phone for you," she called, as Suzanne jumped up from the couch with the two other kids following.

"Kathy? Kathy? Is that you?"

"Suzanne? Is this really you?" She started to cry when she recognized Suzanne's voice.

"Yes. I'm so happy to hear your voice." Suzanne was crying as well.

"Where have you been? What's happened to you? Are you all right?"

"I'm fine. I'll tell you everything when I see you. First, you have to do me a favor. I need some money. How much can you get your hands on?"

"Oh, I don't know, maybe fifteen hundred."

"Good. Get the cash. I'll explain later, but I can't come until tonight. I'll be over as soon as it gets dark."

"That may not be a good idea. You know Frank, the electrician at the studio? About a month ago he told me that my phone line had been tapped, but he fixed it."

"Tapped? Why would anybody tap your line?"

"I think the FBI had my line tapped in case you contacted me. Are you alone?"

"No, someone is helping me."

"Tell you what, have that person come to where we used to have lunch on those miserable days and order what we always ate for lunch. I'll leave a number in a bag for them. Say, an hour."

Suzanne looked at Dexter. "Can you go somewhere for me, Dexter?"

"Sure. When?"

"One hour?" she asked, and Dexter agreed.

"Okay. They'll be there in one hour. Bye. See you later."

Dexter met her at the Roadside Cafe off of Route 10. The cafe sold barbecued chicken sandwiches, and alligator tail meat, but Suzanne and Kathy had only eaten the chicken sandwiches. This was the safest method for them to communicate.

But, in a Seven-Eleven store two blocks from Kathy's house, two men were calling Todd Sandchester. The FBI had ceased tapping Kathy's phone, but Sandchester had kept up surveillance on Kathy and Suzanne's apartment. The two men told him of Suzanne's reappearance.

Sandchester was shocked by the news of Suzanne's reappearance. He ordered them to follow her. However, Kathy had left the house, undetected, by the time they arrived looking for her car. When they didn't find Kathy, Sandchester contacted Deputy Chief Phillip Waller.

Kathy had withdrawn fifteen hundred dollars from the bank, and then ordered a chicken sandwich at Roadside Cafe. There were only five people in the store at the time, all white customers. Although apprehensive about entering this environment, Dexter, having received a good description from Suzanne, approached Kathy.

"Suzanne sent me, he said.

Kathy struggled to smile, handed him a bag with a chicken sandwich, her cellular phone number, and directions to the location where they would meet. Dexter returned to Suzanne with that night's instructions.

* * * *

Malcolm walked into his office at the firm at one-thirty that afternoon, and was surprised to see his belongings neatly packaged in boxes. His secretary wasn't there, but someone new asked him what he wanted.

"What do I want? Last I remembered, this was my office."

Malcolm stormed into Walter Baer's office.

"You know, Walter, I don't know who's worse—those hate mongrels in Louisiana, or the ones here in New York."

"Have a seat. I assume that you've been to your office," Walter said.

"Yes, at least they could have given me some sort of notice that I was fired."

"Now don't go off on some tangent. You're not fired. Last month, Weinstein had a brain aneurysm, and Callucci has taken over the firm's day-to-day operations. And like a good dog, Rothman is standing by his side. Last week, he told me he was going to contact you. He'd decided that the firm has had enough bad publicity from the pro bono case in New Orleans. Clients are objecting to our firm's defending a terrorist for free."

"Walter, I've been making some headway. And with a little more time, I can prove Clarence Reed's innocence," Malcolm said.

"That may be true, but they're ready to pull the plug now."

"So, what does that have to do with my office?"

"I don't know, but they must assume that, knowing how strongly you feel about this case, you'd rather quit the firm, than give it up."

"When do we meet with them?"

"I'll try to arrange it right away."

Calucci agreed to meet with Malcolm and Walter at nine the next morning.

"All is not lost. I'll tell you what, let's go to dinner tonight and, oh...I forgot. I'm taking my wife to the opera. You like the opera?"

"I'm really not up to an opera, Walter."

"Don't worry. Join me tonight, and we'll work this out somehow. Remember, we've worked out the problems before."

"Yeah, you're right. How many tickets do you have?"

"Four. Thinking of bringing a guest?"

"Yeah. Can I use your phone?" Malcolm asked, as Walter gestured for him to be his guest.

"Hello, may I speak to Sara?"

"How are you?"

"You're in New York?"

"Yes, are you free tonight?"

"Sure. What did you have in mind?"

"Dinner and the opera."

"Don't you remember that both of our children were conceived on nights we attended the opera? What's on your mind, Mr. Stinson?" she asked, flirtatiously.

"I just want to talk about the children, all right?"

Malcolm met Walter on his way out. "I'll meet you at the opera. I need to talk some things over with her. Sara will be with me tonight."

"Reconciliation?"

"No. Just a parent meeting, that's all. I'll pick up the tickets at the box office."

"Lincoln Center, eight o'clock. See you tonight."

* * * *

At five-thirty that evening, Suzanne called the designated number, a cellular phone that no one knew about. Kathy suggested that, since rain was coming down in waves, they should meet earlier than planned.

The plan was for Dexter and Willy to pick up Kathy at her apartment on the other side of town. At five-fifty-five, Dexter, Willy, and Suzanne pulled up in front of the apartment building, and Kathy ran out carrying a small umbrella. Two of Sandchester's men intercepted her.

"Going somewhere, Ms. Sommers?" the bald man said, flashing a phony police badge.

"What do you want?" she shouted, as he grabbed her arm.

"Come with us, please. We want to ask you some questions about Suzanne Joret," the other said.

Suzanne got out of the car.

"Let her go. Who are you, and what do you want?" she shouted over the pounding rainstorm.

"Okay, good. You just made our job easier. Let's go, sister." He released Kathy and grabbed Suzanne.

Dexter and Willy were observing all of this.

"Willy, I think that guy is trying to take our reward money."

"You approach them from the front and I'll cover the rear. Use the silencers we took from that redneck in the bayou."

"You must've been reading my mind," Dexter said, as he slipped out of the car.

"Excuse me, sir, but them there ladies is with us," he said.

"Take a hike, nigger," the short stocky one said.

"I'm getting wet and you calling me names," Dexter said, as the stocky one reached for his gun. Through the falling rain, three bullets could barely be heard ripping through the stocky man as he fell to the ground. The bald one saw Willy pointing his gun, but before he reached for his, Dexter fired four rounds into him. Sandchester's henchmen lay dead on the grass.

"Let's go, ladies. Staying around here isn't very wise right now," Dexter told Suzanne, who was devastated by the killings.

"Listen, it was either them or us. He would have shot Willy, your friend there, and me. And taken you away," Dexter said to the trembling women.

"Slow down, man. Take it easy. You driving like that going to get us busted for sure." Dexter wiped the rain off his gun.

"I'm sorry. I've reported about killings after the fact, but I've never witnessed one." Suzanne was breathing heavily and holding Kathy.

"Who were those men? And what did they want?" Kathy blurted out. "And who are they, Suzanne?"

"Sitting there is Dexter. And the one driving is Willy. I don't know your last names," Suzanne said.

Willy pulled up onto Route 10.

"Good. Let's keep it that way now that we all know each other," Willy said. The windshield wipers were working at top speed, but the visibility was still low as he tried to enter the highway in the heavy rain. "Listen, we need to get off this highway before we get killed. So, where you want to go, Ms. Suzanne?" Willy asked.

Dexter looked at him cross-eyed. "What's the matter with you?"

"I was just being polite. Try it some time."

"Ms. Suzanne? What, you driving Ms. Daisy?"

Suzanne noticed some hostility developing between them.

"Let's head north to Arkansas."

"Arkansas? What the hell is in Arkansas?" Dexter asked.

"My parents live there. And it will give me some time to set up your reward money. Besides, don't you think we need to get out of town for awhile?" Suzanne asked, as Kathy gave her a scared and strange look.

"She may have a point there, Dex. Let's pick up a few things and split," Willy said, heading back to the Desire housing projects.

When they were nearly five miles outside of New Orleans, Dexter decided he wanted to go back to leave his girlfriend some money.

"Why you want to go back now, Dex?" Willy asked.

"I got to take care of my baby. She don't have any money, and it took me nearly half the night to calm her down when I left town for a week. Sorry, ladies, but I got to take care of my family. It won't take long...just let me pop in and give her a couple hundred dollars. You do have some money, Suzanne?" Dexter asked.

"Sure, ah, did you get the money, Kathy?"

"Yeah, I have it right here."

"Good. Turn this mother around, Willy," Dexter commanded.

It took nearly an hour to make it back. By the time they reached the projects, the police had surrounded Dexter's building.

Parked just outside the project, they could see the flashing lights of the army of police cars.

"Come on, Willy. Let's check it out," Dexter said, opening the door.

"Are you crazy, man? Look at all them po-lice. Man, they gotta be looking for us. That's your building," Willy replied, as he got out of the car.

"We'll be right back, ladies." Dexter and Willy nonchalantly strolled to the outskirts of the police barricade.

"Suzanne, what the hell is going on here? Let's just drive the hell out of here. These black guys murdered two men," Kathy said.

"Calm down, Kathy. It's a long story, but these two guys saved my life, and I owe them."

"You owe them? Suzy, they're cold-blooded murderers. Besides, they're black."

"So is the man I love, and he's not a cold-blooded murderer. Or have you forgotten? As I recall, he always treated you well."

"Will you listen to yourself? We're not talking about Clarence, Suzy, but about two killers. How long have you known them?" Kathy asked frantically, looking out of the window for Dexter and Willy.

"A couple of days. What do you think they're going to do? Rape and murder us?"

"That's something to consider," Kathy said.

"Yeah, I didn't think of that. Okay. Let's go. I'll call them later. They know how to get around in the hood." Suzanne climbed into the driver's seat. She put the car in reverse and stepped hard on the gas, and then slammed the brakes on and turned the steering wheel. The car spun around on the wet surface. She switched the gear into drive and screeched down the street.

"Damn, Dexter. There goes our reward money, man. Damn you, man. You had to come back," Willy screamed.

Dexter had pulled out his gun to shoot at the fleeing car, and then quickly replaced it.

"Come on, Willy. Let's get out of here." Dexter kept his back to the police and walked calmly away.

"I ought to shoot your black ass. One hundred thousand dollars, man. We ain't never had a score like that," Willy whined.

"All right, I screwed up. Can't trust white people for nothing. But all is not lost. I'm willing to bet that her friend put her up to this. She was cool with us. That Kathy broad was a ball of nerves."

"So if you saw that the chick was nervous, why did you just want to leave them alone in the car?"

"Forget that, man. Listen, brother, suppose Suzanne was telling us the truth about her father having a place in Arkansas."

"Sure, we're going to just look in the Yellow Pages and find the address. What you been smokin'?" Willy asked.

"The Yellow Pages is for business, Willy. We'll find the house. She is going to pay us for rescuing her, or she'll wish she'd stayed with that bayou redneck. Now, let's find a car. We can stay with my cousins in Biloxi till things cool down. Don't worry, Willy. We are going to find Ms. Suzanne Joret."

Dexter watched the red tail lights of Suzanne's car disappear into the dark, rainy night.

CHAPTER 24

Jasper and Jerry Dalton arrived in New York City shortly before noon on Friday, without any luggage. Jasper's plan differed from Joret's: Joret wanted him to watch Malcolm Stinson; instead, Jasper was on a mission to kill Reuben Caulfield.

They took the subway to 145th Street and Eighth Avenue, the heart of Harlem. The buildings still showed some evidence of the beautiful neighborhood it once was. Now, half of the buildings were sealed up with condemned posters nailed onto their doors. They approached a row of five buildings that were still livable.

Four years earlier, Jasper had supplied some Connecticut militia groups with arms, and a black associate introduced him to a Black Haitian voodoo princess, better known as Mama Letrec. Though she still practiced voodoo, the fifty-one-year old ran a very efficient arms-selling operation that neither the New York City police, the ATF, nor the FBI had been able to break for five years.

Mama Letrec had renovated the basement into a luxury apartment and had thirty Haitian men working for her. Two guards at the front door stopped Jasper and Jerry. "What be your business?" asked the tall and muscular guard.

"Tell Mama Letrec it's the White Crow," Jasper replied, and the message was relayed by walkie-talkie. Jasper and Jerry were allowed to pass the two guards, only to be picked up by four men waiting inside. All were armed and kept their fingers on the triggers. Jerry thought he was on a safari when he entered Mama's apartment, decorated with the bright reds, oranges, and yellows of West India, and the furniture upholstered in tiger prints.

Sitting in a leather chair, Mama Letrec smoked a cigarette from a holder planted in her teeth, exposing her gold tooth, shaped like a skull. She slowly turned to face Jasper and Jerry, who were surrounded by ten armed men who watched their every move.

Mama had thought she'd never see Jasper again after their last encounter four years ago, when she ran her operation in the Bedford Stuyvesant section of Brooklyn, New York.

Jasper had just bought his rifles and Mama's men had loaded up his car, when, much to their surprise, fifteen cops and four detectives raided her operation. Jasper had escaped out the back, carrying an automatic rifle and seven magazines of ammunition. He circled the building and re-entered through a side window, from which he killed every cop. When the others roared in to help their fellow officers, Jasper killed them, too. Only one of the nineteen cops survived and eventually testified that a white man had been the killer.

Mama Letrec had escaped to Haiti for two years, and had just returned ten months earlier and gone back to business as though she'd never left.

That was four years ago. Now she owed him a favor for saving her from being arrested. And Jasper came today to collect.

Jasper had made several calls to find Mama Letrec.

She was not happy to see Jasper, but didn't want to cross him after what she had witnessed four years earlier.

"So, what brings the White Crow back to New York? I would think you'd be out bombing government buildings...isn't that what you do?" she inquired, in her French West Indian accent.

"That's what I like about you, Mama; you have such a sense of humor."

"What can I do for you?"

"I need a little protection while I'm here in the city."

"Such as?"

"Small, but efficient."

"I have just the thing for you. A new shipment's just come in." Mama nodded her head to one of her men, who returned in less than a minute with a Beretta .93 R complete with a silencer.

Jasper was impressed. "Mind if I test the merchandise?"

"Toba, take the gun and demonstrate for White Crow," Mama Letrec said.

"I'd rather do it myself, if you don't mind."

"I do mind. Let Toba show you how the gun works."

"Don't you trust me, Mama?"

"You are correct. So, do you want to see the gun demonstrated, or do you wish to take it as is?"

"I'll take it as it is. I trust your merchandise. I need three more. And a few rounds of ammo," Jasper said, examining the gun.

Toba brought out three more Berettas and ten boxes of bullets. The boxes were taped and put into a bag along with the four guns. "So, how much do I owe you for the extra guns?" Jasper asked, moving closer to Mama Letrec by leaning on the desk. "The light is not so good down here, but you're looking as pretty as ever. A little bit of gubba dust and I could fall in love with you." Five semi-automatic weapons were instantly pointed at Jasper.

Mama Letrec waved them off.

"Would you be interested in some, as you call it, gubba dust? I can tell your love life is not what it should be. I see that you have things crossed up." She smiled, as Jasper's face twisted into a frown.

"It's been a pleasure, Mama. See you around sometime," Jasper said, as he turned to walk out.

Jerry didn't budge an inch the entire time.

"White Crow, let this be the last time we meet. Next time could be fatal," she said, as Jasper and Jerry were being led out.

"For whom? You or me?" Jasper smiled, and blew Mama Letrec a kiss.

The men led them to another door that led to a tunnel. "Where are we going, boys? This ain't the way we came in," Jasper said.

"We never know who's outside watching, so we are going to take you through this tunnel which leads to a park down the street. From there you go where you want," Toba replied.

The walk from Mama Letrec's house to the park was about a quarter of a mile in the dark, wet, and rat-infested tunnel. They came to a ladder that Toba said would lead to a manhole in the park. They climbed out, and bid Toba and his men farewell. They walked into the park, and behind some bushes, they loaded their guns and stashed the ammo in their coats. Jasper and Jerry were armed and ready.

"We need to get some transportation for the next day or so," Jasper said, looking for a cab.

"We are going to rent a car?" Jerry asked.

"No. Borrow one."

"I tell you, Jasper, being around them niggers with guns made me nervous. How do you know that witch woman?" Jerry asked.

"You meet strange people in this business. She served her purpose, and that's all that counts." Jasper flagged down a gypsy cab, which dropped them off at the corner of Delancey and Houston in the bowery. Twenty minutes later, the cab Jasper was looking for came to a stop at the traffic light. Wearing a turban, the cab driver's identification card revealed he was Pakistani.

"Where to?" he asked, in a thick Pakistani accent, as Jasper and Jerry got in.

"143rd Street and Riverside Drive," Jasper said, as he studied the credentials of the cab driver. The partition was open between the front and back seats. "You drive a lot, huh?" Jasper asked, striking up a conversation.

"Yes, I put in twelve, sometimes fourteen, hours a day," the cab driver answered.

"Your family must miss you—gone all those hours every day," Jasper probed.

"My immediate family is still in Pakistan. I live here with my brother and his wife. I am bringing my family later this year. I will have enough money saved by then," the cabby said proudly.

"So, you see your brother's family every day?"

"Hardly. He's a cabby, also. He works the opposite shift that I do. And his wife works with my cousin in a food market they have in the Bronx. Sometimes I don't see them for three or four days. I'll probably catch up with them day after tomorrow," the cabby said.

"That's too bad," Jasper said, pulling out a thin steel wire. He had two handkerchiefs that he wrapped around each of his hands, and gave a little slack to the wire. Then he leaned back to enjoy the ride. He pulled out a piece of paper and wrote down for Jerry to have his gun ready.

Just as the cabby was about to reach 143rd Street, Jasper told him to pull over. The cabby told him the fare was thirteen dollars, and picked up his clipboard to mark down his trip. Jasper moved through the partition and lassoed the cabby around the neck, pulling the wire taut. The cabby struggled so violently that his turban fell off.

Jasper was losing his grip and the cabby was trying to escape. "Shoot him, dammit!" Jasper yelled at Jerry, who took his gun with the silencer, and shot the cabby in the head. Blood splashed everywhere.

"Quick! Move up front and get us out of here." Jerry pushed the dead cabby over and they drove up the Henry Hudson Parkway to the Dyckeman Street Exit, where they threw the cabby's body into a dumpster behind a nearby hospital. They had transportation for the evening.

Jasper stopped by Malcolm's apartment building and asked the doorman if Mr. Stinson had come in yet—or if he had seen him lately. The doorman, reluctant to give out any information, simply stated that Mr. Stinson was not in right now, and asked who was calling on him. Jasper gave a fictitious name, claiming to be a client. Jerry and Jasper would return later so that they could follow him the next day to meet Reuben Caulfield.

They arrived a little early in the lobby of the Metropolitan Opera House, so they ordered drinks.

* * * *

"You know, the kids are taking this divorce pretty hard. I'm starting to see the signs of it," Malcolm said, sipping his drink.

"What sort of signs?"

"They want us to be a family again. Serena cries for you, and Joshua is mad at both of us. I keep them pretty active, but they always fall back into wanting their mother. I don't know how you're going to do it, Sara, but these are your children, too, and you need to see them more."

"Swell, that's pretty hard with you having them in New Orleans," she said, as tears began to trickle down her face. "Malcolm, I am a good mother. Do you still hate me?"

"I don't hate you…it's just that after ten years, and two children, I don't understand how you could turn on me like that." Malcolm looked her straight in the face.

But Sara just stared out the window.

"What do you want me to say? I screwed up my life with you and the kids. You once told me that in love, forgiveness is the rule." She turned to look at Malcolm. "So, son of a preacher man, can you forgive?"

"Forgiving is not the hard part. It's forgetting."

They sat in silence for the next ten minutes. People, who had been held up in traffic coming in from Long Island, entered the opera hall.

Just as the lights were dimming, Walter and his wife came into the balcony booth.

"Sorry we're late. Traffic was horrendous," Walter apologized. He and Malcolm sat between the two women.

"So, what exactly is going to happen tomorrow, Walter?" Malcolm whispered.

"I fear for the worst, my friend…I believe they are going to pull the plug on the whole shebang. And to make matters worse, they're going to ask you to return to the firm immediately, and take on the Giamanco case."

"Are you serious? Even if they pull out of the case, I'm not going to do that." As Malcolm's voice rose, the people in the neighboring boxes looked on in disgust.

"Surely we can make an arrangement for you to stay on, while you find another lawyer to take the case. There are dozens of lawyers who want to take on Clarence Reed as a client," Walter said, confidently.

"Walter, if they pull the plug on me in this case, I'm quitting the firm—no ifs, ands, or buts. Ten years is long enough, anyway. I can join another firm, or better yet, start my own practice…where, I don't know—New York or Louisiana. That, I'd have to decide later."

"That does sound like a good idea, but you're still going to need money and assistance for this case," Walter said. "Malcolm, think about this. You make over five hundred thousand a year. Do you really think someone is going to pay you that kind of money?"

"Walter, there's no price for peace of mind. I've got some money saved and I have a stock portfolio. I can sell the condo," Malcolm said, sounding unsure.

"So what will you do?" Walter asked.

"Start looking for help in New Orleans. Walter, what do you know about the Southern Poverty Center in Alabama?"

"They're a reputable firm that usually delves into civil rights' cases. They might help, but they may also want to take over as lead counsel."

"We'll see about that."

"Please mull this over before making any sort of rash decision…we're talking about ten years with the firm, and a good salary."

"You know, my daddy says that sometimes God has a way of moving you out of your comfort zone, and putting you where you're most needed. I think a change will do me good. Walter, I'm not going to hem and haw with them tomorrow. If they tell me it's over, I'm just going to resign and head back to New Orleans."

"But, Malcolm, really…"

"Enjoy the opera, Walter." Malcolm leaned back in his chair, and glanced at Sara, who was trying to figure out what was going on.

After saying goodnight to Walter and his wife, and settling on the time to meet him in the office, Malcolm and Sara walked up Broadway to a restaurant named Ernie's.

"So, what were you and Walter arguing about?"

"Nothing much, just some life-changing issues."

"Life-changing? Like what?"

"I guess I can tell you. I'm planning to resign from the firm. I don't know exactly what I'll do yet. Either go to another firm, or better yet, start my own practice."

"It's about time. Remember how we used to talk about that...what, three, four years ago? You'll start here in New York?" She looked over at Malcolm, as she ate her baked clams.

"I don't know. New Orleans could use a good lawyer."

"I was afraid you'd say that. What about the kids? How would we do that?"

"When I come to that bridge, I'll cross it. So, how did you enjoy the opera?"

"Better, if I'd known what it was about."

"Well, it was Mozart's "Cozi van Tuitte." It's about two men who place a bet on their fiancées' faithfulness. They return in disguise to see how faithful they are."

"Oh."

They enjoyed their meal while reminiscing about their life together.

After nearly two hours in the restaurant, they left like the loving married couple they had been for ten years. Malcolm hailed a cab and rode with Sara to the apartment.

"Malcolm, can we both stay at the apartment tonight? Just this once?"

As much as Malcolm longed to hold Sara again, he couldn't forget the deep hurt that she had caused in his life.

She waited patiently for his answer. "Perhaps if we just stayed in separate rooms," she said in a sultry voice.

"All right, just for tonight. This is no form of reconciliation—it's just for convenience. Driver, west side of 84th Street and West End Avenue."

As the cab dropped them off and they went upstairs, Jerry nudged a dozing Jasper. They were sitting in the taxicab across the street.

"What's the matter? What's wrong?" Jasper asked, coming out of his nap.

"Our lawyer boy is, and he brought home a little piece for the night," Jerry grinned.

"Good. At least we'll know where he is for the night. Now let's take shifts; two hours on, two hours off. I'll go first since I'm already half asleep," Jasper said and fell back to sleep.

CHAPTER 25

Malcolm arrived one hour early for his nine o'clock meeting with Calucci and Rothman. Walter was waiting in Malcolm's empty office. He had a worried look on his face.

"Why the strange look on your face, Walter?" Malcolm asked, sitting down at his desk.

"If only Weinstein were here, we could cut these bastards off," Walter said.

"A month's extension to work with some jury consultants on a mock jury, hell, I'm in Louisiana. I don't know what they're thinking down there."

"Then maybe that should be our strategy," Walter said, running his hands through his thinning white hair.

"You know what's funny, Walter? Here in New York, I'm very comfortable in the courtroom. I can almost predict what a jury will do. But in New Orleans, I have no idea what will happen. The politicians won't listen; and some of the church folk won't listen to what I'm telling them. And the ironic thing is, that it is my hometown...you'd think they would embrace me. The only one on my side is my father. That's why I may start over in another city—Atlanta, Chicago, or maybe even Los Angeles," Malcolm said, as he wrote something down on a pad.

Walter walked over to the rose-colored leather chairs in front of Malcolm's desk. "You ever read about Jesus when the people of Nazareth, his hometown, didn't accept him? He was considered a prophet without honor. He had done wondrous works everywhere else, but in the town where he grew up, they would hardly acknowledge him."

"This is great. I've got a Jew quoting to me from the New Testament. Shows what kind of day I'm going to have." Malcolm smiled.

"Just because I'm Jewish doesn't bar me from reading what the Christians believe."

"Well, you must have paid close attention to be able to tell me about Jesus in Nazareth."

"I read about a lot of religions. Now, we want at least another month or so before you're back in New York."

"Another month? Yes. Whether I'll be back in New York after that, I can't say, Walter." Malcolm glanced at the picture of Reuben Caulfield lying on his desk.

"Another client?" Walter asked.

"Ah, no. More like an informant, I think. Well, I'll know later today. Let's go, Walter."

They left Malcolm's office, and took the elevator to the fifty-fifth floor, where Rothman and Calucci were waiting in the conference room like the Gestapo waiting to pass sentence. Malcolm and Walter sat across from them.

"Good morning. I guess you know why we've called you here, Malcolm. In light of everything that's going on in Louisiana—I'm talking specifically about your father's church being blown up—the negative publicity has had a tremendous effect on the firm. Now I know how strongly you feel about this case. But after careful deliberation, Mr. Calucci and I have decided that it would be better for Clarence Reed to find other counsel," Rothman said in a modest attempt to be diplomatic.

"What kind of negative feedback have you been receiving? Have we lost any clients?" Walter asked.

"No, not yet, but we fear we will, once the actual trial begins," Rothman replied.

"Have you ever considered that the man is innocent?" Malcolm inquired.

"Look, we don't want to be known as the firm that defended a terrorist," Rothman snapped.

"Malcolm, you've been with us for nearly eleven years," Calucci interjected. "You're an excellent lawyer, and I understand your passion for this case. But we feel that you would be better suited working here in New York on a case sanctioned by the firm."

"Don't hand me that condescending BS. You don't like a black lawyer representing a black man at the firm's expense. This is not the first time you've pulled this, but it's all right if I represent someone like Giamanco—a well-known underworld kingpin. That doesn't hurt the firm's reputation."

"Only you have brought race into the discussion," Calucci said calmly.

"What's the difference between a man accused of bombing a riverboat, and a widely-known mafia boss suspected of dumping many bodies into the Hudson River?" Malcolm said, leaning over on the table.

Calucci and Rothman were trying to keep their composure. Walter whispered in Malcolm's ear to think about the month's time he'd need, and to take it easy.

"Okay, so when does this party end?" Malcolm asked, calmly.

"We'll give you one month to find new counsel. We'll try to intercede with the court in delaying the trial while Reed's new counsel takes over," Rothman said.

"What about money? I need at least one hundred thousand to clean up matters," Malcolm said.

"One hundred thousand? For what?" Rothman almost choked.

"I have to pay the people working for me down there: the forensic specialist, bomb experts, and the legal aids. The list goes on and on," Malcolm said.

Against the wishes of Rothman, Calucci nodded his head in approval and gently shoved a three-inch file over to Malcolm.

"What's this?" Malcolm asked, slowly opening the file.

"Your next case. Look it over in your spare time, and be prepared when you return in a month," Calucci said with a sneer.

Malcolm almost shoved the case right back at Calucci, when Walter interceded by grabbing the folder. "Will there be anything else, gentlemen?" Walter asked, as he nudged Malcolm to leave.

"One month, Malcolm, and I expect to see you here, ready to work on Giamanco. He's one of our revered clients," Calucci said. Malcolm said nothing, but glared angrily at Calucci and Rothman.

Malcolm stopped just short of the door, and then slowly turned around with a funny smirk on his face. "Is this one of those family things, Mr. Calucci?

"What exactly do you mean?" Calucci sneered back at Malcolm.

"It just seems strange to me that you used the word revered when you mentioned Giamanco. I thought it was just one of those last names ending in a vowel type thing."

Malcolm walked furiously toward the elevator. Walter knew that he was upset by the outcome of the meeting.

"Walter, you're a good friend, but I'm telling you, there's no way I'm coming back here to work for those two jerks. It's time to go. There are no more reasonable people here making proper decisions."

"Malcolm, I want you to know that whatever you decide—whether you're here or not, I support you. I'm a partner, but I don't swing most of the weight around here. However, there's more than one way to skin a cat," Walter said, as the elevator doors opened.

"Walter, I've taken most of my things out of my office. When I call you, just send the rest to me in New Orleans."

"Here, maybe you should take this Giamanco file with you."

"For what? I don't need it. Wait a minute…this just might come in handy. After all, I'm still employed, at least for the next thirty days." Malcolm took the file, and hugged Walter for all his help. "Come down in October and see the trial. I'll make sure you get a court-side seat."

"Maybe I'll just do that. I haven't been to New Orleans in twenty years. Yeah, I'll even bring the Mrs. She would enjoy some light gumbo. Think they prepare it that way?" Walter asked innocently.

"Why not? Take care of yourself, Walter."

Waiting outside the firm's building on busy Fifth Avenue, two FBI agents still watched Malcolm's activities.

Malcolm put down his convertible top on the 1969 restored Mercedes 250 SL and drove to his next appointment downtown at a restaurant in Little Italy. Actually, there was a caravan headed for Little Italy: Malcolm was in the Benz, the FBI in their Ford Taurus, and Jasper and Jerry in the yellow cab.

* * * *

Henri Joret was having lunch with a Louisiana women's organization at the Holiday Inn in Lafayette. Henri was dazzling the women, when Sandchester politely excused Henri from his supporters.

"What the hell is so important that it couldn't wait?" Henri barked.

Sandchester led Henri to an isolated balcony.

"Last night, in the Desire housing project, two of my men were killed." Sandchester looked around making sure that no one overheard him.

"I'm sorry to hear that, but that's no excuse to interrupt me. Make the necessary arrangements, and send my condolences to their families," Henri said, sarcastically.

"No, Henri. That's not it. Before they were killed they reported to me that they'd found Suzanne."

"Suzanne? Oh, my God! She's alive! But how did they find her?"

"I had been watching her friend who works with her at the news station. Well, bingo! Suzanne shows up with two black guys driving her green BMW. That was the last thing they reported before they were killed, I presume, by the two black men."

"Why was she with two black men? Damn, wasn't it bad enough she was going out with that nigger, Reed? Must surely be something in her blood—she's not of my lineage, you know."

"It gets better. The cops normally go into the Desire housing projects looking for criminals. So, after shaking down some thugs, the cops find out that a white woman was staying at the apartment of a Dexter Holland."

"Dexter Holland? Have the police found him?"

"No, not yet, but it won't be long."

"I assumed that Suzanne had been kidnapped all this time…but by whom and why?" asked the puzzled Joret.

"Think about this logically, Henri. There could only be two reasons. One, she was being held for ransom, but no one was ever contacted for money. Or, two, our friend Monet knows something about Suzanne."

"What the hell do you mean 'knows something about Suzanne?'" Henri asked. "What's going on in that devious little mind of yours?"

"That's it. How I could I have been so stupid?" Sandchester smacked himself in the head.

"Damn it, man, what are you talking about?" Henri yelled so loud it got the attention of the fundraisers inside the ballroom.

"Suppose—and this is purely conjecture on my part—that your brilliant little investigative reporter stepdaughter somehow put you and Monet together, and Monet found out about it. And suppose he was holding her hostage, for God knows what, to use against us."

"Why in tarnation would Jean Claude do something like that? He has a vested interest in this deal."

"What if something went wrong? He wanted some sort of guarantee. What if he wanted more than what we agreed upon, more control, more money…"

"How do you explain the two black guys?"

"I haven't figured out that part yet, but we need to contact Superintendent Waller, and have him keep us informed minute by minute. Henri, Suzanne must know something about you and Monet—and even worse, the bombing. She could hinder the entire run for governor."

"Let me tell you something, my little friend. You better hope she doesn't, or the gators will be chopping on your bone marrow for a healthy meal. Find her and find her now!" Henri ordered, as he scurried off to his patiently waiting participants of the fundraiser.

* * * *

Malcolm arrived fifteen minutes early for his eleven o'clock appointment at Sabino's Restaurant. The FBI used telephoto lenses to photograph him entering the restaurant. There were no patrons in the restaurant yet, and he had to wait twenty minutes for Giuseppe Martini.

The old man was seventy-five years old. He wore thick, black framed glasses. He had large and strong hands that revealed he'd done manual labor in his youth. His thinning white hair was neatly combed back on both sides. When he smiled, he showed expensive dentures. He was an elegantly aging man.

Malcolm slowly walked toward the back where four big bodyguards stood around the small old man. Two slowly walked toward Malcolm with their hands inside their jackets, no doubt waiting for any false move. One man with greased, black hair, and a weightlifter's body, spoke to Malcolm. "You hold it right there. Who are you, and what's your business?" he asked, as his partner frisked Malcolm.

Not letting on that he was nervous, Malcolm answered. "I'm Malcolm Stinson. I realize I'm a little early, but I do have an appointment with Mr. Martini."

"Who set this appointment up?" asked the bodyguard.

"Frankie Sabino."

"Come over here so I can see you better. Have a seat. Stinson, right?" Mr. Martini questioned, smoking a big Havana cigar. "Would you like a cup of cappuccino?"

"Sure," Malcolm replied, as the old man's goons surrounded the table. "Bring the lawyer a cup. And back off. I don't believe Mr. Stinson means me any harm. So, Mr. Stinson, how's that brat of a nephew of mine?" Martini asked, blowing cigar smoke into the air.

"As far as I can tell, he's doing fine. Staying out trouble, at least."

"Good. My sister has aged twenty years over that little punk. But he treats her good now, so I agreed to do him a favor by meeting you. So shoot. You've got five minutes," Martini said, looking over his thick, black glasses.

The waiter brought Malcolm the cappuccino. Martini examined Malcolm as he sat with his legs crossed; his four goons were just two feet behind the table sitting in a semi-circle around him. Just as Malcolm was about to speak, another man, dressed all in black, walked briskly up to Martini and whispered something into his ear. As the man spoke, Martini slowly turned his head toward Malcolm, bearing a grim look. He stared at Malcolm for a moment. Malcolm felt his palms begin to sweat. No one knew he was meeting with the head of a New York crime family. The man seemed irate with him for no reason.

"Is something wrong?" Malcolm asked, gently.

"Do you have a habit of bringing the FBI with you?" Martini asked, coolly.

"I can assure you that I'm not working with the FBI. They were even following me in New Orleans. I didn't think they were going to follow me here," Malcolm said, turning around looking at the front door.

"Good boy. You're honest—I like that. I knew they'd been trailing you in New Orleans. Don't worry about it. They come around every once in a while to get pictures for their scrapbooks. They can't touch me. So, now you've got three minutes," Martini said, signaling for his toast to be served.

Malcolm leaned his right arm on the table. All eyes followed his every movement. "Mr. Martini, as you may know, I am representing Clarence Reed who's accused of bombing the gambling riverboat in New Orleans. I believe he's innocent and that he's been framed. I'm here to simply ask if there's a war going on among any families," Malcolm said, stirring his coffee with the spoon in his cup.

Martini bit a piece of his whole wheat toast with grape jelly, took a sip of his cappuccino, picked up his napkin, and gently dabbed the corners of his mouth.

"If there is a so-called war, as you say, what makes you think that I would tell you?" Martini stood up using the cane that was leaning on his chair. "I should throw you out on your ass just for asking me that question." Martini stood next to Malcolm and spoke without looking at him. "But if I told you that there is no war, who would be your next suspect?"

"Ahh, I don't quite know, but in all probability a hate group—the Klan, Neo-Nazis, Aryan Nation, those sorts."

Martini put his hand on Malcolm's shoulder. "I'm an old man, Mr. Stinson, and through the years I have ordered justice for injustices done. You know, Louisiana is a tough place. Marcello ran that place with an ironclad hand. He dies, and a few years later, bombs are going off, destroying hardworking people's property," Martini said, turning to look down at Malcolm. "I must be getting weak in my old age. There is no war going on, Mr. Stinson. So we must find out who did this hideous crime. You got any leads yet?"

"I'm working on some, but the process is very slow."

"Hmm, you know Arty Luppino?"

"No, but I've heard of him."

"When you go back to Louisiana, see Arty and Victor Zano. You know Zano, don't you?"

"I met Mr. Zano once."

"They'll give you all the help you need. On one condition…I want to know everything before the police or the FBI know. I'll take care of these hate group motherfu…"

"No offense, Mr. Martini, but if I find out who these people are, I may need to have them arrested in order to free my client. Inspector Tulle is going to be a hard nut to crack; convincing him that someone other than Clarence Reed committed the bombing is going to be tough. This is going to be more than proving a case beyond a reasonable doubt."

"That's not my problem, Mr. Stinson. Tulle, you say, hmmm. You see, we both have a common enemy. When you know something, I want to know it five minutes later," Martini said, then looked at his watch. "You've had more than your five minutes. Have a good day, Mr. Stinson. The boys here will show you out."

"Mr. Martini, this puts me in a very precarious position."

"I know. It should make you work more proficiently."

Malcolm got up from the table without finishing his cappuccino. Two bodyguards led Malcolm to the front door. As the door was being opened, Martini shouted, "Listen, one other thing, don't concern yourself about representing Giamanco."

"I never intended to represent him."

"Very good." Martini turned to walk into a back room of the restaurant. "Oh, and one more thing, I almost forgot. You should keep an eye on that China doll working for you. I have reason to believe that she doesn't have your best interests at heart."

Malcolm walked out into the bright, midday light, mumbling to himself about Lucy, the China doll working for him. He wished he'd asked Martini exactly what he had meant by that statement.

Riding up Mott Street in Chinatown, Malcolm checked his rearview mirror. He couldn't spot the feds, so he drove to Lolita's Restaurant on Church Street in Soho. Since he had over ninety minutes before his meeting with Caulfield, he called Pete Neil in Louisiana on his cellular phone.

"Hello?" Pete answered cheerfully.

"Pete, where are you?"

"I'm at the professor's house going through some pictures, trying to find a match for our sketch. Why? Where are you?"

"Forget that for now. Listen, I want you to follow my assistant legal counsel. Don't ask me why yet, but just for today, keep a tail on her. See who she talks to and if she meets with anyone."

"Is the pretty lady a problem for you?" Pete inquired.

"She may be, and then again she may not be. I want to make sure."

"How long?"

"Round the clock. See if you can find out who she has called from her hotel room. I don't think she has a mobile phone."

"You sound serious about this. What happened?"

"Like I said, I don't know yet. But for now, keep an eye on her," Malcolm said.

The waitress came to take Malcolm's order of a house salad and turkey burger. He kept a steady eye out for the FBI. Questions were now running through his mind. How and why would Martini know about Lucy? He tried to remember everything about her coming on the case. He called Walter at the firm, but he wasn't in. Had she been telling the truth about her parents owning a restaurant in Fort Lee, New Jersey? He didn't have the time to drive to Jersey and be back before his meeting with Caulfield.

His food came. He ate it, but didn't really taste it.

His mind was running on all cylinders. What more did Martini know? Why did the mafia have people following him?

He had to lose the FBI before his one o'clock appointment with Reuben Caulfield. Malcolm suddenly felt the anxiety that he'd experienced with Giamanco's son's trial—the mafia threat hanging over his head. Not this time, he thought. Damn the old man. Damn Tulle. Let them come after me this time, I don't care.

* * * *

Suzanne and Kathy made it to Arkansas and the Joret home where Henri had built a barn house on the White River. Suzanne had come here many times with her mother and brothers when they were children, and sometimes, she used it as getaway from her hectic life as a TV journalist. She knew exactly where the key to the house was stored in the garage. Kathy helped her push the old Ford pickup out of the garage, and Suzanne put the green BMW in it.

Other than some cobwebs, the house was exactly how she'd left it last spring when she and Clarence had used it for a weekend. The house had a burglar alarm and guns. After unlocking the rifle cabinet, Suzanne pulled out two hand guns and a shotgun. While she cleaned the guns, Kathy was in the kitchen looking for canned goods.

"Suzy, there's really not much of a selection here. We need to go to a store. And how long do you plan on being here?" Kathy asked.

"There is a store about ten miles from here. You'll have to drive there," Suzanne said, cleaning out the barrel of the shotgun.

"Not me. I don't know anything about this part of Arkansas. And what would you do?"

"I don't want to be seen just yet. Kathy, I don't know if this guy, Jasper, and the Dalton brothers kidnapped me on their own, or if it was ordered by somebody else. Either way, if somebody thinks that I know something, they'll want me dead and out of the way."

"Why don't we just go to the police and let them sort it out?" Kathy asked.

"The police are the last people I trust. Don't you remember when Jim Dalton told me that a police department higher-up is the one who set Clarence up with the FBI? And besides, I don't know how Henri is involved. For all I know, he may have ordered the kidnapping."

"My God, Suzy, he's your stepfather. Why in the world would he do something like that?"

"Because he wants to be the governor of Louisiana, and the President of the United States. I know his track record, and nothing is beneath him. I know if he was involved in my kidnapping and my mother found out about it, she'd blow his brains out."

"Suzy, why do you say that?"

"Although my mother may have some love for Henri, she always knew that he resented me. But in his political climb to the top, he needed my mother's family and money to advance his career—it was a marriage of convenience."

"How convenient could it be if your mother had three more children?"

"Right! All boys, just like him. Many times my mother argued with him about how he treated me differently from his sons. And besides, he's a racist."

"Can't be too much of a racist if he has Campy Frazier as a running mate."

"Don't let that fool you, honey. I'm quite sure he has plans to dump Campy somewhere down the line. I can't tell you how many times the Ku Klux Klan leaders would meet with him when he was running for Congress and the Senate. Little secret meetings when my mother was at social gatherings.

"There were always rumors about that, but no one in the press could ever prove it," Kathy said.

"Oh, they are true, all right. I couldn't wait to get out of that house. Why do you think I went to college in New York City? I hated leaving Mama, but she always had a grand time shopping in New York. You find anything to eat?"

"Some pineapples in a can. There's some tuna here, too. We should be all right for tonight. So what's our next move?" Kathy inquired, searching for a can opener.

"Why do you think those men were stalking your apartment?" Suzanne questioned.

"I haven't the foggiest idea. But they must have been watching me for a while, those dirty bastards."

"The police wouldn't stake out your place that long. Someone else had to do it on the long term."

"Who?"

Suzanne gazed out the window and watched the river as it reflected the noonday sun. "Jim Dalton talked about working for a man in Montreal. So, let's suppose that our friend Monet suspected I had heard something that day he called Henri..."

"...then he ordered you to be kidnapped, which means your stepfather knows about it," Kathy said.

"Yes and no. I mean Monet could have done this. Henri is smart, but my mother is smarter. She would have gotten that information out of him a long time ago, and fed him to the gators. No. Monet, or maybe someone else that works for Henri—someone close."

"You always told me the closest people to your father were your brothers and Sandchester."

"Bingo! Good thinking. I've got to figure out how to approach him. And I need to contact Clarence's lawyer. What do you know about him?"

"Just what I've read and seen on television. He seems very capable, and the D.A.'s office sure isn't taking him lightly."

"Can he be trusted? Can I trust him?"

"You know his father, Reverend Josiah Stinson."

"That's good, I guess. The reverend is a good man. May I have some of that pineapple? You know, Kathy, we could go down to the river and catch some fish."

"I didn't know you were such an outdoorsy-type person."

"It's called survival. I need to figure out what to say to Sandchester. And I need to meet with Malcolm Stinson, but how? And I want to talk to Mama. Let's go," Suzanne said, as she loaded a .38 caliber pistol. She offered a .22 pistol to Kathy, but she refused to take it.

Near the waterfront in the mud, they found some worms. They sat on the pier with their bare feet dangling over the river for the rest of the afternoon, talking and fishing. For the first time in months, Suzanne felt safe and had a sense of peace.

CHAPTER 26

As Malcolm drove uptown to meet Caulfield, he thought about the portfolio of Caulfield's history as a journalist that Lucy had provided him before he had left for New York. He was an impressive newspaperman who'd faced many dangerous assignments. What kind of incident would scare him so much that he felt he had to duck out of town?

Malcolm remembered that Caulfield's partner had been killed while doing a story on the homeless. What information could Caulfield have to help him prove Reed's innocence? Malcolm hoped this was the break he needed. Malcolm missed his turn off the Henry Hudson Parkway at Tenth Street, so he rode up Hudson Street and turned the corner to 11th Street, driving by the park full of children and their parents. With the exception of a few bums, everything seemed normal—but this was Greenwich Village.

In a bookstore across from the park, the Daltons were browsing through some books, while watching Malcolm park his Mercedes on Perry Street and then walk back to the park. Sitting on a bench wearing a Cincinnati Reds hat, was a clean-shaven Reuben Caulfield. He was reading a newspaper and had another newspaper next to him on the bench. The brothers hadn't noticed when he'd slipped into the park. Malcolm nonchalantly sat next to Reuben.

"Nice day for Memorial Day weekend," Malcolm said.

"Whatever you do, Mr. Stinson, don't look at me when you talk. Pretend that you're asking to look at that paper," Reuben replied, as he kept looking into his paper.

Malcolm picked up the paper. "Be very careful, Mr. Stinson. That is a very special paper. Now slowly hold up the paper and turn to page two."

"If you don't mind my asking, what are you afraid of? You've been in New York all these months, and I assume you haven't had any problems."

"I worked with the Chicago police for five years and mastered the art of a stakeout. What I'm concerned about is if anyone has followed you. Now follow me as I lead you through the pictures. See the picture marked number one? Do you recognize that man?"

"No, can't say that I do." Malcolm studied the picture intently.

"He's the deputy chief of police of the third district in New Orleans."

"So?"

"Notice the other three men?"

"Yes."

"Do any of them look familiar?"

"Maybe this one with the ponytail…"

"Look at photo number two."

"It's a picture of me and my kids on Easter Sunday."

"Correct. Now look at the blown-up photo on the next page."

"Same men as the ones in the photo with Waller." The picture was focusing in Malcolm's mind.

"These men were with Waller the day after the riverboat bombing. I was doing an undercover story on the homeless. In the coffee shop, I overheard Waller tell the man with the ponytail that the feds fell for it—hook, line and sinker. 'They'll arrest that nigger for the bombing in a matter of hours,' he'd said. I left when the man in the ponytail started looking at me. I met my photographer down the street and instructed him to take pictures of this little band of thieves with his telephoto lens. But they noticed and chased us. I escaped. Bob Cummings, the photographer, was killed. He did manage to get several shots. Before we split, he kept the camera and I took the film. These men are following you, Mr. Stinson."

"Why me? I'm just the lawyer," Malcolm said, still studying the photo. "My God! It's him."

"It's who?" Caulfield was watching Jasper and Jerry leave the bookstore and stand on the corner. Caulfield recognized them immediately.

"It's him—the man in the sketch that Clarence Reed's mother said came by the house the night before the bombing, posing as a gas and electric man. The utility company said they had no record of sending anyone to the Reed home that evening."

Hiding behind his sunglasses, Caulfield kept an eye on Jasper and Jerry, and then noticed a car coming down the street. Two cops—at least that's what he thought. They parked on the corner near Jasper and Jerry, who also noticed them and moved down the block to their parked taxicab. Caulfield was thinking of an escape route.

"Hurry now, Mr. Stinson. We haven't much time. Turn to page forty-five in the entertainment section." Malcolm found an answering machine tape attached to the page, and written under it was Suzanne Joret's phone number.

"What's this?" Malcolm asked

"I had some business in Baton Rouge around the first of the year. I made a call to Suzanne Joret, who I was supposed to meet at a hotel there…"

"She's Joret's daughter. Do you know her well?"

"Very well. We dated for a while before she started seeing Clarence Reed. But she never showed, so I cut my long hair and beard and dressed like a tourist, and traveled into New Orleans to find out what happened to her. It's not like Suzanne to not keep an appointment, particularly if it's about a story. Who better to investigate the murder of Bob Cummings than Suzanne Joret?"

"Weren't you putting her life in danger?"

"That may be true in hindsight, but then it seemed like the logical thing to do at the time. I went by her apartment, making sure that no one was staking the place, gambling that she'd left her key in the same place from when I was dating her. Sure enough it was there. Nothing seemed out of order in the apartment, but just as I was about to leave, I pushed the playback on her answering machine. A man wanted to meet her in the bayou with information that could lead to the freeing of Clarence Reed. Suzanne probably went, not thinking of her safety, just trying to help Clarence. I assume that whoever's voice was on the phone, is the same one who abducted her…I hope to God she is still alive."

"Well, maybe she is. I mean, no one has come up with a body, so maybe they just kidnapped her. But why?"

"Why? Maybe for the same reasons they want to know your whereabouts."

"Maybe she knows something."

"I know you checked me out before you came here, just as I checked you out. You're an aggressive litigator and quite an investigative lawyer. They think you know more than you should, the same with Suzanne. Mr. Stinson, who else knew you were going to meet me?"

"Let me see…just my assistant. Why?"

"Do you trust her?"

"I've only known her for few months."

"Anyone else know?"

"No, no one else. I've been so busy that the only person who knew I was meeting you was Lucy. Why?"

"Now, don't panic, but the two men in the photo just walked down the street. And I bet those other two men are cops or feds. We need to leave here. Now."

"How can you be sure?"

"Because they've been watching us from that bookstore and from the corner the whole time we've been sitting here. They must have walked down the street when they saw the authorities. Keep that paper with you, and if we get split up, I'll be in touch with you in New Orleans. This is the village, so it's not unusual for two men to walk closely together."

"How close?" Malcolm said, finally looking at Caulfield.

"Please, Mr. Stinson. Our very lives may be at stake here. Let's just walk up Perry Street," Caulfield said.

They walked to Washington Street. Caulfield thought that if they could make it to Washington Square Park they'd have a good chance of losing the feds and Jasper. The FBI agents drove slowly behind Malcolm and Caulfield, and Jasper and Jerry were not far behind.

"Our reporter friend is on to us. Look up ahead. I'll bet he's trying to get to the park. We need to do this now—they could lose us there," Jasper said, checking his gun for ammunition.

"What about the feds?" Jerry asked.

"What's that? A church? A school? We'll do it there. Pull alongside. I'll take the driver and you get the other one. Then quickly move after the reporter and Stinson," Jasper said, as Jerry stopped the car for Jasper to hop in the back.

St. Joseph's Catholic Elementary School was just ahead. It was a one-way street, and the cars were parked on the right-hand side only. The FBI agents were slowly making their way up the left side of the street, leaving room for cars to pass. Jerry sped up alongside the FBI car.

"Excuse me, sir, but which way to Soho?" Jerry asked in his Cajun slang. The agents kept moving, waving Jerry on. Again he asked, "Which way to Soho? I'm lost." He held his gun just below the window level. Jasper had his window open, sizing up the angle for his shot. The agent rolled down the window. "Just head downtown, you can't miss it."

"Now!" Jasper whispered. Jerry shot the driver squarely in the head. The other agent reached for his gun, but Jasper had already fired three shots into the back of his head. Both agents were slumped over as their car, the windows covered with blood, veered onto the sidewalk and hit a small tree.

Malcolm and Caulfield had been walking briskly, about thirty yards in front of the FBI agents. Malcolm turned as the car rammed the tree, glancing quickly from the FBI car to the taxicab. Reuben Caulfield was already running. Malcolm caught up with him at Sixth Avenue, and they ran through the traffic light, even though the light was green.

Jerry was almost sideswiped by a Poland Springs water truck that stopped short of crashing, right in front of Jasper and Jerry. When the truck driver started shouting ethnic expletives, Jasper jumped out and pointed his gun at him, but the truck driver threw his truck in gear and moved on.

Suddenly traffic bottled up at the intersection. Malcolm and Caulfield were nearly at Washington Square Park, when Jerry careened onto the sidewalk, hitting two men.

"There they are, just ahead. We'll get them in the park," Jasper said, as he watched Malcolm and Caulfield jump the three-foot iron fence and make a dash for the other end of the park. Jerry slammed on the brakes and Jasper ran to the fence and started firing. Jerry hopped the fence and pursued them on foot. Jasper zeroed in on Caulfield and, with ever so light a squeeze of the trigger, hit him in the upper right thigh. Caulfield tumbled as blood spurted from his leg. Malcolm was ahead of him, yet stopped to help him. As Malcolm leaned over to pick Caulfield up, another shot ripped into Caulfield. It landed in his right arm. The blood splattered all over Malcolm's face. He turned and, not knowing what to do, started charging toward the barreling Jerry, who had a silly smile on his face and was now taking aim at Malcolm.

Jerry was twenty feet away, with his finger slowly pressing on the trigger, when one, two, three shots rang out, sending Jerry to the ground like a running back being tackled on the football field. In a panic, Jasper searched for the origin of the foreign shots. To Jasper's right, about thirty yards away, was an undercover cop. Jasper didn't return fire because the cop's attention was on Jerry. Jasper ran to the cab and drove off as the cop quickly descended upon Jerry, making sure he was alive.

Jerry was in agony and was lying in a pool of blood. He'd been shot twice in the right rib cage, and once in the leg. The undercover cop still handcuffed him and asked Malcolm if he was all right. Malcolm said he was. The cop pulled out his radio and called for back up, and then he chased after Jasper, who was dodging his way through traffic. He saw no escape and slid out. The rushing cop was taken by surprise when Jasper popped out from the rear end of a car and fired four shots, knocking the officer backwards.

Sirens filled the Saturday afternoon, as Jasper forced open the door of a Volvo station wagon. At the sight of the gun, the driver jumped out, and Jasper sped off.

Twenty seconds later, the police were everywhere. People were pointing in the direction of the Volvo. Malcolm, covered with blood, stayed with the still unconscious Caulfield.

"Get out of here. You don't need this headache," Caulfield said in a faint voice, when he finally came to.

"I can't just leave you here," Malcolm said. The cops were approaching the park, searching for the scene of the crime.

"Damn it, man. Get out of here. Take that paper. Find Suzanne. If they have kidnapped her, that means she knows something. Get to her, Stinson, before it's too late. I'll be fine," Caulfield coughed.

"Okay, I'll find out who did this to you. I'll be back to see you soon," Malcolm said, as he gently laid Caulfield down.

"You'll get them. But you'd better watch your own ass. You were lucky today." Caulfield continued to cough, as his face contorted in pain.

Malcolm made a clean escape from the crowded park while people were still scatting for cover. With blood on his shirt and pants, he threw his shirt in a trash can and held the newspaper in front of his pants to hide the blood. He walked shirtless to the other end of the park, drawing no one's attention, then casually walked over to Eighth Street and flagged a cab. A man dressed only in bloodstained pants caused no alarm to the Greenwich Village cab driver.

* * * *

Jasper drove the car all the way to a parking lot on the West Side Highway and simply walked away. While New York police cars were flying north and south, Jasper casually walked back to Eleventh Street where Malcolm's Mercedes was still parked.

A men's clothing store was on the corner. Jasper was wearing jeans, a red shirt, and a baseball cap with his ponytail hanging out. He bought some white pants, sneakers, and a yellow tee shirt. Then, he bought a pair of scissors from a drug store, went into the restroom of a nearby restaurant, and cut off his hair. No one noticed.

Browsing in the window of another store, he nonchalantly checked on Malcolm's car. He planned to hot-wire it. He had discarded the gun in a sewer opening, but had another one strapped to his leg.

All of a sudden, there was Malcolm, half-dressed, getting out of a cab. Malcolm had the newspaper rolled up in his back pocket. He was walking briskly to his car and searching for his keys. Malcolm got into his car and tossed the newspaper behind the driver's seat. Jasper kneeled down next to Malcolm's car, as though he were tying his shoes, and pointed his gun at the car window.

In a loud whisper, his neck veins bulging, he said, "Open the door, Counselor, or you'll die right here."

Malcolm reluctantly unlocked the door.

"Who are you? What do you want?" Malcolm asked, not yet recognizing him. Jasper climbed into the passenger seat and pointed the gun at Malcolm's ribs.

"Just drive toward Eighth Avenue."

"Look, fellow, I don't have any money. Don't let the car fool you. I borrowed it from someone," Malcolm lied.

"Now, Counselor, we're getting off on the wrong foot on our little journey. I know that this is your car. Lucky for you, I was about to borrow it. Now, no more lies. What was the gist of your conversation with the former Louisiana journalist?" Jasper asked, pointing for him to turn onto Twenty-Third Street.

"What are you talking about?" Malcolm looked into Jasper's face, trying to recognize him.

"My patience is wearing thin. Now, what were you talking about?" Jasper poked the gun further into Malcolm's ribs.

"He was telling me about a friend of his, who's missing in New Orleans."

"Did this friend have a name?"

"Ah, yeah, Suzanne Joret."

"What else about her?"

"Nothing much, other than he was supposed to meet her in New Orleans a few months ago, but she never showed. That was about it."

"You're lying. If you don't want to communicate, we will just pull off onto one of these side streets. What else did you talk about?"

"The upcoming Clarence Reed trial. You know of it?"

"Yes, it's national news. He's the terrorist, right?"

"Then he told me that he thought someone was watching us. He thought that the FBI was tailing me."

"Um, funny he never mentioned me, but then he rarely does." Jasper broke out in laughter.

"I wouldn't know. Where are we going?"

"Penn Station will be just fine," Jasper said, as he noticed all of the police swirling around the streets. "Not a problem. They're not looking for me," Jasper mumbled, as they pulled up in front of Penn Station. "Well, Counselor, you get to see your children again, but next time you may not be so lucky."

Jasper got out of the car, put his gun away, and turned to Malcolm. "Oh, if you tell anyone about what happened today, you're a dead man. I know where you live and I will kill you all. If you're thinking about being a hero right now—I'll kill you, and anyone in the general vicinity. So long, Counselor, until we meet again."

Jasper bought a train ticket to Philadelphia, then took a taxi to the airport, and flew to New Orleans.

* * * *

Malcolm drove to the apartment. When he got there, he saw Sara and the kids playing in their bedroom. "When did they get here?" he asked her.

"Pete flew with them this morning."

He wanted the kids as far away from New York as possible, and as soon as possible. Malcolm was carrying the newspaper that Caulfield had given him.

"What in the world is the matter, Malcolm?" Sara was astounded by his bizarre appearance.

Malcolm walked straight to the bedroom with the children and Sara was right behind him.

"Sara, who's your friend, the one who lives in Amherst, Massachusetts?" Malcolm asked, as he took off the bloody pants. "Could you get me a paper bag, please?"

"Not until you tell me what's going on," Sara demanded, as she pushed the children out of the room. "Let's go, Serena. Daddy has to change his clothes."

"I've seen Daddy change his clothes before." Serena was jumping on the bed.

"Me, too," Joshua said.

"Go into the living room now, and make it pronto!" Malcolm shouted to the children, who immediately left the bedroom. Sara was, however, getting angry and impatient with him.

"Look, there's been a murder, the two FBI agents who were following me. So I need you to go to the phone booth on the corner, call your girlfriend in Massachusetts, and ask her if we can visit her for a few days, just until I sort some things out with the FBI."

"Did you shoot them?" she asked, with her hands covering her mouth.

"No, woman, I just witnessed it, but the man I was meeting was critically wounded. Hell, I hope he's still alive. Sara, please call your friend. I figure we've got maybe a half-hour before the FBI is knocking at the door. Tell the doorman to bring the station wagon up from the garage on the next block. We'll leave through the back alley. Hurry, Sara. We need to leave," Malcolm said, not realizing he was standing naked in front of her. The previous night's missed opportunity flashed through her mind before she was off to call her friend.

Malcolm took a two-minute shower, and put on fresh clothes. He threw the bloody pants, sneakers, and socks into the paper bag. The children sat still as he rushed through the house, but he stopped when he saw their stricken faces.

"Come here, you two," he said, as they hung their heads as if he would punish them. "Daddy's sorry. I was upset about something. Do you forgive me?" When he wrapped his arms around them, they both hugged him.

"Daddy, are we going on a trip?" Joshua asked.

"Yes, we are."

"Mommy, too?" Serena asked, excited.

"That's right, Mommy, too. Now go and get the things you want to take with you," Malcolm said, as the children tore off to the toy chests in their rooms. Sara came rushing back in.

"Well?"

"She said okay. She's seven months pregnant and would enjoy the company."

Malcolm gathered everything he could carry for himself and the kids. They went through a tunnel in the basement that led to the next building. The doorman unlocked the door, and they were on the next block. They loaded the Ford station wagon and were on their way to Massachusetts.

* * * *

Jon Tulle was in District Attorney Ducruet's office reviewing some notes about the case and talking about the jury selection that would take place in three months. Tulle wanted to make sure that every aspect of the trial was covered. It was 4:55 when agent Mitch Benner interrupted the meeting.

"Inspector Tulle, I need to talk to you right away," Benner said, as discreetly as he could.

"Don't you see I'm busy here? Wait outside. I'll be with you in a few minutes," Tulle answered, and turned back to Ducruet, who continued to look at the agent who hadn't moved.

Tulle turned around again. "Is there something in what I said that you don't understand?"

"With all due respect, Inspector, I feel that I must inform you that two of our agents were killed this afternoon while on duty in New York City."

"Not the two agents that were following Stinson?"

"Yes, sir, I'm afraid so."

"Excuse me, Ducruet. I'll talk with you later. Let's go, Benner," Tulle said. He and Benner scurried out of the office.

"Now, I want you to call the airport and have the plane ready for New York. Call the chief there—Inspector Hennessy—and have him meet me at the airport. Also, contact the NYPD and put out an APB on Malcolm Stinson. Have some agents look for him at his firm and his apartment," Tulle said, as he and Benner walked down the steps of the courthouse.

"Inspector Tulle, we have preliminary reports that the NYPD has eyewitnesses that two white men were seen shooting the agents, and are the same two men who were observed shooting another white male, who is in critical condition. A black man was seen assisting the victim. He was also being shot at, but he fled the scene. If the suspected black man was Malcolm Stinson, he didn't do anything, except avoid being shot," Benner said. They hurried to the car.

"I don't care. Arrest him for leaving the scene of a crime," Tulle said. He got in one car and Benner got in another.

Ducruet looked outside the courtroom as Tulle and his men rushed off. He had the telephone in his hand, waiting for Henri Joret to come to the phone.

"Yes, Ducruet, what is it?" Henri asked, vexed by Ducruet's call.

"There is a problem in New York. Two FBI agents were killed and Tulle was just here. I can only assume that he's on his way to New York. I think it would be fair to assume that these two agents were following Malcolm Stinson. Tulle said some cleaning up needs to be done, like right this minute," Ducruet said. Henri hung up the phone without saying a word.

CHAPTER 27

The next day, Pete went to the professor's house, searching for Lucy. When he got there, he spotted the license plate of her rented Ford Taurus. He circled the block further up the street.

It was nearly noon, and the temperature was already in the low-nineties. Most of the neighbors were either in church, or on a Sunday afternoon junket. Pete rolled all of the windows down, and waited to see if Lucy would come out of the professor's house.

The professor gazed at Lucy as she combed her black velvet hair that cascaded half-way down her back. He wanted to cook her breakfast, but she had an appointment that afternoon.

When Lucy strolled into the living room fastening her dress, she noticed the professor's print of Picasso's "The Guitar."

"Why does this painting seem so morbid?" She peered at the painting.

"That one? See how the man holding the guitar is colored blue? Picasso painted it during his four-year depression. Can't I fix you something?" the professor pleaded.

"I'd love for you to, Thomas, but I have some work to do for Mr. Stinson."

"You work too hard. God gave man six days to work, and the seventh to rest...even lawyers." A big smile brightened Lucy's face.

"By the way, did you ever connect a name to that sketch?" she asked.

"As a matter of fact, I did, just minutes before you arrived. My friend ran the picture through NCIC last night. Interesting, who it is—so interesting, that I suspect your boss is going to be very happy," the professor said.

Lucy stopped at the door and walked back to gently kiss the professor on the lips. "So, who is this person? I mean, after all, I'm going to know anyway," she said, pressing her body close to his.

"Yeah, but let me tell him. After all, he wanted me to find out this man's identity," he said, as the blood began rushing through his body again.

"I promise. Just don't tell him that you told me." She put her arms around him. They were standing in the doorway for the entire neighborhood to see, including Pete, who watched them through his binoculars.

A neighbor woman, standing on her front porch, was watching Pete, so he put down the binoculars.

"His name is Jasper Yates, a former captain in the Navy SEALs."

"Navy SEALs? What's that?" she asked.

"It's a special unit for difficult tasks."

"Interesting. Jasper Y-A-T-E-S?"

"Yes," the professor said, leaning in for another kiss. She looked at her watch and rushed off.

"I'll talk to you later," she shouted over her shoulder. As she pulled off, Pete rolled up.

"Pete! Pete!" The professor saw him and hollered. Pete stopped, but kept his eye on Lucy.

"Hey, how's it going, buddy? Where's your boss? I have some good news for him."

"He's in New York. Look, I have to catch up with Lucy. Did she say where she was going?"

"No, just that she had an appointment—something to do with the case. Why?"

"I've got to go. I'll talk to you later..."

"Wait a second. I'll come with you. I just have to close the door."

"All right, hurry!"

Pete screeched down the street, but it took about ten blocks before he caught up to her, but then stayed a safe distance behind Lucy.

"She's a beautiful woman," Pete said. He turned onto Highway 10-South.

"Yes, she is, and intelligent, as well."

"So, have you two have gotten chummy?"

"We're getting to know each other."

"What have you told her?"

"Like what?"

"Anything pertaining to the case. Any information you have found out about the hate groups. How about that sketch—did you get a name yet?"

"I told her about American hate groups and my course at the University. I did tell her the name of the man in the sketch. But she was there when the sketch was drawn, so what's the big deal?"

"What's his name?"

"Jasper Yates. He's a former Captain in the Navy SEALs. When he retired he did missionary work overseas, but he has been suspected of helping different militia groups and hate groups here and abroad. Why? What's the difference?"

"You told her all of that?"

"No, just his name, and that he was a captain in the SEALs. Why are you interrogating me?"

"Because, my friend, we think she's working for the enemy."

"No way, that's preposterous," the professor said. Pete made a quick turn, almost missing the exit. They followed Lucy to a hotel where she boarded a bus, then followed the bus for nearly an hour and a half after it left New Orleans. The bus stopped at an old slave plantation. Lucy was playing the role of a tourist.

Pete parked outside the old plantation gates, and watched a man, dressed in black, park in front of him and run onto the plantation grounds. He was carrying a camera and a bag, and was obviously in a hurry. The man piqued Pete's interest.

There were over a hundred tourists milling around.

"Look, she'll recognize you. So stay here in the car"

"I will not! I'm as curious as you are as to why she's here. Let's go!" the professor said, as he exited the car.

A man, wearing wire frame glasses and sweating profusely, suddenly jumped into the tour and started talking to Lucy.

Out of nowhere, the man in black started taking pictures of Lucy and the stranger.

They walked out into a garden behind the mansion. The man was holding Lucy by the arm, obviously trying to skirt the crowd.

"So, what do you have for me today?" the man asked.

"I'm tired of being your spy, and I want out, now," Lucy demanded.

"We had a deal, Ms. Yee."

"Mr. Hurst, I've done everything you've asked. There is nothing more to tell."

"So, what did you learn from this professor?"

She took a deep breath, and then reluctantly said, "The picture they had made from a sketch came back with a name."

"What is it?"

"Jasper Yates. Some former Navy captain, with the Navy SEALs." Hurst wrote down everything she said.

"Has Mr. Stinson returned from New York?"

"Not that I know of."

"Well, Ms. Yee, your work here is almost done. The firm will withdraw from the case in less than thirty days, and you'll be back in New York for the Fourth of July.

Pete and the professor were standing in a column of hedges and noticed the man in black was eavesdropping on Lucy's conversation from the house. When Lucy and Hurst started back toward the mansion, the man in black followed.

"That's it. Let's go back to the car," Pete said, rushing ahead of the professor.

Pete followed Lucy and Hurst, and the man in black, back to New Orleans. He dropped her off by the car, and then Hurst drove to the Meridian on Canal Street. The man in black also went inside, followed by Pete. Hurst wrote something down and had the desk clerk fax it for him. He went to his room, but, within fifteen minutes, he left the hotel again.

The man in black approached the desk clerk and grabbed him by the collar, and then suddenly let him go. Clearly upset, the clerk, after some conversation, gave the man a key. When the man in black entered the elevator, Pete flashed a badge in front of the clerk and identified himself as an FBI agent.

"I'm Agent Dixon. I couldn't help but observe that man treating you rather rudely. Who is he?" Pete inquired.

"His name is Jack Boutte, pronounced Boo-tay, a former NOPD officer," the clerk said.

"Why former?"

"The brute got caught in an extortion scam a few years ago, and your people busted him. Well, after working as a security guard in Natchez, Mississippi, I hear he's become a private detective for Benny Dubois—another piece of scum."

"What did this guy want?"

"I'd lose my job if I told you."

"You'll lose it if you don't tell me."

The clerk looked around and leaned over to tell Pete. "He wanted to see Hugo Hurst's room. Mr. Hurst is a lawyer from New York. Just bust him and take him away, can't you?"

"Give me a key to the room," Pete demanded, then rode the elevator to the fourth floor. He listened at Hugo Hurst's door and he heard Boutte in the room.

After about five minutes, as Boutte was leaving the room, Pete jumped him. They scuffled for a few minutes, until Pete pinned Boutte face-down on the ground.

"Let's make this short and sweet. What were the Asian girl and Hurst talking about?"

"What's it to you?"

Pete twisted Boutte's arm farther.

"What were they talking about? Make it quick."

"Something about a guy named Jasper Yates."

"And what else?"

"Something about her not having to do this much longer."

"We're almost done, Mr. Private Eye. Why were you in Hurst's room, and who are you working for?" Pete dug his knee into Boutte's back and twisted his arm farther yet.

In pain, he answered faintly, "To see who he faxed a message to in New York. I work for Benny Dubois, and you'll be sorry about this, my friend."

"Okay, who did the fax go to?"

"Someone in Long Island, New York," Boutte said, just before Pete whacked Boutte on the head with his gun and grabbed the film out of his camera. Pete dropped off the key to the clerk, and spotted the professor waiting outside in the car.

"What did you find out?"

"That you'd better start thinking with the head on your shoulders—I don't know who Ms. Lucy Yee is working for, but it's not us."

* * * *

Jasper Yates arrived in New Orleans late Saturday night, then hitchhiked out to the bayou and walked three miles from the main road to the Daltons' shack. But Jim didn't come out to meet him. It wasn't like him. The alligator that had been killed by Willy and Dexter had been dragged back into the water by the other alligators, and Jasper noticed floating debris. Unarmed, because of the plane flight, he dashed up the stairs and dove into the room. Jim was tied up on the bed and stared at Jasper listlessly.

"What the hell happened here?" Jasper shouted. He untied Jim, who slowly stretched his arms.

"Two niggers ambushed me."

"But you're a Navy SEAL! You should be ashamed of yourself, damn it." Jasper released Jim's chain handcuffs and ankle brackets.

"They had guns, Jasper, pointed at my head. If I had tried anything, they would have shot me."

"You would have been better off dead trying. What about the girl?"

"They took her with them."

"That's no surprise, what did they look like?"

"Two African-Americans, but I'd recognize them again if I saw them. What do we do now?"

"I should throw your ass in the river for alligator bait. How could you be so incompetent?" Jasper watched the alligators ripple through the water.

"Where's the cellular phone?" Jasper shouted.

"In that cupboard over there."

"Get it for me." Jasper dialed Sandchester, and the phone rang six times before he answered.

"Mr. Sandchester, Suzanne Joret has been under my protective custody for the last few months. And two days ago she escaped with two Negroes, probably criminals..."

"Why were you holding her hostage?"

"Because she had information that jeopardized the entire operation," Jasper replied.

"You're probably right, but now we have bigger problems—like why the hell did you kill those feds in New York?"

"I'll explain that later. How can you help me recover Ms. Joret?"

"You know, Yates, you have some damn nerve keeping the girl hostage for months, then out of the clear blue sky asking me to help you. But this must be your lucky day. She showed up at a black guy's house in the Desire housing project. His name is Dexter Holland, a short skinny guy with a gold initial D imbedded in his front tooth. The police are looking for him, too. She was there a day or two, and then disappeared. Okay, Jasper, for now we keep this from Henri; he has got enough on his mind. Call me the minute you find Suzanne, and I'll give you instructions on what to do next. Do we understand each other?"

"Ten-four, loud and clear." Jasper hung up. "Jim, do you know where the Desire housing projects are?"

"Yeah, that's the African haven for two bit criminals."

"Let's go. Dexter Holland is our man. And you better not mess up again."

"Where's Jerry?"

"I left him in New York to take care of some things.

* * * *

Malcolm arrived late that night from Boston and took a cab to Pete's hotel, where he sat sipping bourbon in the hotel bar.

"Your New York trip must've been exciting; the FBI have been here twice looking for you."

"Some weirdo shot two FBI agents in cold blood, and then tried to kill me and Reuben Caulfield."

"Caulfield, the newspaper guy?"

"Yeah, how did you know?"

"The lovely Ms. Yee enlightened me. Malcolm, she's up to something that is going to be a problem for you."

"What did you find out?"

"She met a man and told him the man's name in the sketch. She has also given out other information, maybe insignificant information, to this Hurst fellow."

"That's Hugo Hurst? He works for Rothman at the firm. How did she get the name from the professor?"

"A man in love will spill his guts for a woman. But there's more. I took these photos from a private dick named Jack Boutte, who works for Benny Dubois."

"What in the Sam Hill is going on, Pete?"

"That's the tip of the iceberg, my friend. Cephus paid me a visit a couple of hours ago. And the hush word at the police station is that Suzanne Joret..."

"Henri's daughter?"

"...is thought to be alive. She's been held hostage somewhere. But why, and by whom, is the question."

"Because she knows something about the bombing?" Malcolm asked, as he saw two men approaching them.

"Mr. Stinson?" the ruddy-looking man asked.

"Who wants to know?"

"I'm Agent Carlson, FBI. We'd like you to answer some questions at our headquarters."

"About what?"

"You'll find out."

"Unless you're arresting me, I'm not going anywhere."

The agent walked away to use his mobile phone, and then walked back to Malcolm. "Stay around town, Mr. Stinson. We'll talk later," Agent Carlson said, and walked out of the bar.

"What was that all about? I thought we were going to bring him in?" the other agent questioned.

"We have to wait until Tulle gets back from New York. He wants to interrogate Stinson himself," Carlson said. He and the other agent got into the car and drove off.

"So, what do you make of that?" Pete asked.

"I bet they'll be back. What do I do with Lucy?"

"You're the boss."

"You better move out of this hotel. They'll be looking for you, too," Malcolm said, and ordered a cranberry juice with a twist of lime. "Arrange for a meeting with the professor tomorrow."

"And what are you going to do?"

"Talk with David Segal, and set up something with the Southern Poverty Law Center. I'll be along as soon as I dump Ms. Yee. The trial starts in six weeks. We don't have much to go on."

* * * *

It was four-thirty-nine in the morning when the FBI came knocking on the Stinson door. The thunderous banging awakened everyone in the house. Malcolm looked out of the window and saw the government cars.

"Who in the devil is banging on that door like that?" asked Reverend Stinson.

"Now listen to me carefully, Papa Joe. I want you to call Cephus, David Segal, and Pete. Tell them to meet me at the FBI headquarters, or the police station—I don't know which, yet. Okay?" Malcolm said. He scurried down the stairs.

"Where are the children, Malcolm?" Lois asked.

"I left them in New York with Sara," he lied. "They'll be fine. Malcolm opened the door.

"Malcolm Stinson? FBI. We need you to come with us," Agent Carlson said.

Papa Joe did as Malcolm had asked when the two agents grabbed him by the arms and hurried him off to a waiting car.

The FBI took Malcolm to the woods, where ten agents were waiting with Tulle.

"Good morning, Counselor," Tulle said.

"What's this all about, Tulle? Not enough criminals for you to chase?" Malcolm replied.

"Just tell me how you assassinated two of my agents."

"Me? You asinine fool." Malcolm laughed. Tulle felled Malcolm with a hard punch to his right cheekbone.

"So, this is routine FBI interrogation? You forgot one thing, Tulle. I'm an officer of the court and will bust you for this." Malcolm wiped blood from his mouth.

"You're in Louisiana, remember. Now, what the hell happened up there?" Tulle asked. He nodded to Carlson to hit Malcolm in the groin.

"I was walking, shots rang out, and I saw two men dead in the car. I panicked and ran."

"Who was with you?"

"Why?"

"He's in critical condition and we don't know his name," Tulle said, as Carlson threw another punch. Malcolm ducked and threw a left hook that landed Carlson on his butt.

"Know this one thing, Tulle. You better put a twenty-four hour guard on that man."

"Why?"

"He can identify who killed your agents," Malcolm said, catching his breath.

Four cars, one with lights flashing, came speeding toward them on the deserted road.

"What's John Doe's name, Stinson?" Tulle asked again.

"I guarantee he can identify the killers. Didn't you arrest one of them?" Malcolm asked, as Tulle picked Carlson off the ground.

Cephus, Pete, David Segal, and ten other men, all armed, ran down the road. The agents had their guns pulled, and were ready for action.

"Now everybody take it easy. We were just assisting Mr. Stinson here. He felt rather ill, didn't you, Counselor?" Tulle asked.

Cephus made his way through the agents. "You all right?" Cephus asked Malcolm.

"Don't forget what I told you, Tulle. Twenty-four hour protection," Malcolm said.

"And who might you be, son?" Tulle asked Cephus.

"Cephus Pradier, detective homicide, NOPD. And I ain't your damn son."

Tulle waved his men back into their cars, and in an instant, they were gone.

"How did you find me so quickly?" Malcolm asked Cephus, as they walked to the car.

"Your father's neighbor across the street followed the caravan of cars, and called us from a phone booth," Cephus replied.

"Just for starters, Malcolm, we can sue the pants off of the FBI for violating your civil rights. We'll destroy Tulle," David Segal said.

"Maybe, but I might need that bargaining chip later to get something big from Tulle."

CHAPTER 28

Malcolm met the professor and David Segal at a picnic fundraiser for his father's new church. Church folk and politicians from all around the state were there, and a black Zydeco band played while choir groups prepared to sing.

The Reverend Josiah Stinson was the fundraiser's gracious host. Sixty thousand dollars has already been contributed, and that didn't include a ten thousand dollar contribution from a white minister from Shreveport.

Malcolm and the reverend greeted everyone. "Listen, son, I'm going to the National Baptist Convention next week, and I'd like you to spend a day or two there," the reverend said.

"Papa Joe, I'd love to, but there are only five weeks before the trial and I still have a lot to do. Where is it being held?" Malcolm asked, while shaking hands with some hospitality women from the church.

"Memphis. I want to present you to the audience when I speak about this injustice to Clarence Reed. You said we were going to need money, and what better place to make our first pitch for Clarence's defense fund?"

"Let me see how things go next week."

"Okay. Now that your mother ain't around, are you going to tell me why you left the children with their mother whose head ain't wrapped too tight?"

"It's too long a story to tell today, but when I get some things taken care of, they'll be back. They needed to be with their mother for a few weeks. Trust me, Papa Joe, everything is all right. Hey, there's David Segal. I'll talk with you later, Papa Joe." Malcolm met David and his guests—a man and a woman with two children.

"David, how are you? Glad you could come," Malcolm said, as they shook hands.

"Malcolm, this is my wife, Teresa, and my two boys, Kelvin and Andrew. And this is Conrad Hingley. Why don't you two talk, and I'll join my family for some baby back ribs."

"Well," Malcolm said, "I don't know what David has told you, but the basic theme here is S-O-S. My firm has pulled out of the case, citing bad publicity. I have one assistant. She's on her way back from New York, and will be here shortly. So, I'm between a rock and a hard place."

"We've been watching this case. How can I help you?" Hingley asked, with a welcome grin. They talked for two hours.

The reverend walked over with a plate of ribs, potato salad, and corn on the cob.

"Thanks, Papa Joe. This is Conrad Hingley, from the Southern Poverty Law Center. He's agreed to help with the Reed case," Malcolm stated, as Hingley and Reverend Stinson shook hands.

"We just don't know where to set up shop," Malcolm said, grabbing some ribs.

"Let me see," the reverend said, sitting down to engage in the rib festivities. "Deacon Thomas, right down the street, moved out of his house a couple of months ago. I know the realtor, and, as a matter of fact, she's here. I'll talk to her. Surely, we can work out some sort of rental deal."

"We'll also need some electrical work done for computers, and some living accommodations," Malcolm added.

"I've got church members who are electricians. They'll be happy to donate some time to work on the house. How many people are we talking about here?" Papa Joe mumbled, with a mouthful of ribs.

"Papa Joe, can you eat this food? I thought Mama said you needed to stay away from pork and beef," Malcolm said, looking around for his mother.

"Mind your business, boy. That's why they make Pepto Bismol. Now you were saying, Mr. Hingley. How many folks have you got coming?"

"I believe five law clerks and three lawyers."

Malcolm took a deep breath. "Maybe the good Lord is shining his face down on me, for a change."

"I've told you that the Word says that He would never leave or forsake you." The reverend watched a deacon approach them with a white man.

"Excuse me, Reverend, but this gentleman is from the Henri Joret campaign," the deacon said.

"Reverend Stinson, on behalf of Henri Joret, who is at a political fundraiser in Lafayette today, please accept this check for twenty-five thousand dollars toward the rebuilding of your church."

"What's your name?"

"Allen McAllister."

"Um, let me wipe my hands."

"Mr. McAllister, you tell Mr. Joret, thank you very much for his contribution." The reverend studied the check and put it in his pocket.

"You're going to accept a check from that scoundrel?" Malcolm questioned, discontentedly.

"Son, you really need to read your Bible more. Forgive him. Mr. Hingley, this is rather embarrassing—the son of a preacher-man not knowing the ways of the Lord. The Word says that the wealth of the wicked is laid up for the righteous. Hallelujah! And we'll take it to build up God's house again. Thank you, Jesus."

The reverend nudged Malcolm and pointed in Roberta's direction.

When Malcolm approached Roberta, he saw something different. She appeared to have had a make-over.

"So, you've been busy?" Roberta asked, in her sultry voice. "I haven't heard from you in a while."

"You know...the case and all. And yourself?"

"Busy at the hospital. Why are you looking at me like that?"

"You seem to have changed."

"Just my hairstyle...and a little different makeup."

"Trying to pick up some man?"

"Well, I was told that a lawyer would be attending this fundraiser." She grinned at Malcolm, as she looked around him.

"Seeing that he's not here, will I do?"

"Did you spend some time with your wife?"

"My ex-wife. And yes, Sara and I went to the opera and talked about the kids."

"Was she as happy to see you as I am?" Roberta questioned, as she and Malcolm started to walk.

"It was just dinner, the opera, and talk."

"About...reconciliation?"

"You're just full of questions today." Malcolm walked her into a wooded area out of sight to hold her in his arms, and feel her sultry lips upon his.

"I'm not married to her anymore, and I'm making no attempt at reconciliation, and if she has plans for that...well, she had her chance. I'm interested in a woman who may or may not be interested in me. And that's all I need to know about my love life," Malcolm said, whispering in Roberta's ear.

They heard Reverend Stinson calling Malcolm's name, but held each other for another five minutes, before walking back, hand in hand like new lovers.

* * * *

Jasper and Jim Dalton waited for five nights outside the Desire Housing Project, without finding Willy or Dexter. At ten-thirty on Saturday night, Deputy Chief Waller and his driver pulled up to their van.

"Where have you guys been? Joret is looking all over for you," Waller said.

"What the hell does he want?" Jasper sneered.

"Says he needs to have a little chit-chat with you."

"What do you have for me?" Jasper asked.

"That nigger, Dexter, has a cousin in Biloxi, Mississippi. Here's his address—hurry up, and do what you have to do."

Waller backed up as Jim drove off in the direction of Mississippi.

Two hours later, the brothers walked into Dexter's cousin's bar. The black patrons froze and stared at them.

Jasper handed the bartender a one hundred dollar bill and asked him to point out Dexter. He nodded toward the corner where Dexter was whooping it up with two sassy women.

Dexter was drunk. Willy wasn't around.

"Excuse me, are you Dexter Holland?" Jasper asked, politely.

"Who wants to know?" Dexter's eyes were half shut.

"That's him," Jim whispered to Jasper. "I don't see the other one."

"May I sit down?" Jasper again asked politely.

"Take a load off your big ass," Dexter slurred.

"Dexter, could we take care of our business privately?"

"Money? We are going to talk about money?"

"Absolutely."

"Go on, bitches, get out of here. I got business with my friend here."

Even in Dexter's drunken state, he recognized Jim—but said nothing.

"What's on your mind?" Dexter asked.

"I have a gun pointed directly at your family jewels. If you tell me what I want to know, I'll think about letting you live. If not, I'll kill you right here," Jasper threatened, as Jim smiled.

"What you want to know?"

"Where is Suzanne Joret?"

"That bitch! Dumped me and my partner."

"Where did she go?"

"If I tell you, I don't get shit out of the deal. Oh, yeah, you were going to let me live. Boy, don't you know you wouldn't make it out of here alive? Ain't a person in here who don't have a pistol."

"I'll take my chances," Jasper said, pressing the gun against Dexter's family jewels.

"Don't get so jumpy. She mentioned something about going to her parent's summer home in Arkansas."

"That's it?" Jasper asked.

"Do you think that if I knew where this place was, that I would be sitting in this rat hole talking to your dumb asses?" Dexter leaned back and took a deep breath. "So, if you going to shoot, do it, cause I got to take a piss. Excuse me."

"You sit your black ass down until we tell you to leave," Jim said, reaching to push Dexter back in his seat, when he felt a cold gun barrel on his neck.

"If the man says he has to take a piss, he takes a piss. I've been watching you for the last couple of minutes, and it's time for you boys to leave. So look here, Boy Scout, put that pistol right back into its home, and walk out of here alive."

"You tell him, Willy. I got to go piss. Excuse me, dogface. We should have took care of your ass when we had the chance." Dexter got up from the table. Willy had two guns pointed at Jasper and Jim, and some other patrons had put their guns on the table, just in case.

Jasper and Jim walked out of the bar with Willy still pointing his guns at them.

"Thank you for your time, gentlemen. We'll be leaving town now," Jasper said.

Willy walked back in after Jasper and Jim drove off.

"Come on, Dex. Let's get the hell out here. That's enough excitement for one night." Dexter had sobered himself up, a little, by the time they said good-bye to Joe and walked out the front door.

The shots rang out, grazing Dexter and knocking him down. Willy was hit in the shoulder. They scrambled behind cars in front of the bar, and fired at the white van. Jim roared away unharmed, but Willy and Dexter were left bleeding on the ground. A few local boys took them to Doc Axle's, who wasn't a doctor, but he had experience patching up bullet wounds.

When they got back to Dexter's cousin's bar, Joe was still cleaning up the mess from the early morning gunfight.

"Look here, Dex. Take your dumb ass back to New Orleans. I ain't never had a gunfight in here. I'd take that troublemaker with you, too," Joe said.

"Show a little mercy, cousin. We are leaving. Just come to get my things out of the back."

"Don't bother. Your stuff is sitting right there on the end of the bar. And that whore you messing with in New Orleans keeps calling—don't call her because she thinks her phone is tapped, but call this white gal in Arkansas, pronto. There's the number. Now get to steppin'," Joe said.

Willy and Dexter stopped at the first phone booth they could find and called Suzanne collect.

"Where have you been? I've been trying to reach you for two days," Suzanne asked.

"Let me get this straight," Dexter said. "My partner and me save your life and you ditch us. And you ask where I've been? Well, darling, I better get my reward money, because I done took a bullet for your ass."

"What do you mean?"

"That guy who was holding you hostage, and another weird-looking white guy, showed up here in Mississippi, and shot up my cousin's bar. They hit me and Willy."

"Oh, my God."

"What are you going to do now?"

"I need to meet with Clarence's lawyer, Malcolm Stinson. Can you set it up?"

"When?"

"Wednesday. I'll be in Lafayette for a couple of days before we meet in New Orleans."

"Why not in Lafayette?"

"Because it's my safe haven. I was thinking about something on the trolley car this morning, but we'll talk about it later."

"Hold on a minute. Willy, what's the number for your grandmother in Plaisance? 555-2540. Okay, got that number?"

"Yeah."

"Now listen to me, missy. Last night, when them boys come looking for me, I was a little drunk, and had a little slip of the tongue. I told them you were somewhere in Arkansas. If they can find me in Mississippi, they can find you in Arkansas. They've had enough time to get there, so get the hell out of there now. Hello? Hello?"

Suzanne had already hung up.

*   *   *   *

As Jasper and Jim crawled along the river's edge, the clouds rolled in, and a light rain began to fall. As they trudged through the water, Jasper complained. "If you weren't so incompetent, we wouldn't be wading in waist-high water right now."

"What would you have done if two pistol-toting niggers came sneaking up on you?"

"I would have fought them, guns or no guns." Jasper pulled out his twelve-inch hunting knife.

Jasper grabbed Jim from behind, violently driving his hunting knife up his back. He died instantly.

The rain was falling heavier. Jasper let Jim's body flow down the river. He climbed onto the shore and headed towards the house, and Suzanne.

*   *   *   *

Suzanne had a fully-loaded .38 magnum ready to use, and put a .22 pistol in Kathy's hand. On their way out, they heard a windowpane break downstairs.

Suzanne reached for her gun.

"Hello. I know you're in here, Ms. Joret. Now this might seem like a strange request, but I need you to spend a little more time with me. But no harm will come to you—and this can be as easy or as difficult as you want." He was slowly climbing the stairs, holding his knife in the air.

"Over my dead body, you Nazi bastard," Suzanne shouted.

"Now, is that any way for the future governor's daughter to act?"

Jasper wanted Suzanne alive. He kept his gun in its holster. Suzanne was kneeling behind the couch. Kathy's bladder was about to burst. Jasper hesitated before he turned the corner. "Now, Suzanne, you're being more difficult than your boyfriend, Clarence."

"How's that, since you tricked him into helping with the bombing?"

"Actually, it was rather simple. I posed as a businessman who needed three divers for a job. Your boy volunteered, for a small fee."

"I can't believe Clarence would volunteer to kill innocent people."

"No, he didn't. We were miles away from the riverboat. I had his two pals terminated and rendered him unconscious. Then, I conveniently moved him to a strategic spot, where he would be arrested," Jasper said, while checking his gun.

"So, how many of you were there?" Suzanne inquired, keeping an eye on the stairs, waiting for Jasper to come to the top of the stairs. She waved for Kathy to head for the window.

"It was normal Navy SEAL routine; seek and destroy. Five men with scuba gear were in place in the Mississippi River. It's very hard to detect anyone at night there. We placed the C-4 explosives on the boat. I picked my men up and they flew back to the bayou undetected. It was a perfect mission. And your lover got hooked for the crime," Jasper said, slowly peeking around the corner. Suzanne took aim and shot.

"You seem to be able to handle that weapon very well; now why don't you put down it down and bring those luscious lips over here."

"Why would I do that? According to Jerry, my lips are not the kind you like. What I would pay to sit around a campfire with your Klan buddies, telling them about your love life, you terrorist fag."

Jasper became angry and came around the corner firing. He hit Suzanne, once in the right arm, then again in the left leg.

"Suzanne!" Kathy screamed.

"One last question…who do you work for?"

"Ask your daddy," Jasper said.

Jasper fell backwards when the bullets hit him. Jasper tumbled back down the stairs, in agony. Suzanne slapped Kathy, who was still screaming out of control. They climbed out an upstairs window onto the roof and shimmied down the drainpipe. The rain made it slippery, but they both got halfway down the pipe before falling to the ground.

They drove the BMW right into a mud hole. The wheels spun, but the car wouldn't move. While trying to switch gears, Suzanne saw Jasper holding his arm and dragging his leg. He made his way toward them in the pouring rain. The car rocked back and forth, digging deeper into the mud. Jasper was getting closer, and reached for his gun. Suzanne turned the front wheels as she switched into reverse, pulling the car out of the mud.

They were within twenty feet of each other when she sped off. Jasper aimed, hopped toward them, and got a shot off as he tripped over some driftwood. The bullet smashed the back window out. Jasper seethed in the mud as he watched Suzanne escape.

CHAPTER 29

At eight o'clock on Sunday morning, Lucy stood at Sun Reed's front door, feeling guilty about her betrayal of Malcolm and Clarence.

Sun Reed was having breakfast before she went to church in a makeshift tent on the vacant lot where the church once stood. Sun was delighted to have Lucy join her, but knew something was on her mind.

"What troubles you so much, my child, on the day of the Lord?" Sun asked.

"I feel I have been a detriment to your son's defense. So much so, that I hope I don't get disbarred."

"What did you do?" Sun Reed asked.

"Well, my boss in New York ordered me to report all of Malcolm's actions in the handling of your son's case to him."

"That doesn't seem so bad."

"I thought the same thing, but he insisted that I not let Malcolm know about the information I was funneling back to New York."

"Maybe you should talk to Malcolm."

"They promised me thirty thousand dollars extra a year, plus a ten thousand bonus at the year's end. My family is not rich; my parents sacrificed plenty to get me through law school. So if I tell Malcolm what's been going on, he'll kick me off the case, and I may lose my job in New York."

"I'll talk to Mr. Stinson."

* * * *

Malcolm called Sara's girlfriend's number in Massachusetts. Serena answered the phone.

"Hallo? Who dis?"

"Hello, baby. Why are you answering somebody else's phone?"

"Hi, Daddy. Mommy told me to. Where are you?"

"At grandma and grandpa's. Are you and your brother behaving?"

"Yes, I want to talk to Grandma, Daddy."

"You don't miss me? How about talking to me for awhile? Besides Grandma isn't here right now."

Malcolm could hear Sara in the background asking Serena who was on the phone. She yelled out, "Its Daddy."

"Hi, Dad," Joshua said, excited to hear from Malcolm. "You coming to get us?"

"In a few weeks. Don't you want to spend some time with your mother?"

"Yeah, I suppose so…but why can't she come to Louisiana? I'd rather be there."

"We'll see what can be done in a few weeks. I'm involved in a big case, and I don't have time to spend with you and your sister."

"That's all right. We can still play with the kids at church. This place is boring, Dad, just a lot of trees. Besides, Mom has been going out at night, anyway."

"Josh, let me speak to your mother."

"Its Daddy, Ma."

"Hello?" Sara said, somewhat irate.

"Hello. How's it going?"

"The kids are stressing me out a little. You know, Malcolm, you've been too easy with them. They act wild, and resent it when I tell them something."

"I wonder why."

"Don't start, Malcolm. I'd like to take them to my parents in Connecticut."

"Hold on a minute, Sara. There's another call."

"Hello?"

"This here is Malcolm Stinson, attorney at law? I got a message for you from a lady named Suzanne Joret."

"Look, I have someone on the other line. Hold on."

"Sara, I'll call you back in a few minutes. It's an important call."

"Things never change with you, do they? I was just getting ready to give them breakfast. Call back tonight. Bye." She slammed the phone down.

"Sorry. Now, what's this about Suzanne Joret?"

"Meet her on Tuesday morning at ten on the trolley that goes through Carrollton. Come alone. The deal is off if anyone else is with you. Any funny business, and somebody is going to get hurt, and it ain't going to be Suzanne or us. Get my drift, brother?"

"Okay. Carrollton. Ten o'clock. What will she be wearing? How will I recognize her?"

"She'll find you. Catch the trolley in Palm-Air and enjoy the ride. Ten sharp. Don't be late or there is no date." Dexter hung up.

"Well, I'll be…she's alive at least…we'll see…" Malcolm said, out loud to himself.

Malcolm gazed out at the church service going on just up the block from the porch of the new Reed defense headquarters. If all went well, Malcolm and his new colleagues could be up and running within twenty-four hours. There were two weeks until jury selection would begin. Malcolm was starting to see some light in Clarence's defense, but there was still much to do.

Just before the service was over, Malcolm stood with his clipboard, checking off his to-do list. He turned and saw Sun Reed, Lucy, and Professor Hickman walking toward him. Pete came to Malcolm's side as they approached.

"I'll handle this, Pete."

"Let me have fifteen minutes with her. I'll get her to tell me everything, and save you a lot of diplomatic time," Pete said.

"Good afternoon, Mr. Stinson. I've missed the sermon. What did he preach about?" Sun Reed said, looking up at Malcolm through her dark sunglasses.

"I believe our growing faith in God."

"May I speak with you for a moment, Mr. Stinson?" Sun Reed asked. She took Malcolm's arm and walked.

"Ms. Reed, I really need to talk with Miss Yee," Malcolm said, looking back at Pete and trying to keep an eye on Lucy.

"Don't worry. She's not going anywhere. Malcolm, how is my son's case going? You don't mind if I call you Malcolm?"

"No, I don't mind. It's coming along well. We've had a few setbacks, but I'll be ready come trial time. Is something wrong?"

"I had a very interesting talk with Ms. Yee this morning, and she confessed some things to me that seem unethical. Actually they aren't; it's more of a case of loyalty."

"I don't quite understand."

"She'll explain everything to you. Now I know you're my son's lawyer and that's why I've had you investigated. I know that you have a spotless reputation, but you're having some problems with your law firm in New York. If you need any money, please, son, don't hesitate to come to me. I'm not a rich woman, nor am I a poor woman, either." She stopped and took off her glasses, turning her back to the sun. "This is my son, Malcolm, and I pray every day that you won't succumb to these viper politicians here in New Orleans. I hope you'll give your whole-hearted effort to exonerate Clarence."

"We'll free Clarence, Mrs. Reed."

"I would also appreciate your keeping Lucy Yee as co-counsel, even after you have your little conversation. My son stood for the rights of all minorities, black, as well as Asians."

"I understand."

"Do you? I mean, do you really understand that the growing Asian community will also be watching this trial very closely?" Sun Reed stated, and turned towards the tent meeting. They said nothing else, and she left Malcolm when she saw a friend of hers. She winked at Lucy Yee as she walked by.

"Can we talk now, Mr. Stinson?" Lucy said.

"Let's walk to my parents' house."

"I told Mrs. Reed what happened, but I wanted to be the first to tell you." Lucy took her sunglasses off and squinted up at Malcolm.

"What is it?"

"When I was asked to work with you, my job was to assist you, but I was also to report back to the office on your progress."

"And who were you supposed to give this information to?"

"Hugo Hurst."

"Did Rothman put you up to this?"

"Mr. Hurst approached me, and said that as an Asian woman, I could go far in the firm in a hurry. He upped my salary by twenty thousand, and promised another twenty thousand dollar bonus by the end of the year, with a five percent increase for next year. At first, I didn't think anything was unethical."

"So, divine intervention came over you, to give a moral sense of conviction. And more importantly, what exactly did you feed back to Mr. Hurst?" Malcolm listened with rapt attention.

"During my last meeting with Mr. Hurst, I wondered why—if we're working for the same firm—do they need all of this information about the case, like who are our key witnesses and where do they live? How many times have we visited them? Who else is helping in the case? He emphasized that I not mention any of this to you, and to spend even more time with you. They wanted to know about your social life while you were here."

"What have you told them?" Malcolm asked.

"Nothing about your personal life. He knows about Jasper Yates. He knew about your trip to New York to meet Reuben Caulfield."

"Who else knows about Caulfield?"

"No one but Hurst."

"Hmm, that might explain some things." Malcolm wiped the sweat that was forming from the beating sun off of his forehead. "Something's not right about this."

"What?"

"If Rothman was behind this, chances are he'd have you contact him. Hurst is his flunky, but Rothman is a hands-on type person. And you've never had a conversation with him?"

"Not once."

"It couldn't be Calucci, because Hurst would have told Rothman and he would have defied Calucci, and contacted you. Unless…"

"What?"

"How did you transfer the info to Hurst?"

"Telephone, fax, and personal visits.

"Whose side are you on, Lucy?"

"Once I stop feeding information to them, I'll be fired."

"Well, maybe you should leave now—make up some excuse about family problems. I need you to help me throw them off the track, but first, who's getting the information, and what are they doing with it?"

"I'll need a job. You probably don't trust me right now, but I did come to you and tell what was going on."

"I appreciate it, and I need all the help I can get. You can work with the law clerks coming this week from the Southern Poverty Law Center. I assume they know about that?"

"Yes."

"Lucy, if you betray me again I'll do everything I can to have you disbarred, and while I'm working on that, my friend, Cephus, the cop, will find a way to keep you in a Louisiana jail for a while. Are we clear on this?"

"Yes, sir, thank you. I won't let you down."

"For now, keep playing their game, but only feed them the information that I give you. Understand? I want to know the second they contact you, and what they want to know," Malcolm said.

Just then, the professor approached them.

"Counselor, I feel that part of this problem is my fault, too."

"Yeah, you have a big mouth."

"No great injustice has occurred here. So, if we could talk a minute..."

"Everything is straightened out. When you have information about this case, tell me first. I am the defense lawyer. By the way, Lucy, the firm will be pulling out of the case in the next week or so. Get with me tomorrow. We have to find you another place to live...if you don't already have one," Malcolm said, looking at the professor standing next to Lucy.

* * * *

Deputy Chief Waller came to Arkansas to pick up Jasper, and took him to a hotel room in Gretna. A doctor, who did not ask any questions, treated Jasper's wounds. There was no news of Suzanne's whereabouts, but Waller had put out an APB for a fugitive, a bogus murder charge, in Texas. This made the trail fresh and hot.

Henri Joret wanted to see Jasper and Waller, so they came in the dark of night to the meeting. Jasper was brought through the Joret mansion's back door, to the study where Sandchester and Henri Joret waited.

"Monet told me that you were the best. Want something blown up, no traces? Jasper can do it. Want somebody removed from the face of the earth? No problem. Jasper can do it. He follows instructions to the letter. As long as he's paid well, the job gets done. No questions asked. Now look at you. Whoever you're trying to kill seems to be getting the best of you. So, refresh my memory. When did I tell you to go to New York and start shooting everybody up?" Henri's face had turned beet red.

"It couldn't be helped. It was unfinished business, and doing it in New York was a perfect opportunity," Jasper replied.

"Why is that, Mr. Yates?" Sandchester asked.

"Because it could have had ramifications that would later lead back to you and Monet."

"What the hell are you talking about?" Sandchester said.

"I'm tired and wounded..."

"Were you injured in New York?" Henri asked.

"Yeah."

"Looks fresh to me. Anyway, I don't need you around here anymore. Malcolm Stinson knows your name, and it won't be long before the FBI does, too."

Joret pulled out ten thousand dollars and threw the money on the desk close to Jasper.

"There you are, ten grand. Go back to Monet, or wherever the hell you came from."

Jasper gave Henri a crazy look. "Ten thousand? Our agreement was for five hundred thousand until my employment ended, or until the election was over, whichever came first. I have other people to take care of."

"Not my problem—you're lucky you're getting the ten grand," Henri said. Jasper picked up the money, turned, and started to walk toward the door. When he reached the door, Henri said, "Oh, by the way, your unfinished business is still unfinished. That reporter, Caulfield, lived through the ordeal, and now the FBI has him under twenty-four hour guard. Your colleague, Jerry Dalton, is under arrest and is also under twenty-four hour protection. The only unfortunates were the FBI agents that you killed, and the New York City cop that died yesterday. Good-bye, Mr. Yates."

A black Chevy Blazer, with three of Joret's men in it, was waiting to take Jasper back to New Orleans, instead of Waller. Jasper only had an eight-inch hunting knife strapped on his right leg. They took a detour to a less traveled dark road that went through the bayou. Jasper sensed that something was going down, and slowly reached for his knife in his boot. He could hear the two men in the back handling guns, and figured they planned to feed him to the gators. He grabbed the steering wheel, forcing the car to swerve to the other side of the road, and stabbed the driver in the heart. He jumped out before the car careened into a gully beside the road. The two henchmen jumped out—one searched for Jasper, while the other checked the driver.

"He's dead. Let's get the bastard. There's a flashlight in the glove compartment."

Jasper picked up the driver's gun next to him and fired two shots into each of their heads, killing them both.

Jasper pushed the men's bodies into the marsh and drove off into the night. He had friends that the Daltons had introduced him to in New Orleans; Klansmen and military militia. He thought of two things: first, getting the money Joret owed him, and secondly, how he would kill Henri Joret afterwards.

CHAPTER 30

Malcolm's entire operation was being set up like an army on foreign soil, preparing to attack the enemy. People from all over the communities of New Orleans were chipping in to help. All sorts of equipment, computer tables, desks, and chairs were being donated. Food was prepared throughout the day. Cephus had arranged for at least two armed guards to be on duty twenty-four hours a day.

Everyone had been working since the early morning hours. At nine a.m., Malcolm slipped away to meet Suzanne Joret.

* * * *

Willy and Dexter would follow Suzanne through this whole ordeal, and if any trouble arose, they were prepared to protect their interest at any cost, even if meant killing someone. And this time, Suzanne would not escape.

After the New York fiasco, the FBI had ceased tailing Malcolm. Unaware of that, Malcolm carefully watched his back as he boarded the trolley at the Palm-Air Station. When the trolley turned down Carrollton Avenue and stopped in Black Pearl, Willy got on.

Suzanne insisted that Willy and Dexter change into jeans, sneakers, and Xavier University T-shirts, with knapsacks that carried their guns. Except for his Tulane University T-shirt and his matching hat and sunglasses, Malcolm was dressed the same.

When the trolley stopped at Gert Town, near Xavier University, Willy sat down in front of Malcolm and turned toward him. "How you feeling today, brother?"

"Good," Malcolm politely replied, with an air of suspicion.

"Looky here, my man, we about to stop up here at St. Charles Street, just at the bend in the road by the river. You get off there, at the bend in the road by the river, and walk to the Camellia Grill. You hungry?" Willy asked, exposing his capped gold tooth. "I hear they got some mean burgers in there, with some fancy sterling silver and cloth napkins. Ms. Joret is wearing a short blonde wig, cut-off jeans, and a black LSU hat. You can't miss her with them nice legs. Just sit down and chat. Anything happens, I'll be right there," Willy said. He turned around and stood, waiting for the trolley to stop.

Malcolm walked into the grill and saw Suzanne Joret sitting in the corner, drinking a cup of coffee. Dexter sat in the truck outside. Willy opened a book and pretended to be studying.

"Sit down, Mr. Stinson. Long time, no see," Suzanne said. The restaurant was about half full, and they were sitting by themselves at one end of the restaurant.

"So, where have you been all this time? Next to Clarence, you ran a hard second two in the news," Malcolm asked.

"With three crazy racists—Jim and Jerry Dalton, and their leader, Jasper. I don't know his last name. They abducted me six months ago," she whispered.

"How did you escape?"

"That's not important now. What you need to know is that the Dalton brothers, Jasper, and a few other men—how many, I don't know—were responsible for the riverboat bombing."

"You know this for a fact?"

"Absolutely! This all started on Christmas Day when I overheard a conversation between my stepfather, Henri, and a man named Jean Claude Monet, a Montreal mob boss."

They ordered two cheeseburgers with fries and iced tea when the waiter stopped to take their order. She continued her story. "I don't know if Henri is involved."

"Why not tell the police, and get this whole thing over with?"

"Mr. Stinson, I'm a television news reporter—at least I was six months ago. You don't know much about the New Orleans Police Department."

"I've heard some stories."

"Stories! Hitler wished he'd had such a staff—they're the last people I want to reach out to. I'll come back when the time is right. If I did now, I might endanger my mother and Henri. And if Henri is involved, I still may be endangering my mother. She's my primary concern."

"What did you overhear that was so threatening?"

"Just the plans for the bombing, and how they would get rid of the civil rights activists. And very recently, my suspicions were confirmed by the man named Jasper Yates. He tried to kill me, and I don't think he'll stop at just one attempt. He is the one responsible for the bombing and framing Clarence Reed."

She stopped her story as the waiter came back with the food.

"How is Clarence?" she continued, once the waiter left.

"He's managing. I don't know how much more he can take, being in jail. Angola is not a nice place to be. So, why did they hold you hostage instead of just killing you?" Malcolm asked.

"Somebody disobeyed an order. Whenever I pissed off Jim, he'd say they should have killed me, like they were supposed to. I assume they wanted some sort of ransom down the road," she said.

"So, you mean to tell me, that this Jean Claude Monet may have collaborated with Henri to blow up the riverboat by hiring Jasper and these other men?"

Suzanne nodded in agreement.

"But why?"

"To push out the New Orleans mafia, and take over the operation themselves. Do you know how much money is involved?" she asked.

"They'd have to know that other crime families, particularly in New York and Chicago, probably have millions vested in the riverboat casino."

"You've worked with the mafia before?"

"We're not exactly strangers. What do you want me to do for you?"

"So far, everything we've talked about is just a bunch of good theories. Wouldn't you agree that we need some concrete evidence?"

Two white NOPD detectives sat at the counter and glanced at Suzanne and Malcolm.

"Don't look now, but we have company. Let's continue our little chat another time."

"How do I contact you?" Malcolm asked.

"I'll contact you. The fewer people that know where I am, the greater chance I have of living," she said.

Willy peered in to see if everything was all right. Suzanne nodded her head toward the two cops. Willy motioned to Dexter across the street, and Dexter got out of the truck.

The cops were scrutinizing them. One pulled out a photo of Suzanne, with long brown hair, and then the squatty-looking cop walked over to them. Willy raised his arm to Dexter, while still looking into the restaurant. Dexter shot three rapid shots in the air, got back into the truck, and drove off. The cops heard the shots and rushed out into the street. Willy pointed in the direction of some young black kids running and playing, and the detectives took off after them.

Malcolm turned back to Suzanne after hearing the bullets. She was standing and ready to leave.

"There may be some evidence at my parent's house. I'll be in touch," she said.

* * * *

Cephus Pradier drove to the Stinson home, where Malcolm, Pete, and Hingley were reviewing evidence for the upcoming trial.

"Hey, Cephus, come on in," Malcolm said, holding the door open.

"Look, it's almost seven, and I told the missus I'd be home by seven-thirty. I think it would be best if you came out here," Cephus said with a serious look.

"Something happen?" Malcolm asked.

"I checked out what happened in New York. The shooter in New York is from right here in New Orleans."

"Here?"

"Jerry Dalton—lives out in the bayou with his brother, Jim. Both are former Navy SEALs."

"But what's their motive?"

"Don't know. Dalton is a member of the Louisiana Klan. When Waller's men checked out the house per request of the police chief, it was clean."

"No guns, nothing out of the ordinary?"

"But there's more."

They walked over to the chair and couch, and sat down in the cool of the evening.

"Jerry Dalton's brother, Jim, was found dead in the White River in Arkansas last week—less than a quarter mile from Henri Joret's vacation house."

"I haven't the foggiest," Malcolm said, with rapt attention. "Joret has a house in Arkansas?"

"My cousin is a cop over in that district, and he was telling me about some ol' boy from Louisiana they found floating in the river. They investigated all of the houses around the area to see if anyone had noticed anything. The back door of the Joret house was broken into, there were fresh bullets in the wall, and blood was splattered all over. They dusted the place down, and just this morning I was told that they found fingerprints…"

"Belonging to Suzanne Joret," Malcolm interrupted, to Cephus's amazement.

"How did you know?"

"I met with her earlier this afternoon," Malcolm said. Cephus sat back and thwacked his leg.

"So, that's what it was all about."

"What?"

"I heard that two detectives claimed they saw Suzanne Joret with a black man at Camilla's Grill off of Carrollton Avenue. today. There's an APB with Suzanne's description out to all of the NOPD, but they're not calling her by her name. They're saying she's a fugitive. I'll be damned. Waller is behind all this."

"So, what happens now?" Malcolm asked.

"They just keep looking for her. If they matched your face with her today, Waller will send some boys to visit you. If they do, just beep me—put in the word help. I'll go to the mayor. Waller hates the fact that New Orleans has a black mayor."

"Thanks, Cephus."

"Where has she been?"

"Kidnapped by the man you just told me about, and his dead brother."

"Malcolm, it's Walter Baer on the phone," Pete said, coming out on the porch.

"Look, Cephus, I'll fill you in later, and thanks for the info," Malcolm said.

"Hello, Walter. How are you?"

"Fine, son. Have you hired legal representation for Reed yet?"

"I've gotten help from the Southern Poverty Law Center. The NAACP is pissed off because I wouldn't let them in on the case, and there is a lot of pressure from politicians. Other than that, we're making progress. I have to see this through, Walter," Malcolm said.

"Well, if that's your decision. I assume Lucy Yee will be back."

"Someone in the firm has had her spying on me, but I don't think it was Rothman."

"Why not?"

"Because she reported to Hugo Hurst."

"He works for Rothman."

"What she has told me doesn't add up to his way of doing things. I wonder why he would push for me to drop the case if he wanted her reports."

"I'll poke around and see what I can uncover. Hugo Hurst, huh?"

* * * *

That weekend, Malcolm sat on the convention floor surrounded by nearly twenty thousand Baptist preachers, ministers, prophets, apostles, men, and women. It was nearly noon, when the Reverend Josiah Stinson, of New Orleans, was introduced. He led the entire convention hall in prayer, and then he launched into his speech. The reverend came with a prepared speech—much like he did for a sermon at church—which he'd glance at for the first ten minutes, then put away, and let the spirit of God take over.

"My brothers and sisters, I will not waste your time today. I want to talk about something God has put on my heart. America is in a state of turmoil and Satan is winning the war. A few years ago, our white brothers made an apology to the black race for their forefathers' sins, and for the institution of slavery. Now, I come to you today as a follow up to that, for reconciliation among men.

"God's church is not black, white, or any other color. Let me draw your attention to II Corinthians, chapter five. God talks about reconciliation, and we can learn a lesson from this in dealing with different races..."

Malcolm crossed his legs and spread out his arms over the empty chairs on both sides of him. Without asking, a minister, dressed all in black, sat down next to him. Malcolm removed his arm and continued to listen to his father. The minister leaned toward him, with his left arm inside his jacket, then put his arm around Malcolm, and pulled him ever so gently toward him. Malcolm gave him a strange look and started to pull away, when he felt the sharp object poking into his ribs.

"We meet again, my friend. Small world, isn't it?" Jasper said, smiling at Malcolm.

"What the hell do you want?" Malcolm questioned, calmly.

"I just came to warn you. If for any reason my name comes up at the trial, I will kill your elegant father up there, your mother, and your children. Now, I need a little information." Jasper pressed his knife harder.

"Such as?"

"Have you heard from Suzanne Joret?"

"I thought she was dead," Malcolm said, looking around to see if anyone noticed what was going on.

"Keep your eyes focused on me, Counselor. Don't worry. I'll find her."

"Why did you blow up the riverboat?"

"That doesn't concern you. You just defend your client, whom I have no doubt the jury will convict."

"Whoever put you up to this must have paid you well." Perspiration began forming little beads on Malcolm's forehead.

"That's none of your concern."

"The mafia boys don't believe that Clarence did it."

"You don't say?"

"Even if Clarence is convicted, they'll keep looking for you."

"Before they catch up with me, every member of the Stinson clan will be buried six feet under...and that is a promise, Counselor."

"That's why you killed Jim Dalton in Arkansas?"

"My, my, you've been very busy. They say you're a stickler for details—half detective, half lawyer. I suggest you pay more attention to the lawyer aspect—your family's well-being depends on it."

When Malcolm tried to pull away, Jasper tightened his grip. "I can kill you right here in the midst of thousands of people. I'd be out of the building before you fell to the ground. So sit still until I'm finished." Malcolm heard his father introduce him as Clarence Reed's lawyer, and asked for him to stand up. A spotlight searched for Malcolm, who stood up and waved to the audience, moving away from his chair to put more space between him and Jasper. He made a three hundred and sixty degree turn to the crowd, who gave him a modest round of applause.

Jasper was gone. As he raised his arms to the crowd, he felt an acute sharp pain in his side, where there was now a trickle of blood.

* * * *

The following Monday morning, at Malcolm's insistence, church security guards provided twenty-four hour protection to his parents, Roberta, and her daughter. Malcolm risked that Jasper didn't know the location of his children. He told Cephus what happened in Memphis, and two of his fellow officers volunteered to protect the Stinson house, above and beyond the security already provided.

Professor Hickman wanted Malcolm to meet him at the Williams Research Center because he had some important information about Jasper Yates that Malcolm was anxious to learn.

At ten-thirty in the morning, Malcolm passed rows and rows of books on the history and culture of Louisiana, until he found the professor sitting alone, reading.

"Did you have a good trip?" Malcolm asked, sitting down.

The professor leaned forward with his hands clasped and a serious look on his face.

"I visited an old high school buddy of mine. We've kept in touch throughout the years...Captain Winford Collins...he knew a little about Jasper Yates. Twenty years of Navy service; eighteen of it as a SEAL. The SEALs are a special unit within the Navy: the name is an acronym for SEA, AIR and LAND. They are trained killers and authorized terrorists. Captain Collins showed me a training film of Jasper teaching his young recruits." The professor pushed the manila envelope across to Malcolm.

"My friend called Captain Ron Smithers, a white captain investigating hate groups in the Navy, who told us that he personally knew that Jasper recruited young Navy cadets into hate groups. The Navy never could pin anything on Jasper. He said Jasper is an expert with explosives, and that his last mission in the service was Desert Storm. Jasper has trained hate groups in Germany. After he left the service, the only information about Jasper was related to the military missionary work he did in third-world countries. Before Desert Storm, Jasper had been commissioned for several jobs by the CIA."

"Does he live here in Louisiana?" Malcolm asked.

"He supposedly lives somewhere in Idaho. Before he left the service, he took two Navy cadets under his wing—Jim and Jerry Dalton. They live here in New Orleans, and they are also explosives experts. They won Medals of Honor in Desert Storm, and left the service six months after Jasper retired."

"Thanks, professor. The pieces are starting to fall into place now. Anything else?" Malcolm picked up the manila envelope that contained a tape.

"They both warned me that Jasper could kill a person as easily as he could blink an eye. Be careful, was their only advice..."

"Does Lucy know all of this?" Malcolm asked.

"She was very helpful. Look, I can't tell you how to do your job, but can't you give her another chance? She really wants to help you win this case."

"Is that your heart speaking, or your professional opinion?"

"It's the part that understands that people make mistakes. You've made them as a young lawyer, haven't you?"

"I was always watching my back, not trying to stab somebody else's." Malcolm shook the professor's hand.

"If it makes you feel any better, professor, I need all the help I can get. But, if she makes one wrong move, there will be a trial in Louisiana for me, for what I'll do to her."

Chapter 31

Malcolm waited impatiently in front of Angola Prison with another man. Rothman was to bring the release papers from the firm for the Reed Case. A cab pulled up and Hugo Hurst exited it. This was better than he expected.

Hugo instructed the cabdriver to wait. He greeted Malcolm and they went inside to see Clarence. The other man stood six foot eight, two hundred and eighty pounds, and looked as mean as he was big. His name was Cherry Watkins, and he was Clarence's cousin. Cherry told the cabbie to leave, once Malcolm and Hugo had gone inside.

Malcolm had already explained everything to Clarence, who signed the release papers. Malcolm told Clarence that he'd return later in the week, and left with Hugo. When they came out of the prison, Hugo saw that his cab was gone.

"Guess your cabbie had another call. You can ride with us," Malcolm said.

"Did I introduce you to Clarence's cousin? Cherry Watkins, this is Hugo Hurst. He's from the law firm that just dropped Clarence." Hugo cut his eyes at Malcolm for saying that. Cherry took up the entire back seat.

"I wish I could say the pleasure was mine, but your pulling out on my cousin like this don't sit well with me."

"Just business, Mr. Watkins, nothing personal." Hugo looked to Malcolm for help. "Mr. Stinson is also leaving the case."

"Haven't you heard, Hugo? I'm not leaving the case. I'm quitting the firm." Malcolm smiled.

"That's news to me." Hugo's hands started to twitch.

"Since I'm no longer obligated to the firm, let's get right down to it. It has come to Cherry's attention that, from time to time, the firm that sent you here is spying on me. I'm quite sure you'll be happy to tell Cherry the reason for that."

"I am not at liberty to discuss my business with you or Mr. Watkins."

"That's a shame. We were hoping that you would be a little more cooperative than that. Cherry, why don't you tell Hugo that story you were telling me earlier." Malcolm turned onto a dirt road that followed the bayou.

"Back in Louisiana and Florida after the Civil War, white men used to take black men and tie a rope around their chests and hang them six feet over the water. Any alligator that could jump that high would pop out to snap at the black man. When the alligators came flying out of the water, the white hunters shot them.

"They also used that method to obtain information about any crime committed in the area. After they had killed enough gators, and hadn't gotten the information they wanted, they cut the rope and fed the black man to the gators."

Malcolm pulled up to the river, where a rope was hanging from a tree.

"Get out, Hugo," Malcolm said, watching Hugo's face turn pale.

"What do you want? What are you going to do?" Cherry led Hugo by the arm and secured the rope around him, then lifted him up, and released the rope that sent Hugo out over the water. Malcolm assumed that Hugo would tell him what he wanted to know and then they could leave. Standing atop the car, Malcolm shouted out to Hugo, who was hanging over the water about ten feet in the air. In no time, there were five alligators swimming underneath Hugo.

"Now, Hugo, Cherry just wants to know who you passed the information you got from Lucy Yee to."

"I'll lose my job." Hugo never took his eyes off of the alligators swirling underneath him.

"Hugo, my friend, if you tell Cherry what he wants to know, you'll at least have your legs to find another job."

"Why are you doing this to me?"

Suddenly, an alligator flew out of the water and took a swipe at Hugo, who quickly pulled up his legs. The alligator missed by a foot. Malcolm motioned to Cherry to pull him up another foot.

"That was close, Hugo. You were saying the person was…?"

"Alright, I'll tell you—just get me down from here!"

"Tell me now."

First, one gator, then another, jumped, barely missing Hugo's dangling legs.

"Weinstein, damn it. Now, let me down!"

"It wasn't Calucci or Rothman?"

"They know nothing about it. If they had, they wouldn't have dropped your client. Weinstein's bad health is why they did it. Now please, get me out of here," Hugo pleaded.

"One more thing. Why does Weinstein want the information?"

"I don't know, Malcolm. Believe me. I'm telling the truth," Hugo said, crying as the alligators swam beneath him.

When they pulled Hugo in, he fainted in Cherry's arms. He put Hugo in the back seat, and they drove back to New Orleans. That's when Malcolm woke Hugo.

"Hugo, wake up. Where are you going?"

"Oh, my God!" His breathing was heavy. "To the airport; I just want to get the hell out of this state!"

"Hugo, don't mention this to Mr. Weinstein yet. Or I might bring Cherry to New York to visit you."

Cherry turned and smiled at Hugo.

* * * *

The Fourth of July was more like Memorial Day than a celebration. In New Orleans, it had been one year since the bombing. Stories that reflected on the bombing were on television, radio, and printed in the newspapers. Their coverage began with pictures of the aftermath of the bombing, but switched to pictures and stories about Clarence Reed.

Malcolm and his crew were hard at work on this holiday, although Reverend Stinson planned a small barbecue for them in his backyard. The Stinson home was nearly a police state, and every security man had pictures of Jasper Yates.

It was a little after four in the afternoon when Cephus brought his family over. As he sat down with a plate of ribs, he handed a manila envelope to Malcolm.

"What's this?" Malcolm asked, cleaning his hands with a wet towel.

"Some interesting photos."

"My God! Who is this?" Malcolm looked at a grotesque picture of a naked man with knife marks on his back. His right ear was missing.

"It's Jim Dalton. You may need that if you talk with Jerry Dalton."

"Yeah. It's definitely convincing."

"Something else you should know. There are a lot of mafia folk in town. Word is, the feds are in a frenzy—no one knows why."

"Maybe Benny Dubois can tell us."

"All the players are in place; let the games begin."

Malcolm noticed Roberta. This would be their last night together. They laughed and joked late into the evening. Malcolm spent the night, while two bodyguards watched over Roberta's house.

* * * *

After three weeks of discovery and preparing witnesses, Malcolm and Hingley walked into the courtroom, accompanied by Lucy Yee, and two Southern Poverty Law Center lawyers. The atrium was already crowded with people.

The courtroom held three hundred and fifty people, and they saw one hundred and sixty prospective jurors on the first day. Ducruet had four jury consultants and was watching all of their facial expressions.

Over the years, Malcolm had become an expert jury consultant. Hingley had also selected juries before. Malcolm and Hingley studied prospective jurors for five days. On Friday, at two in the afternoon, they had their twelve jurors and three alternates. There were seven white, four black, and one Asian. The alternates were one white male and two black females.

The Honorable Martin L. Grunwald was fifty-nine years old, a Democrat, and up for election next year. He wanted one more term before retirement. He was a no-nonsense judge who had put many black criminals away, which didn't sit well with Malcolm.

Judge Grunwald instructed the jury for over half an hour. He expected the trial to last at least two months, hopefully no more than three.

Ducruet had six lawyers at his table, and Malcolm had five. Sandchester and his assistant sat in the back row, behind the media and local observers. Two hundred and fifty-five people filled the courtroom on this Friday. On Monday, the court would be filled to the rafters. Outside the courthouse, all the news networks were reporting from the courthouse steps.

Judge Grunwald said that opening statements would begin at ten on Monday, August third. After the judge dismissed the jury, Ducruet walked over to Malcolm.

"You sure you don't want to take my offer—life imprisonment with no possibility of parole? That way, he at least avoids the death penalty. Think about it. On Monday, there's no turning back." He smiled at Malcolm and offered his hand.

Malcolm took his hand and calmly replied, "Enjoy your weekend, Ducruet. Monday begins a big week for you. Hope your future boss, Henri Joret, still considers you for Attorney General after you lose this case."

Ducruet's smile faded, as Malcolm and his crew left the courtroom.

Reporters bombarded Malcolm and Hingley with questions, and Malcolm refused to answer. Instead, he made a statement.

"Monday, we start the process of exonerating Clarence Reed from the charges against him. Thank you."

Malcolm felt a queasy feeling in his stomach, the same feeling he'd had when he handled his first case out of law school.

* * * *

Malcolm and Pete stood on the front porch of the Stinson home. It was unusually cool for an August night. Pete pulled out a cigarette and leaned against a post.

"You seem anxious about this case," he said, taking a drag.

"This is new turf, and from what Hingley says about this judge, it's not going to be a picnic. You need to pack up and head for New York."

"What for?"

"One of Hingley's law clerks dug up a profile on Jerry Dalton. He's a pure racist. I've added him as a witness."

"What makes you think that he'll testify for the defense?"

"I'm not a gambling man, but if presented properly, his brother's murder at Jasper's hand should convince him. Let's just hope the old blood-is-thicker-than-water theory will apply here."

"If he confesses, he goes to jail," Pete said, flicking his ashes over the bushes.

"He's going to jail for killing the FBI agents and shooting Reuben Caulfield. He knows that. But the thought of letting Jasper walk free for killing his brother has to stir something inside of him."

"It's worth a try. And if I don't succeed?"

"Then I'll come aggravate the hell out of him."

"How?"

"Maybe a black face, convincing him that both Clarence and Jasper will walk, may push him over the edge."

Pete shrugged his shoulders and went inside.

Malcolm sat up for another two hours, thinking about Sara and the kids. And where was Suzanne Joret? Jasper Yates? What about the jury? He fell asleep on the porch as three security guards stood guard.

CHAPTER 32

The sun was shining brightly on Monday morning, but the humidity was unbearable. It was seventy-eight degrees by nine o'clock.

The media was out in full force, and reporters, sweating profusely, were trying to keep their equipment dry.

Ducruet showed up first, with at least six lawyers. He stopped briefly to say that he would give a statement after the opening statements. Ducruet gave the press the impression that he was a pleasant man, working for the people, just trying to get at the truth, and bring justice for the riverboat bombing. Those closest to him knew that he was arrogant, pretentious, and a generally unlikable character. He was Henri Joret's kind of man, who would do whatever was needed to convict Clarence Reed.

Malcolm, Hingley, Lucy, and two other lawyers, made their way through the television cameras. "Good Morning America," "The Today Show," and several other morning shows picked up live coverage of the lawyers entering the courthouse. The court proceedings would be presented on television with a thirty-minute tape delay.

Judge Grunwald couldn't guarantee all the victims' families seats in the courtroom. Fifty television monitors were placed in another courtroom for the overflow. The judge allowed only sixty members of the media—television, radio, and newsprint—so a lottery would be taken for a week at a time to determine who sat in the courtroom to cover the trial.

When Judge Grunwald entered the courtroom, the voice of the court clerk rang out.

"All rise. The Superior Court for the Parish of Orleans is now in session, the Honorable Martin L. Grunwald, judge presiding. God save the United States and this honorable court. The People of Louisiana vs. Clarence Reed."

The judge called Malcolm and Ducruet to the sidebar for a few words on procedure, and then ordered the bailiff to bring in the jury. After he gave them more instructions, he turned to Ducruet for his opening statement. Ducruet glanced down at his notes one last time before he strolled slowly toward the jury.

"Imagine a cool breeze on a warm night, coming off the Mississippi River on the Fourth of July. Folks moving about on the boardwalk could hear the sounds of laughter and slot machines coming from the riverboat…a gambling riverboat that held some one thousand people that night. Out of nowhere came a tremendous boom. Suddenly, it felt like a war zone. Hundreds of innocent lives were lost."

Ducruet stopped for a moment, and then walked toward Clarence, who was sitting next to Malcolm.

"Why? Why would someone commit such a hideous crime? We will show you how it was committed, when it was committed, and why a man, who thought this was a divine intervention in the name of God, committed it. Now don't get me wrong. I'm a church-going Christian man, but sometimes we take the Lord's Good Book into our own hands. This time, an ex-Navy SEAL, a trained government killer, acted on his moral beliefs for what he thought was a menace to society."

Ducruet talked for another forty-five minutes about the evidence and the motive, then ended by mildly slandering Clarence's character. Ducruet thanked them and cut his eyes at Malcolm, as if to challenge him to top that.

The judge looked over his reading glasses and spoke to Malcolm.

"Mr. Stinson, the defense opening?"

"Good morning, ladies and gentlemen. Let me begin by stating that the riverboat bombing was a tragic event for the victims, their families, the state of Louisiana, and our country. The state asked a question—why? And that's the same question I put to you. Why would a Navy SEAL, who was decorated with honors for single-handedly saving the lives of thirty-five soldiers, commit this crime? Did he stop to ask those soldiers whether they believed gambling was morally wrong? Why would a Desert Storm hero commit this crime? While serving his country, he got news that his father had been killed by police officers in New Orleans. He came home with a heavy heart, witnessed the trial, and watched the men, who had assassinated his father, walk free. Then, this young man took up the banner to speak against injustice. Oh yes, you're going to hear that he was arrested fifteen times, not for criminal offenses, but for charges like loitering outside an abortion clinic, or a sweatshop, where people work fourteen hours a day and get paid under minimum wage. They won't tell you about his work helping unwed mothers provide for themselves. They won't tell you about his helping teenagers get off the street and stop committing crimes, or helping them come off drugs. They won't tell you about his protesting injustices, like this one, in courtrooms like this one. No, ladies and gentlemen, there is no motive. The state can't prove that Clarence Reed committed this pernicious crime. Why? The real terrorists are at home enjoying this fiasco on television. By the time this trial is over, you will see that my client couldn't have committed this crime. Thank you, and may God direct you in your verdict."

All of the female jurors smiled at him and the men seemed impressed with his opening.

Malcolm turned to Ducruet and tried hard not to break a small smile at him. Ducruet nodded with approval.

The judge instructed Ducruet to bring his first witness.

"Your Honor," Ducruet said, "The state calls Kevin Dunlap."

The courtroom's rear doors opened and the deputy stood aside so Kevin Dunlap could walk in. He was one of three surviving people on board the riverboat when it exploded. The other two had only been released from the hospital two months earlier and weren't strong enough to come to the trial.

Dunlap, a husband and father of five children, was once a robust forty-five year old man who'd driven tractor-trailer trucks for twenty years. After spending nearly six months in the hospital and in rehabilitation, he walked with a cane. His long-sleeved shirt covered the burn marks. Ducruet had wanted him to wear a short-sleeved shirt, but would wait until the questioning started, before exposing his arms.

Dunlap slowly made his way to the witness box, while the jury looked on in awe. Dunlap made it onto the stand with the help of two deputies. He took a deep breath and adjusted the patch over his right eye. Part of his face had been burned, and he wore a rather cheap looking wig. He waited for Ducruet to start the questioning.

"Sir, would you state your name for the court."

"Kevin Calhoun Dunlap," he said, with a raspy Northern Louisiana accent.

"Mr. Dunlap, before this tragedy, what was your occupation?"

"I drove an eighteen-wheeler for twenty years."

"I know this must be hard for you, and I promise I won't keep you long. I, as well as the court, offer my heartfelt thanks for your testifying here today." Dunlap simply nodded his approval.

"Mr. Dunlap, would you tell the jury where you were on the Fourth of July, last year?"

"My wife and I came to New Orleans from Shreveport to visit her sister's family."

"And exactly what did your day consist of on the Fourth?"

"Well, we had a barbecue and watched the kids play, cut the cud for a while."

"Cut the what?"

"Talked."

"So, what else did you do that day?"

"Well, my brother-in-law Earl suggested that we take a ride down to the riverboat and try our luck on them one-arm bandits. We arrived just before sunset. We seen this black boy preaching about how gambling was wrong. I don't remember his entire speech, but he did mention something about the judgment of God on all those who partake in games of chance."

"If that man is in this courtroom today, could you point him out to the court?"

Dunlap struggled with a shaky arm and pointed at Clarence Reed.

"So, you listened to his speech?"

"We caught the tail end of it—probably fifteen minutes worth. The crowd applauded and we went onto the riverboat," Dunlap said, as the jury smiled at him.

"What happened on the riverboat?"

"I had about one hundred dollars. I didn't want to lose that much, but I did. As a matter of fact, we both ran out of money at the same time. It was a hot night and the air conditioning was a little too much for me. So I walked outside with a beer, and leaned over the railing."

"About what time was this?"

"Oh, I can't recall the exact time, but it must have been near nine."

"Then what?"

"Well, Earl come outside and we both was joking about how I was going home to tell the missus that we didn't have any money to get back to Shreveport. As we leaned over the railing, we seen two boys in the water with them wet suits on."

"Two? And just how far were you from the water?"

"Hell, we were on the first level. One of them divers gave a signal with his arm and the other one came with a raft that had some sort of box in it."

"Didn't this make you suspicious?"

"Heck, no. I just thought they were doing some work on the boat. Wasn't any of my business."

"What else did you see these two men do?"

"Not much. They grabbed the box, deflated the raft, and disappeared underwater."

"Go on."

"We stood there for a while, but never saw them boys come up again. About a half hour later, we got tired of watching the dirty black water, so we turned around, still leaning on the railing, to watch the folks exercising their arms on the bandits." Dunlap's voice started to weaken as he came to the next part of his story. Ducruet delayed it with one more question.

"Did you hear or see the divers clearly?"

"Can't say that I got a clear view of them. Even with all the lights from the boat, it was night and the water was black."

"Tell us what happened next."

"Round about ten, I suppose, we decided that we should leave. We must have taken two steps…and the next thing I remembered was a loud noise, and then I was in the Mississippi River. I never saw Earl again."

When Dunlap started to cry, Ducruet offered his handkerchief. He glanced over at Clarence with a look of accusation.

"No more questions, Your Honor."

Malcolm sat still until Ducruet made his way to his seat—he'd come out of the gate fast and hard. Dunlap was almost an eyewitness, and he had gained the juror's sympathy.

Malcolm would need to be careful not to hurt him in any way. That could turn the jury against him from the start. He thought about not asking any questions at all; the man had suffered enough. What harm had he done? He saw nothing but two men in wet suits that he couldn't identify. The only damaging testimony was the speech Clarence gave about God's judgment on gamblers.

He decided he would only ask him a few questions.

"Your witness, Mr. Stinson," Judge Grunwald said, daring Malcolm to attack Dunlap.

"Good morning, Mr. Dunlap."

"Morning."

"Now, Mr. Dunlap, you just testified that you saw two men in the water that night on the riverboat. How long did you say you were outside?"

"Must have been over an hour, I suppose."

"And isn't it true that you and your brother-in-law, Earl, were drinking beer while standing out on the deck?"

"Yep."

"How many do you think you put away that night?" Malcolm said, with a slight grin.

"Hell, I can't remember back that far. Shucks, we'd downed quite a few before we even got to the riverboat."

"So, you would say that you weren't feeling any pain?"

"Objection, Your Honor. He's attempting to put words in the witness's mouth," Ducruet stood and shouted out.

"Objection overruled, but I do hope this is going somewhere, Mr. Stinson," Judge Grunwald said, peering down over his glasses.

"Yes, Your Honor. Mr. Dunlap, isn't it true that you just had your driver's license suspended two weeks prior to your trip to New Orleans?"

"Yes." Dunlap sensed where Malcolm was going.

"Objection, Your Honor. This is a form of badgering the witness, under the circumstances."

"Sit down, Mr. Ducruet." Judge Grunwald pointed his finger at Malcolm. "Get to your point, now. Objection overruled."

"Wouldn't it be fair to say that since you were drinking that night, you really couldn't see that well?"

"Objection, Your Honor. Really, what is the relevancy here?" Ducruet sensed he was going to lose the drama of his first witness.

"Objection overruled. Answer the question, please, Mr. Dunlap."

"You could say that I'd tied one on that night, but I did see what I saw in the river. And, God rest his soul, if my brother-in-law Earl was here, he'd tell you the same thing," Dunlap said, in defense of his testimony.

"No further questions, Your Honor," Malcolm said. He sat down again.

"I'd like to redirect, Your Honor," Ducruet said. The judge nodded approval.

"Mr. Dunlap, isn't it true that before you took your family to New Orleans for the holiday weekend, you had spent three weeks in an outpatient rehab?"

"That's true, but I slipped that night in New Orleans," Dunlap said, coughing after he gave his reply.

"No further questions."

"No re-cross?"

"No, sir," Malcolm said, to the astonishment of the court. But he had gained ground with the jury by not attacking poor Dunlap a second time. Dunlap left with the help of the deputies, and the jury watched with compassion.

Ducruet would spend the rest of the day, and week, calling witnesses who had been victims of the bombing.

By Friday, Ducruet had gone through eyewitnesses who had seen the actual bombing. Policemen testified to the aftermath of the scene. An FBI agent would testify on Monday. Ducruet had a lot of boring material he had to bring forth, and the jury quickly tired of this line of questioning—besides, it was all circumstantial. In criminal cases, circumstantial evidence can lead to only one person: the defendant.

The first week for Malcolm and his group was not as bad as they'd anticipated, but rough times loomed once Ducruet started his character assassinations.

Up early Saturday morning, Malcolm came down to sit on the porch, and he saw Pete already sitting there, drinking coffee.

"Haven't heard from you all week; good to see you're alive. How did it go?" Malcolm asked.

"Not good. With all my friends on the force, not one could get me in to see Dalton. He's being treated like he's just killed the president," Pete said, as Malcolm sat down in his father's chair.

"So, we're going to need help?"

"Don't you know any New York politicians that could help out? Maybe the second-term mayor owes you a favor for the Giamanco case?"

"I'll give him a call, but this is his last term and he's trying to make a good name for himself. We need someone who can open doors for us without any problems."

"Who?" Pete asked, watching the strange look on Malcolm's face.

"Tulle. He can get us in to see Dalton."

"The man hates your guts—and isn't he supposed to testify soon?"

"Leave it to me. Did you check with Walter on that other issue?"

"You're not going to like what he has to say."

"What?"

"He can tell you. I'm bushed." When the telephone rang, it was for Malcolm.

"Hello, Malcolm Stinson?"

"Yes."

"Do you have a cell phone?"

"I do, but who is this?"

"Don't say my name," she said. "Someone you've met before will be by in a little while for your cell phone number, and then we'll talk."

Malcolm recognized Suzanne Joret's voice.

Twenty minutes later, a security guard stopped Willy when he came to see Malcolm, and then cleared him to come through.

Willy scribbled the number Malcolm gave him. "Expect a call in about fifteen minutes, my man."

Willy left as quickly as he came.

"Malcolm?" she said, when he answered the cell phone.

"Suzanne?"

"Yes. I've been watching the trial. Boring, but I've seen Ducruet in action before and it looks like he's going for a slow kill with Clarence. Would you object to some help?"

"I'm listening."

"Of all the terrible things my stepfather is, organized in his affairs, he's not. Let's suppose he's involved in the riverboat bombing with the Don of Montreal. I bet there's a contract to replace the riverboat somewhere at my mother's house. It's just a matter of finding it."

"If what you're saying is true, why would he have a contract in his name with the Montreal mob boss? And how do we relate those two to the bombing?"

"I'm a reporter. You're the lawyer. I can just supply the information that I think you're going to need. I bet you don't have diddly squat."

"Close. But they don't have anything but the box with some explosives and his fingerprints. It doesn't put him at the scene of the crime."

"Circumstantial and you're in New Orleans, Mr. Stinson. We need to find the real culprits and soon. How long before you think you'll put him on your case?"

"Probably in mid-to-late September."

"That gives me some time. Keep this phone with you at all times. I'll be in touch again."

"When?"

"I don't know. I've got to work some things out…Mr. Stinson?"

"Yes?"

"Will you do me a favor?"

"Name it."

"Please visit my mother and tell her I'm all right."

"What if she doesn't believe me?"

"Tell her I said to water my baby blues. She'll understand. Good-bye."

*　　　*　　　*　　　*

Jasper teamed up with some Klansmen at Cooter Point, north of New Orleans. Some old Navy buddies had taken him in so he could heal his wounds. He watched the trial, but thought it was too early to do anything. Caulfield would be a problem if he recovered enough to finger him for the FBI killings. At a library, he read a late report in the New York Times that Caulfield was still in critical condition. Regardless of police protection, he needed to get to New York and finish that job.

While fishing with some of his fellow Klansmen, he borrowed a cell phone to call Monet.

"Hello?" Monet said, sounding slightly hung-over.

"I thought a busy man like you would be up at this hour." Monet quickly sat up in his bed.

"Where are you?"

"Never mind. I help you with your friend Henri Joret, and then he turns around and tries to kill me…"

"I know nothing about this. I haven't heard from you in weeks—serves you right for not listening to me."

"What are talking about?"

"About that damn girl. If you'd killed her when I told you to, there wouldn't be any problems."

"When I find that girl, I'll kill her and her daddy. I suggest that five hundred thousand be put into my Cayman account in the next twenty-four hours. Or you, Jean Claude, will also be on the endangered list."

"Don't threaten me, Jasper. You're not the only mercenary I know."

"Believe me, Monet. I'll be the last one you'll know. Pass that message along. Twenty-four hours, and then I will kill both of you for free."

CHAPTER 33

For the next three weeks, Ducruet questioned all of his technical experts. They went over the autopsies, blood types, fabrics, and fibers from Clarence's house and the area where they'd found the C-4 explosives. The sequestered jury was giving Clarence funny looks.

On Friday, September fourth, Ducruet wanted the jury to think about his last witness over the long Labor Day weekend. The judge would not listen to Malcolm's objection to the hostile witness, and told Ducruet to proceed.

"Your Honor, the state calls the Reverend Josiah Stinson," Ducruet said, with a solemn look. On his way to the witness stand, the reverend nodded to Malcolm, assuring him it would be all right.

"Glad you could make it, Reverend Stinson," Ducruet said. His team of expert lawyers and jury consultants had all advised him against bringing forth this hostile witness. Whatever ground he might gain in questioning, Malcolm could make up twice as much in his cross. Ducruet ignored the advice.

"Now, is it true that the defendant Clarence Reed was a member, and a regular attendee, of your church?"

"That's correct."

"Well, before I ask you about Clarence..." Ducruet hesitated and walked to the jury box. "Is it true that you marched with the late Martin Luther King?"

"True."

"And during those times, back in the fifties and sixties, you were arrested?"

"For the sake of equality and justice, if that's what you're asking."

"I'm talking about the riots in Selma, Montgomery, Memphis, and Chicago." Ducruet gave him a suspicious look.

"Those were peaceful marches. Outsiders started the commotion."

"The outsiders were white. I assume that's what you're saying."

"You said it, not me." The courtroom filled with laughter and the judge called for order.

"Now, through the years you've adhered to those same tactics that you've taught your, shall we say, disciples?"

"I don't understand"

"Isn't it true that you taught men, like the defendant Clarence Reed, to defy the authorities?"

"I object, Your Honor. Testifying for the witness," Malcolm stood and shouted.

"Objection overruled. I hope you're going somewhere with this, Mr. Ducruet, and quickly," Judge Grunwald said.

"Yes, sir. Let me rephrase that question. Do you sanction people from your church protesting abortion, affirmative action, judicial actions, state and city laws, and gambling?"

"You missed a few, but yes is the answer."

"And by what authority do you do this, sir?"

"By God's Word, the Bible."

"So, you interpret the Bible for your own moral satisfaction?"

"I don't understand your question, sir."

"Let me put it to you this way. Maybe you're chanting protest songs."

"I object," Malcolm said.

"Objection overruled. Now sit down," the judge said to Malcolm. "Mr. Ducruet, make your next sentence get to the point."

"Yes, Your Honor. May I approach the bench?" Ducruet asked, and the judge waved Malcolm up to the sidebar.

"Your Honor," Ducruet said. "I'm trying to show that the reverend here has a history of protesting issues, and I think it's only fair to show where the Desert Storm hero learned his techniques."

"This is totally irrelevant to the case," Malcolm said. "The reverend is not on trial here. What do Reverend Stinson's actions of thirty years ago have to do with today?"

"Ducruet, cut the crap, and get to the point, or I'll end your direct in the next vowel," Judge Grunwald said.

"Did you ever encourage the defendant to take stronger methods to get his protesting points across?" Ducruet asked the reverend.

"Your Honor?" Malcolm said, with his arms spread.

"Answer the question, Reverend."

"I don't know what you mean by stronger."

"Well, what I mean is..."

"He answered your question, Mr. Ducruet. Now continue with your next question."

"No further questions at this time, Your Honor," Ducruet said, and sat down.

"Your witness, Mr. Stinson," the judge said, and looked at his watch. It read five minutes after three.

"Reverend Stinson, how long have you been a pastor?" Malcolm asked, standing directly in front of the witness box.

"Thirty years, right here in New Orleans. We started the church with five people."

"So for thirty years, you've been teaching the Word of God? Have you ever been arrested for that?"

"No, but I see times like that coming."

"The state would like us to believe that you taught the defendant things about destroying life and property."

"The Bible teaches that God alone will judge adultery, fornication, uncleanness, lasciviousness, idolatry, witchcraft, hatred, strife, murder, and drunkenness, to name a few. Nowhere does it say that man is to punish man for committing these acts. As Christians, we do have an obligation to warn people about these things. That's all."

"When you walked with Dr. King, was there ever talk of violent retribution for the racist acts committed against blacks or Jews?"

"Tension flared among many, but there was never a plan to commit a violent act. I was arrested twenty-nine times for protesting discrimination in the workplace and inequalities in education. Outside of that, I have never had any run-ins with the law."

"Your church was recently blown up."

"Objection, Your Honor," Ducruet interrupted. "Although my heartfelt sympathies go out to Reverend Stinson for the loss of his church, this line of questioning is irrelevant to the case."

"Objection sustained. Get to the point, Counselor."

"Your Honor, you allowed the state to make accusations about alleged practices that the reverend was teaching at his church."

"Like I said, Counselor, get to your point."

"No more questions," Malcolm said.

The judge then spoke to the court.

When he had concluded his remarks, he asked, "Do you have any further witnesses, Mr. Ducruet?"

"No, Your Honor, the state rests its case."

"We'll stand in recess until Tuesday morning at nine a.m., beginning with any motions," the judge stated, and then he gave the jury their instructions for the weekend. Judge Grunwald didn't pay attention to Malcolm's glares. He simply slammed his gavel, and court was adjourned.

The reverend walked over to Malcolm.

"Listen, son, you did fine. Now, let's get ready for our case next week."

"Did you see what they were trying to do?" Malcolm inquired, gathering his papers. "They wanted to portray you as some radical preacher from the church of what's happening now. It was an attack on your character, Papa Joe."

He turned his attention to Clarence. "Either Hingley or I will see you this weekend."

Suddenly, tears welled up in Clarence's eyes. The guards waited as he sat back down to whisper into Malcolm's ear. "During the last few weeks, the prosecution has made a monster out of me, they've twisted the truth all kinds of ways. Do we have a chance?"

"Yes, we do. Now here's some good news for you to think about over the weekend. Suzanne is alive and free."

Clarence was stunned. All he could do was mumble something about what, where, who, when.

"I'll fill you in later with the details, but she's safe—that much I do know," Malcolm said, as the deputies escorted Clarence back to jail. Turning back to look at Malcolm, Clarence wore a big smile.

As one of his legal aids handed him his briefcase, Ducruet looked over his left shoulder at Malcolm.

"You got a big wall to tear down, son. Better get plenty of rest. You'll need a big sledgehammer," Ducruet chuckled, and his other dark suits laughed on cue.

Malcolm said nothing.

Outside of the courthouse, Malcolm took advantage of the media's bombardment of Ducruet and to slip out undetected. His team walked in another direction when a burly man, with arms like tree trunks, walked up to Malcolm carrying an envelope. He said only one thing. "Follow these instructions to the letter and don't be late."

Hingley, Lucy Yee and the others were curious, but Malcolm waved them on to their awaiting cars. Only Hingley lingered as Malcolm opened the envelope.

The note read, Come alone tomorrow morning at 8:00 a.m. to an airport just outside Belle Chasse. You will be met there and receive further instructions. Signed, Victor Zano.

"What are you going to do?" Hingley asked.

"I'm going to go. I have an idea of what he wants. Make sure you see Clarence tomorrow, and prep the first witnesses. You'll start on Tuesday." Malcolm noticed the media blitz heading toward him.

"These people are dangerous, Malcolm," Hingley warned. They picked up their pace to avoid the media.

"It'll be more dangerous if I don't go," Malcolm replied, as they entered their waiting van and drove off, leaving reporters shouting questions into the air.

* * * *

Once in New York City, Jasper got into the hospital through a service entrance, and put on a set of doctor's surgical scrubs that he had found in a laundry room. Disguised as a doctor, he managed to get to the fifth floor, where he saw two NYPD uniformed officers posted outside Reuben Caulfield's room, along with a plain-clothes FBI agent.

Jasper stepped into an empty room and attached his silencer to his nine millimeter, released the safety, and placed it under some towels on a rolling tray. He walked to the opposite end of the hall, where the FBI agent intercepted him.

Jasper began shooting. The agent went down, and before the uniformed cops could pull their guns out, Jasper had killed them. He entered the room and saw Caulfield connected to IVs and other electronic equipment. When he pulled down his mask, Caulfield's eyes widened.

"Remember me?" Jasper asked. He shot three bullets into Caulfield's already bullet-ridden body. As police cars roared to the hospital entrance, Jasper was making his way to the stairway. People in the hallway were screaming. Jasper ran madly through the crowd into the stairwell, and down into the basement, where he eased into an empty ambulance, and slowly drove away. Within minutes, sirens were blaring throughout the area. Jasper switched on the flashing lights and stepped on the gas. On York Avenue, he double-parked the ambulance and walked up to Ninety-Sixth Street. He caught a cab to the LaGuardia Airport for a flight to New Orleans. He made his flight with ten minutes to spare.

* * * *

Malcolm was dropped off at the small public airport used for private and public planes. A fat man with deep olive skin approached him.

"Follow me," he said. They went to the section of the airport where the helicopters were located.

The FBI was again following Malcolm. They called in for instructions, but by the time they got word from their superior, Malcolm was already in the air. No traceable flight plan was given. They stood in the morning sun, and cursed as Malcolm flew off.

The flight took thirty minutes. As they landed, Malcolm could see another helicopter already on the ground. They were in Pilot Town, a national wildlife refuge located near the Gulf of Mexico.

Zano stood alone, smoking a cigar. Two men walked Malcolm toward him. They frisked him and checked him for wires; Malcolm was clean. Victor Zano welcomed him with open arms. Victor wore sunglasses, a white cotton shirt and khaki pants—not his normal attire. "I'm glad you could make it. I suppose you're wondering why I went through all this trouble to see you."

"It did cross my mind."

"Let's walk. Here's the deal. For the last few weeks, I've watched the state bombard your client. Hey, they even had me convinced that no one could have committed the crime but your client. The media has all but convicted him, as well. So, the way I see it, you've got a big wall to bring down," Zano stated.

"I don't think it's that bad…mostly circumstantial. Other than the box with the C-4 explosives, they don't have a case."

"Look, you're an experienced lawyer. When you have a case with circumstantial evidence, and it all points to one person, who do you think the jury's going to believe?"

"We'll get through it."

"I think not. So, I have come to offer my help, and I'm well-versed when it comes to jury matters."

"Really, Mr. Zano, I don't need any help."

"Oh, yes, you do. If they convict your client, those scumbags will still be roaming free to hit again. Now with business overflowing into Biloxi, Mississippi, we're trying to renovate New Orleans and I would hate to go through all of this again."

"Mr. Zano…"

"Wait, let me finish. I'm on your side, Malcolm. I believe your client is innocent. We have resources within the bureau as well. So...what do you have for me?"

"Have for you? Like what?"

"Don't act stupid with me. You're presenting your case next week. So, what do you have?" Anger flared in Zano's eyes.

Malcolm was prepared for Zano. He had to give him something while he handled the trial. He brought photographs in an eight-by-twelve manila envelope. Malcolm pulled them out for Zano.

"And who are these lovely people?"

"That is a picture of Deputy Chief Waller of New Orleans. With him, are Jasper Yates, and Jim and Jerry Dalton. Jim is dead; Jerry's in jail in New York City, and Jasper's at large."

"I'm listening."

"Now, this is not gospel, but pretty close. Waller informed the FBI that my client committed the crime. I believe these men are the riverboat bombers." Malcolm pointed to the photograph. "There may be more...we don't know yet."

"So, this Jasper is the ring leader? What's his story?"

"It's all there on the back of the photo—his bio as best as we know it," Malcolm said. Zano flipped the photo around to read about Jasper Yates, the former Navy SEAL commander turned militia mercenary.

"And this is the bastard who blew up the riverboat?"

"Yep, but there is more..."

"Go on." Zano was looking right at Malcolm's mouth.

"I believe Jasper was working for this man." Malcolm pulled out another photo. But before Malcolm could say a word, Victor's eyes lit up.

"Jean Claude Monet."

"Yes. Jasper's been working for him for a while."

Malcolm's over verbalization of information went beyond what he knew to be fact, but it would keep Zano occupied while he gave Joret to Tulle, later, he hoped.

"Very good, Mr. Stinson. Now, let me reciprocate," Zano said.

"That's not really necessary, sir."

"Oh, it is. I have an envelope for you, but before you open it, you have two scenarios that win this case. The mistrial is in the envelope, or I can fix the jury for you."

"Jury tampering? Always heard about it, but never been involved in a case where the culprits got caught."

"Never do. Since the day they picked the jury, we've had portfolios on your jurors. We have enough information to get you an acquittal ten minutes after the jury convenes," Zano said, smiling as if he'd won the case for Malcolm.

"And the envelope?"

"Open it."

Malcolm reluctantly obeyed. There were five obscene pictures of an old man with two boys, no older than twelve or thirteen. The same young boys were in all of the pictures, engaging in various sexual acts with the smiling old man…Judge Grunwald.

"I know you use Pete O'Neil, but if you really want a good private dick, consider Boutte."

Malcolm couldn't believe Judge Grunwald was a pedophile. He had to ask.

"How do I use these pictures for a mistrial?"

"Do I have to draw you a picture? You walk in and tell him you want a mistrial, or you'll use the pictures."

"I'd get disbarred."

"It never would happen. We did our homework on him. Twenty years on the bench. He wants to retire in another three years. Why would he risk his retirement and reputation? No, my friend, everything is in your favor. Let's just say you can use the photos for leverage."

"I, uh, have to think about this one, Mr. Zano."

Zano slapped Malcolm on the back. "Look, you've been very helpful today. And I have what I want, so I'll tell you what I'll do. Start your case on Tuesday, and I'll give you three options. Jury tampering, the pictures, or try to win the case outright. But let me know by Tuesday what you're going to do. Just dial the number on the envelope, and punch in, yes, if you want my help, or no, if you don't. Call from a public phone right after court on Tuesday. I'll take care of Mr. Monet and his cronies—everyone involved will be dealt with."

Malcolm nodded and turned toward the helicopter, but remembered another question, and walked back to Zano.

"One thing I forgot to ask you…"

"Yeah?"

"Jerry Dalton, the guy who's in jail in New York. I need him to testify at the trial." Malcolm hollered over the helicopter noise.

"Okay, just for the trial. If you opt to try the case, he testifies, and you still lose. I don't figure he'll testify in an appeal. Oh, by the way, what's with all the security at your father's house and the other places with your lawyers?"

"Jasper threatened to hurt my family if I brought up his name at the trial…"

"Don't worry, Benny and his boys will help you out."
"Doesn't Benny work for Luppino?"
"And who do you think Luppino works for, Counselor?" Zano questioned.
Zano watched as Malcolm flew off in the helicopter.

CHAPTER 34

Jasper still had some unfinished business to clean up. Caulfield was dead, but now he had to deal with Joret. His beeper was ringing; it was Henri Joret. He was reluctant to respond to the call. He dialed the number.

"Hello, Jasper."

"Yeah?"

"I'm glad you called. In spite of your refusing my orders, I want you to know that I had no part in what happened when you left here that day. Sandchester made that decision. But anyway, don't worry about him. After the election, I'm going to get rid of the little bastard, but I could use a man like you."

"Hmm. So, what do you want?"

"News came to me about Caulfield being killed. That was very good. I knew it had to be you. And since you're cleaning up loose ends, I think there's one more, no, actually, two more that need to be cleaned up."

"Like who?"

"Like Deputy Waller and my stepdaughter, Suzanne. I can't have anything in the way of my future political plans."

"And my money?"

"I'll wire the five hundred thousand to you in the next forty-eight hours."

"Good. When I see that's done, I'll take care of the rest."

"Well, you'll have to find Suzanne later, but for now, Waller needs attending to. Come on. Let's show a little faith in each other here."

"If my money is not in my Cayman account in forty-eight hours, you won't have a political future."

"Agreed."

"I'll be in touch," Jasper said, then hung up.

* * * *

Malcolm dressed, then put together a package of photos and information into a large manila envelope. He walked out to the porch and talked with one of the guards.

"Good morning. Anything new?"

"No, sir, other than a van parked down the street with three white guys sitting in it. They've been there for about an hour and a half. On the other end of the block are the two black FBI agents. And further down the street is a local pimp, a hustler named Benny Dubois, with three guys," the off-duty cop said. Cephus had hand-picked these men for this job, and Malcolm knew they weren't doing it for free. This brought to mind something Malcolm had to do. Money was running low for housing, and the upkeep for the legal help down the street. He had brought in a dactyl-gram expert to read fingerprints. The most convincing evidence against Clarence was the fingerprint on the box of C-4 explosives found at the time of his arrest. Put that and a motive, together with the circumstantial evidence, and Clarence was as good as convicted.

Malcolm needed two things: money for expenses, and one of the criminals that committed the crime. He decided that he now needed Tulle's help. He turned and left the guard and went inside to where the reverend was reading about his testimony in the paper for the third time this weekend. He was talking to Lois about the bad picture they had taken of him.

"Papa Joe, I have to go out for a while. We're going to need some money for expenses. I'm not concerned about the lawyers and the legal aids down the street, but we need money for other things."

"How much we talking?"

"Ballpark figure, fifty thousand, at least," Malcolm said. His father put his hand to his chin and contemplated the matter.

"That's some ballpark. Be here tonight around seven. We'll have a meeting with our old friend Campy. I'm quite sure he'll come up with a solution for us. He is very good at raising money," the reverend said, with a smile.

Malcolm smiled back and said, "You sure you didn't miss your calling as a politician?"

"No. I'm doing what the good Lord intended for me to do. Politics is just a sideline, if you will."

Malcolm patted him on the back, grabbed some biscuits, and started to leave.

"When are those children coming back here?" Lois asked, while washing dishes in the sink.

"I don't quite know yet. I spoke with Sara this morning. The kids are fine. Hopefully, I can bring them back real soon. I have to go. See you later," Malcolm said. He grabbed his package, then walked outside and told the men they didn't have to go with him. He walked in the direction of the two FBI agents and caught them off guard. They didn't expect him to be walking. One of the agents spilled coffee on himself, surprised by Malcolm's appearance on foot.

Malcolm didn't break his stride when he talked to the agents. "Start your car and stay right here. I'll be right back."

He continued on about three houses farther and walked over to Benny Dubois in his car. "Morning, Benny. Gentlemen. Listen, I would appreciate if you would do me a little favor. You see that car right there? Well, that is the FBI, but the problem is, there are three white guys sitting in a van down the other end of the street. Maybe you can convince them to leave the neighborhood. You know what I mean?"

"You sure they're not cops?" Benny asked from the front passenger side of the car.

"No, they're not cops. They are probably from a racist organization."

"No problem, Counselor. We'll take care of it for you," Benny said. The driver started the car, and slowly drove past the FBI agents to the other car. Malcolm walked back, and as soon as he saw Benny turn the corner, he hopped in the back seat of the FBI agent's car.

"Let's go. Quick! Turn around. Take me to see Tulle now," Malcolm said. The agents hesitated for a moment, then turned the car around, and headed for the FBI headquarters in New Orleans. The agents radioed in that they were bringing Malcolm to see Tulle. Jon Tulle and two of his assistants were waiting in a small conference room when Malcolm was escorted in.

"I want to talk to you alone. You've probably got the room bugged, but that's all right if you want the whole world to know what I'm going to tell you," Malcolm said. Tulle picked up the phone and ordered no taping of their conversation.

Malcolm sat across the table and pulled out his tapes and photos. Malcolm told Tulle the story about Jasper and the Dalton brothers. He showed him the pictures of Jasper and Waller, explained about his connection with Reuben Caulfield, and explained why Tulle's agents had probably been killed in New York. Tulle's resistance was slowly dwindling. The pieces were beginning to fit and make sense, and he hated that. He still felt that Clarence had been part of the bombing.

"So, what do you want from me?"

"First, I need you to analyze the voice on this tape from an answering machine, and the voice on this video tape."

"Who is it?"

"The tape is the voice of Jasper when he lured Suzanne Joret into the bayou before he kidnapped her."

"So, you're going to tell me that a tape is going to convince me she was kidnapped by this Jasper character?"

"Oh, yes. She's alive. I met with her recently."

Tulle sat straight up and put his forearms on the table. "What do you mean, you met with her?"

"She called me and I met with her at a cafe on Charles Street. She told me about Jasper and the Daltons' involvement in the bombing of the riverboat, and the bombing at my father's church."

"Where is she?"

"That, I don't know. She contacts me. She doesn't quite know who all the players are, so she's still afraid for her life. Forget about the NOPD. She doesn't trust them…or the FBI, for that matter."

"What's on the videotape?"

"Jasper Yates training a Navy SEALs class. He was a commander before he retired seven years ago. Tulle, I know you want the truth about what happened."

Tulle made a call on his phone. In a matter of seconds, an agent came into the room. Tulle handed him the tape and the video, and rushed a voice analysis. "So, now what?"

"I need another favor."

"I'm not in the favor business, Counselor."

"I'll forget about what happened in the woods that night in exchange for this favor," Malcolm said. Tulle leaned back and started to chuckle. "Why go through all the legal rigmarole? I have witnesses to what happened."

Tulle pondered the thought and asked, "What sort of favor did you have in mind?"

"Let's take one of your private jets, go to New York, and have a little chat with Jerry Dalton."

"What for? He's not going to talk to you. He's already got a lawyer from the ACLU, I hear."

"Not after he sees these pictures." Malcolm brought out another envelope containing the grotesque pictures of the dead Jim Dalton.

"From what I understand, these brothers were very close. Once we show these photos to Jerry and tell him it was Jasper who killed his brother, I think we might get some of the pieces of the puzzle we've been missing." Malcolm leaned back, waiting for Tulle's reaction.

"Let's wait to see what the voice analysis comes back with, and I want to see the girl."

"Tulle, I have no control over the girl. She contacts me when she wants to. But if it's any consolation, she did tell me the other day that she would be in contact with me soon."

"Okay. Forget that for now. I'm curious. Where did you go on your helicopter ride?"

"I'm not at liberty to talk about that. When this is all over, I'll tell you," Malcolm said, lying. He wouldn't tell Tulle about his meeting with Victor Zano. He knew Tulle wouldn't understand.

"Okay. You're running a little scared about your client. Suppose I say no to all of this?"

"Not a problem. I'll do what I have to do to get Jerry Dalton. And when the truth comes out, the only thing I'll be able to say to the press is that the FBI had this information all along, but chose to suppress it for their reasons. You'll have to explain that to the public."

Malcolm picked up his picture of Jim Dalton. He left the remaining pictures with Tulle. "I'll be waiting for your call."

Malcolm caught a cab to the Orleans Hotel in the French Quarter. Walter Baer was up and watching television, when Malcolm knocked on the door.

"Malcolm, I was just going to give you a call."

"Walter, I need to know what's going on in New York. Hugo Hurst told me that he didn't report to Calucci or Rothman, but to Weinstein. Why?"

Walter took a deep breath and walked over to the couch. "I visited Weinstein just before I came down here. He told me that they used Lucy Yee to gather information that you had obtained about the case, and I think you better sit down for this."

"Go on. I'm okay."

"They were funneling the information back to Henri Joret."

"To Joret? Why?"

"Joret has a big account with the firm under a dummy corporation name. Also, there are future political ties involved, but since Abrams was running the show, it made it easy for him to use Lucy Yee. Malcolm, she only did what she was told, and she knew no more than her contact with Hugo Hurst."

"So Joret was feeding all the information to Ducruet. But why did they pull out of the case, if this was so convenient for them?"

"They—I should say Weinstein—didn't want to, but when he became ill…Thank God Calucci and Rothman were running things, because they really felt it hurt the reputation of the firm when they pulled out of the case. I understand that when Weinstein was feeling better, he ripped into Calucci and actually wanted him to let you continue and use Lucy Yee."

"So, that explains a lot of things. Why didn't you tell me this earlier?"

"I figured the worst was over, and you had enough on your mind with the trial and all."

"You should have told me…anyway, I need you to help Hingley this week in court. I might leave one day and go to New York. Maybe while I'm there, I'll visit Mr. Weinstein."

"What's in New York?"

"Jerry Dalton. Walter, we don't have squat. We need an eyewitness, and Dalton was in on the bombing."

"You know that for a fact?"

"Yes. But I need Dalton in the courtroom. I'll just have to convince New York to extradite him as a witness once I convince him to come—if I can convince him to come. See you in the morning," Malcolm said.

He was walking up Bourbon Street when he noticed a couple cuddling together. It was midafternoon. He stopped and tried to keep from staring. Malcolm watched the man holding her tightly and kissing the woman as they walked down the street. He turned and walked in the same direction but on his side of the street. He walked faster, crossed the street, and walked right toward the couple. Then nonchalantly, he lifted his head while he was walking, but almost past the couple.

He spoke to her.

"Hello, Roberta," Malcolm said, smiling and looking at her companion. She was startled to see Malcolm walking in the streets of the quarter.

"Hi, Malcolm, uh…this is Ed," she said. The two men just nodded at each other. "Funny seeing you out here on the holiday. I would think you would be preparing for your case tomorrow."

"I am preparing. I'm learning new things every day. Well, don't let me hold you up. Have a good day," Malcolm said, then quickly walked away and crossed the street. While crossing, he saw her glance over her shoulder with a forlorn look. He thought to himself, another no-good woman—that's it for her. He couldn't think about it now. There were more important matters to deal with, and Roberta was now of no consequence to him.

Malcolm turned away in anger. Suddenly, a man with a sweater over his hand poked a sharp knife into Malcolm's back.

"Just keep walking, nice and easy, Counselor."

"What do you want?"

"I know where your wife and children are. They are not protected like your parents, are they?"

"If you knew where they were, you would know if they were protected or not."

"Very good, Counselor, but I will find them."

"Not if the FBI and mafia find you first, Jasper Yates. Oh yeah, a fellow by the name of Victor Zano heads the crime families in New York. He doesn't believe Clarence did the bombings. And he knows all about you and your buddy Jean Claude Monet. Don't think Henri Joret can help you, either."

"You've been very busy. I should just kill you right here in broad daylight. It would just be another murder in the streets of New Orleans."

"Not quite. You see, Dalton is in jail, and he knows you killed his brother, and he wants your ass. So, no matter what you do to me, he'll testify in court against you."

"We'll just see about that boy," Jasper stated. He saw two cops walking in their direction. He spotted some young black boys tap dancing on the sidewalk for money. Jasper pushed Malcolm into them. Malcolm slipped on the money box and fell over one of the kids. Jasper dashed into a store and through the back exit.

The police arrived and asked if anything was wrong. Malcolm picked himself up and shook his head no.

He thought to himself that Jasper knew that Sara and the kids were not in New Orleans. But he had to do something to protect them. Bringing them back to New Orleans seemed to be his best option.

CHAPTER 35

The Stinson house was full of lawyers and legal assistants enjoying a delightful dinner that Lois Stinson had made. Campy arrived late. He ate, then waited in the living room as the other lawyers and legal aids left to prepare for the trial. Malcolm brought coffee into the parlor for the meeting with Campy and the reverend. They sat down at seven-thirty.

The phone rang. Lois called Malcolm and told him that it was for him. He replied that he didn't want to be disturbed. She shouted out that it was a man named Jon Tulle, so Malcolm answered the call.

"The report came back confirming the voice analysis. Listen to me carefully; you'd better be right about this, Stinson. You know that airport that you took your little helicopter ride to?"

"Yeah?"

"Meet me there at six o'clock in the morning."

"Tomorrow's the first day of our case."

"Not my problem. You work it out. Six A.M., Counselor. And you get back to New Orleans on your own. I have to stop in D.C. on the way back," Tulle impassively said, then hung up.

"What's the matter, son?" the reverend inquired, when he saw the disdainful look on Malcolm's face.

"Nothing, I'll take care of it," Malcolm said, and sat down.

"Listen, son, if you have something that you need to do, I can take care of this with Campy."

"As a matter of fact, I do," Malcolm said.

He walked down the street to the legal headquarters to discuss the motions that they needed to make tomorrow with Hingley, since he would be going to New York.

He called Walter about tomorrow's events, slept for a few hours, and left the house at five A.M. with Cephus, who had slept in the living room.

They arrived at the airport at exactly six A.M. Two agents approached them and drove them to the hangar where the FBI jet waited. Tulle brought three more agents for the flight to New York. There was no conversation during the entire flight. A car was waiting when they landed at LaGuardia Airport.

They were taken to a visiting room at Riker's Island Prison, where they stood behind a glass-mirrored window. Tulle had radioed ahead and made all of the necessary clearances. Jerry Dalton was brought in.

His wrists were shackled and a chain connected them to his shackled ankles. He wore an orange prison uniform. His face was unshaven, but he managed to keep his military-service style haircut. He walked with a light limp from the bullet he had taken in the park. Aside from that, he was in generally good health, with a pesky disposition. The guards shackled him to a metal loop attached to the steel table. Tulle would talk to Jerry alone first. Tulle sat in a chair only three feet away from him. Jerry slumped in his seat, but looked attentively at Tulle.

"Mr. Dalton, I'm Inspector Tulle of the FBI." Jerry's eyes narrowed as he scrutinized Tulle. "The reason I'm here is to talk to you about the bombing of the riverboat casino last July fourth, in New Orleans. We have reason to believe that you, your brother, and a man named Jasper Yates were all involved." Tulle was bluffing, but his preliminary reports on Jerry Dalton's background may have had some validity.

There was still no response from Jerry. "That's just for openers. We still have the issue of the two dead agents, the dead New York cop, and the attempted murder of Reuben Caulfield."

Jerry raised his head in surprise to Tulle's statement about Caulfield.

"I don't have anything to say to you, G-man," Jerry snapped viciously.

"Even if you don't confess about the riverboat bombing, you're still facing first degree murder in the FBI and New York cop killings."

"We'll see when I get to court."

"It doesn't matter. You're facing the death penalty. Why do you want that black boy to be convicted for something he didn't do? So just tell me about it," Tulle said.

"Personally, I think they ought to give him a medal. Can I go now? I'm missing the midday news," Jerry said, with a smile.

Tulle got up to leave the room without saying a word.

"They should have more niggers like Clarence Reed. Ha, ha, ha," Jerry laughed, as Tulle was about to leave.

"I may not prosecute you on the riverboat bombing, but I'm sure as hell going to make you burn for killing those agents," Tulle threatened. He shot a cross look at Jerry and left the room.

"Your witness, Counselor," Tulle said. He joined Cephus and the others on the other side of the two-way mirror window.

Malcolm took his manila envelope and walked into the room. Jerry's eyebrows lifted at the sight of Malcolm.

"I guess I don't need to introduce myself. Your face tells me that you know me," Malcolm said, sitting in a chair next to Jerry.

"What the hell makes you think I'm going to talk to you?"

"Oh, I have some information that you may be interested in knowing about. Let's see," Malcolm said as he began reading from his reports. "Jerry Dalton joined the Navy in 1981 with his brother, Jim. In 1983, they became Navy SEALs. They served in Desert Storm under commander, Jasper Yates. You and your brother left the service in 1993. You moved back to New Orleans and did missionary jobs here and there with your ex-commander. It paid the bills and you lived for the better part of eight to nine months, give or take, in peaceful co-existence in the Louisiana Bayou."

Jerry stared with anger, but said nothing.

"Unlike Inspector Tulle, who may not prove that you had anything to do with the riverboat bombing, I have an eye-witness who is going to testify that you, Jasper, and your late brother kidnapped a woman, held her hostage in a shack in the bayou, and that you confessed to your part in the River Queen bombing."

Malcolm then pulled out a picture of the Dalton home and placed it directly in front of Jerry.

"Suzanne Joret. Remember her, Jerry? She escaped with the help of the two black men that left your late brother Jim tied up. She's safe and protected. You are in jail, and Jasper can't get to her."

"I don't know what you're talking about, and what do you mean by my 'late brother?'" Jerry asked, with a puzzled look on his face.

"I'll get to that in a minute, but first look at these photos. Here's a picture of you and Jasper outside of my father's church, weeks before you blew it up."

"You're full of crap, nigger. Guard, I want to leave now," Jerry shouted out, looking at the mirrored window.

"Your buddy, Jasper, has left you here to rot, and with good reason. Recognize these pictures of you, Jasper, Deputy Chief Waller, and your late brother Jim, moments before you tried to kill Reuben Caulfield, just before you killed Bob Cummings, the photographer…?"

"I ain't going to tell you again, nigger. I'm not answering any of your questions. Now, get me the hell out of here. Guard!" Jerry shouted. He spit at Malcolm, while trying to lunge at him.

Behind the mirrored window, the warden was saying, "Enough of this, Jerry is entitled to have a lawyer in there." Tulle stopped him.

"Dalton's rights are not being violated. Let him continue," Tulle said, holding the warden's arm.

Malcolm sat back in his chair, pulled out a handkerchief, and calmly wiped Jerry's spit from his face and jacket.

Jerry sat there smiling and laughing. "Kinda pisses you off, huh, nigger?"

Malcolm reached inside his envelope for ten more photos and placed them face down. He motioned to the mirrored window for Cephus. He turned back to Jerry. Cephus entered the room and stood on the other side of the table, next to Jerry.

"What the hell is this, some sort of coon convention? At least bring back the white FBI guy," Jerry said, in a rage.

Tulle came into the room and stood next to Malcolm.

"Look, I'm not saying anything without my lawyer present, so Mr. Nigger lawyer, don't ask me any more questions. And that goes for you, too, Mr. G-man, and this big buck, too. What are you doing? Bringing in this big buck to rough me up? Take these chains off and let's see how much damage you can do," Jerry said, vehemently.

"Jerry, this is Cephus Pradier." He's a homicide detective in New Orleans. He's here for one reason…for you to identify these photos," Malcolm said, quietly.

"I'm not doing anything for you. Now get the guard or the warden, so I can get the hell out of here," Jerry said, screaming and trying to stand.

Malcolm turned the first photo of the dead Jim Dalton over and placed it in front of Jerry.

"You're the next of kin. Cephus just needs you to identify your brother."

"Is this some sort of sick joke? That ain't my brother," Jerry said, not taking his eyes off the pictures, as his voice cracked with every picture Malcolm showed him. Jerry examined them closely; there was complete silence as he wept at the sight of the pictures.

"No, it's not a joke, Jerry. And here's the part you're really not going to like. Your brother was stabbed in the back and found floating in the White River in Arkansas. If you notice the picture numbered four, the house in the background belongs to Henri Joret. Suzanne was hiding out there for a while. Jasper found her, and we know it was Jasper because Suzanne said he was the only one who broke into the house and chased her. The coroner's report matches the time of death, almost to the minute, that Jasper was there pursuing Suzanne."

Malcolm continued. "This is only a theory, but one that fits, nonetheless. You get shot and arrested. Jasper returns to New Orleans. He goes back and finds that Suzanne has escaped. He's furious with Jim, but takes him in search of Suzanne. There, somewhere along the bank of the river, they are canvassing the house. An argument ensues; Jasper comes up behind Jim and stabs him in the back, pulling the knife in an upward motion. Isn't that how they teach you to kill in the SEALs?"

Jerry was still weeping bitterly, but attentively listening to Malcolm's theory. He flipped to the pictures of the knife wound in his brother's back, a typical SEAL killing. He had seen it before.

Malcolm glanced over at Cephus, who, in turn, glanced at Tulle. "Jerry, Lieutenant Pradier needs your confirmation that the pictures are of Jim."

The four men stood in silence for nearly five minutes as Jerry tried to regain his composure, shuffling the pictures over and over again.

Then Jerry broke the silence in the cold steel room. "Have you caught Jasper yet?"

"Not yet," Malcolm answered, leaning over the table and even closer to Jerry.

"Suppose I told you that I didn't kill those agents, the cop, or the photographer."

"Who did then?" Tulle asked.

"I drove the car; Jasper did all the shooting. I did shoot Caulfield, but you said he's still alive."

"And the photographer?" Cephus asked.

"My brother Jim killed him. Caulfield can vouch for that; I was chasing him."

"What about Waller? What's his involvement in all this?" Cephus asked, sitting in the chair, expecting a mystery to unfold.

"Before I answer any more questions, I want a deal."

"A deal? I hardly think you're in a position to ask for a deal," Tulle cried out.

"I'm not talking about these killings...I'm talking about the River Queen bombing," Jerry said, watching the expressions on everyone's faces.

"I'll just subpoena you, and extradite you to New Orleans," Tulle exclaimed.

"Fine, I'll get on the stand, won't remember a thing, and you'll be looking for clues like finding a turd in the Mississippi River. What do I have to lose? You'll pin the agent murders on me, I go to jail, and the others walk scott-free to strike again," Jerry said, still trying to convince Tulle to make a deal.

Tulle motioned to the agents outside the window mirror to cut off the recorder. He walked to the far side of the room with his hands folded, and stroking his chin, he turned to Jerry. "What exactly are you looking for?"

"Don't take me for some sort of country bumpkin. Remember, I'm a highly decorated soldier of Desert Storm. So, this is what I want: to be placed in the witness protection program out of the country," Jerry said.

Malcolm offered his spit-on handkerchief for Jerry's runny nose.

"In exchange for what, exactly?" Tulle asked, leaning over, standing face to face with Jerry.

"For the names and addresses of everyone involved, including the main man who hired us for the job."

"What part does Clarence Reed have in all this?" Tulle asked.

"I'll tell you that when we have a deal," Jerry said, looking at Tulle, and ignoring Malcolm.

"I'll need some time to work this out, if it can be worked out at all. We'll have a deal only if the information pans out, Mr. Dalton."

"Not to worry, it will. Can I have these pictures?" Jerry asked, while gazing at the pictures of Jim. Malcolm looked at Cephus, who shrugged his shoulders as if he didn't care.

"Sure. They are rather morbid," Malcolm said.

"Yes, I know. I want to keep them to remind me every day of Jasper. You see, if you don't find him, and this deal goes through, I will. I want to show him the photos just before I cut out his heart." Jerry sobbed, and Malcolm and Cephus left him to his grief.

Tulle was outside now, walking ahead, talking on his cell phone with some official at the FBI headquarters in New York. In a matter of minutes, he was brought documents that, with his authority, and the approval of a local federal judge, he knew he could use to move Jerry back to New Orleans. This would give him time to work on a witness protection deal.

After twenty-seven years on the force, he was hesitant to offer this deal. He called the airport to have the FBI jet readied for departure in two hours. He also called ahead to New Orleans to make arrangements for transport of a prisoner. A member of Tulle's staff, a fourteen-year veteran, Chad Spragins, took the call. Spragins had found a friend in Henri Joret.

Once Spragins completed all of Tulle's instructions, he went outside for a cigarette, then used a cell phone to call a private number that Joret had given him. The information was greatly appreciated by Joret. A vote of confidence went out to Spragins from Joret. He said that once he became governor, he would find a spot for Spragins on his staff.

Then Henri beeped Jasper, who returned the call and took the information. Jasper assured Henri that Jerry Dalton would never testify in court. Henri still didn't feel confident in Jasper's handling this delicate situation.

Tulle walked back with orders and a faxed document from the judge, in a matter of thirty minutes. Orders were given to move Jerry Dalton to the John F. Kennedy airport for transport to New Orleans. The warden was leery of this move, and wanted to make some calls, but Tulle assured him that everything was legitimate. After a brief debate, the warden gave in; he needed the room anyway.

Tulle had one of his agents draw up a document offering the witness protection program. Jerry wanted his legal counsel to review it, but Tulle insisted that there wasn't time.

"How do I know this is legal?" Jerry asked, reviewing the document.

"You can read, right? My signature is on there. It's legit," Tulle replied.

Malcolm said nothing in defense of Jerry or in favor of Tulle. Cephus stood to the side of this sham. Malcolm pulled out a small notebook from his coat pocket. Tulle slid a recorder in front of Jerry, and Cephus sat back to listen. Jerry hesitated for a moment, then signed the makeshift witness protection agreement.

"There were six men chosen from militia groups in five states," Jerry began. "Arizona, Florida, South Carolina, Pennsylvania, and Louisiana. We all came from the Aryan nation, The Klan, and the World Order. Each man was paid one million dollars, with five million promised to their respective organizations. Each of us was a former member of the elite Navy SEAL unit and, at one time or another, had served under Commander Jasper Yates. Everyone's last mission had been Desert Storm. We all were explosives experts.

"The mission was calculated to the second. It was divided into two phases, and then a third phase was added at the last minute.

"First, we entered the Mississippi River and carried nearly three hundred pounds of C-4 explosive on a raft. We each followed the blueprints of the River Queen, and had a designated area to plant the bombs with timers. Once the bombs were set, we sunk the raft, and Jasper picked us up, one by one, just like a Navy SEAL drill. We were then taken to the shore on Metairie, where we took off our scuba gear. Man, that was the toughest body of water I had ever been in. Those currents kept pulling. We almost lost two men."

"What time was this?" Malcolm interrupted.

"Oh, I believe it was about 2150 hours. Nine-thirty. Anyway, we unloaded our gear. I don't know how Jasper disposed of the scuba gear, but then we put on our Para motors."

"Para motors?" Malcolm asked.

"It's a sort of harnessed flying machine, in layman's terms. You have a motor attached to a propeller, with a parachute attached. You turn on the motor, the propeller fills the parachute, and you take off flying. Jasper had the motors and the parachutes painted black to blend in with the night sky. We all took off. Jasper took care of the scuba gear because he was the last to come. He wore a black jogging suit to cover his white linen suit underneath."

"What was the reason for that?" Tulle queried.

"That was the next part of the mission. We flew over the Jefferson Bridge and into the bayou. Jasper made a call to Suzanne Joret, but we would deal with her later. First, we had to position ourselves for Clarence Reed, that civil rights lawyer, Gere, and the other black boy, Akins. They thought they were going on some sort of special mission for five thousand apiece...that was funny." Jerry chuckled, but none of the others laughed. "I guess you had to be there...well, Smitty and I went back into the water to make sure the explosives were set."

"Who's Smitty?" Tulle asked.

"Linus Smith, from South Carolina, is a brother from the Klan. Well, we made sure the bombs were all right, and then went back onto shore and out of sight. We held the detonator and waited for Jasper's signal."

"Now, you said that Jasper was dressed differently, how so?" Malcolm asked, trying to catch up on his notes.

"Yeah. He was dressed like this German businessman who went by the name of Oppenheimer."

"Bald head, reddish gray moustache, with a chubby gut?" Malcolm asked.

"That's right. He had Gere and Akins go into the water first, then Clarence. They all were wearing head gear that allowed them to talk to one another and with Jasper. Just before Jasper gave the signal for us to detonate the bomb, Jasper called Clarence back up for some bogus reason, equipment, I think—and then Smitty detonated the bomb. Jasper whacked Clarence on the head. We went back into the water and picked up the bodies, brought everyone on board, then piloted the boat near the River Queen, and dropped Akins and Gere back in the water. We headed back for the bayou, threw Clarence Reed onto the bank, and left. You know the rest."

"So did Waller have anything to do with this?" Tulle asked, curiously.

"He was the final phase, to lead you to Clarence."

"And the explosives in his house?" Tulle continued.

"That was Jasper and me. We disguised ourselves as gas and electric men, and planted the explosives in Clarence's room."

"What about Harpo Stevens?" Cephus inquired.

"We...took care of Harpo afterwards."

"And the girl, how does she fit into all of this?" Tulle asked.

"Well...it seems my employer felt that she knew something about the bombing and..."

"And who is your employer?" Tulle asked.

One of his agents came into the room and told him he had a phone call.

"Not right now; tell them I'll call back later."

"It's the chief of the Bureau in Washington, and he says right now."

"I'll be right back. Hold that thought about your employer," Tulle shouted and left the room. The FBI men, prison guards, and the warden stared through the window. Malcolm wrote something on a piece of paper and pushed it in front of Jerry. It read, Don't mention that your employer is Jean Claude Monet. Not yet; they can't be trusted. Jerry was surprised, but shrugged his shoulders and agreed.

Tulle returned and picked up his tape recorder. "I'm afraid that we'll have to finish this later. It will take a few hours to get a judge to sign your release papers."

"We goin' to N'Awlins?" Jerry asked, with a smile.

"Yes, New Orleans, I'm afraid. Counselor, you're going to have to take commercial flight back. Mr. Dalton here will be taken care of, but I have to report to Washington immediately. I'll see you in New Orleans tomorrow. We'll continue there," Tulle said. He shook hands with Malcolm and Cephus, and left in a hurry.

The prison guard came and shuffled a stoic Jerry away. Malcolm and Cephus caught a ride to Manhattan with an FBI agent. They had lunch at BBQ's on West 72nd Street on the east side. Malcolm tried to contact the Weinstein house, but there was no answer.

After lunch, they were making their way uptown to a Chase Bank on 72nd Street. Just as they were about to enter the bank, two big stocky olive-skinned men jumped in front of them and instructed them to turn around and get into the waiting limousine. They backed up and turned to see who was in the limo.

Malcolm whispered to Cephus, "Follow my lead." This puzzled Cephus, but he went along nonetheless.

Malcolm darted into the street, amid the oncoming traffic. Cephus was dead on his heels. The two goons stood there, startled for a moment, by Malcolm and Cephus's actions.

Malcolm and Cephus had made it across the street, but the goons got caught in traffic. The limo dashed into the oncoming traffic. They turned the corner at 80th Street and ran all the way up to Madison Ave. Eightieth Street was a one-way, going the opposite direction that they were running.

Cephus was having a hard time keeping up. By the time they reached Madison Avenue, they were both out of breath. They looked for a cab. One pulled up, but then suddenly a limo blocked the cab from moving. Out of the limo came two goons and someone Malcolm recognized. Boutte exited the limo with his hand in the air.

"Easy fellows. Remember me, Counselor? New Orleans…your private dick gave me the once over. Now, Mr. Zano would like a few words with you. So, let's go. And don't make a scene," Boutte said, as he led them to the limo.

Sitting alone in the car was Victor Zano. "Is this how you act when someone wants to offer you a ride?" Zano questioned.

"What can we do for you, Mr. Zano?" Malcolm asked, still breathing heavily.

"Let's just cut to the chase here. You leave New Orleans in the wee hours of the morning with your FBI friends. You come to Riker's Island to visit an inmate. Had you asked me, I could have set up an appointment for you without the FBI."

"In this case, the FBI was needed," Malcolm answered.

"So, mind sharing with me some information about your morning visit?" Zano asked.

"And if I don't?"

"Well…Malcolm, how rude of you not to introduce your friend."

"This is Cephus."

"I'm Detective Pradier. Homicide, New Orleans Police Department," Cephus said, offering his hand to Zano.

"Delighted," Zano sneered.

"And if you don't, is what you were saying. I thought we had an understanding? But it could be something rather regretful on my part."

Malcolm said nothing for a minute. There was complete silence in the limo as it made its way up Fifth Avenue.

"Stop the car for minute," Malcolm said. Zano instructed the driver to pull over in front of Bloomingdale's.

"Cephus, could you excuse us for a minute?" Malcolm said to a bewildered Cephus, who complied nonetheless.

"You have twenty-four hours to see your friend Jean Claude Monet. The prisoner, Jerry Dalton, fingered him as the conspirator in blowing up your gambling riverboat. And a Navy captain named Jasper Yates. Twenty-four hours, Zano, before the FBI knows, and by then, they'll be all over him."

"Thank you, Mr. Stinson. Can I drop you anywhere?"

"Kennedy Airport."

"If you get out here, I'll have the other limo take you there directly."

They had a quiet comfortable ride to the airport. Malcolm charged two tickets for the six o'clock flight on Delta to New Orleans. He made a call to the Stinson headquarters and talked with Pete.

"Pete, listen very closely. I have the names of the bombers of the River Queen. We'll have to move quickly to get to them one by one. The closest is a man named Linus Smith in Lauren, South Carolina. Take down this list of names: Jesse Faxon in Arizona with the Aryan Nation; Lee Thomason in Pennsylvania with The Order; Bill Riley in Florida with the Aryan Nation; and Jim and Jerry Dalton, of New Orleans. Oh yeah, I almost forgot the ring leader, Jasper Yates. Get these names to the professor and then head for South Carolina. Tell him I need information on these thugs, like yesterday. And, Pete, be careful with this Smith character," Malcolm cautioned.

"And what am I supposed to do with this Smith guy?"

"Nothing. When you locate him, let me know. We'll take it from there. Trust me."

Malcolm returned to Cephus, who was still upset that Malcolm had had a private conversation with Zano. He didn't appreciate being put out of the car.

"So, who was that guy, and what was that all about, Malcolm?" Cephus asked about their experience.

"I didn't want to get you involved with anything since you are an officer of the law. He's a crime boss here in New York. It's in your best interest, and for your safety, that you weren't there to witness our conversation."

"So what did you tell him?

"I...told him who blew up his riverboat. Period. No more questions, please. I know what I'm doing, Cephus."

They read The Times and The Daily News while they waited. Across the waiting area were two of Zano's goons, and thirty feet from them were two FBI agents.

CHAPTER 36

Malcolm was anxious to tell Hingley the good news on Saturday morning. His plan was to put Dalton on the stand as soon as possible, but no later than Wednesday. Tuesday would be spent building up Clarence Reed's character. Ducruet had painted a poor picture of Clarence to the jury—a picture Malcolm needed to change before bringing on Dalton. Then, as frosting on the cake, Suzanne Joret would testify of her ordeal and present the information Jerry Dalton had given her about the bombing. Malcolm knew that Ducruet would attack Dalton for the murders of the FBI agents, but Suzanne's credible recollection would give Dalton credibility. That's why Suzanne was needed—she'd been a victim and would be a credible witness.

* * * *

At four-thirty, Suzanne gathered Kathy, Willy, and Dexter to reveal the plan she'd been devising for the last three days. Everyone sat around the table for an early dinner.

"Everyone's getting restless sitting out here in the country, so it's time to make a move. Willy, Dexter, I appreciate everything you've done for me and Kathy."

"I'm glad, but what about our money?" Dexter asked, with a mouthful of dirty rice.

"I'll get to that. First, we'll meet with Malcolm Stinson. Things aren't going well at Clarence's trial. I'm sure I'll need to testify. I'm scared about my safety, but I have a plan."

"I'm listening," Willy said, lifting the fried catfish to his mouth.

"I've been searching my memory for any legal documents that Henri might have on the riverboat. If he's in business with the Canadian crime boss, there must be a contract for a new riverboat. That's where you come in, Kathy, since no one suspects you of anything. You deliver a note to my mother and explain what's been happening. The note will be asking for the delivery of Willy and Dexter's money. And, hopefully, she can find a legal agreement about the riverboat in the house."

"Suppose your father has it in a safe?" Kathy asked.

"My mother knows everything that goes on in that house, and if Henri has a safe, which he does, she can get into it and find what we need. This is where you guys come in. My mother probably has a couple of bodyguards assigned to her. First, gentlemen, we'll contact Malcolm Stinson and arrange to meet privately. The bayou will probably be the safest. Willy and Dexter will come with me to the rendezvous point. We'll need a map to give Mr. Stinson. The sooner he has the documents, the better."

"And what if there aren't any documents?" Kathy asked.

"At that point, Willy and Dexter get their money. I will be under the protection of Malcolm Stinson. I understand he has a fortress at his parents' home. Kathy, maybe you should stay with your sister in California until this is over..."

"That sounds like a good idea, but I'd rather stick around," Kathy said, cautiously.

* * * *

Sunday morning, Louisianans woke up to the headlines in The Times Picayune:

LOUISIANA MAN EXTRADITED HOME TO TESTIFY FOR DEFENSE IN RIVERBOAT BOMBING

The small caption underneath the headline asked a question. Will his testimony free Clarence Reed?

The news spread like wildfire from the deputies that brought Dalton to Angola Prison. Louisiana had the exclusive; the rest of the country had to broadcast the news. The news traveled so fast that the white inmates cheered Dalton as he walked through the prison in handcuffs and leg chains. The black inmates threatened the hatemonger. They vowed he wouldn't leave the prison alive. Jerry

Dalton paid little attention; the FBI would protect him. He had immunity from the bombing charges, as well as the witness protection program.

A few hecklers made comments—one got his attention for a moment.

"Hey, Clarence, you gonna show some love and forgiveness to the man that set you up?" the lone voice shouted out. No answer from Clarence Reed, who was just one hundred feet away from Dalton.

Jerry slept peacefully, even though many hate groups were planning to attend the trial on Tuesday. He was a traitor who needed to be dealt with.

The people Jerry Dalton had persecuted over the years were now responsible for his safety. Before he went to sleep, he whispered, "God bless America."

* * * *

Alva fixed herself a morning mint julep with some soft-shell crabs for breakfast. Henri sat at the other end of the dining table. His face was aghast at the news of Daltons coming to testify. He started for the phone when Alva intercepted him.

"Henri, my life has been a living hell these past few months."

"Not now, Alva. I have to make an important call."

"Not on my ass. You better sit there and listen to what I have to say."

"Suzanne may not be of your blood lineage, but she is of mine. And frankly, Henri, I'm rather distraught at your attitude toward her disappearance. You see, any parent of any age would be overwhelmed with the loss of a child. But you just seem to keep rolling along with this campaign. To tell the truth, I was hoping that you would withdraw from the race until we found out what happened to Suzanne," Alva said, strolling along the dining room table could seat sixteen people.

"The FBI and the local police are doing everything in their power to find out what happened to Suzanne. What else can I do; I'm not a private investigator," Henri said, sternly.

"I'll tell you what you could do. You could march down to the bayou, roll up your pant legs, and walk through the marshes amongst those four-legged critters—just like you do with these two-legged ones—and find her."

"That's a little preposterous," Henri answered.

"No, my darling, I'll tell you what is preposterous. If I find out that that Canadian bastard, or any of your many enemies, had a hand in harming Suzanne, and you could have done something about it, you will regret the day you were born. I've stood by you all these years and watched you manipulate people, but I draw the line when it comes to my children. That, Henri, is when I will become your worst enemy," Alva said, then left the room.

Henri waited for her to walk out of the house and into her greenhouse. She always went there when she was upset. He dashed for the phone and called Sandchester.

"What the hell is going on with this Dalton coming to town for the trial? But before you answer that, get a hold of Jasper and have him tell you where Suzanne is. I just have a gut feeling he knows. And move quickly, my friend. Alva is losing it, and I don't want the Corlans involved. Her daddy in Texas can cause us a lot of problems. I want to know if she is dead or alive. I don't care, just find out," Henri said, and slammed the phone down. He went to the backyard and walked around, thinking that if she was alive, and Monet or Jasper had her, what would she know? If she knew anything, would she turn on him, too? Henri was determined to find out.

CHAPTER 37

The courtroom was filled to capacity with reporters, deputies, court clerks, lawyers, and family members of the bombing victims. Malcolm's appearance brought smiles to the jurors' faces.

"All rise, the Honorable Judge Martin L. Grunwald, presiding," the bailiff said.

"Glad you could join us today, Mr. Stinson," Judge Grunwald said, peering over his glasses. Ducruet smiled.

The first witness sworn in was Justin Cortez, the third black mayor of New Orleans. The mayor testified to Clarence's character. Malcolm also called other character witnesses, including the schoolteachers Clarence had helped in the strike a year ago, the nurses who needed support in their strike, and the garbage men and the city municipal workers that Clarence had aided in their dispute with the city. The jury also heard testimony from the shrimp fishermen, the child care center in the city, the drug rehabilitation center that the government had wanted to shut down, the teenage girls with unwanted pregnancies, and the ex-cons looking for work. Even the new police chief vouched for Clarence Reed's character.

Malcolm quickly questioned each group's representative to restore Clarence Reed's credibility. Ducruet made a feeble attempt to discredit them in his crosses. The jurors didn't seem to be biting, and Ducruet sensed that they might hold his attempts against him. His theory was, "Yes, Clarence was a good guy with a dark side that led him to bomb the riverboat, proving his point that gambling was morally wrong."

The day went by quickly, and Malcolm felt he had gained some ground. Ducruet would not be so lenient tomorrow. Court adjourned at exactly four o'clock.

* * * *

Around seven-thirty, Malcolm, Hingley, and Lucy Yee paired off into another room to discuss the strategy of questioning Jerry Dalton.

"Dave, you visit him tomorrow, and I'll see him on Wednesday and Thursday. On Friday, he'll be our star witness—something for the jury to think about over the weekend. Hopefully, Suzanne Joret will contact me by then, to collaborate his story." Malcolm had his feet up on the coffee table looking at Dalton's questions, when a church deacon—turned bodyguard—came into the room.

"Excuse me, Mr. Stinson, but there are two characters outside saying they want to have a word with you. We tried to brush them off, but they're insistent. And they claim you know them."

"Who are they? What do they want? We're busy here."

"Willy and Dexter," the deacon said. Malcolm flew to the front door.

"Come right in, gentlemen. I'm so glad to see you again."

"Sure, likewise," Dexter said. Malcolm led them into the kitchen, the only unoccupied room.

"Look here, Counselor. Suzanne wants to meet with you Thursday night, seven sharp," Dexter said. He pulled out a map and laid it on the kitchen counter. "You'll have to get a boat here, and ride to this point," Dexter said, pointing to a spot on the map. "It's a little island in the bayou. Suzanne will ride with you. Willy and I will be there once your meeting is over. She said to bring no more than two people with you, and to not be late, or she'll disappear on you again," Dexter said.

"Tell her I need her to testify at the trial and I'll provide all the protection she'll need. Tell her that Clarence's life depends on it."

"You can tell her yourself tomorrow, but she said to give you these two letters. Only open the one with your name on it—it tells you what to do with the other letter. Goodnight, Counselor," Dexter said.

Willy nodded his head in agreement. Dexter stopped at the front door. "One more thing, my man. Don't blow this. Your meeting with her is very important for me and my partner."

They disappeared into the dark, steamy Louisiana night.

* * * *

Malcolm's letter said to visit Suzanne's mother, Alva, before they met on Thursday, and hand her the letter. Her mother would know what to do after that. When Malcolm dialed Alva's private line, she answered the phone.

"Hello, Mrs. Joret. This is Malcolm Stinson."

"Really? And to what do I owe the pleasure of this call? And how did you get this number?"

"I need to see you, and then I'll explain to you how I got your number. Mrs. Joret? Are you there?"

"Mr. Stinson, I'm really not in the mood to see anyone."

"I understand how you must feel, Mrs. Joret, but I have information about Suzanne."

"Really? What sort of information?"

"I'll come to your house. I'm conducting the morning session, so we could meet around two."

"I'll be waiting on the porch," Alva said. "One last thing, please don't mention our meeting to anyone. Suzanne's safety will depend upon your being discreet about this matter. Goodnight."

Malcolm went back into the war room, where Hingley and Lucy Yee still were, and told them about his change of plans for tomorrow.

Alva had no idea that Henri had tapped her private line, and that the house was being recorded twenty-four hours a day.

* * * *

Wednesday morning was the same rush and tumble, with the press asking when Jerry Dalton would be put on the witness stand.

Malcolm would conduct the morning session, and Hingley would be back in time for the afternoon session. Malcolm questioned his fingerprint expert faster than he'd previously planned, then questioned Sun Reed about her son's whereabouts on the night of the bombing. Time ran out, so Hingley would finish questioning her in the afternoon.

Malcolm arrived at the Joret mansion shortly before two. He was cleared at the gate entrance and drove through fifty rows of chinaberry trees leading up to the mansion.

Malcolm saw Alva Joret sitting in a rocking chair, drinking a mint julep.

"Good afternoon, Mrs. Joret," Malcolm said, wiping the beads of sweat that were trickling down his face.

"You don't mind sitting out here, do you, Mr. Stinson? We're being watched."

"Not at all. May I ask who is doing the watching?" Malcolm glanced around as he walked up the steps and sat down.

"It's rather strange. The man standing over by that tree is usually with my husband's bodyguard team, but this morning he tells me that my husband reassigned him to me—something about added security. A bunch of bull," Alva said, sipping on her drink.

"Do you think your phone is tapped?"

"I can't say for sure, but I'm going to look into it today. I won't tolerate being a surveillance object in my own house."

Alva stared at Malcolm, and tears started to well up in her eyes. "You said my baby is still alive? You've seen her? How did she look? Has she lost weight? Did they hurt her?"

"She's fine, Mrs. Joret. They had her hidden deep in the bayou in chains and handcuffs, but for the most part, she's in good health. She wants you to find some documents that could be very helpful in the trial. This may be hard for you to understand, but the pieces are coming together to prove that Clarence Reed didn't commit this crime."

"Why didn't she tell me she was involved with him? What did she think I was going to do? Turn my back on her?" There was a long pause as Alva wept quietly. "I'm sorry, Mr. Stinson, but this is the best news I've had in months. She's my first-born. Not Henri's daughter, but that's another story. I'm sorry. You were saying something about some documents?" Alva wiped the mixture of sweat and tears from her face.

Malcolm handed her the envelope from Suzanne, which Alva ripped open immediately. The note asked her mother to get twenty-five thousand dollars for the men who had rescued her, and that she would explain later. She wanted Alva to find any documents that Henri might have with any company building casinos. She stressed not to mention any of this to Henri.

Alva looked up at Malcolm with tears of happiness. "This is really her handwriting. Thank you, Mr. Stinson. I'll take care of everything and see you on Thursday."

Alva was weeping as she went back into the house. Henri's bodyguard came over to ask if anything was wrong.

"No, nothing. Please see that Mr. Stinson gets out. Thank you."

Malcolm walked past the guard, who watched him every inch of the way. After Malcolm drove off, the bodyguard got on his cell phone and called Henri Joret.

* * * *

During Wednesday's court session, Judge Grunwald and District Attorney Ducruet appeared to be in a tag team combat against Malcolm; his questions triggered objection after objection all morning.

The judge overruled nearly every objection Malcolm made in Ducruet's cross-examination. Sidebars, lengthy discussions, and arguments were all against Malcolm. By lunch break, he felt that the judge and Ducruet had spent the night plotting against him.

The afternoon was not any better. Judge Grunwald threatened to have Malcolm placed in contempt of court. Malcolm was relieved when four o'clock came. Something was wrong. The jury seemed more interested in the many arguments between the judge, the prosecutor, and the defense, than in the witnesses that appeared that day. Now, Malcolm was apprehensive about bringing on Jerry Dalton.

He faced the barrage of reporters wanting answers about today's hearings; they deduced it wasn't a good day for the defense.

With his defense team following him, Malcolm saw Sara standing outside the courtroom. He was slowly making his way toward her when Professor Hickman approached him, insisting on talking immediately. Malcolm worked his way back to an empty courtroom and motioned for Tulle to join them.

Professor Hickman seemed wary of talking in front of Tulle, but Malcolm reassured him. "What's so important, professor? Did you find out anything about our militia men?"

"I'm afraid I did...you see, in my research of locating these men...I found out that...well, the names of the men...they are all dead."

"Tulle! I knew I shouldn't have trusted you."

Malcolm just dropped his head.

"Well, he might not have given you bad information."

Both Malcolm and Tulle gave the professor their attention.

"What do you mean?" Malcolm asked.

"I'm saying that the names of the men—I located each town they lived in. But the strange thing is, they all died in the last seventy-two hours."

"How?" Malcolm asked.

"Each one's house went up in flames while he was asleep. The information I have is skimpy, at best. The last was Linus Smith in South Carolina, yesterday morning. All the men and their entire families were killed in the fires."

"Tulle, you and I were the only ones that knew about them. You bastard! You went and had them killed." Malcolm charged Tulle. They threw punches at each other until they were both on the floor, and the agents outside the door came in to separate them.

"Guess the FBI will do anything for a conviction," Malcolm screamed. The two agents held him back.

Tulle waved them out of the courtroom.

"Now you listen to me, Stinson. I don't know what happened, but I'll find out. What do you take me for? I made a deal, for a man who killed two of my agents, to free your client. I'll be in touch with you tonight," Tulle said, as he left the courthouse.

"Have you heard from Pete, professor?" Malcolm asked, still breathing heavily.

"Not a word. I assume he's still in South Carolina."

"Yeah. Let me know the moment he calls you." Malcolm left the courtroom and walked into Sara.

She was leaning against the wall, looking just as beautiful as ever. Malcolm gently grabbed her by the arm and asked, "What are you doing here? Don't you realize you're putting yourself and the kids in danger?"

"I'm sorry. I couldn't stay cooped up in Massachusetts any longer. The kids are fine. They're at your parents' house. What's going on with all the bodyguards?"

"My point, exactly. There have been threats made against my whole family. We don't know who saw you come down here. Besides…"

Roberta walked slowly toward them, looking Malcolm directly in the eyes. His mouth dropped open. "Hello, Malcolm. I need to talk to you about the other day." Her eyes moved from Malcolm to Sara.

"That's not necessary. Excuse me. This is Sara. Sara, this is Roberta." Malcolm tried to walk past Roberta, but she grabbed his right arm.

"Listen," he said. "The other day was self-explanatory. We needn't continue this conversation any longer. It was over before it started."

"A little problem comes up, and the first thing you do is call your ex-wife?"

Malcolm kept walking as the reporters tried to make sense of what was going on. "We'll talk about this later, Roberta. Right now I have other things to attend to. Surely you can understand that. I thought you had a little integrity. I thought maybe you were different, but I was wrong. I don't see what you're upset about."

"Upset? Yeah, I'm upset that you're with this hussy ex-wife of yours. The one that did you wrong..."

"Wait a minute," Sara said. "Who are you calling a hussy? Girl, you don't know me. We can take this outside right now," Sara threatened, with her hands on her hips and her face flushed.

"The time we spent together didn't mean anything to you?" Roberta asked.

"Obviously, it didn't matter to you, did it?" Malcolm replied.

"Who is she, Malcolm? I should go back there and bop her one," Sara said as Malcolm whisked her down to the waiting car.

"Just somebody I know. No big deal."

"Well, she seems to know you very well—particularly the time you and she spent together. What's up with that?"

"I met her and spent time with her. What was your excuse?"

Sara bit her tongue. She got in the car and complained about everything but Roberta.

Malcolm wanted to go to the airport and put her on the next plane.

As they pulled up to the Stinson home, the children came running.

"Daddy, Daddy, I missed you, Daddy," Serena shouted as Malcolm picked her up and kissed her.

"And daddy missed you, honey. What's up, son? Boy, you're getting big."

Lois and Josiah were glad to see the family reunited. Before they were in the house five minutes, the phone rang.

"Malcolm, it's for you," Lois said.

"Hello?"

"Well, Counselor, seems like homecoming, huh? Got the whole family in town now," the voice said.

"Jasper?"

"You remember me. New York City, Greenwich Village, or perhaps you remember our meeting in Memphis at the Baptist Convention, and of course, again just the other day," Jasper said.

"Turn yourself in, Jasper, and we can end all this."

"My, my, I didn't know we were on a first-name basis. I just wanted to thank you for taking care of all those people for me, even though I hated losing all those frequent flyer miles."

"You're telling me you didn't kill those people?"

"I'm good, but that was quick, even for me. You don't know who did it?"

"You must have some sympathetic friends."

"You're probably right, Counselor. So don't go letting your family tour around New Orleans too much. They may be so sympathetic to the cause that they might even help take care of your family, as well."

"You bastard. Come anywhere near my family, and I'll personally skin your hide."

"Now, now, Counselor. Is that any way for the son of a preacher-man to talk? I'll tell you what...you go and let Jerry Dalton testify all you want. The district attorney will tear up his testimony, but if you don't want anything to happen to your kids and your wife, I'd strongly suggest you keep Suzanne Joret off the stand. Don't say I didn't warn you. Au revoir."

Click, and the phone was dead.

"Sara?"

"Yes?"

"Until the trial is over, you and the kids must not leave this house."

"Now, Malcolm."

"I'm trying to keep you all alive."

He walked down the street to prepare for Jerry Dalton's questioning the next day. Now he had the trial on his mind, and the concern for his family. And where would Jasper make his next move?

CHAPTER 38

In Thursday's Times Picayune, the cover story was based on the what-ifs of Jerry Dalton's testimony.

Extra county police were on duty at the federal courthouse, and every major and local television station was parked outside. Rumor had it that Jerry Dalton's testimony would break the case.

Once past the media and into the courtroom, Tulle whispered into Malcolm's ear that it was important that they talk privately after the meeting.

"I had a conversation with Jasper Yates yesterday," Malcolm said. "He wanted me to thank those individuals that so graciously helped him out in eliminating his former colleagues."

Tulle gave him a puzzled look and left.

The sun was bright this morning. The courtroom had three ten-foot windows on the side where the observers were seated.

Judge Grunwald entered the courtroom, promptly at ten, and asked Malcolm to call his first witness. Malcolm called Jerry Dalton, who was brought in shackled. His face was scruffy and he needed a haircut. The jury glanced at him like he was some animal they'd never seen before. He smiled at them and for the cameras in the rear. He smiled at the judge, and even at Malcolm. Jasper Yates watched the activities through his Redfield power scope from the top of the Tulane Medical Center. His M-14 had a range of eleven hundred yards, and he used 165 pt. bullets. After he adjusted his Krieger barrel, his target was in sight. Jasper waited for the signal to squeeze the trigger.

Malcolm asked Jerry Dalton to state his name for the court.

"Jerry Dalton..."

"Mr. Dalton, where do you live?"

"Right now I'm in Angola Prison."

"Before you were incarcerated?"

"My brother and I lived in the bayou here in N'Awlins."

"Were you ever in the armed services?"

"Yes, I was in the Navy SEALs for ten years."

"What was your expertise?"

"Hell, I did everything, but I was trained in explosives…extensively."

"When did you leave the Navy SEALs?"

"My last commission of duty was Desert Storm."

"And whom did you serve under in Desert Storm?"

"Lieutenant Commander Jasper Yates."

Malcolm walked over to his table where Clarence Reed was sitting and pointed at him.

"Mr. Dalton, do you know this man?"

"No, can't say that I do."

"Have you ever seen him before?"

"Yes." Malcolm picked up a picture.

The deputy sat by the ten-foot window. He had been paid five hundred dollars, no questions asked. His assignment was to pull out a red handkerchief and rub the back of his neck when Dalton started talking about the bombing. Standing six-foot five, the closet-Klansman slowly moved by the window and gave the signal.

Malcolm walked back over to Jerry Dalton with pictures of the riverboat before it was blown up. "Do you recognize this photo?"

Dalton's last word was "yes."

Malcolm turned to the judge. "I submit this picture as defense evidence number…"

The shot pierced the glass of the courtroom and penetrated over Jerry Dalton's right eye. He slumped over as the blood gushed out of his forehead.

Another shot grazed Malcolm's shoulder. The courtroom panicked, and everyone hit the floor. The jurors stormed out the door to leave the courtroom, as did the victims' families and the media. Deputies drew guns and squatted down, looking for a target to shoot back at. None could be found.

The judge went under his desk. The entire courtroom was in hysteria. Ducruet and his team of lawyers tried to crawl out, but froze on their knees for fear of being trampled by people fighting each other to get out.

Jasper dropped the M-14. There were no fingerprints. He walked back into the medical center and changed into green operating scrubs. He made it to the main floor and walked out of the medical center to a waiting car. His timing was perfect. It would be at least fifteen minutes before they'd figure out where the shot had come from.

Jasper was soon on I-10, flowing with the morning traffic out of New Orleans.

* * * *

At five o'clock, Cephus Pradier came by the Stinson home, reporting that Dalton had died instantly from the assassin's bullet. The feds had found the M-14 rifle on top of Tulane Medical Center, nearly three hours after the shooting. They were still questioning people, but no one at the medical center had noticed anything unusual. The killer had escaped without a clue. The feds were taking fiber samples, but had nothing to go on.

Malcolm's shoulder wound was just a grazing from the bullet. He knew in his heart who had done this, but he couldn't prove it. He needed Suzanne more than ever. Malcolm, Cephus, and the professor were about to leave for their rendezvous with Suzanne, when Chief Inspector Jon Tulle came to the house.

"I just came by to let you know about Dalton."

"I know. Detective Pradier just informed me."

"Are you all right?"

"I'm fine, thank you."

"Can we speak in private for a moment?" Malcolm led Tulle to the back porch.

"In spite of our indifferences, I want you to know that I had nothing to do with the murders of those men. We are investigating, and as soon as I find out something, I'll let you know. Believe me, that's not the way I wanted to see Dalton die. He killed two of my men; that I know for a fact. The riverboat bombing is yet to be proved. I never thought I would hear myself saying this, but be careful. There are other factors involved in this case that I have no control over. I can tell that these other factors want to see Clarence Reed convicted of the crime, whether he did it or not."

"A militia fanatic is threatening my family, I'm dealing with some noted criminals, and you're telling me to watch my back because the government wants Clarence convicted?"

"What's with the crime families?"

"They've been pressing me for information about identifying those responsible. They don't believe Clarence did it and don't care what happens in the trial. They just want the real criminals who blew up their boat."

"Who are they?"

"Tulle, I've already told you too much. But you rest assured that I don't now, or ever did, work for them."

"It's Victor Zano, isn't it?"

"This much I will tell you. These militia men that were killed all worked for a Canadian crime boss named Jean Claude Monet."

"I've heard of him. Why didn't you tell me this before?"

"Because I couldn't. My family comes before divulging information to the FBI. And besides, we weren't on the best terms anyway."

"Would you like for me to leave some men to guard your house?"

"No, we'll be fine. Thanks anyway. If I hear anything, I'll be in touch."

Tulle left with his men. Malcolm watched him leave, and wondered if Tulle could be trusted. And just who were those unknown factors out there, wanting him to lose the case?

* * * *

It was near 6:45 p.m. when they arrived at the spot where the professor had docked the boat. He'd borrowed a test boat that his friend, who worked for the Textron Marine & Land Systems, was testing for the coast guard. The forty-seven-foot boat had twin 475-horsepower Detroit Diesel engines and was made of aluminum, with a deep-V hull.

Hey, this is one heck of a machine, professor. Where did you get it?" Cephus asked.

"I borrowed it from a friend, in case we need to make a quick getaway. The boat has four seats with safety belts. Please use them."

Night was beginning to fall on the bayou as they rode to the island of Zair, their meeting point. Neither Malcolm nor Cephus had ever been to this part of the bayou.

They quietly passed the bewitched oak trunks with gnarled branches that seemed frozen in torment. From their agony hung gray moss, tattered like old feather boas. Just above the surface, behind the reeds and the trees, eyes peered out at them. The moon dodged in and out of the gray sky. The silence sounded like death. Cephus remembered old folklore that said this place was the devil's retreat. Malcolm put the light on the water to watch the cotton-mouth snakes slither across the water's surface.

When they reached the island at eight-fifteen, Suzanne and Willy were waiting on the shore. Five minutes later, another boat appeared with Dexter and Alva Joret. The two women raced to lock in an embrace. Tears flowed, and then smiles and laughter lit up the dark night in the bayou. Malcolm tried to let them have a little time to enjoy their reunion. Cephus kept trying to place Willy and Dexter. The professor stood at the shore listening to the night.

"Listen, Willy and Dexter, right?" Malcolm asked.

"Yeah, what can we do for you, governor?" Dexter answered.

"Just as a precautionary measure, you guys stake out over there in case we get any visitors, and we'll take care of any water arrivals."

Wiping her eyes, Suzanne said, "Please, Dexter."

"Okay. Did she bring the money?"

"Yes. Right here in my bag," Alva said, smiling.

"Don't I know you fellows from somewhere?" Cephus asked, trying to get a better look at Willy in the moonlight.

"Naw. We're from Nebraska. Let's go, Dex. We'll be just beyond those bushes." Willy took hold of Dexter's arm, and put as much distance between them and Cephus as possible. "Ladies," Malcolm said, "I hate to interrupt this joyous moment, but this place gives me the creeps. Did you find any documents, Mrs. Joret?" Her nose sniffled from crying.

Alva pulled out a document from an Irish boat company, a tentative agreement for a riverboat to be built and delivered in the summer of 1999. The company in Montreal would be part owner. Malcolm felt the dummy company could be traced to Jean Claude Monet. It was just too much of a coincidence.

"We'll have to do some research, but I think we're on the right track," Malcolm said, reading the document under a flashlight.

Suddenly, there was a movement in the still waters that the professor couldn't figure out. At first, he thought it might be alligators. But before they could escape, three air boats were upon them. Jasper and his storm troopers came jumping off the boat with rifles in hand, like they were on a raid of Normandy. Nine men surrounded them with AK-47 rifles, and Jasper Yates, like the commander he was, approached the inner circle.

"Wonderful night for a family reunion. Nice to see you again, Suzanne," Jasper said, softly stroking her face with the back of his hand.

He turned to Malcolm. "They said you were good at gathering information for your cases. If I ever need a lawyer, you're hired," Jasper laughed. "But I don't see a need for a lawyer in the near future. And besides, you won't be around. Tsk, tsk. Your race must be very proud of you," Jasper said, as the commandos joined him.

"You just might need a lawyer," Malcolm said. "I understand the FBI has your picture circulating around the country for the killing of those agents in New York. Before you know it, you'll be atop the Most-Wanted list."

"Too bad you won't be around to see how long my fame lasts. So, what do we have here—a black police officer and...oh yes, the professor."

Jasper walked over to the professor who was standing on the bank. "We ought to make you an honorary member. That collection of data that you had in your secret wall is invaluable; too bad we had to burn it. Don't want that sort of information getting into the wrong hands."

"What have you done?"

"Let's just say you're no longer a homeowner," Jasper said. The professor lunged at him. A soldier knocked the professor aside the head, causing blood to gush out of his ear. When Cephus reached over to assist him, Jasper said, "Check our policeman for weapons. We don't want him to shoot himself accidentally."

"What do you want, Jasper?" asked Malcolm.

"Nothing from you. Tomorrow I'll call your co-counsel and tell him that if he doesn't give his closing statement by Monday, you'll never be seen again."

"He'll never do it." One of the soldiers had his rifle in Malcolm's back.

"Oh, yes, he will. See, I'm going to call your daddy, and that pretty wife of yours. That should convince him to move forward. The truth of the matter is that you'll never see any of them again, but for purposes of this trial, it'll work out just fine. I think you'll enjoy jumping off that nice boat tonight to go swimming. I'm a sporting man. I'll tell you what. I'll have a few of my men take you to a place the Daltons showed me—it's alligator heaven. They'll enjoy the night swim, too," Jasper said, laughing along with his new-found troops. "With the exception of Alva here, Henri and I have some unfinished business."

"Henri will have nothing to do with you," Alva said.

Jasper walked over to Alva. "Isn't it the wife who is always the last to know? Didn't he tell you that Suzanne was keeping me company these past few months?"

"This is preposterous!" Alva cried out.

"No, it's reality. And now, hopefully for your sake, he cares more about his wife than his stepdaughter."

"You're saying that Henri knew you had Suzanne locked up?"

"Well, he is my employer, but don't concern yourself about that. Enough questions. Take my friends swimming."

Jasper pointed to one of his new recruits. The men opened the circle to let them get back into the professor's boat. While they were huddled together, the professor whispered for them to buckle themselves into their seats. Malcolm and Cephus sat on the two seats at the rear of the boat, and Suzanne sat in a seat just opposite the professor who was steering. Three men got on the boat with them, and three more followed in an airboat.

One soldier walked up to Jasper and asked, "What about the two niggers out there?"

"You three go find them," Jasper said.

"And when we find them?"

"What do you do when you go coon hunting?"

"Let's go, fellows," the soldier said, as they ran into the bushes looking for Willy and Dexter.

"You, my lovely lady," Jasper said. "...will come with me. Your husband and I have some unfinished business. And I'll take that bag with the money for our expenses..."

"How did you know that we were here?" Alva asked, as Jasper led her by the elbow back to the airboat.

"Your husband has an in with Southern Bell," Jasper said, laughing.

The motors were started, and Malcolm and company went one way, while Jasper and the crew headed another. Willy and Dexter saw the three militia men approaching with their guns ready to fire.

"What we going to do, Dex?"

"We should follow the money and take them out. I'm pissed that she didn't bring all the money. Fifty grand ain't nothing to rich people."

"So, we are going after them boys with the money?"

"Naw, let's help Suzanne and the lawyer so we can get the rest of our money. For saving their asses, we'll up the ante another twenty-five G's. First we got to take care of these cub scouts, and quick, before we lose the others. Circle over there, and we'll ambush them when they come through this pass."

"We shooting or cutting?"

"Shooting. That's what they planned on doing to us."

The three Klansmen were using flashlights to scan the area.

"Come on out, boys. No reason to be scared. We just want to talk to you."

Dexter and Willy had two 9mm guns apiece. Dexter waited till they were within ten feet, then gave Willy the nod. "Who answered the Klansman's call" was a game they played.

"Mister Man, please don't shoot," Willy said, standing up, hands behind his back.

"Good boy," the Klansman said. "Now, where's your friend?"

"Right here, boy." Dexter fired at the two men closest to him, while Willy took the third man. The barrage of bullets told Jasper his men's machine guns had found their prey.

Willy and Dexter emptied their guns into the Klansmen.

"Let's go. Grab their machine guns," Dexter said as he and Willy ran to the airboat. "You know how to drive this thing?" Willy asked.

"Yeah, nothing to it," Dexter said. He started up the giant propeller and they were off. It didn't take them long to catch up with Malcolm's boat, so they slowed down and watched for a moment from a distance.

The moon was shining on a still body of water surrounded by land. Hundreds of red dots reflected off the moonlight of the water's surface.

"What kind of bugs lay on the water like that?" Suzanne asked.

"Not lady bugs—even they don't sit in pairs," Malcolm said, starting to sweat. His childhood fears haunted him.

"Oh, they're bugs alright, lady…with big teeth. Now you steer this boat out there into the middle, boy," the Klansman told the professor.

The professor had the spotlight on, and realized a large oak tree in the water was his only chance. He pushed hard on the throttle, rocking the boat side to side to keep the Klansmen off balance. In seconds, he brushed against the oak tree as he made a hard right turn. The boat flipped on its side, and the Klansmen flew into the water.

The quiet pool of water became a rush of rapids as alligators rushed for the unexpected night meal. In less than ten seconds, the boat turned right side up, but Malcolm, Cephus, Suzanne, and the professor were still buckled in. As they turned upright, a four-foot alligator managed to make its way on board. The professor struggled to get his seat buckle off. He finally got loose, grabbed the alligator by the tail, and flipped it off the boat, while the others panicked.

As the men in the airboat came alongside their screaming comrades to shoot at the alligators, the professor pushed hard on the throttle and bumped his way through the mass of alligators and out of the little cove.

One of the Klansmen started firing at them, but within seconds, the three were sucked into the alligator bayou. The rest, in shock and cursing, watched as the professor turned the airboat in pursuit.

Dexter and Willy waited in the dark.

"Ah, Suki, Suki, now. Let's go, Dex," Willy said. Dexter pushed full throttle on the airboat. They heard machine guns firing.

The professor had all 475 horses moving, but bullets were ripping the boat. A bullet charged into Cephus's shoulder and almost caused Cephus to fall off the boat, but Malcolm grabbed him just in time.

"Get them below," shouted the professor.

"Any guns on the boat?" Malcolm shouted over the roaring engines.

"No—it's just a test boat for the coast guard," the professor yelled back.

"What kind?"

"Rollover rescue boat."

Dexter pulled up alongside the Klansmen as he and Willy waved, and then fired at them. The Klansmen fired back hitting Dexter in the leg, and damaging their airboat. However, the Klansmen had all been injured and they fell off the airboat, which crashed into the bank.

Willie called out with a bullhorn to the speeding professor to stop. Dexter slowly pulled alongside.

"Glad to see you boys," Malcolm said to Dexter, who was clutching his leg.

* * * *

Jasper tried to contact the men he'd left behind on a walkie-talkie, but there was no response. He ordered everyone back to the island.

Jasper and his men found the abandoned boat and took to the swampland searching for the others. Two men went into the water, but did not last long against the mob of alligators. Malcolm could hear their screams. Three alligators attacked as Jasper's men showered gun fire into the murky waters. The men were able to survive, but with deep bite wounds. Jasper ordered three of the men to help them back to the air boats, even though he would have preferred to leave them there.

The rest continued in the search.

* * * *

Malcolm and company traveled all night, reaching the road just before dawn, tired, dirty, and scared. They kneeled down on the road knowing Jasper wasn't far behind. "We have four guns. Let's take a position and fight it out with these guys." Dexter was delirious, having lost a lot of blood. Cephus was barely conscious.

"Maybe Dexter's right," Suzanne said. "Let's just fight them off." A helicopter flew over their heads.

"Who's that?" she asked.

Malcolm looked up as the helicopter hovered over them for a minute, then left as quickly as it had come.

"Come on, folks. Let's stay off the road and keep moving." Malcolm was weary himself.

Just ahead, in the middle of the road, stood Jasper and his men. Suzanne ran to Malcolm.

"Bon Dieu avoir pi tie'," she said.

"Oui," answered the professor.

Jasper walked toward them. "Now before anybody gets hurt, I suggest that you put your weapons down."

The Klansmen came closer with their rifles poised to fire. Behind Jasper, cars raced down the road, and the helicopter appeared again. Just as Malcolm was about to tell everybody to run for the woods, a voice boomed out of the helicopter.

"Put down your weapons. This is the FBI."

Although Jasper commanded that the Klansmen stay and fight, they dispersed back into the woods. Jasper stood alone in a matter of seconds.

"I'll be in touch!" he shouted, and he also fled into the woods.

The sun was coming up as the helicopter landed on the road. Its door slid open and Benny Dubois stepped out. There were ten cars on the road, each with five men and automatic weapons.

"If you hadn't been so successful in giving me the slip, you wouldn't have had this problem," he shouted over the roaring blades of the helicopter.

"How'd you find us?" Malcolm asked.

"I was enjoying my late-night dinner at Dooky Chase when these two foxy chicks came looking for me. It was that Asian gal, Lucy, and your wife, Sara,"

Benny said looking around. "We had better get out of here before the real FBI shows up."

"Benny, see if your men can catch a couple of Klansmen," Malcolm said, while helping to lift Dexter.

"Why?"

"They've kidnapped Alva Joret."

"My job is to protect you—not search and rescue."

"Mr. Luppino and Zano would appreciate the favor, once I talk to them."

"Alright."

"Are all these men yours?" Malcolm asked.

"Some are, but most flew in from Chicago and New York at Victor Zano's request. Victor Zano is very appreciative of the information you gave him about that Monet guy in Montreal."

"What happened?" Malcolm questioned.

They laid Dexter down in the helicopter seat.

"While you were out here gator hunting, Zano and his boys closed in on Monet and his crew in Montreal."

"What happened?"

"Zano and Monet's conversation got pretty heated and accusations were thrown around. Next thing you know, bodies were dropping like a Wild West show. Zano and Monet both got out without a scratch. But Zano killed most of his men. Zano cooperated with families from Chicago, Detroit, Atlanta, and Vegas, so the place was surrounded and his men outnumbered Monet's men five to one. It was like the Valentine's Day Massacre."

Benny gave the pilot the okay to take off.

"The mafia knows about Monet?" Suzanne whispered to Malcolm.

"Yes."

"Do they suspect Henri, too?"

"Not unless Monet told. I'm hoping to save it for the feds."

"I agree that the time isn't right yet."

"Benny, can you have a car ready to take Cephus and Dexter to the hospital?"

"I'll do you one better, Counselor. I'll have two ambulances waiting," he said, smiling at his authority.

"Benny, can I borrow that jacket of yours? I need to be in court by 9:30."

"I don't know. It cost me seven hundred bucks in Los Angeles last year. And you smell like the swamp."

"I need to get some clothes. I can't go to court like this."

"I got some threads in the car. I'll hook you up."

The helicopter landed at the airport twenty minutes later. Two ambulances were waiting, but so were two police cars—not by Benny's request. Benny led the way to his limo. Malcolm found a hose used for cleaning planes, and washed the bayou funk off. He put on the white linen suit, with a red shirt and red shoes that Benny had found in the trunk of the limo. He picked up a white tie as well.

Suzanne washed and wore one of Benny's girl's dresses, then accompanied Malcolm to court for her public debut.

The professor and Willy escorted Dexter and Cephus to the hospital.

* * * *

At 9:30, Suzanne and Malcolm arrived at court. Security screening far exceeded the previous days, and a courtroom without windows was provided. The press was out in full regalia.

As they climbed the steps to the courthouse, one reporter started pointing. Then another. Reporters from Suzanne's television station called out to her. There was a new story today. Suzanne Joret was alive. Clarence Reed became second page news for a day. She held Malcolm's arm as they made their way through the reporters.

Once inside, Malcolm and Suzanne were checked for weapons. They stopped Suzanne from entering until Malcolm cleared it with the judge.

Hingley and Lucy were surprised by Malcolm's attire, but glad to see him. Ducruet was on the phone to Henri Joret.

"Thanks for contacting Benny," Malcolm said to Lucy.

"You're welcome. When you didn't call us back last night, I went to your parents' house and spoke with the reverend and your wife."

"Ex-wife."

"Yeah. I remembered your mentioning Dooky Chase's, and that Benny Dubois was your bodyguard, so I went to meet him."

"Thanks again." Malcolm hugged Lucy. "Listen, everyone. I want you to meet Suzanne Joret." He gently took Suzanne by the elbow. "She's going to testify about her abduction and everything the Dalton brothers told her." Everyone was happy and surprised to see her.

But Suzanne wanted to talk to Malcolm in private, so they sat in the empty seats three rows behind the defense table.

"Now don't take this the wrong way, Malcolm, but I just can't testify."

"Why not?"

"Those animals are holding my mother captive somewhere out there in the woods."

"Don't worry. Benny's men will find out where she is. I promise we'll get her back in no time."

Judge Grunwald entered the courtroom. Only the lawyers, court clerks, and deputies were allowed in the courtroom today.

"In light of yesterday's events, I'm canceling the proceedings for today," he said, glancing at Malcolm's outfit. "Over the weekend, we'll make every preparation for a safe court—either in this courtroom or another. The jury has been dismissed for the weekend. On Monday we'll start with motions, and Mr. Stinson can then proceed with his case. I'm sorry your witness was killed, but we must continue. Are there any questions, gentlemen?" the judge asked, looking over his reading glasses.

Neither Ducruet nor Malcolm had anything to say.

"Then you are dismissed. I'll see you on Monday, and Mr. Stinson, do something about your wardrobe by Monday. Thank you," he said, then left the courtroom.

The reporters attacked Ducruet when he came out first. Live reports that Suzanne Joret was alive had been reported on the radio and television. They waited for her. The deputies held them off as Tulle helped Malcolm and Suzanne escape into a van through a side entrance. Tulle also wanted to hear Suzanne's story. She gave Tulle the details about her months of captivity as they drove back to the Stinson headquarters.

Malcolm interjected the events of last night. Tulle was limited in what he could do, but he would help in Alva Joret's rescue.

Thirty-five minutes later, Malcolm was dropped off at his house. The reverend and Lois Stinson didn't know it yet, but they had another houseguest. Malcolm didn't know it either, but he already had another one waiting in the house.

* * * *

Alva was tied up in the woods south of New Orleans. Jasper had Alva guarded by twenty men outside the house. It was a maneuver for Jasper to get the money owed to him. To the Klan militiamen, it was an exciting event. Images of Waco, Texas, and the Freedmen of Montana filled their thoughts.

This was their notch in history. Holding a prospective governor's wife hostage until the jury handed down a guilty verdict was their goal. At least this was the propaganda Jasper had presented.

Still pumped with energy, Jasper's first call was to Henri Joret. When the private line to the cell phone rang, Sandchester answered it.

"Yes?"

"I want to speak to Henri."

"This is Sandchester. Jasper? Anything you can say to Henri you can say to me."

"Put Henri on the phone this instant, and Sandchester, I won't forget that little stunt you pulled. I owe you one. Get Henri."

"What is it, Yates?"

"I have your wife here with me. You have till noon Monday to wire the remaining one million dollars to my Cayman Island account. If it's not there by noon, kiss your wife goodbye…and you'll never spend a full day as governor. That, my friend, is a promise."

"What the hell are you talking about? I don't owe you a million dollars."

"Between you and Monet, the balance is a million. You do want to see your loving wife again, now don't you?"

"You're not blackmailing me."

"Hold on a second." Jasper covered the phone.

"Just say hello. Anything else and I'll rip half your face off."

"Hello?" Alva said, her voice cracking.

"Alva? Alva?"

"Satisfied? I tried to detain your stepdaughter last night. I wasn't as successful as I wanted to be. So in addition to having the money wired on Monday, contact your stepdaughter and strongly advise her not to testify."

"Where is she?"

"You'll find her with the nigger lawyer, Stinson. Henri, don't let your wife down."

"You listen to me, do what you have to do, but I'm not paying you a million dollars—and Suzanne is not a problem."

"My dear friend, Henri, if she testifies and they even halfway believe her, my photo will be spread in every post office in America. If she implicates you, your political future is in the dumpster. Think over your choices very carefully. Good-bye."

Jasper played back the recorded conversation for Alva Joret. "Maybe your daughter is more interested in saving your life than your husband is."

Jasper was beginning a call with Malcolm, when one of his soldiers came in for instructions on lining up a defense. He promised to offer Malcolm a deal for her life later.

* * * *

The professor stood in front of the burnt-out shell of his house; his only solace was a back-up copy of his diskettes in a safe deposit vault in the Bank of Orleans. His last download was that of the dead Navy SEALs, which was at his office at Tulane University. Jasper hadn't bothered to check there.

* * * *

Malcolm's children ran to greet him. Sara was so happy to see him alive that tears filled her eyes. Malcolm's emotions were mixed.

"You seem angry," she said.

"Well, yes and no. I'm grateful that you and Lucy went to see Benny, but you put yourself in grave danger," he said.

* * * *

Sunday morning, Malcolm, Suzanne, and three of the church-appointed bodyguards went to Angola Prison. He hadn't spoken with Clarence since Jerry Dalton had been shot. The prison guard led him to the field where Clarence and forty other initiates had just finished the morning's work. On Sundays, they only worked half a day. They were chained together at their wrists and ankles. Tears streamed down Suzanne's cheeks when she saw Clarence. The inmates marched in double time, singing a song.

"He must be a Christian Zealot," one of the prison guards said to Malcolm.

"Why do you say that?"

"It takes a hell of a man to get those hoods to conform like that. Ever since he's been here, all he does is witness the Word of Christ to these men. Usually they come here and join a gang. He seems to enjoy himself," the guard continued. As the men approached, their song could be heard:

"I'm running for my life

I'm running for my life

I'm running for my life

I'm running for my life

If anybody asks you what's the matter with me

Tell them that I'm saved, santicified,

holy ghost filled, and fire baptized
I got Jesus on my side and
I'm running for my life."

As they sang the chorus heading back into the prison yard, the guard pulled Clarence from the Sunday chorus line.

"You have visitors, Reed," the guard said. Clarence followed him, still humming the chorus.

They led Clarence to the room where Malcolm was waiting.

"How we doing, Counselor? We're getting close to the truth, but the devil's still fighting, huh?"

"That's a good way to put it. How are you doing after that court fiasco?"

"Fine, but a lot of people want to make sure I'm executed or at least go to jail for life."

"We know you didn't commit the bombing—we just have to prove it to the jury. Usually in a murder case, the defense doesn't put the defendant on the stand, but I may make an exception. We still have a good shot—we located one of the bombers, and Suzanne is going to testify."

Chapter 39

Benny's men captured one of the fleeing Klansmen. It took two hours to convince him to divulge where Alva Joret was being held hostage.

Fifty men were assembled for Alva Joret's rescue mission. They drove two trucks into the woods at six-thirty that evening. As they approached the hide-out, two armed guards stopped them, instructing them to turn around.

"This here is private property, so turn this vehicle around, boy, and high-tail it out of here," the Klansman guard stated, holding and pointing his rifle at the driver.

Using silencers, two men jumped off the rear of the truck and shot the two Klansmen guards.

The convoy continued on to where a shack sat in a clearing. Jasper was about a hundred yards away when the two trucks unloaded and opened fire on the unsuspecting Klansmen. Jasper ran toward the shack to grab Alva Joret, but was intercepted by two Klansmen who told him that retreat was the only course of action now. Jasper regretfully complied and escaped with them.

* * * *

Malcolm and Alva stood on the porch talking the next morning.

"Suzanne and I have discussed her testimony. And I don't want you to implicate Henri in this."

"With all due respect, Mrs. Joret, Henri may very well be an intricate part in this fiasco."

"On the surface that may be true, but we have a way in Louisiana of taking care of our own."

"I'm sure you do, but this is the law..."

"Malcolm, my maiden name is Corlan. My daddy is a powerful man in Texas. Maybe you've heard of him?"

"Corlan Industries?"

"Yes. When I was pregnant with Suzanne, my daddy was madder than a hot poker. He was ready to send me off to Paris, France, and let me raise my child with a nanny for a couple of years before returning to Texas. But then I met Henri, who wanted to be a politician. His rich Cajun father was totally against it, so he blackballed him out of his family. Henri wanted to be Louisiana's next Huey Long. He showed great compassion for wanting me while I was carrying another man's baby. Four months later, Henri asked me to marry him. I said yes because I had feelings for him, and because it was my escape from exile in Paris."

"I understand your plight here, Mrs. Joret, but..."

"Just hear me out, please. My daddy reluctantly accepted the idea of my marrying Henri...his political aspirations intrigued him. So through the years of city councilman, congressman, and state senator, my daddy provided Henri with everything he needed to be a successful politician. Then six years later, after we'd had three more children, Henri broke away from Daddy and got involved with Luppino and the casinos. This made Daddy angry, who had enjoyed the idea of having power in Texas and a son-in-law aspiring to be the governor of Louisiana.

"Our family was so rich that it wouldn't have gone over well with the voters if a Corlan had run for president of the United States. So for the last five years my family has been grooming Henri to be governor of Louisiana, and after that, president of the United States. Henri doesn't like the idea of Daddy telling him how to run things if he were president, so, now, my family will make sure he never becomes president. Governor would be it."

"Mrs. Joret, your husband may be responsible for the deaths of thousands of people."

"Malcolm, with all the people he knows, do you think they'll ever convict him? What proof do you have? Will Ducruet prosecute him? I don't think so. Will Monet testify?"

"You know Jean Claude Monet?"

"Henri introduced him to me about three years ago when we were vacationing in Montreal."

"Your husband may be part of a terrorist conspiracy."

"Malcolm, isn't it your only concern to prove beyond a reasonable doubt that Clarence Reed is innocent?"

"Yes."

"Then why do I get the feeling that you're taking this case so personally?"

"Probably because one of those riverboat fatalities was my sister," Malcolm said.

"I'm sorry. I didn't know."

"I didn't think it would show."

"Well, it does. Trust me that Henri will be dealt with in due time."

"But you're his wife."

"Malcolm, I stopped being his wife years ago—the other women, the travel. You're a preacher's son. Doesn't the Good Book tell us, 'vengeance is mine, saieth the Lord?' By the way, your parents are wonderful people—I see where you got your good points," Alva said, then left the room.

"And what do you say?" Malcolm asked Suzanne.

"She knows what she's talking about. If you ask me about Henri's connection in any way, I'll clam up. I swear."

"Okay. No Henri questions. Ask Pete to come in here, please," Malcolm asked Suzanne as she left. Two minutes later, Pete entered the room with his arm in a sling.

"How are you feeling?"

"A little sore, but I've been worse. Bad break today in court, huh?" Pete inquired, settling onto the couch.

"I need the envelope, Pete."

"A very risky move, my friend."

"The only one left that can help win the case."

"How about if I give him the envelope? What can he do to me?"

"No. I want to see his face."

"When are you going?"

"As soon as you hand me the envelope," Malcolm said, then left to see Judge Grunwald.

* * * *

Henri Joret paced the floor, while Sandchester sat in the leather chair and stared out of the window. Ducruet leaned back behind his desk.

"Well," Ducruet said. "We caught a break today, but that doesn't mean Stinson won't try to bring in his new witnesses. You may have to talk to Judge Grunwald, Henri."

Henri stopped pacing and ran both hands through his white hair. He cocked his head back and took a deep breath. "From what I understand, all the men involved are dead. That leaves only my stepdaughter, the little witch. Who else could he possibly have?" Henri turned to Sandchester.

"Waller's the only other loose end…we need him to disappear." Sandchester pushed himself up to the edge of his seat.

"Whoever they are," Ducruet began, while loosening his tie. "You've got to make sure Grunwald doesn't let the testimony in. The trial can go either way now. His remaining witness can't hurt us, and my closing will get us the conviction. But if Suzanne gets on the stand and tells her story about being kidnapped by the bombers, she'll look very credible. This jury just might buy her story."

"Let's go, Sandy—nice night to visit a judge. Then we'll stop by to see Suzanne and Alva," Henri said.

"Where has Alva been?"

"With Malcolm and his friends."

"Henri, I don't like to tell you what to do, but this Jasper Yates is a huge liability," Ducruet said, looking at Sandchester.

"It's being dealt with as we speak," Sandchester said. "Henri, I don't think it's a good idea to go by the Stinson's. Campy can find out what we need to know." He stood to leave.

"You may be right," Henri said. "We'll see Grunwald and call Campy. Ducruet, you prepare your closing argument and make it good. We should wrap this trial up by the end of next week. So damn close to the election."

"Don't worry about me. Just make sure Grunwald keeps Suzanne off the stand."

* * * *

Judge Martin L. Grunwald lived alone in an old Victorian home in the Garden District. It was just before nine p.m. Only one light was on in the house when Malcolm got out of Suzanne's green BMW and walked slowly to the front door with a manila envelope. He banged on the door, and after a long pause, a tired voice spoke from behind the door. "Yes? Who is it?"

"Malcolm Stinson, sir. I need to speak with you for a minute." There was another hesitation before the door opened slowly.

"Mr. Stinson, I hope this is not about the trial. You'll be in violation of ex-parte," the judge said.

"May I come in? This won't take long," Malcolm said. The judge nodded his head and led Malcolm into his study.

"How can I help you, Counselor?"

"Judge, I can prove my case with these three new witnesses."

"You should leave, Mr. Stinson. You're on the verge of some serious charges here." Grunwald stood up.

Malcolm looked at him but didn't move.

"Sit down, Judge. I've got something to show you," Malcolm stated. The judge sat back down at his desk.

"I've tried to be patient with you," the judge said. "But you leave me no choice. Take yourself off this case and let your team finish."

"Now you listen to me, Judge. Tomorrow I'll make another motion for my witnesses. And you'll cooperate by letting me use them."

"Who the hell do you think you are, boy? What would possibly make me do such a thing?"

"Open the envelope." Malcolm gently placed the envelope before Grunwald.

There were thirteen pictures of the judge naked with young boys. Malcolm leaned on his desk in front of him.

"Unless you want the country to see that the Honorable Judge Grunwald is a pedophile."

The judge put the pictures down on the desk. He took a deep breath.

"This is blackmail. How did you get these pictures?"

"That's not important now. What's important is that you let my witnesses be heard."

"You just want them to testify?" Judge Grunwald questioned humbly.

"No. Since you made sure I had such a short preparation time for this case, give Ducruet only one week. And after the trial, win or lose, you resign. You really can't dispense justice."

"And the pictures?"

"When my witnesses go on, and you resign after the trial, I give you my word the negatives will be destroyed. The only one you'll have to answer to is God. Goodnight, Judge," Malcolm said, and he left.

The judge wept bitterly at his desk. The phone rang twenty minutes after Malcolm left, but the judge turned out the lights and didn't answer it. Henri Joret was calling, but he didn't care. He drank nearly half a quart of Remy Martin, and slept until his driver awakened him in the morning.

* * * *

The buzz in the courtroom was that the defense would end its case this week. The question in the media and newspapers all read the same: "HAS THE DEFENSE PROVEN REASONABLE DOUBT?"

The media surveyed the people, and the consensus was that Clarence Reed was guilty. Ducruet, aware of this, would let his underlings question the remaining witnesses. The courtroom was full, and Judge Grunwald looked hung over.

The jury came in, and then the judge asked if there were any motions to be made. Ducruet replied no. Then Ducruet offered the floor to his esteemed colleague, anticipating the judge's denial of any motions Malcolm would make.

"Your Honor, based on information that was not available to the defense at an earlier time—information we believe is crucial—we ask that three new witnesses be allowed to testify."

Ducruet rose in protest. "Again we object to any new witnesses at this late hour, Your Honor." Ducruet stood, listening for the judge to deny Malcolm's motion before he sat down.

"Seeing that this case is very high profile, and months have been given to discovery on both sides, and seeing that the defendant should be given every opportunity under the law to have a fair trial, I will allow the witnesses to be heard."

Ducruet nearly wet his pants. He rose and addressed Judge Grunwald, his voice cracking.

"Your Honor, just yesterday you denied this very same motion."

"That was yesterday and this is today. And, Mr. Ducruet, never tell me what I can do in my courtroom. Since you're so concerned about the length of the trial, you'll have two weeks to prepare. Anything else?" Grunwald asked. "In that case, we'll adjourn till nine o'clock Tuesday, September 29th."

The courtroom went from complete silence into a total frenzy. Ducruet turned to look at Malcolm, who glanced over and winked.

* * * *

Henri was in Judge Grunwald's study waiting for him to come home. The judge was perturbed that Henri broke into his house, but expected it nonetheless. The judge threw his briefcase in a chair and poured himself a drink. "Care for something, Henri?"

"I don't have much time. You know why I'm here...so tell me, what the hell happened in there today?"

"After reviewing the matter, I felt that due process wouldn't be served if I didn't allow the witnesses to be heard," the judge stated, taking a big gulp of bourbon.

"Since when are you such a stickler for due process?" Henri was enraged.

The judge poured another drink, stared back at Henri, and lifted the shot of bourbon to his lips. When he reached for the bottle again, Henri stopped him.

"Malcolm was here last night, wasn't he? Don't tell me he knows about your little disgusting life," Henri said. The judge's guilty expression gave him away. "You damn fool. So he blackmails you?" Henri walked, took a deep breath, and rubbed his hands through his hair.

"He had pictures—how, I don't know."

The judge poured another drink and flopped into his chair behind his desk.

"Okay. Then we bring him up on charges of ex-parte," Henri said.

"He'll expose me if I do that. We discussed it last night."

"Who cares? We bring him up on the charges. You deny it's true and say that the pictures were fixed to frame you."

"The initial thought of it would still ruin me."

"Who cares? Hell, take it like a man. Finish the trial, retire, and move to Florida. In a year or so, this will all blow over and nobody will even care. Yes, that's what we'll do. Malcolm will be disgraced and that will give the jury even more reason to think Reed is guilty. It's splendid. I'll set up a press conference for tomorrow."

"Henri, I'm not going to do that. I couldn't bear the embarrassment."

"You haven't been listening to me. I don't give a damn about your being embarrassed. There'll be a press conference tomorrow," Henri said, then grabbed his hat to leave.

"Henri, I've been a judge for twenty-five years. And a man who's only known me through a trial is showing some mercy. I've known you for twenty-five years and you want—at the flip of a hat for your own political gain—to feed me to the wolves. So I'll tell you what, Henri Joret," the judge said, fixing his lips for the savory taste of his bourbon, "the witnesses will be heard in two weeks. I'm going to visit some family in Florida for a while and gather my thoughts. And if you expose me to the public, I, in turn, will expose you. Can you afford scandal, weeks before your election?"

"You're finished in Louisiana. You'll never reside over another case. I'll make sure of that." Henri stormed out of the house to the echoing sound of the judge's laughter.

CHAPTER 40

Two days later, Deputy Chief Waller went through intense interrogation by Ducruet, who wanted to know how he was connected to the case. Waller denied any involvement and swore that he would stick to his position.

Malcolm had not yet given Ducruet the pictures of Waller and Jasper. Waller was angered by Ducruet's questioning. Then, shortly before eleven p.m., a phone call came through. Ducruet simply answered a few uh-huh's, and then let Waller go.

Waller, sweating profusely from the long hours of questioning, waddled down to his waiting car to be taken home. He walked into his empty house, fed his goldfish, and made kissy noises to his two parakeets. He grabbed a bottle of beer and sat down in his favorite easy chair.

The birds began chirping uncontrollably and flapped their wings wildly. The shining knife glared in the living room. Waller told them to shut up or he would cover their cage. The intruder swiftly grabbed Waller under the chin, forcing his head back against the chair. Then, in a swift swipe, the twelve-inch hunting knife cut Waller's throat. Waller died instantly. The intruder cleaned his blade on Waller's shirt sleeve, turned out the lights, and walked out the back door.

* * * *

Jon Tulle arrived at the Reed defense headquarters at ten-thirty in the morning. Malcolm and Hingley were laughing, and wished that they could have been there to see the expression on Ducruet's face when he showed Waller the pictures of himself, Jasper, and the Dalton brothers together.

Suzanne was cooperating nicely, but Waller would be a challenge as a hostile witness.

Tulle walked into the room looking forlorn. Malcolm and Hingley stopped laughing.

"Have something on your mind, Tulle?" Malcolm asked.

"You haven't heard?"

"What?" Malcolm asked.

"The police found Waller dead in his house this morning. His throat was cut."

"Good Lord Jesus!" Malcolm shouted out. They all stood up and faced the window. "What do I do now?"

* * * *

The early polls showed that Henri was behind his opponent in Shreveport; the campaign needed a boost in this area. Campy Frazier was campaigning day and night in nearby Monroe. Henri had called a press conference for Sunday afternoon.

There'd been a lot of speculation about Alva Joret's absence in recent weeks. After his usual campaign rhetoric, Henri explained that Alva was visiting family in North Dakota, where the Red River was flooding again, but not to the severity that it had overflowed in 1997. The press looked into the matter, but Alva was nowhere to be found.

Malcolm and Hingley had decided that more time was needed before bringing Suzanne onto the stand.

Security was increased even more than it had been before. The reverend had an entourage of ten men everywhere he went. Church services continued on Sunday afternoons at Mount Zion Baptist Church, because the construction of the new church on his original site wouldn't be completed until the latter part of January.

In the light of Deputy Commissioner Waller's untimely death, they had to realign their defense strategy.

On September 29th, arrangements were made with the court to bring Suzanne in through a side entrance.

Bill Wettington was a court deputy, but also a close militia friend of Jasper Yates. He had arranged for Jasper to have a uniform and a pass to move about in the courthouse. Wettington's only other job was to make sure Malcolm and his group of lawyers were not allowed in the side entrance.

Malcolm and Suzanne arrived shortly before nine o'clock. The guards informed them of their new orders not to let them in that entrance. Furious, Malcolm went to the front of the Federal building, where armies of reporters were waiting. He wrapped his arm around Suzanne, who was wearing a blue dress with dark sunglasses and a black scarf over her head. They entered into the media frenzy as reporters lashed out questions to their former colleague, asking about her role in the case. She looked down at the steps as Malcolm led her up the stairs. The sea of people got thicker with every step.

Jasper nonchalantly placed himself in Malcolm and Suzanne's path, where he was surrounded by reporters. He pulled out his gun with his right hand, and pulled out a silencer with his left. He didn't look down at what he was doing; his eyes were fixed on Malcolm and Suzanne. With his gun at his side, he stood still as Malcolm and Suzanne approached him.

There was only one tier of humans between him and his target. He eased his wrist up and pointed the gun. An opening for a shot was all he was waiting for. Jasper slowly eased on the trigger, just as a photographer jumped in front of Malcolm and Suzanne to take a picture. Jasper let the bullet fly, and the man fell to the ground.

Jasper stepped backward as the crowd panicked and blood streamed out of the photographer's back. Jasper kicked a reporter down the steps, along with the gun. Some noticed the man and the gun tumbling down the steps. Deputies were racing to the scene. Malcolm stopped in front of the shot photographer. Suzanne tried to let out a scream, but couldn't. Malcolm noticed a deputy walking in the opposite direction. Jasper stopped and, for a brief moment, locked eyes with Malcolm.

Malcolm walked around the wounded photographer, and into the courthouse, while watching Jasper slip away. Malcolm didn't point Jasper out, in fear that he'd shoot someone else.

The jury seemed anxious to hear Suzanne's testimony—many knew her as a television anchorwoman and had heard about her mysterious disappearance earlier that year.

Judge Grunwald ran through the preliminary business, and instructed Malcolm to call his witness.

Suzanne took the stand and was sworn in. Malcolm calmly approached her, and she seemed relaxed in his presence. He asked her name, age, occupation, and how long she had been working.

"Ms. Joret, how did you first learn of the riverboat bombing?"

"Well, Reuben Caulfield, a colleague of mine who worked for the Times Picayune, gave me a tip about some men he'd heard talking about a bombing..."

"Where did that conversation take place?"

"In New Orleans at a little restaurant where homeless people hang out."

"What was he doing there?"

"Working undercover, writing a story on the homeless of New Orleans."

"Go on."

"He noticed Deputy Chief Commissioner Waller meeting with another man," she said. Malcolm walked over to retrieve the blown-up pictures Caulfield had given him.

"For the record, could you identify Chief Waller in this photo?"

"Yes, that's him." She pointed to the photo.

"I would like to show you another photo of Chief Waller with three other men. Can you identify them?"

"Yes, there's Chief Waller, Jasper Yates, and Jim and Jerry Dalton."

"And how do you know these men, Ms. Joret?"

"I was supposed to meet Reuben, but then got a phone call from Jasper Yates, who told me to meet him just outside the bayou at seven o'clock. He had information about the riverboat bombing."

"Did you go?"

"Yes."

"And then?"

"I was knocked unconscious. The next thing I knew, I was deep in the bayou, in a shack surrounded by alligators."

"And what did the Daltons want?"

"Jasper and the Daltons wanted to know what I knew about the bombing. I told them I knew nothing—that was the truth. Jasper and Jerry left Jim behind to guard me."

"How long were you kept captive?"

"I was in handcuffs and leg chains for nearly six months."

"Would you please show the court your wrists and ankles?" Malcolm looked at the jurors' faces following her story. He had a captive audience.

"So how were you made aware of the bombing?"

"Jim told me that he was a Klan member here in Louisiana. His brother and Jasper worked for a man who was sympathetic to the injustices the government was inflicting on fine, working, white Americans."

"Did he ever mention Clarence Reed?"

"Yes. He said they had to shut down the Reed boy because they didn't want to see a resurgence of a movement, like that of the late Dr. Martin Luther King, Jr. He talked about eliminating affirmative action, abortion rights—all the social injustices that still remain in America..."

"Objection, Your Honor. This story is unfounded and irrelevant to the case," Ducruet stated.

"Overruled. Get to your point, though, Mr. Stinson," Grunwald said.

"Did Jim Dalton ever tell you that Clarence Reed was involved in the riverboat bombing?"

"They thoroughly planned the framing of the bombing on Clarence. He bragged about how they blew up the gambling riverboat and had the authorities arrest Clarence. He called it a typical justice in America—arrest a black man and the rest will be easy."

"You said that you were held hostage in the bayou. How did you get out?"

"Well, two men, Willy and Dexter—I don't recall their last names. They came looking for some gas for their car and stumbled across Jim Dalton holding me hostage. I pleaded for them to help me. Jim tried to throw them out but they subdued him and released me."

"Why didn't you go to the police or the FBI?"

"With all due respect, I didn't trust anyone at that time. I went with my friend, Kathy Sommers, to my parents' home on the White River in Arkansas, but Jasper showed up there, too. We escaped from him and went to another house my brother owned in Lafayette. That's when I contacted you."

"Why didn't you go to your father?" Suzanne froze for a moment. She hadn't expected Malcolm to ask her that question.

"My father was busy campaigning for governor, and if those people—Jasper and the Dalton brothers—were to jeopardize my parents' lives in this whole ordeal..."

Her answer impressed Malcolm.

"Did you know that this man..." Malcolm pointed to the blown-up photo of Jerry Dalton. "...was arrested that same weekend, May 30th, in New York City for killing two FBI men, and one NYPD officer, and fatally wounding Reuben Caulfield?"

"Not until weeks after it had happened..."

"Your Honor, this is speculation on the witness's part," Ducruet said.

"Your Honor, if it pleases the court, we can stop Ms. Joret's testimony and bring on any member of the FBI that is present here today to verify this point for the government."

"Mr. Ducruet, do you have any objection to this?"

"No, Your Honor. The government concedes that these are actual facts. But we do object to their being tied to this case."

"Mr. Stinson, can you tie this in with the case?"

"Yes, Your Honor, I can. Ms. Joret, before you escaped from the shack in the bayou, how often did you see Jasper and Jerry?"

"Oh, maybe once a week. They usually called every day."

"How do you know that?"

"Jim was very talkative."

"Did you ever see anyone else?" Malcolm reached for another blown-up poster.

"Yes, a man they called Smitty."

"And what did Smitty do?"

"He was an old friend of theirs from the Navy—an explosives expert."

"So why was Smitty there?"

"Smitty laid the blueprints for how the bombs were to be placed on the riverboat. But this particular night he was brought in for a job, one that Jim went on as well."

"What was that?"

"They were to bomb the Reverend Josiah Stinson's church," Suzanne said. The courtroom stirred.

The judge hit his gavel to quiet the courtroom.

"Objection, Your Honor," said Ducruet. "All this testimony is hearsay, and circumstantial evidence. The Dalton brothers can't testify unless we're going to witness a resurrection service here. This mystery bomber, Smitty, where is he? And what of this Jasper Yates? Who knows where he is?"

"Your Honor," Malcolm said, still holding the poster in his hands. "The witness is giving her account of being kidnapped. She has gone through a great deal of trepidation just to come here to testify."

"For the most part," Judge Grunwald said, "the evidence is hearsay, but considering Ms. Joret's integrity and the alleged ordeal she was put through, I would instruct the jury to weigh her testimony against the strength of the evidence presented by both parties. Objection overruled. Continue, Mr. Stinson."

"I just have a couple more questions. At anytime did Jim or Jerry—or even Jasper Yates—tell you who was sponsoring them?"

"Absolutely. Jim called him a dirty old man not to be trusted, even though he paid well. His name was Jean Claude Monet. Sometime in April, Jim said that

Monet was upset that I was still alive. For some reason, Jasper Yates wanted me alive."

"Where was Jean Claude Monet located?"

"He's a mafia boss in Montreal."

"Why would these so-called righteous militia men work for a crime boss?"

"Jim said Monet paid them more to supply their cause."

"Don't militia groups take stands against the mafia?"

"Jim said they hated the mafia as much as the government—both rip off the American public."

"Did Jim ever talk about other militia groups?"

"Yes, they network with other groups, like the Aryan Nation, Neo-Nazis, Ku Klux Klan, The World Order. They also recruit a lot from the military."

"Objection, Your Honor. Where are we going with this?" asked Ducruet.

"You're going to sit right in your seat. Objection overruled. Get to your point, Counselor."

"Your testimony indicates that you spent the majority of your captivity with Jim Dalton?"

"Practically the entire time. Jasper and Jerry just popped in every once in a while."

"Did Jim ever say who comprised this bombing team?"

"Jasper worked with former Navy SEALs who were sympathetic to his causes."

"In what way?"

"They did other missions, such as the bombings of black churches."

"Objection, Your Honor. This is ludicrous. She's telling the story of a dead man who can't testify," Ducruet interjected, nearly pushing Malcolm away from the lectern.

"Mr. Ducruet, I am well aware that Jim Dalton can't defend these statements. But under the circumstances, there may be some validity to her testimony. Objection overruled."

"Did he talk about how he assembled these men?"

"Jasper kept a file on all his recruits who wanted to join hate groups once they left the service. He had contacts with nearly every hate group in America."

"Did he tell you about the men involved in the riverboat bombing—how many there were, where they were from?"

"He said six men were involved: he and his brother from Louisiana, one from Arizona, South Carolina, Pennsylvania, and one from Illinois. The only name I knew, besides the Dalton brothers and Jasper Yates, was Smitty from South Carolina."

Malcolm turned on the projector for the jury to see the list of names and newspaper articles verifying the dates. "Your Honor, we have a list of men from the states that Ms. Joret just named, along with a newspaper article from each one of their towns. Two weeks ago, within a seventy-two hour time period, an arsonist killed all of these men and their families. All of these men served under Jasper Yates, who is still at large. Jim was found in the White River outside the Joret Arkansas home. Isn't that true, Ms. Joret?"

"Yes. That's where Jasper tried to kill me and my friend Kathy."

Malcolm moved over to a tape recorder and prepared it to play.

"Ms. Joret, do you know the defendant, Clarence Reed, on a personal basis?"

"Yes...we are very good friends. We met a couple years ago when I was covering a story about Afro-Asian children."

"Please listen to this tape from your telephone answering machine."

Malcolm played it three times for the jury, and then played just the audio of Jasper's training tape. "Do you recognize that voice, Ms. Joret?"

"Yes, I do...it's Jasper Yates."

"Now, please watch these videos without the audio and tell me if you can recognize these men."

Malcolm first showed the video of Oppenheimer in Harpo Steven's office. While the video was playing and the lights were dim in the courtroom, Malcolm said, "Please notice how these two men gesture with their hands." He then showed the tape of Jasper Yates addressing young Navy SEAL cadets. The jurors watched with rapt attention. Malcolm turned back to the defense table, and then he caught the eye of a U.S. Marshal standing in the back of the courtroom. Malcolm froze. Jasper couldn't be in here, he thought as he turned back to Suzanne.

"Now, Ms. Joret, did you recognize either man?" Suzanne identified the soldier as Jasper Yates. Malcolm thought for a second about asking Suzanne to look at the U.S. Marshal in the back of the court, then grabbing her and diving for the floor. He'd either look like an idiot, or be a hero capturing a terrorist. He stretched out his arms on the witness box railing with his head looking down.

"Mr. Stinson, are you alright?" Judge Grunwald asked, concerned with Malcolm's delay. Malcolm looked at the judge.

"Yes, Your Honor, I was just thinking of my next question." He headed back to his table for notes and glanced to the rear of the courtroom. Now only two U.S. Marshals were there. The blood rushed through Malcolm's head. Jasper is in the courtroom.

Without turning back to the judge or Suzanne, Malcolm said, "I have no more questions at this time, Your Honor, with your permission to redirect, if necessary."

"Since we didn't break for lunch, we will take an hour. It's one fifty-eight, so we'll return at two fifty-eight, at which time, Mr. Ducruet, you may begin your cross-examination," Judge Grunwald said, getting ready to hit his gavel as he noticed Ducruet rising to speak.

"Yes, Mr. Ducruet?"

"Your Honor, in light of the new testimony and evidence that we have learned today, the People would ask that you allow the state to review this evidence about the five men and their mysterious deaths and let us begin cross-examination first thing tomorrow morning."

The judge thought for a moment. "Motion granted. We'll reconvene at nine o'clock tomorrow morning."

"Your Honor," Malcolm said. "May we approach the sidebar first?"

Malcolm and Ducruet approached the bench.

"Your Honor, a reporter was shot on the steps outside as we were coming into court today by a man in a U.S. Marshal's uniform."

"Are you sure about this?" Judge Grunwald asked.

"This is preposterous, Your Honor!" said Ducruet.

"Then check the video of the courtroom and compare the picture of Jasper Yates who is dressed as a U.S. Marshal," Malcolm said.

"You're telling me that this so-called terrorist, Jasper Yates, was in my courtroom today, dressed as a Marshal?" Judge Grunwald asked.

"Your Honor, you can check with Chief Inspector Jon Tulle of the FBI. He has his men combing the country now for Yates," Malcolm said.

"Your Honor, this is ridiculous." Ducruet, wanting to leave the sidebar, moved away for a second.

"I'll check it out, Mr. Stinson. Expect a conference call tonight, gentlemen. Good day," Judge Grunwald said.

"I would like permission for my staff and Suzanne Joret to leave through an alternate exit, Your Honor."

"Very well. Once the court has emptied out, you can leave through my chambers."

* * * *

Malcolm and Suzanne were greeted at his parents' home by six black Lincoln Continental limousines. Alva was waiting on the front steps with her two brothers—a Senator from Texas, and the president of the Dallas First National Bank. There were fifteen bodyguards lining the steps to the house. Cephus, Willy, and Dexter were also standing on the front porch.

"Hello, Mama. What's going on?" Suzanne asked, hugging her mother.

"I think we've imposed enough on the Stinson's. I'm going to Grandpa Casey's house in Texas for awhile, until I can sort things out," Alva said.

She turned to hug Lois Stinson. "Thank you so much for everything you and your husband have done for Suzanne and me. Promise you'll come visit me in Texas. I'll have someone pick you up and take you to Daddy's private plane at the airport. We'll have a fun time," she said, with tears in her eyes. "I never knew people could be so friendly without wanting anything from you."

"God bless you, honey. May the good Lord watch over your every step," Lois said.

"You take care of yourself and make sure you go to that church I told you about in Dallas/Fort Worth," Reverend Josiah said, as Alva gave him a big hug and kiss on the cheek. She waved good-bye, and then walked up to Malcolm.

"If there's anything I can do to help you...your father and I were talking about some of your legal debts. I left a number with him. Call and we'll work them out. Thank you. You're a brave man. Your friends are, too," she said, as tears rolled down her face. "Well, honey," Alva asked Suzanne, "are you coming to Texas?"

"I have to go back to the trial, hopefully, for just one more day." Suzanne looked at Malcolm.

"Tomorrow should be it for you," Malcolm answered.

"If you don't mind, Malcolm," Alva said. "I'll leave six of Daddy's hired hands to watch over ya'll. Just tell them what you want them to do." Then she whispered in Malcolm's ear. "Whatever you do, be careful. There is no limit to what Henri will do to have his way. He wants to be president of the United States and he'd make a deal with the devil to get it."

She backed away and added, "Take care of those precious little children and that beautiful wife of yours. Don't say a thing...I know the whole story. Women talk when they have time on their hands. Some say it's better the second time around." Alva kissed Malcolm and pranced into the limo as the media flashed away.

The senator and the bank president walked by Malcolm, and one of them said, "We thank you, and our daddy thanks you. Please call if we can be of any assistance." They got into the limo with Alva and most of the media followed them as they drove off.

Malcolm found Willy and Dexter smiling on the porch. Alva had paid them one hundred thousand dollars and offered funding for any legal problems they had recently incurred.

"Cephus, Jasper Yates was in the courtroom today dressed as U.S. Marshal," Malcolm said.

"You sure about that?" said Cephus.

"He stared right at me."

"You're just imagining that—their security system wouldn't let something like that happen."

"Yeah? Well, he shot a reporter on the front steps of the courthouse as we were going in."

* * * *

"Damn it, Henri," Ducruet said. "Your little girl got the sympathy of those jurors today. She may have thrown our entire case down the pooper by naming people, times, and places. And what about the judge? Grunwald acts like I'm a Nazi defending Hitler in a room full of Jews—he objects to everything I say or do." Ducruet paced the floor of Henri's study.

"Only one thing to do," Sandchester said, while cleaning his fingernails.

"Wait! Before you say anything," Ducruet interrupted, lighting a cigarette. "Malcolm claimed that Jasper Yates was in the courtroom this afternoon, get this...dressed as a U.S. Marshal! Can you believe this boy's paranoia?"

"What did Grunwald say?" asked Sandchester.

"We're having a conference call tonight. Malcolm also thinks that Jasper tried to kill Suzanne before court this morning," Ducruet said.

"You have to discredit her."

"How, Mr. Campaign Manager?"

"Simple. Talk about the problems she'd had with her stepfather over the years. Talk about her affair with Clarence Reed. Maybe the jury will feel she was getting back at her stepfather...that the kidnapping was a ploy to humiliate him."

"Stick with your evidence in the closing statement," Henri said. "No more scandal. I'm going to try to make peace with Alva, and then she'll bring Suzanne around, and maybe by Election Day, we'll look like a family again. Sandchester, make sure my boys are more visible to the press."

Henri poured some scotch. "Don't blow this, Ducruet."

"What do we do about this maniac Yates?" Ducruet asked.

"Don't worry about him. My boys will be on the lookout tomorrow. If he's around, we'll get him. I could kill Monet for ever introducing him to me. He's efficient, but not worth the trouble," Henri said.

The telephone rang. Henri picked it up and handed it to Ducruet, who nodded in agreement to everything the other party was saying.

"What was that all about?" Henri asked.

"The judge wants to see Stinson and me in his chambers in one hour."

Sandchester answered a knock on the door. Corky Nackles limped in; he had a small hump in his back from a childhood disease. He was born in Mississippi, educated at Yale, and made his home in Louisiana. Nackles was neither Republican nor Democrat. He was a political opportunist. Years ago when Governor Edwards was running, Nackles had been a liaison between Governor Edwards and the black community. He had an uncanny ability for bringing groups, cultures, and races together to support the politician that would benefit them. For Henri Joret's election, he was a liaison between the Ku Klux Klan and the Neo-Nazi groups.

Henri had forgotten about their scheduled meeting.

"Corky, I've lost track of the time. If you could wait outside, I'll be right there," Henri said.

CHAPTER 41

Ducruet and Malcolm arrived at the same time. The judge sat behind his desk. A monitor had been set up. Three deputies, a court clerk, and one U.S. Marshall were also in the room. The judge offered coffee, introduced the others, then excused the deputies, but asked the Marshall and the court clerk to stay.

A split screen on the monitor showed the picture of Jasper that Malcolm had submitted in court, and the photo of the U.S. Marshall.

Jasper had added a fake nose and glasses, but everyone agreed that the photograph of the Marshall was Jasper Yates.

U.S. Marshall Greenwood turned off the projector. "We found the dead Marshall's body in a hotel room this afternoon. My people and the FBI are investigating this matter, so even if Yates isn't involved in the riverboat bombing, we want him for murder."

"I don't understand how this could have happened," Judge Grunwald said. "But we'll continue tomorrow as scheduled. Any questions, gentlemen?"

"What kind of protection can I expect for my defense team and Suzanne Joret?" questioned Malcolm.

"I have three men that I can personally vouch for," Marshall Greenwood said.

"One other thing: Jasper shot that woman on the front steps today," Malcolm said. There was no response.

"Shall I have my men pick up your people and bring them to the courthouse?" the Marshall asked.

"Just give me your number and we'll call you tomorrow morning."

"Very well." Greenwood wrote down a cellular phone number and handed it to Malcolm.

* * * *

When Malcolm and company arrived at the courthouse, a couple hundred skinheads were lined up by the side entrance that Malcolm had arranged to use with Marshall Greenwood. The skinheads shouted obscenities at Suzanne, calling her a nigger lover and a traitor to her race. The FBI filmed the skinheads, as death threats and ethnic slurs flew. If Clarence was acquitted, they promised that he'd be dead in twenty-four hours.

Malcolm scanned the heathen crowd for Jasper. No one had expected a demonstration this morning, but Suzanne's testimony had made these people angry.

The judge entered the courtroom, the jury came in, and Suzanne took the witness stand.

Ducruet glanced at his notes one last time before approaching her. She looked relaxed and quite stunning.

Ducruet proceeded gingerly, even though he wanted to destroy her credibility.

"Ms. Joret, how long have you done investigative reporting for Channel Eight News?"

"About three years."

"So…you would find out about a story, and then check it out?"

"My first year at the station, I was in the field one hundred percent of the time, and reported the story from the scene."

"Then you moved into the anchor position…what…during your second year?"

"Yes."

"So what percentage of the stories that you reported did you actually investigate? Ten…twenty…thirty percent?"

"I can't put a number on them, but field reporters fed stories back to me at the news station, if that's your question."

"Exactly!" Ducruet said.

He hesitated before asking the next question. If Henri Joret didn't win the election, his promised job with the state—attorney general—was lost, and he'd be criticized for going easy on Suzanne if he lost the case. Henri would have his ass, but he had to ask Suzanne the next questions.

"Ms. Joret, how long have you known Clarence Reed?" Ducruet glanced at Malcolm, who wanted to object, but didn't, for fear the jury would think Suzanne was hiding something.

"About three years. As I said yesterday, we met when I was doing a story about Afro-Asian children in Louisiana," she said.

"Did you and Clarence Reed socialize from time to time?"

"Objection, Your Honor," Malcolm said. "I don't see how this line of questioning is relevant to the riverboat bombing."

"Objection overruled. I'll allow this line of questioning to continue only if you make your point now."

"Yes, Your Honor," Ducruet said.

"Yes, we saw each other quite often."

"Isn't it true that you were planning to marry?"

"Objection, Your Honor. She's answered his question," Malcolm said.

"Sustained. Counselor, make your point."

"So you're seeing Clarence Reed for three years. The riverboat bombing occurs in July. Then some six months later, you tell us that a terrorist has kidnapped you. Why was no ransom asked for your release? Did Clarence Reed ever talk about bombing the riverboat or anything that was against his Christian—or your—principles?"

"No."

"Well, that's strange, because we have his testimony that he wished God's judgment would be visited on people that promoted gambling, abortion, and affirmative action. And you're telling this court that he never talked about stopping these activities in society?"

"Yes, he did, but…"

"Thank you for answering the question. Now, you testified that Jim Dalton volunteered all this information to you. A person who didn't ask for any ransom."

"I assume they planned to kill me when the time suited them. Only one time Jim asked me how much I thought that my parents would pay for my release."

"What was your answer?"

"Someone came into the shack," Suzanne answered, remembering Rusty.

"And who was it that came knocking on the door in the middle of alligator heaven?"

"I don't know. I was tied up and couldn't answer the door," she said coolly, to the delight of the jury.

"Were Willy Johnson and Dexter Holland the two black men who rescued you? Can you identify these photos?"

"Yes, it's them."

"Did you know that they are wanted for a multitude of crimes?"

"No, I didn't. When you've been held hostage for six months, you don't ask for references," Suzanne said.

Ducruet frowned and walked back to his table. "No further questions, Your Honor," Ducruet finished, surprising Malcolm, who thought he'd grind out Suzanne's previous day's testimony.

"Since it's nearly lunchtime, we'll start tomorrow morning with the defense presenting their closing argument."

"Yes, Your Honor," Malcolm said, wondering what Ducruet's game was.

The judge told the jury that they should have the case to decide within the next two days.

* * * *

There was a media frenzy outside the courtroom the next morning. The skinheads had returned in force, but this time there were Clarence Reed supporters in the hundreds, too. Churches from all over the country had come in support of the closing arguments. People of all races and religions—black, white, Asian, Hispanic, Christian—came to show their support for Clarence Reed.

Malcolm surveyed the crowd for any glimpse of Jasper Yates, but saw nothing. On the side of a tractor trailer someone had painted a picture of an Oriental man in an Afro-style hairdo, with a stick of dynamite sticking out of his mouth, ears with fuses, and three hands off the side with lit matches moving toward the dynamite. The next picture said: AFTER THE TRIAL GIVE THE BLACKIE-CHINK TO US.

The cast for the day's proceedings was in place and Malcolm began his closing argument.

Malcolm stood about ten feet from the jury, cupping his hands over his mouth till each juror gave their rapt attention. Malcolm gave his closing statement in forty-five minutes, and Ducruet followed using fifty minutes.

There was a moment of silence in the court. The judge rifled through some papers on his desk, then turned to the jury and instructed them on their duties before they left to deliberate. The jury was dismissed and the judge adjourned court for the day.

* * * *

It was Election Day, November 3rd, and the jury had been out for nearly four weeks. Rumors were flying that it would be a hung jury.

Early polls showed Henri Joret had a substantial lead in southeastern Louisiana, but was slightly behind in the north.

Malcolm was at home, sitting on the porch with Sara and the kids, when the phone rang at five-thirty. He knew this was the call. Reverend Stinson walked out to the porch and quietly said, "It's time to go. The jury has reached a verdict."

Malcolm was in the courtroom in less than an hour. Ducruet and his team were there, too. Tulle and the FBI stood against the back wall.

Henri and Sandchester forgot about the polls and turned on the television. Jasper Yates watched from a motel in west Texas. Victor Zano and his henchmen drank Cappuccino in a little restaurant on Mulberry Street in New York City. Jean Claude Monet was hiding out in a ski town near Ottawa, Canada.

Clarence sat perfectly still, as a few beads of sweat formed and rolled down his face. Malcolm could hear Clarence whispering, "If God be for me, who can be against me?"

Suzanne sat behind them. The announcement of the jury's verdict halted the entire nation for a moment. By NOPD estimation, at least four or five thousand Reed supporters were outside the courthouse, as were nearly equal numbers of militiamen, Klansman, Neo-Nazis, and those Louisianans who thought Clarence Reed was guilty.

At the governor's request, the mayor called out the National Guard, who wedged themselves between the two groups. The networks used split-screens to show inside the courtroom, and the crowd outside. For the time being, no one was interested in the next governor, senator, or congressman—everyone was concentrating on the Big Easy.

Pete was enjoying a beer and po-boy sandwich with Willy and Dexter in a bar in the French Quarter, when a hush fell over the restaurant. Peter Jennings began the report of the trial.

"You are watching a live picture from the Federal courthouse in New Orleans. A lively crowd has been gathering outside the courthouse. The jury has been seated. The foreman is juror number seventy-one, a life insurance salesman, Tom Salis. Let's listen in," Jennings reported.

"Have you come to a verdict, Mr. Foreman?" Judge Grunwald asked.

"Yes, we have, Your Honor," Tom Salis said. The bailiff took the verdict from the foreman and handed it to the judge, who glanced at it without expression. Then the bailiff returned the verdict form to Tom Salis.

"Please read the verdict," Judge Grunwald said.

"We, the jury in the case of the United States vs. Clarence Reed, for the crime of murder and terrorism on United States soil, find the defendant...not guilty."

A roar came from Reed's supporters. Clarence hugged Malcolm and kept repeating, "Thank You, Jesus." Suzanne rose to hug Clarence, while jubilation burst out at the defense table.

Suzanne and Clarence were locked in an embrace and crying when yells came from the back of the courtroom for Clarence to speak to the press.

Ducruet offered his hand to Malcolm. "Congratulations, Counselor, on a job well done. Any plans for staying in New Orleans?"

"Thanks. Tell Henri I had my reasons for not dragging him into this. Also tell him that I know everything." Malcolm saw a bewildered look on Ducruet's face, and then looked at the judge who returned the look without expression.

Outside the courthouse, the National Guard stood between the Reed supporters and the hate groups, who were calling for Clarence Reed's blood.

Pete, Willy, and Dexter congratulated each other while the white patrons were in shock. Willy said, "Similar reaction in the Simpson verdict."

Peter Jennings' voice came on again as the television showed the scene outside the courtroom.

"We have a reaction from one of the family members of the riverboat bombing. Can you hear me?" Peter asked the elderly Roy Alters, whose wife and daughter were killed on the boat that night.

"Yes, I can."

"Tell us what this verdict means to you."

"I'm disappointed. The government put on an excellent case and the jury has let a mass murderer go free. I'm sorry, sir. I can't talk about this right now. It's like reliving the news about my wife and daughter," Roy Alters said, as tears choked him up.

CHAPTER 42

A thousand people had been invited to the Joret mansion for the Inauguration Party. Wanting to make amends with Suzanne, Henri invited Clarence, Malcolm, Cephus, Pete, and Lucy Yee, who all arrived together.

The maid Colette answered the door, letting Malcolm and the others in, as two security guards in black tuxedos looked them over. In the entryway, a portrait of Huey Long, the famed Louisiana politician, hung in a huge gilted frame.

Voices echoed throughout the house. Zydeco music blared, and hundreds of balloons were perched in a net on the ceiling, waiting to be released later that evening.

Clarence found Suzanne conversing with some local politicians. Campy was in a corner of the room with all of his backers—politicians, businessmen, and clergy.

The atmosphere was joyful, even though Klansmen walked around without their hooded sheets. This was the new look of Southern politics—black and white,—clergy and hate mongers—all wrapped together for an evening of collecting what Henri had promised them all.

Then Corky Nackles limped past Cephus and Malcolm wearing a black tuxedo with his black Beatles-style wig.

"Is something wrong?" Malcolm asked Cephus.

"A few years back when Edwards was governor, Corky worked with me and my father in registering the black vote. Every time we see each other we always exchange chit-chat."

"Maybe he doesn't feel like talking tonight," Malcolm said.

"You know, it's strange that his wife reported him missing to the police. Three days ago, the officer in charge of missing persons told me that two days earlier he had visited Corky's wife and there was no new information. Now he shows up here at the party without her. He's a lowlife, but a dedicated husband."

"So he comes to the party without his wife. What's the big deal?" Malcolm questioned, signaling with a slight wave of his hand to the waitress coming around with the hors d'oeuvres.

"I'm going down here to see Campy for a minute. You coming?" Cephus asked.

"No. I'll just mosey around and check out the scenery."

It wasn't long before the guests noticed Malcolm, and folks surrounded him, talking about the trial and future job opportunities.

He saw Clarence leaving Suzanne at the bottom of the spiral staircase; they kissed and exchanged loving glances. Just as Suzanne was about to take the third step up, Corky Nackles approached her. Malcolm couldn't hear their conversation.

"Good evening, Suzanne. We haven't talked since your terrible ordeal," Nackles said, stepping next to Suzanne.

"Hello, Mr. Nackles."

"I don't suppose you know your father's whereabouts?"

"I believe he's upstairs with Mr. Sandchester, preparing his victory-party speech," she said.

"I really need to talk to him beforehand," Corky said.

"I'll check and see if he can see you," she said. Nackles took another step toward her. As she turned her back to walk upstairs, Nackles reached for a gun in his pocket, and put his left arm around her, placing the gun just below her left breast.

"Mr. Nackles…!"

"Now keep very quiet, Suzanne, and your boyfriend will still have two handfuls."

Suzanne felt a ball of anxiety harden in her stomach. She hesitated at first while still stepping up the spiral staircase. Corky led her upstairs to the room Henri and Sandchester were in.

"Corky, what the hell are you up to, man?" Henri blurted out, as he bolted out of his seat.

"Sit down, Henri, and don't let me have to tell you again," Corky said, waving the gun back and forth at them. He reached for his neck and, in one motion, pulled the flesh mask off his face, and then removed the wig.

"Damn, that thing was getting hot. Whew! Never thought you'd see me again, huh, Henri?"

"My God!" Henri said.

"Well, it looks like you got off scot-free. The FBI, ATF, and every cop in America are looking for me. But Henri Joret is the governor of Louisiana. I'm just here to collect my money," Jasper said, reaching for a piece of paper in his coat pocket. The paper had the number of a bank account in Zurich, Switzerland. The number read 739 228 AS.

"Now, get on the phone and wire one million dollars to that bank account."

"You've got to be crazy. The banks are closed!" Sandchester replied.

"Not in Zurich, Shorty. If I hear one more word from you, I'll remember that you sent your goons to kill me. Now start dialing, Henri. We don't have much time. You don't want to keep your guests waiting," Jasper threatened, pointing the gun at Henri. He began dialing slowly.

*　　*　　*　　*

Malcolm was curious about the way Nackles had just walked upstairs with Suzanne. She had seemed nervous.

Without knocking, Malcolm barged in.

"My, my, our party is getting bigger by the minute," Jasper stated, grabbing Suzanne and pointing the gun at her head.

"Mr. Stinson, I'm sure you don't want to see this little lady's brains splattered all over. Now carefully move over there by Henri. I see we have a slight communication problem. Maybe I can fix that for you," Jasper said. Jasper held the gun up in the air and a bullet pierced through Sandchester's head. His head jerked back from the bullet and blood gushed from his forehead. "Now, who's next?" Jasper asked.

The group quickly dropped to the floor.

"You won't get away this time, Jasper," Malcolm threatened.

"Henri, you should be finished dialing by now," Jasper said, pointing the gun at him.

"It's done," Henri replied.

"Good. Now we'll just wait for my confirmation on the other end, and I'll bid you people goodnight," Jasper said. Malcolm gave Jasper an evil look.

"You shouldn't be angry with me, boy. Henri's the one who caused all this trouble."

Everyone looked at Henri.

"He's lying," Henri said, with a half smile.

"Am I? Well, if you ever catch up with that French swamp rat, Monet, he'll tell the truth. After all, who do you think gave Waller the information that the gullible Inspector Tulle used to arrest Clarence? Jerry Dalton and I planted the C-4 explosives in his house," Jasper admitted, then turned his attention to Henri.

"I'm curious, Henri. How did you kill all of my men in such a short time? You did me a favor. When I saw that the counselor here was on my trail, that was my next move. Even though you missed Smith, I caught him for you."

"The Dalton brothers, you took care of them as well?" Malcolm asked.

"Best shot I ever made...a classic. So, Henri, how did you do that?"

"It wasn't of Henri's doing," said Malcolm.

"Umm...I must have secret allies I don't even know about. Oh, well, a job well done, nonetheless," Jasper said, glancing at his watch. "I think I'm going to have to leave. Henri, if my money is there, you can rest."

"Why did you kidnap Suzanne?" Malcolm asked.

"At first, Monet wanted to kill her because she was snooping around and overheard a conversation here in this house. We watched her for a while, and found out she was onto something. So the next logical thing to do was to eliminate her. But, my lovely, you can thank me for sparing your life. It turned out to be a mistake, though. I disobeyed orders—totally out of character for me. Mistakes like that can cost you, right, Henri?" Jasper asked, looking at Henri. "But a month or so before them niggers rescued her—oh, Henri, he was here, well aware that we had her under wraps. He couldn't do anything about it, because she was my bargaining chip. But he knew." Jasper started laughing. "Your poor mother was so concerned about you, and Henri boy could have cared less. He more or less gave me the okay to terminate you," Jasper said, smiling at Suzanne.

There was knock on the door that distracted Jasper for a second. Malcolm lunged at Jasper in a flash. They rolled on the floor punching wildly at each other. Jasper reached for his hunting knife that was holstered on his waist. He kicked Malcolm's feet from under him, and then threw a leg kick into Malcolm's face. He picked up the gun and pointed at Henri, then shot him squarely between the eyes.

Jasper jumped through the window and landed on the glass roof of Alva's greenhouse and tumbled onto a table of chrysanthemums. A shard of glass punctured his right arm.

Taking a deep breath, bleeding, and in great pain from the fall, the old soldier managed to make it to the road where a car was waiting for him.

The shot brought security guards upstairs, along with the state police, Tulle, Clarence, and Pete. The police pursued Jasper, but he managed to escape.

*   *   *   *

Jasper fled into Mexico with the help of his militia friends from Louisiana. He stayed in a little town just outside of Tam Pico on the Gulf of Mexico, where he rested for six months and recovered from his injuries.

When he was strong again, he donned disguises, and traveled to Sicily, Italy, with a phony passport. He lived a private life there for six months. He paid the locals to shop for his food and clean his house. He was on the FBI's Most-Wanted list and Interpol was looking for him.

After living in Italy, he bought a small farm, forty miles outside of London, where he laid low and worked in a steel mill. He started contacting members of the IRA, but he would never return to the United States.

*   *   *   *

They buried Henri Joret and Tom Sandchester on the same day, and the funeral was national news.

*   *   *   *

Pete Neil returned to New York City and to his detective agency business, while Cephus retired from the police force on disability. Lucy Yee was fired from the firm, but stayed in New Orleans with Professor Hickman; they would eventually marry.

*   *   *   *

Clarence Reed demonstrated for the rights of the down-trodden with an even stronger fervor. He and Suzanne would marry the following December—with the blessing of Alva Joret.

* * * *

Malcolm and Sara were together again, on a trial basis. The kids were happy, as were Reverend Josiah and Lois. Two weeks after Joret and Sandchester's burials, the reverend's new church had a grand opening.

"What are you doing, Malcolm?" Sara asked, watching Malcolm flip through some vacation brochures.

"Before all this happened, I was relaxing on the sandy shores of Maui. I think I'll finish my vacation. Would you like to come with the kids and me? They enjoy watching the whales; it's their mating season."

Sara walked up behind him, sliding her hands down his chest. "Do you plan on doing any mating while you're there?"

"Sure. Why let the whales have all the fun?" Malcolm kissed Sara, while the children watched their parents' reunion with joy.

The ten o'clock news anchorman came on, but they continued their loving embrace.

"Before we report tonight's headlines, we here at Channel Eight News would like to greet our colleague, who took an involuntary sabbatical for a little over a year. We welcome back Suzanne Joret," he said. The viewers could hear the studio employees applauding.

Suzanne disregarded the teleprompter and smiled as she stared out to Kathy Sommers holding a clipboard. "Thank you, Ed, and everyone. It's good to be back." She started to become emotional, but maintained her composure.

"I know that a lot of viewers out there want to hear my side of what has happened to me and my family over the last year. In the weeks to come, I will share with you the events I lived through. I just want to thank Willy and Dexter for saving my life.

"Malcolm Stinson, thank you for the great job you did in exonerating Clarence Reed from a crime he didn't commit. All of Louisiana owes you a debt, sir...and to Reverend Josiah Stinson and his lovely wife Lois..." Suzanne shuffled her papers, looked into the teleprompter, and read:

"In the news tonight, Louisiana's first black governor, Campy Frazier, stated today from Baton Rouge that no new gambling riverboat will be built to replace the one that was destroyed on the Fourth of July..."

END

978-0-595-37477-
0-595-37477-8

Printed in the United States
43338LVS00004B/172-192

9 780595 374779